H. E. Manning

Essays on Religion and Literature

SALZWASSER
VERLAG

H. E. Manning

Essays on Religion and Literature

Reprint of the original, first published in 1865.

1st Edition 2022 | ISBN: 978-3-75258-825-5

Verlag (Publisher): Salzwasser Verlag GmbH, Zeilweg 44, 60439 Frankfurt, Deutschland
Vertretungsberechtigt (Authorized to represent): E. Roepke, Zeilweg 44, 60439 Frankfurt, Deutschland
Druck (Print): Books on Demand GmbH, In de Tarpen 42, 22848 Norderstedt, Deutschland

RELIGION AND LITERATURE.

ESSAYS

ON

RELIGION AND LITERATURE.

BY VARIOUS WRITERS.

EDITED BY H. E. MANNING, D.D.

LONDON

1865.

PREFACE.

THE following Essays were delivered before an Association, the nature and origin of which will be seen in the circular letter which is here prefixed as the best introduction to the volume.

The Essays now printed are only a portion of those which have been so delivered; others having been already published by their Authors in various forms.

Letter of H. E. Cardinal Wiseman inviting certain persons of the Clergy and Laity to unite in the Academia of the Catholic Religion.

'Next to the exercise of its purely spiritual office, the Church has in all ages bestowed its special care on the cultivation of the intellect, and the advancement of science, making the Word of God the interpretation of His works, and His works the illustration of His Word, and the science of God the centre and light of the manifold and various orders of human knowledge.

'For this cause the Church has always given especial encouragement to the studies which demonstrate the connection between science and revealed religion, thereby applying the truths and laws of the intellectual and natural world to the confirmation of the Faith.

'Now this, which is good at all times, at certain epochs is of vital necessity; as, for instance, when a perverse philosophy or a false method in science has introduced a real or an apparent opposition between the natural and supernatural sciences.

'Such an epoch, to pass by the earlier examples, was the beginning of this century, when the sceptical and infidel literature of Germany and France penetrated throughout Europe. It was at that time that a number of learned and pious Catholics formed, in Rome, the Academia of the Catholic Religion, for the purpose of cultivating this special aspect of science, and of promoting the same studies in the youth then rising to manhood. This Institution was approved, in a rescript of the then reigning Pontiff, Fel. Mem. Pius VII.

'The circumstances of our days, and of England, seem to demand an Institution of the same kind, for the purpose of drawing into mutual correspondence and cooperation the many minds capable of rendering service in the great work of sacred literature and Christian science, and of promoting the study of the same by example, influence, and guidance, in the youth of our time and country.

'The intellectual condition of England at this moment is amply enough to alarm the least anxious as to the divergence of sacred and secular science, and the unnatural opposition in which they appear to stand. It would be premature in this place to enter into details. It is enough to note, that rationalistic tendencies of thought in an advanced form have explicitly shown themselves in the most educated centres of England.

'Now it is for the Church, which alone possesses both Divine certainty and Divine discernment, to place itself at once in front of a movement which threatens even the fragmentary remains of Christian belief in England.

'With this view, while suffering from illness last year, in Rome, I obtained the necessary diplomas for the establishment in London of an Academia of the Catholic Religion affiliated to that in Rome; and now being still hindered by the same cause from otherwise carrying this purpose into effect, I desire to invite you, in this form, to associate yourself to this work with the hope of directing it in person hereafter. The Card. Asquini, President of that Academia, at the same time with my full concurrence entrusted to the Right Rev. Mgr. Manning, then also in Rome, its practical foundation, organisation, and direction. To him, therefore, you will be pleased to address your reply.

'The constitution and rules of the Institute shall be laid before you. In the meanwhile, it will be enough to describe in a general way its object and practice, which consists in the preparation of papers on any subject relating to religion, science, art, or literature, or bearing upon revelation, to be read at a meeting held every month or fortnight, as may be hereafter judged more expedient, and followed by conversation. It is hoped that much benefit will arise by the correspondence and cooperation which such interchange of thought will awaken. Should it be thought advisable, and likely to procure additional advantage to the cause in view, steps will be taken for the regular publication of such papers as may be selected for the purpose.

'In the hope that you will lend your aid in this work, I have directed this communication to be made to you; and if you should know of any friends desirous of being associated in this Academia, I would request you to communicate the same to me in the manner mentioned above.

'At first it will be, perhaps, more prudent to associate not more than a hundred members, to whom others may be aggregated, partly as honorary and partly as corresponding members, at home and abroad.

'N. CARD. WISEMAN.

'ETLOE HOUSE, LEYTON: *Easter*, 1861.'

No further explanation appears needed, than to say that the Academia has held its meetings regularly for three years.

H. E. MANNING.

BAYSWATER: *Nov.* 24, 1864.

CONTENTS.

ESSAYS

ON

RELIGION AND LITERATURE.

NOTICE.

Since the beginning of this century, there has existed in Rome a Society, or 'Academy,' whose object it is to defend, or illustrate, the Catholic and Christian religion. Application was made to the President and Council of the Roman Society for permission to found, and to affiliate, a similar society in England, and it was at once conceded.

The following document was, subsequently, addressed by H. E. the Cardinal to a certain number of priests and laity, from all of whom an answer accepting membership was received:—

'Next to the exercise of its purely spiritual office, the Church has in all ages bestowed its special care on the cultivation of the intellect, and the advancement of science, making the Word of God the interpretation of His works, and His works the illustration of His Word, and the science of God the centre and light of the manifold and various orders of human knowledge.

'For this cause the Church has always given especial encouragement to the studies which demonstrate the connection between science and revealed religion, thereby applying the truths and laws of the intellectual and natural world to the confirmation of the faith.

'Now this, which is good at all times, at certain epochs is of vital necessity, as, for instance, when a perverse philosophy, or a false method in science, has introduced a real, or an apparent, opposition between the natural and supernatural sciences.

'Such an epoch, to pass by the earlier examples, was the beginning of this century, when the sceptical and infidel literature of Germany and France penetrated throughout Europe. It was at that time that a number of learned and pious Catholics formed, in Rome, the Academia of the Catholic Religion, for the purpose of cultivating this special aspect of science, and of promoting the same studies in the youth then rising to manhood. This Institution was approved in a rescript of the then reigning Pontiff, fel. mem., Pius VII.

'The circumstances of our days, and of England, seem to demand an Institution of the same kind, for the purpose of drawing into mutual correspondence and cooperation the many minds capable of rendering service in the great work of sacred literature and Christian science, and of promoting the study of the same by example, influence, and guidance, in the youth of our time and country.

'The intellectual condition of England at this moment is ample enough to alarm the least anxious as to the divergence of sacred and secular science, and the unnatural opposition in which they appear to stand. It would be premature in this place to enter into details. It is enough to note, that rationalistic tendencies of thought, in an advanced form, have explicitly shown themselves in the most educated centres of England.

Now it is for the Church, which alone possesses both divine certainty and divine discernment, to place itself at once in front of a movement which threatens even the fragmentary remains of Christian belief in England.

'With this view, while suffering from illness last year, in Rome, I obtained the necessary diplomas for the establishment in London of an Academia of the Catholic Religion, affiliated to that in Rome; and now being still hindered by the same cause from otherwise carrying this purpose into effect, I desire to invite you, in this form, to associate yourself to this work, with the hope of directing it in person hereafter. The Card. Asquini, President of that Academia, at the same time, with my full concurrence, intrusted to the Right Rev. Dr. Manning, then also in Rome, its practical foundation, organisation, and direction. To him, therefore, you will be pleased to address your reply.

'The constitution and rules of the Institute shall be laid before you. In the meanwhile, it will be enough to describe, in a general way, its object and practice, which consists in the preparation of papers on any subject relating to religion, science, art, or literature, as bearing upon revelation, to be read at a meeting held every month or fortnight, as may be hereafter judged more expedient, and followed by conversation. It is hoped that much benefit will arise by the correspondence and cooperation which such interchange of thought will awaken. Should it be thought advisable, and likely to procure additional advantage to the cause in view, steps will be taken for the regular publication of such papers as may be selected for the purpose.

'In the hope that you will lend your aid in this work, I have directed this communication to be made to you; and if you should know of any friends desirous of being associated in this Academia, I would request you to communicate the same to me in the manner mentioned above.

'At first it will be, perhaps, more prudent to associate not more than a hundred members, to whom others may be aggregated, partly as honorary, and partly as corresponding members, at home and abroad. 'N. Card. Wiseman.

'Etloe House, Leyton: *Easter* 1861.'

A foundation was thus laid of the Academy, sufficient to begin building upon; and the Feast of the great Apostles

SS. Peter and Paul having been selected as a fitting day for its inauguration, invitations were sent to members to request their attendance at the residence of the Cardinal Archbishop. Nearly fifty priests and laymen were present at the inaugural meeting.

After a few preliminary words by the President, his Address was read by the Right Rev. Dr. Manning. This was followed by the election of two Secretaries, the Rev. J. L. Patterson and T. W. Allies, Esq.

The Academia is placed under the protection, under God, of His Immaculate Mother and the two great Apostles.

Among the members present were persons representing literature, science, and art, medicine, law, and sacred learning, from which Religion draws her most graceful tributes.

INAUGURAL DISCOURSE

OF

H. E. CARDINAL WISEMAN

AT THE FIRST SESSION OF THE ACADEMIA,

JUNE 29, 1861.

LET a mould be prepared, no matter by what hands, let it be a gem exquisitely engraved by an Athenian lapidary: be it composed but of rough gashes made on the face of a rock, by a carver of runes, or an Indian warrior; imagine it to be a die sunk in steel by the great Florentine medallist: be its instrument the diamond, flint, or iron,—you will not see its form accurately, you will not judge its worth fairly, you will hardly understand it, until you see the impression of it transferred upon some other substance, which will form its accurate counterpart. The seal, the cast, the medal, interpret to you the true intention of the artist, and represent to you his design or his record. If you press the pliant wax into the shape, it will not lose one line of its dimensions, or one grain of its weight, nor will the slightest change occur in its structure; yet it will bear impressed upon its surface the tenderest or the rudest lines, the finest angles or most rugged edges, the figure or the legend, or whatever else was meant to be admired or understood.

Something resembling this plastic faculty has God communicated to His Church, in its contact with the outward world. Without undergoing any organic or substantial modification, without being more or less at one time than another, she presents at every moment a surface to the great life of society, over which this rolls on, and imprints its features, its thoughts, its characteristic and specific qualities. The moral and social history of any age, or even portion of an age, can nowhere be so clearly deciphered as in the legislation, the discipline, the struggles, the literature, the arts, the biographies, nay, paradox as it may appear, in the very blank pages and lines, of the Church. For what tells us more of the world's condition than where the Annals of the Church seem to have had whole leaves, not torn out, but only here and there jotted over by a trembling hand, and its scanty records blurred by tears, or even blood?

We begin with the very first age of its infancy. It was too weak and too poor to raise commemorative monuments of its progress: it buried its memorials beneath the ground; and modern industry has sought and found them. At first sight of some chapels in the Catacombs, the Christian antiquarian is startled, perplexed, almost scandalised. He can scarcely decide whether he has penetrated into a heathen tomb or into a Christian crypt. The freedom of design, the elegance of ornamentation, the vividness of colouring, and the arrangement of the parts in the general composition, recal perhaps to his mind the columbarium of the Augustan freedmen, or of the Nasones; and moreover, he sees as leading figures demigods of pagan fiction, engaged in scenes and actions of a hateful mythology. And yet the place, the disposition of its parts, its tombs, its inscriptions, and its emblems, leave no doubt that we are in a most Christian cemetery, that bears, upon every panel and border, in its pictures and arabesques, on its vaults and walls, the forms of that early Roman art which had faded and vanished even before the later persecutions. The Church had taken up, and represented on its subterranean temples the transitory art of the period, even with its uncongenial stories which, by a happy symbolism, she robbed of their poison; and thus displayed her power of appropriating to herself one of the few good gifts which the most corrupt of worlds still possessed, and could communicate.

But, not to carry this illustration minutely through successive centuries, not especially to dwell on the marked influence, or rather impressions, manifested by the Church in her adoption of the Basilica for her architectural model, and of the Roman law as the part-foundation of her canonical code and the precedent of her juridical proceedings, as evidences of her happier connection with the Empire; recal to mind the later period when Europe emerged from the grave of a departed civilisation, and struggled for one of its own, heaving up the accumulated ruins and soil of the past, like one of Michelangelo's figures bursting from the tomb into the valley of judgment. What sort of times do you call those? You answer, 'Of iron.' And you are right: days of massive, compacted, close-grained, high-wrought iron. And that supposes strong-built frames and well-knit muscles to wield the double-handed sword, or the knotted mace, with unfailing prowess.

Well, even of this almost ferocious power the Church took the stamp; not in the feudal institutions merely, which she partly adopted, and which made barons of her bishops, and nobles of her abbots. No: if the age was iron-cased in its outward fashions, it was steel-tempered in its inward organs, the organs of intellectual life and power. If the Crusader could with ease often cleave to the shoulder, by one blow, the paynim's morion, it was no less the blow of a giant with which a Scotus could smash a sophism that protected error. If the fine-edged sword could cut through and through the truest tempered mail on the infidel's breast, not because of the brute strength with which it was handled, but through the deftness and very delicacy of hand with which it was gracefully waved, no less easily were the intricacies of heresy or false theories ripped open, unravelled, and stripped off, by the intellectual keenness of a Thomas Aquinas, wielding the subtle weapons of the schools. Sturdy intellects rose side by side with stalwart frames, and robust brains shared the youth of noblest birth with sinewy arms. Both were offspring of the same conditions of life, of a fresh, unprejudiced, and original civilisation, of barbarian blood, well combined from different races, under the engentling influences of Christian teaching, and the invigorating training of religious enthusiasm.

The Church took to herself the mighty mental development, and, with it yet clearly imprinted on her surface, retains the evidence of the wonderful vigour and strength of the epoch at once of knighthood and philosophy.

Nor was this all. The age of the troubadour, of the minstrel, of the romancer, and of highminded chivalrous affection, was naturally that of hymnology and sacred song. The tenderest and most plaintive notes in which the Church sings her love, or her sorrows, breathe the spirit of those times. The tenderness of a Bonaventure, the sweetness of a Bernard, the flashing love that breaks out in the few lines left us by St. Francis (the troubadour, as he has been called, of love divine), by the softest heart that ever beat beneath the roughest of hair-shirts,—were the natural productions of times when the rose and the lily as truly symbolised the noble dame like Elizabeth of Hungary or of Portugal, as the helmet and sword did a Tancred or a Godfrey.

Then, when this new social life created, or adapted, its own forms for recording its sensations, where do you look for them, as representative of ideas, feelings, instincts, pulsations, and even involuntary action, which all life must have? Of the royal palaces which every sovereign erected, from Scandinavia to Sicily, scarcely one remains inhabited; of the cathedrals which the Church contemporaneously built, scarcely one has fallen to decay. The few that *have* fallen have been victims of religious fury, or of calculating avarice. As you sail along the Rhine, the feudal castles that crown its crags are but picturesque ruins; the parish churches of the same date, that nestle at their feet, are fresh and filled. Had not the Church preserved, almost intact, *her* share of the monuments of those ages, the beautiful architecture which is yet our model either would have been eternally lost, or would have to be studied in fragments, scarcely less unintelligible than the history on Babylonian bricks.

The rough stem which with a superhuman, or rather with an unearthly, effort had broken into air and light, was soon covered with bright and beautiful blossoms, and delicious fruit. New and different from whatever the world had heard or seen was this sudden and quickly-matured produce. Since the creation of Paradise, there had been no parallel. It began, as was natural, with poetry and art; and ended in the revival, too sadly soon abused, of all classical learning. And by whom was all that was beautiful adopted, nursed, cherished and preserved?

Secularise, for a moment, the 'Divina Commedia;' leave to it only Virgil and Beatrice with the poet; suppress all but the histories of the petty tyrants of Italy, and of their deeds of atrocity and perfidy; let it only chronicle the crimes of men unknown, the passions of parties long forgotten,—and you would indeed erase some tender or harrowing legends; but on the whole you would remain with a dull chronicle, in beautiful verse and rich poetry, but a labyrinth of contemporary history, to be only threaded with a clue of ravelled commentary. You might then safely strike out the epithet of *Divine* from the title of the work: it would be the most human of books. But where the vivid and rich theological thought of the age kindles the poet's imagination, when first, at the end of his 'Purgatorio,' he describes holy mysteries borne as of old on triumphal cars; then in his 'Paradiso' soars from star to star, floats from harmony to harmony upon angels' wings, or rather breath, finds celestial knowledge and divine wisdom in the discourse of the saints whom I have enumerated,—we become conscious how all that is characteristic, unique, and sublime in the poetry of the age to which as yet we owe our sense of the truly beautiful, and withal holy, belongs to the part which the Catholic Church took in the action and movement of that period of revival. She preserves in those enduring records, which she inscribed on the vellum-sheets of Dante as on her most solid monuments, the evidence of her connection with the times of both, the fairest impression of a new golden age, more indelible than the traces of the former one are, in the writings or the edifices of the Augustan period. That venerable old poet, whose countenance is the type of a northern race, sitting day by day, on the stone bench in the Piazza of Florence, watching the growth of Giotto's belfry, is an excellent symbol of that second mighty age.

And as to that great distinctive quality given to it, of which that painter-architect is the aptest representative, it would seem superfluous to say, that if the world at that time gave birth, education, even genius and unmatched skill, to innumerable painters, illuminators, engravers, enamellers, jewellers, medallists, artists in bronze, sculptors in marble, wood, and every other material, such as the world never before saw, all this prolific power would have been wasted and utterly lost if the Church had not happily, in accordance with her mission on earth, received upon her ample surface the most beautiful and the most durable of its productions there impressed. She rushed, like Veronica, with her outspread veil to catch the inspired *effigies* and true images, which genius seemed to have caught in heaven, of things celestial, and hung them up for the admiration and reverence of generations to come.

Who goes to royal palaces, to imperial halls, to national galleries, to contemplate or study the masterpieces of nobler artists? To view, indeed, a few small pictures painted by favour for some noble patron, or perhaps some altar-pieces torn from their places by rapine or revolutionary covetousness. But the mighty works of the great masters are inseparably fixed on the vaults or walls of large churches, or of cloisters, or of religious halls. You go to the deep mysterious grottoes of Asisi or Subiaco to admire the solemn frescoes of early art; you visit the churches of Florence and Perugia for the second period of sacred art; you wander for hours in the halls of the Vatican for the purpose of knowing it in its perfection, whether of grandeur in the Sixtine chapel, of beauty in the Stanze, or of sweetness in the oratory of San Lorenzo. All that has been preserved of the grand conceptions of revived and perfected art, consists of what it has left grandly imprinted upon the Church's hospitable home.

Yet while her outward walls were thus successively beautified from age to age, while she ever appeared to each generation '*circumdata varietate*,' gathered on her surface by the passing of centuries over her, still was her inward structure unchanged, her essential duties were unvaried, her course pursued with equal success. Her Pontiffs all through, with the exceptions which formed the necessary tribute to humanity, were nobly grand, whether martyrs or confessors; her Councils were splendidly dignified, whether general or provincial; her Bishops, in their respective sees, form a track of light through the history of nations; her monasteries and convents, with whatever varieties, rise as landmarks over every flood of devastation, of ignorance, or of impiety, nursing the sacred fire of Christian learning, and of even profane knowledge, till Providence should bring the fulness of time for its manifestation. Yes, without clothed and surrounded with rich variety, but her real glory unchanged within. '*Omnis gloria Filiae Regis ab intus.*'

What a remarkable proof and illustration of this truth is in the very period of which I have just spoken! It was one in which it might have been thought that the world had most mastered the Church. Love of art had been pushed the nearest to luxuriousness, literature had apparently most nighly reached enervation, even ecclesiastical life seemed to have almost touched on voluptuousness. And yet at this moment the jealousy of truth, the ardent love of sound faith, the intolerance of error, broke out with a vigour, a firmness, a brilliancy, such as even at the Arian epoch had not been surpassed, with a learning, an acuteness, and extensiveness never since rivalled. That period of supposed secularism oppressing the Church proved to be the glorious era of the Council of Trent; and the very Pope who has been accused of having yielded more than became him to the weakening and effeminating influence of art, was the very one who seized by the throat the hydra of the new heresy, and grappled with it as it poured out its first words of blasphemy.

And what further evidence we have of this necessary mutual action, in the fact that even S. Charles, so stern in his orthodoxy, so lynx-eyed in his watchfulness over accuracy in faith, yet considered himself bound, in graceful deference to the classical taste of the world, to clothe the teaching of the Church in pure and elegant diction, and employ the tasteful scholar to impress the type of his age upon the unalterable doctrine of the theologian!

Such, honoured Academicians, has been the Church in every age. Whatever is good, whatever virtuous, whatever useful in the world, at every time, she has allowed to leave its seal upon her outward form. And now another day, another generation, another spirit has come with the good will of God, has come through His ever-varying Providence.

By dispensations, which no physical research has yet mastered, cycles come, and run a course, then give place to others; cycles of natural conditions, untraceable to any cause, unconnected with discoverable laws. Year after year, the vineyards of continents are blighted and barren; the olives of provinces are withered and fruitless; the plant which feeds the poor population of a kingdom droops in its stem and rots at its root, and belies all the promises of the spring. We are told that these things have been before, and will come later again; that they follow a hidden law, like ague or neuralgia; like them have a periodicity. And so with the diseases that afflict humanity; for years their type is depressing and debilitating, and then return again the maladies of our forefathers, like sins visited on their children, with febrile energy and sanguine oppression. No study can modify these phenomena, no skill can retard or accelerate their appointed course. The simple-hearted will call them, when they come with violence and destruction in the field and in the body, *visitations*, and raise their arms in prayer; they are visitations of justice.

In like manner, unaccountably, gifts of some peculiar form seem to be poured out on mankind at a given time, and appear to be as visibly withdrawn. Thousands of artists rose simultaneously, and apparently spontaneously, in every part of Europe, at a given period. Art was self-sown in Italy, in Spain, in Flanders, and in Germany, at two distinct periods: just as now hundreds of men gifted with mechanical powers are to be found to answer to any demand for new and wonderful undertaking,—men, any one of whom would have excited admiration, and gained undying fame, a century ago; just as some ages before, every school of science or theology in Europe had its doctors, each surpassing in subtlety of intellect, and accurate learning, the most rarely-gifted professor of our days. This periodical abundance of a peculiar gift, wanted to help mankind forward another step, has no connection with any law of progress. In no instance has the quality granted to Society reached its perfectibility before it is withdrawn.

Is it not so even in the Church? Has she not, too, her periods of martyrdom, of asceticism, of mysticism, of learning, and of active charity? And is not this one more of those parallelisms betwen her nature, and the social growth of man, which the more we find, the more we are convinced, not by demonstration, but by intuition, that one Lord and Master rules and directs all, and that all which I have endeavoured to describe is nothing more than a common moulding, impressed by Him who holds all in the hollow of His hand, and imprints the varied folds and lines of His ever-shifting mercies equally on every part of His creation?

Then, as I have said, there is another change: we are come to a time, or rather a time has come to us, when a new spirit, to use the beautiful language of Him who gives it, is poured out upon the world—the spirit of scientific investigation. Humbly, gratefully, joyfully, I accept it from the treasury, and from the hand of the All-wise and the All-good. It is a new impulse to the intellect which He has bestowed on man; it is a new sharpening of the keenness of the wits which He has given him; it is a new sphere, a new world, which He has opened to his perception of the divine operations *ab extra*. Fool will man be if he misdirects these faculties, and makes not for himself a fresh and brilliant field, where to gather new tributes of admiration and love, and offers up his first and his later fruits in adoration of God, his Creator.

Be this as it may, I feel sure that this new phase of social pursuits will leave its well-marked forms impressed upon the Church, and that generations to come will trace that with admiration there, which we see perhaps with some uneasiness. And has not this been always so?

Did not warm and earnest souls view with alarm the first great boon of assured peace to the Church, and fear relaxation of discipline from the cessation of martyrdom?

Did not S. Bernard vehemently declaim against the beautiful architecture that was springing up, and the richness of decoration and church-ornaments which an infant art was introducing, as a religious effeminacy and unnerving luxury? Did not the followers of severer learning reprobate the introduction of more elegant literature, so as to be caricatured by Protestant critics in the '*Literae obscurorum virorum*'? And were they altogether wrong, when minds like Erasmus's could be allured and seduced from the truth by the elegances of profane letters?

And did not many fear, what, unfortunately, came to pass, that the beauty of art might be perverted to the service of evil passions, and become the food and stimulant of vice?

And, in like manner, be not surprised if something similar should now occur. All these various gifts, granted at different epochs, were brought by the world that received them before the seat of grace, within God's Church. They came, asking for blessing; they approached, praying for guidance; they drew near, kneeling for sanctification. And yet cautiously, timidly, did good and holy men accept them. They feared the world as much as the Trojan did the Greek even when bearing gifts.

But here it is totally different. The science of our day comes forward, not only disclaiming cooperation, sympathy, or good wishes from the Church, or from religion, but as a rival, an adversary, an antagonist. It advances defiant and rampant, and menacing; too often with a sarcasm on its lips, nay, with blasphemies, scoffs, and lies upon its tongue. It 'speaks great things;' and treats with levity and contempt of what we deem most holy. And because we do not run forward, and meet half way, and embrace, and receive a Judas-kiss from this declared foe, the Catholic is taunted as afraid of science, as a lover of darkness, as a foe to progress. When men go forth to welcome the burglar who plainly tells them that he is coming to plunder and despoil them, and lead him into their house, or the incendiary who shows them the torch with which he intends to set fire to their property, and point out to him the most inflammable part,—then we may be expected to fraternise with men whose avowed purpose is to rob and to destroy.

With the researches or discoveries of Herschel, Leverrier, or Lord Rosse, when has a single Catholic quarrelled? Against the chemical transmutations of Liebig or Faraday, when has any ecclesiastical authority warned? Upon even a single fact in geology, any statement of Murchison or Lyell regarding the position of a layer, or the bed of a fossil, when has a word of condemnation been spoken? On science seriously and conscientiously conducted, the Church looks on, fearless but cautious; fearless of facts, but most cautious on deductions. It is indeed a notable fact, that while you will find the Roman *Index* loaded with works on history, treatises of metaphysics, political, or rather anti-social, pamphlets, you will look in vain there for scientific books, astronomical or geological.

No, I repeat it; it is not with the discoveries of honest philosophers that the Church is at war, it is with their application by the unscientific who come against her in the name of natural pursuits, that she feels it almost a degradation to be compelled to fight. In other words, she dislikes, she detests even, that very mode of attack, which the Church of England is at this moment disgusted at, and is trying to repel, such science and philosophy as are put forward in the 'Essays and Reviews.' It is a providential permission, after the outcry and calumny against our Church, that she shrinks from the contact of science, and dreads the application of its principles as a test of her teaching; that another religion which has joined in the taunt, or stood by applauding while it was made, should now not only feel its point and stroke, but should struggle more hopelessly under it, not having any measure of its own resisting or healing power, not having skill or experience in dealing with error, beyond the limits of past toleration. The Church of England has joined in blaming the Catholic Church, because, in place of refuting, she has contented herself with condemning; and now, from the palace to the parsonage, in Upper and Lower House of

Convocation, is the question seriously agitated, whether or no condemnation of some sort, synodical, juridical, convocational, or episcopal, is to be adopted and applied. It does not now seem to enter into the circle of Anglican ecclesiastical consideration, whether the Church of England ought not to welcome free, and even disrespectful, discussion of the objections extorted from science against Revelation, nay, as the phrase is, 'to court' the appeal to individual conscience or intellect, on the disputed claims of geology against the truth of the Old Testament, and of philology against the inspiration of the New.

We may truly call this a just retribution. For while our appearing to dispose easily of perplexing opinions on the principle of a conscious authority, has been put often severely aside, on the high ground of God's never having granted to His universal Church so high a prerogative, so large a dowry of His own unfailing wisdom, our stern reprehender now feels itself in the dilemma, of either putting its doctrine, as defendant, at the bar of private opinion, with infidelity as its plaintiff, or claiming place on the judgment-seat, from which it has attempted to extrude the Catholic Church, as God's judicial representative in the decision of dogma.

But pass by the painful scene of embarrassment and vacillation which the proceedings of Anglicans present, in this unpractised controversy; let us leave them to themselves—in their exercise of dogmatic jurisdiction now first asserted—contemplating with dismay the new patent crop of thistles and briers which have sprung up amidst their flowers, deliberating how to clip, or crop, or pluck them, but not having courage to put the spade beneath their roots, and dig them out, and cast them where they will dry and die harmless: sure that they will pullulate again, and with ranker growth, if left imbedded in the rich soil of tolerated error. Let us rather consider our own position relatively to this new manifestation of scientific warfare.

I will express my sense of it in a few words. I have read one of the confutations, out of many published, of the 'Essay on the Mosaic Cosmogony,' by Mr. C.W. Goodwin, and I seriously declare that I have found in it nothing new. In principle, or in line of argument, or in generalised deduction, I do not see anything which any Roman professor of 'Sacred Physics' (a chair in the Roman University), nay, which as teacher in my own college I, might not have said five-and-twenty years ago. I will even break through the reserve of literary modesty—I have found nothing which I did not say, and print, in Latin first, and lay at the feet of the most learned of modern Popes, Pius VIII., in 1829, and then in English in 1836.

No doubt, since then details have accumulated; the earth and its searchers have undergone the revolutions of one more generation; many new discoveries have been made; past generalities have been detailed and particularised; we know more of the true seat in the downward stages of the globe, of the stories in our terraqueous home, in which its curious and monstrous inhabitants have successively dwelt. Geology has been poetised by Hugh Miller, and the Mosaic history of creation has been turned by him into a vision; but the great feature of the question is the same; and Anglicanism only repeats the arguments of the Catholic, without the grace to acknowledge that it is only second in the field.

But this is taking up the controversy too low. And it is even making unworthy concessions to 'the oppositions of learning falsely so called,' to allow its being considered as an ally where it is in truth a disciple, to claim for it credit when it is really a debtor. The insolent blasphemer Volney wrote a catechism of morality, which pretended to deduce all practical virtue from natural reasonings; but he forgot to tell his readers that he had learnt his 'Christian doctrine' at his mother's knee, or perhaps before the altar-rails, before he had lost his faith. It was like one who had lost his sight in youth pretending that he imagined his descriptions of natural objects.

And something like this has been the case with modern scientific enquiry. To say the least, it has been often ungrateful. The basis of all its study, the clue of its intricate researches, have been, in truth, the Bible. The precurrence of a chaotic condition, indefinite in duration, is found, indeed, vaguely expressed in Hindoo, Scandinavian, Egyptian, and Western cosmogonies; nowhere so definite, so plain, nor so connected with subsequent physical events, as in the scriptural narrative. But in none other is the very groundwork of modern science described as in this—the doctrine of successive production, not vague and confused, but definite, step by step, so as to challenge to proof—to proof not attempted till after thousands of years. It was not geology (no one suspects it) which suggested this system, but it was this untested system that suggested geology. The Mosaic cosmogony was the very handbook of its research: the elder proficients, Pallas, Saussure, Cuvier, even Buckland, may be said to have searched the rocks, opened the caverns, and turned over the *débris* on the earth's surface, with the certainty, drawn from theory, that successive creations had peopled the earth, or that evidences of its last cataclysm would be found recorded on the lines of its strata, or that earth had undergone preparatory revolutions, and rough but careful manipulations, before the hand that made them had fashioned man. From these first steps true science has never departed; nor has it cared to gainsay that first point of departure, though it makes light of its source.

It is, then, a solemn truth—the Bible has created geology: Moses has laid down the first principles, by which the modern science of the earth has been guided, from its first infant unsteady steps, to its present proud and hurried strides.

Nor is this all. Sincere science asks for long indefinite periods to account for gradual developments of organic beings, and for huge accumulations of inorganic matter. Supercilious science objects, that days are not long enough for these purposes, and will nail the commentator to the literal sense for once. And here, for the Church, her best teachers, her ancient Fathers, as if foreseeing the future want, and the future strain upon the text, have long anticipated the whole objection, by bearing their testimony to the all-sufficient interpretation that days may mean periods to any extent, equal to the teaching of any scientific system. I mention this only to show that the two modern theories, either that days mean long periods, or that there was an undefined interval between chaos and order, as now established, are as old as the Fathers; for this second hypothesis is to be found no less in their writings. The Bible has given the rule; the Church, its interpretation.

Then what shall we conclude? That it is our duty to follow without anxiety, but with an unflinching eye, the progress of science. Even when this is in the hands of upright and sincere men, experience has shown—and I could illustrate it by instances—that they may be mistaken even in their statements, and in their observation of facts. There have been too many examples of illusion, and of hasty deduction, for us to repose absolute confidence in any naturalist, especially if he has already formed a theory. But let repeated observation establish a fact, and we need not fear its consequences. How many human skeletons have been announced as found in preadamitic positions! Yet not one has yet been admitted as proved. Let any number of new hideous apes be found in Africa, and hailed as a more remote progenitor by enlightened naturalists, I will be satisfied to end my genealogy at the first of the line endowed with reason, instead of pursuing it into the primevalness of ferocity, and to trace my life to the breath of life inhaled by Adam from the mouth of God, rather than consider him only a link between myself and the respectable, though somewhat unintellectual family of baboons. Probably a gorilla points out man to his apelings as a very degenerate specimen of his descendants.

And if science needs careful watching in its observations, surely it sadly wants it in its inferences. It is chiefly over these that the Church invites her children to be vigilant. For these fall generally into the hands of sciolists, and those half-learned who deal in what Pope has so well characterised as 'a dangerous thing.' It is over their superficial applications, their half-suppressed truths, and half-displayed errors, that we are invited to keep watch and ward, lest little ones be seduced, and the weak-minded be misled. It is for this purpose that we are incorporating ourselves this day. As, in ancient times, those who loved and studied art gathered round its masters or its models to learn its principles, from the instructions of the former, or the inspirations of the latter,—and these were the schools, or *academies*, of art,—so, in later times, have similar institutions been created, for gathering together persons bound by a similar community of pursuits to learn from one another, or from a common source. Such are the learned societies of our own country, such the *Academies* of the Continent.

In the seventeenth century, Rome saw spring up the remarkable Academy of the *Lincei*, or *Lynx-eyed*, whose principal and avowed object was to promote physical science. Its founder was the clever and religious young nobleman Federico Cesi, who, at the age of eighteen, in the year 1606, established it in the house of his haughty and ignorant father, the Duke of

Aquasparta; who, while yet a stripling, was consulted by Cardinal Bellarmine on scientific matters, and was almost rebuked by him for his superfluous display of patristic learning; who, after persecution, almost to death, by his unnatural parent, still persevered through his short life; who inaugurated his Academy by a devout visit of its members to S. John Lateran's on S. John's day, and opened every meeting by prayer; and who has lately been commemorated in science by the name of Caesia, given by Brown to an Australian family in botany. The Acts of the Academy still form a valuable fund of materials in the history of science. His Academy was revived by Leo XII., and has its halls and observatory on the Capitol.

In 1799, the growth of infidelity excited the zeal of the learned Mgr. Zamboni, and suggested the necessity of forming a society for the purpose of checking its rapid and overbearing course over Italy. One man will in vain cast a stone, or roll a rock into a torrent's bed; twelve men, from different tribes, may, by each carrying one, raise a warning mound in the midst of a river's course. The Society held its first meetings privately, and members read their papers to try their strength. In the first year of the century, the holy Pontiff Pius VII. incorporated, blessed it, and approved its rules under the name of the 'Accademia di Religione Cattolica.' From that day it has prospered, has flourished, and has grown. It has counted among its members many illustrious men, and, no doubt, a few less worthy of note.

Among the last, allow me to place myself; and bear

with me, if a second time in this discourse I have the folly to speak of myself. It will be at least an expression of a strong feeling of grateful attachment, and in explanation why I desire to transplant to Catholic England a shoot, which may here take root, of a plant beneath whose shadow I have cultivated my own slender pursuits.

In the year 1830, I had the honour of being, without solicitation, elected a member of this Academy, and the following year I read a paper in it, in presence of Card. Cappellari, Prefect of Propaganda, whose gracious commands I received to extend and publish it. Its title was, 'The Barrenness of the Missions undertaken by Protestants for the Conversion of Heathen Nations, proved by their own Accounts.' The learned Cardinal undertook not only to have the book published at the Propaganda Press, but also to correct the proofs himself. This he kindly did, till the day of his election to the Pontificate in the following year. Not long after, I read a paper on the Pontificate of Gregory VII.

On the 16th of June 1837, I delivered a discourse on the Oxford movement, making it known for the first time in Italy; on the 4th of the same month 1840, I read a paper on Boniface VIII., since expanded in the Dublin 'Review.' None of the others have appeared in English.

I venture, therefore, to come before you, as a veteran of thirty years' standing in these ranks, with some right to seek recruits for our renewed warfare. The Roman Academy, to which I have sent papers from England to be read, in proof of my enduring connection, has encouraged us to form a branch here, as a bulwark or outpost, nearer the front of danger from pretended science, and has granted us a patent of incorporation as a branch of itself.

Our call for associates has been nobly and graciously responded to, and I beg, in the name of our Roman President, the Eminent Cardinal Asquini, my friend and schoolfellow, and in that of our illustrious associates, to thank you and welcome you.

Strong in faith, and secure in revelation, it will be our pleasing task to meet from time to time, to discuss interesting subjects, and bring into and keep in harmony science and religion. The Church's position is lofty, but only thus can she watch over the progress of other institutions. It may be a homely illustration ; but she seems to occupy, in our times, the place of the watchman whom we see standing, ever vigilant, where many iron paths meet, cross, or diverge. His object is not to arrest the rapid career of the panting engine, or the multitudes whom it draws after it, or the wealth which it conveys far away. With one firm touch of his hand, with one gentle pressure of the fine mechanism, he directs its power and velocity upon its right track. One moment of neglect, one mistake in his action, and thousands may be driven into a fatal collision, or turned into a wrong direction. Our office be, in her name, to employ the resources at our command, gently, delicately, yet firmly and strongly, to guide many on the right path, and so earn for ourselves the blessings due to every one who saves another from evil or leads him into good.

THE SUBJECTS PROPER TO THE ACADEMIA.

BY H. E. MANNING, D.D.

THE office of addressing you to-day at the opening of the third year of the Academia, through a cause which we all very deeply regret and earnestly hope may soon pass away, has fallen unexpectedly to me. And though I could wish it in other hands, above all in his who but for illness would have addressed you, I will do as best I can.

When the other day I heard the Congress of Malines recommend the establishment of Academias such as this, as one of the most efficacious means of counteracting the false and anti-Catholic principles abroad at this day, it was not without a lively satisfaction that I remembered that we in England, who are but in the rudiments of our Catholic organisation, have nevertheless for two years had our Academia of the Catholic religion. And on reviewing the subjects which have been treated by its members, we may congratulate ourselves, not only on the excellence of many of the discourses addressed to us, considered in themselves, but also on the timeliness and applicability of those discourses in relation to the errors of the times and of the country in which we live. And this leads me to offer a few remarks, not on any specific thesis, but, as the custom is in Rome at the opening of each year, on an *argomento libero*—a wider and freer subject. I will therefore speak of the nature and intention of the Academia and of the subjects proper for its sessions. Its main intention, as you are well aware, is, to exhibit the truths and principles of the Catholic faith and Church, not only in themselves, but in their relations to the world and to the age, to philosophy, to science, and to politics; and that not too only *absolutè*, but especially in the bearing of these truths and principles upon the errors of the time. The Academia in Rome was instituted, as you well know, in the beginning of this century, to combat the Voltairian infidelity and the anti-Catholic revolution, which from France began at that time to descend upon Italy. It is therefore what the Germans would call the *time-spirit* that we have to appreciate, and, so far as it is hostile to truth, to combat and, by God's help, to counteract.

With a view to such an appreciation, and to mark out in some degree the subjects proper to be treated, I would ask leave to make a few remarks upon the times in which we live.

It is I know a common illusion to imagine that our days are exceptional for good or for evil, and that they surpass in importance the times of our fathers. A slight event before our eyes is more vivid, real, and exciting than the great actions of past history. It needs a calm judgment, and a wide comparative survey of the events both of the past and of the present, not to be carried away by this illusion. Shall I seem to incur this censure, if I say that the times in which we live are exceptionally great, and pregnant beyond most other times gone by with certain mature consequences of past events? Let me, then, endeavour to shelter myself from this fault and from the recoil of my own censure. It would seem to me that the age in which we live, that is the lifetime of our contemporaries, is marked by a crisis of exceptional magnitude and importance.

1. And first, the Protestant Reformation has reached its three hundredth year. It has run the career which is usually permitted to a heresy. Pelagianism and its *reliquiae* infested Africa, Gaul and Britain for less than three hundred years. Donatism ran out in three hundred years. Arianism and its offsets possessed first the political power of the Lower Empire, then the Gothic races, then Lombardy and Spain for about three hundred years. Where is Pelagianism? where is Donatism? and where is Arianism? S. Gregory the Great lived when Arianism was dying out. His pontificate inaugurated the beginning of a new period of Catholic faith and unity. In our day Protestantism has reached its term. As a religion it may be said hardly to exist, for its transformations are such, that the forms of fragmentary Christianity which pass under its name would be disowned by the Protestant Reformers. It has ceased to be a definite and intelligible form of spiritual conviction, or of intellectual thought. It exists as a form of politics, as a plea for social hostility to the Catholic religion, and for revolutionary diplomacy against the Catholic Church.

It is a fact pointed out by Lord Macaulay in his earlier years, when as yet the asperity of the partisan had not soured and warped the candour of the historian, that in every instance Protestantism was established by the civil power; that when the civil power ceased to propagate it, Protestantism ceased to spread; that there is no example of a country becoming Protestant since the first outbreak of the sixteenth century; that there are Protestant countries which have become Catholic again, but no Catholic country which has become Protestant; that whatsoever in the confusions of the last three hundred years has been lost to Catholicism has been lost to Christianity; that whatsoever has been gained to Christianity has been gained to Catholicism.*

Now, as a form of religion or of intellectual thought, it is certain that Protestantism has not been able to perpetuate, much less to propagate itself. In Germany it has passed off into partial or into complete Neology; in Switzerland and France, extensively into Socinianism; in England into a congeries of irreconcilable heterodoxies, which are in a perpetual flux.

Perhaps, in Scotland the original Protestantism retains its character with greater tenacity, partly from the persistent spirit of the Scottish religionists, and partly from its isolation and remoteness from the Catholic nations which by contact powerfully affect other Protestant countries. It is certain, nevertheless, that both speculative unbelief and practical infidelity have made great ravages in Scotland. My object, however, is not to

* Essay on Ranke's *History of the Popes*, vol. iii. p. 253.

enter into farther detail than is necessary for the justification of the assertion which I have made, that is, that Protestantism as a religion is dead. It has departed from its own type. It has generated a multitude of new and erroneous religions, and in them it has lost its identity, and therefore as a religion its existence. What number of professing Christians at this day are intellectually represented by the Helvetic Confession, the Augsburgh Confession, the Westminster Catechism and the Thirty-nine Articles? These things are now what the Thalia of Arius, or the creeds of Sirmium, Ancyra and Seleucia were in the times of S. Gregory the Great.

But I must narrow the ground of our subject, and confine myself to England, alone with which we have chiefly to do.

There are, then, certain signs upon the Established Protestantism of England which mark its advanced decay.

First, its singular isolation. It is out of the unity of the Catholic Church, and therefore of the great Christian society of the world. It is rejected by the Greek Church, with which it endeavours in vain to hold communion. It has no union with the Protestant Churches of Sweden, Denmark, Germany, Switzerland, or France. It is repudiated by the Established Church of Scotland. It is abandoned or rejected by 58 per cent. of the population of England. Of the remaining 42 per cent. much continues in it by mere nominal, traditional, social, political adhesion. Anglican

Protestantism is not only struck with sterility in propagation, but with an incapacity to retain even its own hereditary members. It is remarkable that this is the state of the Establishment, after an unprecedented stir and exertion, in which it must be said that great natural energy and generosity has been manifested during a quarter of a century. But it is evident to all who stand upon the shore, that nothing can save the Established Protestant or Anglican religion from sinking. Its seams are gaping wide, and the waters of dissension, indifference, and rationalism must inevitably draw it under.

Now this, though it be no new fact, is more advanced and more evident than it was thirty years ago. Until then the Anglican Establishment was girded and underpinned by its exclusive social and political privileges. Three hundred years of regal supremacy and legal primacy and religious monopoly had given to it an apparent and fictitious superiority.

The repeal of the Test and Corporation Acts and the Catholic Emancipation threw the Anglican Establishment upon its own centre for support. It could no longer rest upon the legal repression of those who disbelieved or rejected its claims. It had to go alone, to depend upon its own spiritual and intellectual resources. With what result the last thirty years will show. It is true, that what is called freedom of action has called forth much zeal from its members; but it has also called out their antagonisms; if it has multiplied its churches and its ministers, it has multiplied its contentions and its divisions. For three hundred years its bond of coherence was mechanical and external, not internal and dynamical. It was not the unity of thought and will, because it had neither unity of faith, nor even the principle of Divine Faith for its centre. When the outward bonds which swathed it were taken off, it began to separate every way. All its internal repulsions began to exhibit themselves in a more developed activity, and to reach a farther point of divergence; for instance, the two schools which are now dominant in their activity are the Rationalistic and what I must call the Romanising. They are drawing to themselves the vigour, zeal, generosity, and earnestness of the Establishment, and in their vehement departure from each other they are rending the Establishment asunder. And yet thirty years ago these two schools existed only in germ. They who moved the University of Oxford with such a vehemence of alarm to condemn Dr. Hampden's Bampton Lectures, never dreamed that in that very place in a few years Professor Powell would deny the whole supernatural order, and explicit Rationalists would be tutors and heads of houses. They, too, who contended for Tract 90, as if for the body of Patroclus, never dreamed that Anglican clergymen would now be not only burning incense, or writing tracts about low masses, but would be forming sisterhoods and professing to believe the infallibility of the Church.

These things, which are thought to be signs of life, are rather signs of the acute excitement which precedes dissolution. They are like the mental over-activity of men dying of consumption. They rise fitfully above themselves, and then sink by exhaustion. That Anglican Protestantism will ever become one in mind, or opinion, or doctrine, is intrinsically impossible. The law of internal divergence which distracts it, is irresistible and multiplying in its force, and its intellectual antagonisms are becoming every ten years more and more intensely developed. That any one form of thought should prevail over all the others and cast them out is equally impossible. That the Romanising school should ever prevail, no Catholic who knows what an act of Divine Faith is, can for a moment imagine; nor anyone who knows how deep and violent is the hostility of the English laity towards these fanciful imitations of the popery which they hate.

I cannot fail here to notice in passing, an error which unhappily has found among Catholics a few to countenance it. I mean the notion that the duty of Anglicans is to remain where they are with a view to spreading their opinions in the Established Church: in other words that individuals may postpone, or even refuse to submit to the Church in the hope of bringing about what I may call a corporate union of the churches. Such a theory, to make the best excuse I can for any Catholic who holds it, must rest upon the assumption that the Anglican Establishment is as truly a church as the schismatical Greek Church, that it possesses valid orders, succession, sacraments, jurisdiction to absolve, and truth of doctrine, i.e. the principle of Divine Faith. How any Catholic can hold this view without unsoundness I do not see. If all the pretensions of the Establishment were as undoubted as the orders and sacraments of the Greek Church, still no Catholic could maintain such a theory. Every several Greek is bound to submit to the Catholic Church, one by one, without question or thought as to what others may or may not do. Salvation is the first law of conscience, and to hasten out of a state of even material schism or material heresy is an absolute duty. To remain in it *sciens et prudens* would make the heresy or the schism to be formal. If anyone wish to see an example of the error I allude to, let them look at a journal called the 'Union Review;' a singular example of arrogant and pharisaical patronising of Catholics and the Catholic Church, with much petty and malevolent gossip, picked up it is to be feared in Catholic houses, and from Catholics who lend the countenance of their sympathy and, I fear, of their name to this mischievous delusion. But to return. It has always appeared to me that this intellectual movement towards the Catholic Church was providentially intended to restore the line of continuity between the intelligence of the English people and the intelligence of the Universal Church. The Reformation had utterly dissolved it, and the breach was kept open by every means, as by change of language and of terminology, and even change of pronunciation in both Latin and Greek, whereby we have become 'barbarians' to all nations and all nations 'barbarians unto us.' England was so cut out from the faith, the language, the spiritual and intellectual context and communion of the Catholic world, that it ceased to receive from abroad the influences of other races, or to make itself understood by them. Nothing but this can explain the strange ignorance of the English respecting the Catholic Church and faith. I do not mean only among the poor—who in a part of England known to me, call their Catholic neighbours Romans, believing them to be the posterity of Julius Cæsar—but among educated and cultivated men. This solution of continuity between the English intelligence and the Catholic intelligence brings with it also a like separation and variance of all the sympathies and instincts which spring from unity of intellectual judgment and belief. Now nothing, humanly speaking, could have restored this continuity except a line of minds advancing like skirmishers towards the Catholic Church, or like a pontoon bridge gradually thrown across the gulf which the Reformation opened. It is also to be noted that almost at the same moment there sprang up in the Presbyterian Establishment a movement on which the name of Irving has been fixed. This movement has developed into a servile imitation of Catholic doctrine and worship, together with the most fanatical enmity against the Catholic Church. These two parallel movements are not permitted without design, nor will they fail to bear their fruits.

One consequence is already seen. The Catholic doctrines and practices, which, twenty years ago, were defended controversially by our preachers and writers, are now for the most part adopted, preached, and defended by a numerous body among our opponents. They are in mutiny, and have fallen into contention among themselves about our Catholic theology. We may save the time which controversy wastes, and, instead of going out into the battle-field, we may go into the harvest-field to reap and to bind, and to gather our sheaves into the garner.

This, then, is one point in which our times are more critical than those of our fathers.

Another remarkable and unprecedented sign of decay upon Anglican Protestantism is the fact that the young men of cultivation and vigour of mind are turning away from its ministry. It is not enough to say that worldly callings present easier and higher prizes, and that the poverty of the clergy repels young men from ordination. This is not true of the Catholic Church, and that too in our great poverty. The Catholic priests in England certainly do not receive on an average the wages of upper servants. But the sons of our best families, and the highest and best for intellect and cultivation among their sons, give themselves joyously, but humbly and with fear of their own unworthiness, to the priesthood of the Church. It is not poverty which causes this repugnance. It is the doubt, the uncertainty, and the bondage of an incoherent and untenable position, which repels them from Anglican orders. On the other hand, it is the living consciousness of the apostolic power and jurisdiction, the certainty and freedom of divine faith, which draws our youth to the narrow and self-denying path of the priest's life.

The true cause, then, of this ominous desertion of the young men is to be found in their unwillingness to bind themselves by subscription to incoherent and untenable formularies. There have been, indeed, attempts made at other times to abolish subscription to the Articles; but with this difference. In 1688, it was a movement in order to comprehend non-conformists; in 1774, it was a feeble attempt got up by a few Socinianising clergymen. But now it is far more widely demanded. The Rationalistic school, as a body, and the Romanising school, as a body, desire to be free from the Articles. The laity are forward in asking that their pastors should enjoy the same liberty as themselves. No layman holds himself in any way bound by the Thirty-nine Articles. He rejoices in the liberty of thinking and criticising, believing and disbelieving, as he likes. And he asks the same liberty for his teachers.

In proof of this I will quote an authority which must carry no little weight. Professor Stanley, in a letter to Dr. Tait, says:—

'The intelligent, thoughtful, highly-educated young men, who twenty or thirty years ago were to be found in every ordination, are gradually withheld from the service of the Church, and from the profession to which their tastes, their characters and their gifts best fit them. For this great calamity, the greatest that threatens the permanence and the usefulness of the Church of England, there are, no doubt, many causes at work—some transitory, some beyond the power of any legislative enactment to reach. But there can be no question that one cause is the reluctance, the increasing reluctance, of young men of the kind just described to entangle themselves in obligations with which they cannot heartily sympathise, and which may hereafter be brought against them to the ruin of their peace and of their professional usefulness.' *

Again he adds:—'I have been told on good authority that of nineteen young men, within the acquaintance of a single individual, who were within the last few years known to have gone to Cambridge with the intention of becoming clergymen, every one has since relinquished his intention, chiefly on the ground of the present state of subscription. Similar statistics to a larger extent, although of a less definite form, might be produced at Oxford.' †

This again is a new sign of these times, and one which is full of consequences. It has been well said that the opinions of the young men are a prophecy of the future. And certainly a system from which the young men turn away has the sentence of death in itself.

Finally, the rationalism which lay hid in the Anglican Reformation has at last reached its legitimate development. After rejecting the Divine authority of the Church, the tradition of dogma, the Catholic interpretation of Holy Scripture, it is ending by a denial of the inspiration and authenticity of the sacred books. I notice this, not to dwell upon it, but because it is the most signal evidence of the failure of Anglicanism. Its 'Articulus stantis aut cadentis Ecclesiae' is the sixth Article, which affirms the sufficiency of Scripture,

* *A Letter to the Lord Bishop of London on the State of Subscription in the Church of England and in the University of Oxford*, by Arthur P. Stanley, D.D.

† *Ibid.* note, p. 31.

and rests its authenticity and canonicity upon the testimony of the Church. It is precisely here that the last blow has been struck at the Anglican system: and the rationalistic infidelity which has robbed Protestant Germany of its belief in Holy Scripture is beginning to gather and to descend from high places upon England. The Sixth Article has been tried and found wanting; and Anglicanism, which has based itself upon the Scriptures, has generated a spirit of unbelief which has undermined the Scriptures on which it professed to rest. Whatsoever may tend to the exposure and extinction of error must be a cause of thankfulness to Catholics; and yet we cannot but view with sorrow and with alarm the gradual decay and dying out of the fragmentary truths of Christianity which survived the Reformation. A belief in the revelation of Christianity and in the inspiration of the Holy Scriptures may be said to have been universal in England. But it is this which is now giving way in the educated classes and in the masses of the English people.

I might add many more reasons for the belief that Protestantism in general, and Anglicanism in particular, has reached the term of its pretensions, and that we are at the crisis of its decline, but time forbids.

2. Another reason for regarding these times as critical and of singular importance is the condition of the Catholic Church both in the East and in the West. In the East there is a disposition among the populations separated from it to return to its unity: of which movement Russia may be considered as the centre: in the West a similar movement is in progress, of which

England is visibly the centre. The missionaries of the Church are penetrating the East with a vigour and success never known since the missions of S. Francis Xavier: and the Church in the West is renewing its strength and its action upon the old Catholic countries of Europe with an energy never seen since the Council of Trent. Neither is it without a significance that the other day the tercentenary of that great council was solemnly celebrated in the presence of a prince of the Church, delegated from the Holy See, in the ancient city of Trent. For three hundred years its decrees *de Reformatione* have been working deeply and surely in the universal Church. The civil powers have distracted its operations by their jealous maintenance of old abuses of prerogatives and customs; but revolutions have come as the scourges of God to sweep them clean away. After these reigns of terror the Church has renewed itself in a purity, majesty and expansion exceeding all its past. Witness the Church in France, the Church in Holland, and now the Church in Ireland and the Church in England. After three hundred years of penal laws, to which the fabulous cruelties of the Spanish Inquisition are merciful, the Church in England is once more free. I shall not touch even in outline the well-known events of the last thirty years—the Emancipation, the Hierarchy, the expansion of the Catholic Church in England. These three words are enough to show that our days are exceptional: that we are witnesses of one of those miracles of grace, of those resurrections of the Church after generations of death, by which God manifests His presence and His sovereignty. But it is a wonderful and almost articulate Providence that the same event which liberated the Catholic Church to use the freedom of its power should have driven the Anglican Establishment upon the infirmities of its own internal incoherence: that when the State ceased to persecute the Church and to protect the Establishment, Protestantism should have begun to dissolve and Catholicism to expand itself: nothing has held the Church under for three hundred years but the whole weight of a penal code: and nothing has held the Establishment up but the favour and force of the civil power.

Divine Providence has seemed to watch its opportunities to exhibit the office and action of the Church by diametrical contrasts. When the Royal Supremacy becomes visibly intolerable in its pretensions, the Supremacy of Rome enters in its calmness and power. When an article of the Apostles' Creed disappears from the religion of the Anglicans, the definition of the Immaculate Conception is promulgated: while the Established religion is visibly losing its social and political influence in England, the revolutions of Europe in fifteen years of sedition, intrigue and warfare, cannot overthrow the temporal power of the Vicar of Jesus Christ: when the Protestants of Germany and England by the aid of their pastors are denying the inspiration of Holy Scripture and undermining the authenticity of its books, the Catholic Church, the mother of unwritten traditions, against whom they have been perpetually clamouring, stands sole as the pillar and ground of the Truth, the witness and keeper of Holy Writ. 'Hæc non sine numine.' They are like the chips of wood which under the childish hands of Hildebrand, *manum pueri ductante numine*, fell into legible forms and prophesied of the future.

It was, then, in such a time as this that the Academia of the Catholic religion was founded in London. Its object, as we know, was to form a centre to which Catholics, both priests and laymen, who desire to serve the Truth and the Church may be drawn: as a means of communication and correspondence: and as a mutual help for the study and solution of questions which affect the Catholic religion, that is both the Faith and the Church, and that both in speculation and in practice. And first we have to be thankful for its existence and for its continuance, and for the discourses which have been addressed to us, especially for some of them. Nevertheless we have not as yet recognised as much as we may the direct and practical uses for which it may be employed. And with a view to this I would endeavour to suggest the subjects which appear to be proper to this Academia.

They may, I think, be stated as follows:—

1. First, all such arguments as exhibit the relation of reason to Revelation, of reason to the Church, of the Church to the Scriptures, of reason to the Scriptures. These subjects are especially forced upon us by the intellectual condition of England, by the dissolution of Protestantism, and by the influence of these two causes upon many among our own people. It is much to be desired that certain men would subdivide these subjects among themselves, and engage to produce papers upon each of them, to be read before the Academia. From

such, a volume most useful and needful at this moment might easily be formed. We must all desire that the Catholic Church should be seen by all men to stand foremost in the defence of the Word of God, unwritten and written, in these days of unbelief.

2. Next, the relation of the Church to politics requires a new and careful restatement. The great Catholic writers, such as S. Thomas, Suarez and Bellarmine, treated of these subjects in the abstract, and in their bearing upon the forms of political society known in their day. But the last centuries have changed the whole aspect and application of their principles. The political society of the last three hundred years is a new phase of Christian civilisation. The inevitable divorce of the ecclesiastical and civil powers, which is everywhere accomplishing, and the separation of the nations, as such, from the unity of the faith, which brings with it the desecration of the corporate life and action of society—that is of the civil power—is a new and unprecedented fact of a portentous character, charged with a future which we can only contemplate with submission to the will of God and confidence in His care of His Church and people. A multitude of subjects are at once forced upon us. What is the relation of the Church to the civil society of the world? Has it any duty towards it, or direction over it? Do politics enter into morals, and has the Church any jurisdiction within the sphere of politics? Can politics be separated from the faith, and Christian society from the Church? Is civilisation dependent on or independent of Christianity, and therefore of the Church? Was the concurrent

action of the spiritual and civil powers in past ages for good or for evil? Is their present divorce an advance or a retrogression in Christian civilisation?

I need not point out that these questions are inevitable; they are forced upon us; they underlie the whole continental revolution against the Holy See; they are mixed up in the foreign policy of every government; they are ventilated in every newspaper; Catholics cannot meet in a congress without being overtaken by them as by a spring-tide; they enter into the duties of every Englishman who possesses the trust of a vote or the responsibility of influence; they are the fine wedges which are rending us asunder, and throwing many, who are otherwise sound in faith, upon a stream which will carry them not only away from the spirit of the Church, but, at last, into opposition to the Holy See. Do not think I exaggerate, or speak as a theorist. Every parish priest will know that the subtilest form of political sedition is at this moment being propagated among our Catholics in England by brotherhoods, secret societies, and obscure newspapers. For all this we must prepare ourselves. If we need a last reason to attract us to these studies, we may find it in the allocution of the Holy Father at the canonization in 1862, in which all the faithful of every nation and people were warned to beware of the anti-social and anti-Christian principles of modern political theories.

3. Once more, the relation of philosophy to faith lies at the foundation of the chief intellectual problems of the day. Without a clear decision on this subject there can be no sufficient treatment of the first truths of

theology. The most lamentable aberrations of these later years may in some cases be traced to a single philosophical error, which, like a morbid particle in the blood, will produce death.

A certain class of modern metaphysical philosophers has been well subdivided into objective and subjective atheists, and yet these writers are read both without and within the Church in England without scruple or hesitation. Happily many men are not consequent, and many have no conception of the character and reach of the books they read. Inconsequence and unconsciousness preserve them from the evil of the anti-Catholic and anti-Christian philosophy by which they are surrounded.

A still more urgent subject is the relation of Faith and the Church to Science. It would seem to be too trivial to go on repeating, that between revelation and science there can be no opposition; that the works of God are His words, and the words of God are His works, and that both are in absolute harmony. In the Divine mind they are one truth: in the Divine action they may be only partially and successively developed. They may for a time seem to be diverse, and to involve discrepancies of signification; but ultimately and essentially they must be one, even as God is one. 'Deus scientiarum Tu es.' God is the fountain of all sciences. For this cause Catholics have no fear of science, scientifically elaborated and scientifically treated. They have no fear of any accumulation of facts and phenomena, truly such, nor of any induction or conclusion scientifically established. They fear only science unscientifically handled, superficial observations, hasty generalisations, reckless opposition to revelation, and undissembled readiness to reject revelation rather than doubt of a modern theory about flint instruments and hyena's bones. It is indeed true that Catholics have an intense dislike and hostility to such science as this, and to all its modifications. They hold it to be guilty, not only of *leze majesté* against the Christian revelation, but against the truth and dignity of science itself. They abhor—and I accuse myself of being a ringleader in this abhorrence—the science now in fashion, which I take leave to call 'the brutal philosophy,' to wit, there is no God, and the ape is our Adam.

How necessary it is for Catholics to prepare themselves on the relation of society and of science to the Church, may be seen by what passed the other day, as at Malines so at Munich. Catholics cannot meet without being forced into the time-spirit. We do not live in an exhausted receiver. The middle ages are passed. There is no zone of calms for us. We are in the modern world—in the trade winds of the nineteenth century, and we must brace ourselves to lay hold of the world as it grapples with us, and to meet it intellect to intellect, culture to culture, science to science.

For in these last centuries, first politics and now science have fallen away from the faith. This is the paradisaical state according to some. To others it is the dissolution of the Christian society of the world carried out to its last consequence. Now it will be a subject very proper to the sessions of the Academia to discuss whether Science have any dependence upon Faith, or whether it be independent in a province of its own; whether it be scientific to threaten the received chronology with a jaw-bone found at Amiens, or with cities submerged in lakes, or with formations arbitrarily assumed to be slow in their accretion and the like; or whether it be not the part of Science to proceed with the docility of a learner, and the patience of an interrogator, waiting for the answers of nature, who will not be rudely or contemptuously questioned, but demands of its disciples the reverence and the piety of sons to its great Creator.

Lastly—for I must not trespass longer upon your patience—under the name of science is included not only Metaphysics and Physics, but also the scientific treatment of Theology, Philosophy, and History in its relation to theological science. In this sense it goes to the root of faith. I cannot better illustrate my meaning than by quoting the words of a Swiss theologian, Gügler, whose works I do not pretend to know beyond the passage which I have met in quotation. Either that passage does adequately represent the mind of the writer, or it does not. With this I have less to do than with its inevitable effect on the mind of the reader. 'We are to believe,' says the author to his antagonists, 'the voice of the Church, you say, without seeking to understand; but where do we hear this voice? Not in your mouths, certainly, or with the ears of the body; it must be sought for in history, and in the written records of the Church. We must examine each document historically in order to know whether it is the authentic expression of the mind of the Church without interpolation; only then does faith begin.' 'Embrace reason and science, become what you ought to be; and your kingdom will rise again from the dead.'*

First, I would wish to know who *we* are who are bound to examine each document historically? and next, what documents? and lastly, for the establishment of what doctrines? Does it signify that the faithful are to receive the articles of their Baptismal Creed from documents historically examined by each one for himself, and not from the voice of the Church? Or the interpretation of those articles, or the interpretation of Scripture? And is it only after examination of each document historically that faith begins? Have they no faith before baptism, nor after baptism, till they become historical critics?

If by these high-sounding phrases be meant only that we must know *what* we believe, and *why* we believe, before we believe it, or that reason is the preamble of faith, there is no need of such imposing phraseology, nor of any discovery. We may answer with S. Augustin, 'Absit ut ideo credamus ne rationem accipiamus, sive quæramus, quum etiam credere non possemus nisi rationabiles animas haberemus.'† But if it be meant that science precedes faith, and that the unscientific have no faith, I would leave the writer to reconcile himself with the Prophet who says, 'Nisi credideritis non intelligetis,' and with S. Augustin, who with the principle transfixes the pretensions of the Manichees. We are no lovers of darkness, nor of the kingdom of the dead, and we have, I hope, as ardent a love of science and

* *Home and Foreign Review*, July 1863, p. 194.

† *S. Aug. Epist.* cxx. 3, tom. ii. p. 347.

reason as any men of our time; but we have learned in the school of those doctors and saints who teach that faith is a rational act, and that to believe is the condition of understanding, and understanding the reward of faith. 'Si a me,' says S. Augustin, 'aut a quolibet alio doctore non irrationabiliter flagitas, ut quod credis intelligas, corrige definitionem tuam, non ut fidem respuas, sed ut ea, quæ fidei firmitate jam tenes, etiam rationis luce conspicias. . . . . . Et ideo rationabiliter dictum est per Prophetam, "nisi credideritis non intelligetis." '

Again he says: 'Sed prius Sanctarum Scripturarum auctoritatibus colla subdenda sunt, ut ad intellectum per fidem quisque perveniat.'*

And once more, for the principle pervades the works of S. Augustin from beginning to end—

'*Sed sunt quidam*, inquit, *in vobis qui non credunt.* Non dicit, sunt quidam in vobis qui non intelligunt: sed causam dixit, quare non intelligant. *Sunt enim quidam in vobis qui non credunt*: et ideo non intelligunt, quia non credunt. Propheta enim dixit, *Nisi credideritis, non intelligetis.* Per fidem copulamur, per intellectum vivificamur. Prius hæreamus per fidem, ut sit quod vivificetur per intellectum. Nam qui non hæret, resistit: qui resistit, non credit. Nam qui resistit, quomodo vivificatur? Adversarius est radio lucis, quo penetrandus est: non avertit aciem, sed claudit mentem. *Sunt* ergo *quidam qui non credunt.* Credant et aperiant, aperiant et illuminabuntur.' †

* *De peccatorum meritis*, cap. xxi. 16 D. tom. x. p. 16.

† *In Joan. Evang.* cap. 6, Tract. XXVII. tom. iii. pp. 504.

In a word, it is not science which generates faith but faith which generates science by the aid of the reason illuminated by revelation.

In what I have hitherto said, I have assumed one truth as undeniable and axiomatic, namely that God has revealed Himself; that He has committed this revelation to His Church; and that He preserves both His revelation and His Church in all ages by His own presence and assistance from all error in faith and morals. Now inasmuch as certain primary truths—which may be naturally known of God and the soul, and of the relations of the soul with God, and of man with man, that is certain truths discoverable also in the order of nature by reason or by philosophy—are taken up into and incorporated with the revelation of God, the Church possesses the first principles of rational philosophy and of natural ethics both for individuals and for society. And inasmuch as these principles are the great regulating truths of philosophy and natural morality, including natural politics, the Church has a voice, a testimony and a jurisdiction within these provinces of natural knowledge. I do not affirm the Church to be a philosophical authority, but I may affirm it to be a witness in philosophy. Much more when we come to treat of Christian philosophy or the Theodicea, or Christian morals and Christian politics; for these are no more than the truths of nature grafted upon the stock of revelation and elevated to a supernatural perfection. To exclude the discernment and voice of the Church from philosophy and politics is to degrade both by reducing them to the natural order. First it pollards them, and next it deprives them of the corroboration of a higher evidence. Against this the whole array of Catholic theologians and philosophers has always contended. They have maintained that the tradition of theological and ethical knowledge is divinely preserved, and has a unity in itself, that there is a true traditive philosophy running down in the same channel with the divine tradition of faith, recognised by faith as true by the light of nature, and guarded by the circle of supernatural truths by which faith has surrounded it. In saying this I am not extending the infallibility of the Church to philosophical or political questions apart from their contact with revelation; but affirming only that the radical truths of the natural order have become rooted in the substance of faith and are guaranteed to us by the witness and custody of the Church. So likewise, as the laws of Christian civilisation are the laws of natural morality elevated by the Christian law, which is expounded and applied by the Church, there is a tradition both of private and public ethics, or in other words of morality and jurisprudence, which forms the basis of all personal duty and of all political justice. In this again the Church has a discernment, and therefore a voice. A distribution of labour in the cultivation of all provinces of truth is prudent and intelligible: a division of authority and an exclusion of the Church from science is not only a dismemberment of the kingdom of truth; but a forcible rending of certain truths from their highest evidence. Witness the treatment of the question whether the existence of God can be proved, and whether God can be known by natural reason in the hands of those who turn their backs upon the tradition of evidence in the universal Church. Unless revelation be an illusion, the voice of the Church must be heard in these higher provinces of human knowledge. Newton, as Dr. Newman says, 'cannot dispense with the metaphysician nor the metaphysician with us.' Into cosmogony the Church must enter by the doctrine of creation; into natural theology by the doctrine of the existence and perfections of God; into ethics by the doctrine of the cardinal virtues; into politics by the indissolubility of marriage, the root of human society as divorce is its dissolution. And by this interpenetration and interweaving of its teaching, the Church binds all sciences to itself. They meet in it as in their proper centre. As the sovereign power which runs into all provinces unites them in one Empire, so the voice and witness of the Church unites and binds all sciences in one.

It is the parcelling and morselling out of science, and the disintegration of the tradition of truth, which has reduced the intellectual culture of England to its present fragmentary and contentious state. Not only errors are generated, but truths are set in opposition: science and revelation are supposed to be at variance, and revelation to be the weaker side of human knowledge.

The Church has an infallible knowledge of the original revelation. Its definitions of Divine Faith fall within this limit. But its infallible judgments reach beyond it. The Church possesses a knowledge of truth which belongs also to the natural order. The existence of God—His power, goodness, and perfections—the moral law written in the conscience—are truths of the natural order, which are declared also by revelation, and recorded in Holy Scripture. These truths the Church knows by a twofold light — by the supernatural light of revelation, and by the natural light which all men possess. In the Church this natural light is concentrated as in a focus. The great endowment of common sense, that is the *communis sensus generis humani*, the maximum of light and evidence for certain truths of the natural order, resides eminently in the collective intelligence of the Church, that is to say, in the intelligence of the faithful, which is the seat of its passive infallibility, and in the intelligence of the pastors, or the *Magisterium Ecclesiae*, which is the organ of its active infallibility. That two and two make four is not more evident to the Catholic Church than to the rest of mankind, to S. Thomas or S. Bonaventura than to Spinoza and Comte. But that God exists, and that man is responsible, because free, are moral truths, and for the perception of moral truths even of the natural order a moral discernment is needed; and the moral discernment of the Church, even of natural truths, is, I maintain, incomparably higher than the moral discernment of the mass of mankind, by virtue of its elevation to greater purity and conformity to the laws of nature itself.

The highest object of human science is God; and theology, properly so called, is the science of His nature and perfections, the radiance which surrounds 'the Father of light, in whom is no change, neither shadow of vicissitude.' Springing from this central science flow the sciences of the works of God, in nature and in grace: and under the former fall not only the physical sciences, but those also which relate to man and to his action—as morals, politics, and history. Now, the revelation God has given us rests for its centre upon God Himself, but in its course describes a circumference within which many truths of the natural order relating both to the world and to man are included. These the Church knows not only by natural light, but by Divine revelation, and declares by Divine assistance. But these primary truths of the natural order are axioms and principles of the sciences within which they properly fall. And these truths of philosophy belong also to the domain of faith. The same truths are the objects of faith and of science; they are the links which couple these sciences to revelation. How, then, can these sciences be separated from their relation to revealed truth without a false procedure? No Catholic could so separate them; for these truths enter within the dogma of faith. No Christian who believes in Holy Scripture could do so; for they are included in Holy Writ. No mere philosopher could do so; for thereby he would discard and perhaps place himself in opposition and discord with the maximum of evidence which is attainable on these primary verities, and therefore with the common sense not only of Christendom but of mankind. In this I am not advocating a mixture or confusion of religion and philosophy, which, as Lord Bacon says in his work, 'De Augmentis Scientiarum,' 'will undoubtedly make an heretical religion and an imaginary and fabulous philosophy,' but affirming that certain primary truths of both physical and ethical philosophy are delivered to us by revelation, and that we cannot neglect them as our starting-points in such sciences without a false procedure and a palpable forfeiture of truth. Such verities are, for instance, the existence of God, the creation of the world, the freedom of the will, the moral office of the conscience, and the like. Lord Bacon says, again: 'There may be veins and lines, but not sections or separations,' in the great continent of Truth. All truths alike are susceptible of scientific method, and all of a religious treatment. The father of modern philosophy, as men of our day call him, so severe and imperious in maintaining the distinct province and process of science, is not the less peremptory and absolute as to the unity of all truth and the vital relation of all true science to the Divine philosophy of revelation.

In confirmation of what I have said, I will use better words than my own. In the second of the well-known Lectures on University Education,* Dr. Newman, treating of the relation of theology to other sciences, speaks as follows: 'Summing up, gentlemen, what I have said, I lay it down that all knowledge forms one whole, because its subject-matter is one; for the universe in its length and breadth is so intimately knit together that we cannot separate off portion from portion, and operation from operation, except by a mental abstraction; and then again, as to its Creator, though He, of course, in His own Being, is infinitely separated from it, yet He has so implicated Himself with it, and taken it into His very bosom, by His presence in it, His providence over it, His impressions upon it, and his influences through it, that we cannot truly or fully contemplate

* *Discourses on the Scope and Nature of University Education*, J. H. Newman, Disc. II.

it without contemplating Him. Next, sciences are the results of that mental abstraction which I have spoken of, being the logical record of this or that aspect of the whole subject-matter of knowledge. As they all belong to one and the same circle of objects, they are one and all connected together; as they are but aspects of things, they are severally incomplete in their relation to the things themselves, though complete in their own idea and for their own respective purposes; on both accounts they at once need and subserve each other. And further, the comprehension of the bearings of one science on another, and the use of each to each, and the location and limitation, and adjustment and due appreciation of them all, one with another—this belongs, I conceive, to a sort of science distinct from all of them, and in some sense a science of sciences, which is my own conception of what is meant by philosophy, in the true sense of the word.' . . . .

Further on he says:—'What theology gives, it has a right to take; or rather, the interests of truth oblige it to take. If we would not be beguiled by dreams, if we would ascertain facts as they are, then, granting theology as a real science, we cannot exclude it, and still call ourselves philosophers. I have asserted nothing as yet as to the preeminent dignity of religious truth; I only say, if there be religious truth at all, we cannot shut our eyes to it without prejudice to truth of every kind, physical, metaphysical, historical, and moral; for it bears upon all truth. And thus I answer the objection with which I opened this discourse. I supposed the question put to me by a philosopher of the day, "Why cannot you go your wayand let us go ours?" I answer, in the name of theology, "When Newton can dispense with the metaphysician, then may you dispense with us."' . . . .

'Man, with his motives and works, his languages, his propagation, his diffusion, is from Him [God]. Agriculture, medicine, and the arts of life are His gift. Society, laws, government—He is their sanction. The pageant of earthly royalty has the semblance and the benediction of the Eternal King. Peace and civilisation, commerce and adventure, wars when just, conquest when humane and necessary, have His cooperation and His blessing upon them. The course of events, the revolution of empires, the rise and fall of states, the periods and eras, the progresses and the retrogressions of the world's history, not indeed the incidental sin, over-abundant as it is, but the great outlines and the issues of human affairs, are from His disposition. The elements, and types, and seminal principles, and constructive powers of the moral world, in ruins though it be, are to be referred to Him. He "enlighteneth every man that cometh into the world."' . . . .

'If this be a sketch, accurate in substance and, as far as it goes, of the doctrines proper to theology, and especially of the doctrine of a particular Providence, which is the portion of it most on a level with human sciences, I cannot understand at all how, supposing it to be true, it can fail, considered as knowledge, to exert a powerful influence on philosophy, literature, and every intellectual creation or discovery whatever. I cannot understand how it is possible, as the phrase goes, to blink the question of its truth or falsehood. It meets us with a profession and a proffer of the highest truths of which the human mind is capable; it embraces a range of subjects the most diversified and distant from each other. What science will not find one part or other of its province traversed by its path? What results of philosophic speculation are unquestionable, if they have been gained without enquiry as to what theology had to say to them? Does it cast no light upon history? Has it no influence upon the principles of ethics? Is it without any sort of bearing on physics, metaphysics, and political science? Can we drop it out of the circle of knowledge, without allowing either that that circle is thereby mutilated, or, on the other hand, that theology is no science?'

Such being the essential unity of all truth, and such the mind and instinct of the Church, it is no wonder that humble and pious minds not largely cultivated beyond their Catechism should turn with fear and suspicion from the pursuit of science. It is deplorable, but not wonderful, that they should be thereby set against the progress of scientific knowledge. But on whom rests the blame? Without question, on us, who profess to know better, if we so use our better knowledge as to offend and to affright our weaker brethren. Life is short, and at longest there is little time for the pursuit of knowledge. Better to use it for science silently and humbly. There is as little fear of our modern philosophers being burnt for magic, or even accused of it by their ignorant cotemporaries, as of our attaining the intellectual superiority of Sylvester II. or Nicolas of Cusa. Nothing is gained to science, still less to charity, by a tone of pretentious menace: such as, 'If the facts of geology are contrary to the Catholic faith, let the Catholic faith look to it.' We need no such admonitions, be they threats or warnings. It would inspire us with more confidence in their science and humility, if our geologists said: 'If the facts of geology are contrary to the Catholic faith, let geology look to its facts.' It is much easier to trumpet about facts than to fix them. Even in our own short lifetime we have seen the facts of geology to be made, unmade, remade, and made over again, I know not how many times. The nature and origin of man has been so often fixed and unfixed that I am in doubt whether I am descended, as I said, from Adam or from an ape, or from a jelly, or from a capsule, or whether I am created at all, or am a transient manifestation of an uncreated whole, that is whether I am man or Pan, whom I revered in boyhood, but never aspired to be. And this is science. Truly the Catholic faith has not much need to fear it, save only for the half-learned, vain-glorious, pretentious and unbelieving. But they are many.

To illustrate my meaning from a high authority not to be suspected of partiality to us, I will quote the words of Mr. Lewes, the hierophant or archimandrite of Comtism, or as I have ventured to call it in respect to theology, the Brutal Philosophy. After a review in four volumes of the triumph and progress of philosophy along the *via sacra* of ages from the seven friends of our boyhood, Thales, Pythagoras, Solon, &c., through

Anaximenes, Anaximander, to Spinoza, Locke, Reid, Kant, Hegel, Fichte, to Auguste Comte, he sums up the pæan in this melancholy strophe which closes his last volume. 'Modern philosophy opens with a method—Bacon; and ends with a method—Comte; and in each case this method leads to positive science, and sets metaphysics aside. Within these limits we have witnessed various efforts to solve the problems of philosophy; and all these efforts have ended in scepticism.' *

It sounds like the voice of the buffoon in the chariot reminding Cæsar that he is but a man.

The mission, then, of the Catholic Church in England at this moment is a noble and beneficent work, that of calling home, first, truths to their proper centre, and then men to those truths.

It has first to reorganise the elements of Christian belief which lie scattered in fragments around its unity. And this it is already doing beyond all hope: even error is working with it, revealing its own incoherence. It is certain that as the Catholic Church stands at this hour in England the only witness for unity of faith, so in ten years it will be recognised as the only Divine evidence, and therefore the only certain authority, for the inspiration and canon of Holy Scripture.

It is the duty therefore of Catholics to prepare themselves for the future which is before them. They little thought thirty years ago to be as they are now.

They little thought ten years ago of the majestic expansion of the Catholic Church at this hour, and of its dignified attitude of calm in the midst of the religious

* Vol. iv. p. 263.

confusion and dissolution which is around it. Still less can we anticipate what the next ten years may bring. The advance of the Church is in geometrical progression.

And in proportion as it regains the intelligence of the English people, the hearts of men will turn to it *sicut torrens in austro.* It will be seen to be in England also what it ever has been in the civilised world—the mother and nurse of all intellectual culture. The people of England are already beginning to hear its voice and to recognise it as the pleading of truth, charity, and common sense.

THE ACTION OF THE CHURCH UPON ART AND CIVILISATION,

SHOWN IN THE HIGH ALTAR IN THE CHURCH OF S. AMBROSE AT MILAN, SO VALUABLE FOR ITS LITURGICAL TEACHINGS, AND AS AN EXAMPLE OF ANGLO-SAXON WORKMANSHIP.

By DANIEL ROCK, D.D.

AFTER Rome, there is no Italian city so crowded with stirring recollections belonging to the olden times as Milan; and some of its churches have a peculiar interest about them for ecclesiastical antiquaries and artists of all nations, but more especially for every well-read Englishman. Its Gothic cathedral, the daring thought of a Teutonic mind, bodied forth and made to live in marble, with the three thousand statues that people its roof and the outside niches of its walls, is one of the wonders of mediæval constructive science, and takes high rank among the most beautiful erections of Christendom, notwithstanding that its western end is deformed rather than finished by an incongruous front in the Pagan style perpetrated at the beginning of the present century under French usurpation and influences when classicism in government, in arts, and letters was the idol of the day. Its magnificent bronze seven-branched candlestick, called by the Milanese the 'Albero di Maria,' or as we should name it, a 'Jesse tree'—an admirable work of the thirteenth century, and although once so common in England, France, and Germany, is now almost the only one of the kind known of anywhere—makes us deeply regret the still finer one which adorned the abbey church of Saint Remi at Reims, and the finest one of all, that reached almost to the roof of our own majestic Durham. The sacristy, though often plundered, can yet show not a few specimens of some of the oldest and most interesting liturgical appliances, among which, a beautiful ivory holy-water vat, two diptychs, ivory covers for the evangeliarium or book of the Mass Gospels, and one especially precious cover for the same kind of textus in the rare style of framed enamel, are not the least conspicuous; but the underground silver-sheathed chapel, with the gorgeous shrine of S. Charles Borromeo, is, as it always must be, the great attractive point to every pious traveller who will, for the moment, forget arts and archæology, and shut his eyes to the glare of lamps and tapers and the rays of precious stones, and the sparkling of gold and silver, the while he kneels to beg the intercession of one of the best and the most active among the thousands of holy and sainted bishops whom God has given to His Church.

To the lover of mediæval art, S. Eustorgio's will furnish many an object of noteworthy attention; and the English archæologist will not overlook the effigy of Stefano Visconti, wearing about his neck that well-known badge of the house of Lancaster, borne by its followers through many a hard-fought field during the war of the Roses, the collar of SS., or Sanctus, Sanctus,

Sanctus—the name of God, as John of Gaunt's mother said of it—written upon each one of its links; an ornament which Henry VII. had wrought as a border round those twenty-four magnificent copes of cloth of gold which he got made for his chapel in Westminster Abbey, one of which, belonging to Stonyhurst, was lately exhibited in London. This badge, coming down from Catholic times, and speaking of the Catholic liturgy, is yet worn by the Lord Chief Justice of England on saints' days and solemn occasions. This same English collar of SS may be found upon another sepulchral effigy in the Church of S. Ambrose, to which edifice we will now hasten.

The Ambrosian basilic is set out in true orientation—due east and west; it has a square colonnaded fore-court, a wide vestibule opening upon a nave and two aisles, one ambo, a screen between the people and the chancel, an isolated altar beneath a dome-shaped canopy upheld by four porphyry columns, and an apsidal east end, with a marble chair against the wall; bearing in fact, a strong likeness, in very many of its features, to the venerable Church of S. Clement at Rome.

While standing on the threshold of this hallowed building, the mind dreams back to persons and to things gone by more than fourteen centuries ago; and we cannot help thinking of those two great saints and doctors of the Church who so often trod its pavement. We behold, in imagination, S. Ambrose, with a long-drawn procession of clerics and people, bringing hither, at its consecration, the so much longed-for and newly-found relics of SS. Gervase and Protase, and a mob of scoffing Arians and Manicheans hovering round: an earnest cry—a prayer to those martyrs—is suddenly heard, a halt is made, and a blind man that sat by the wayside, poor Severus, known to all Milan as having been blind for years, at his own earnest wish is led forwards by some friendly hand, a linen cloth that overspreads the relics is put upon his eyes, and lo! he sees again: the Catholics shed tears of joy and thankfulness, the Arians gnash their teeth with vexation, and scream out that it is all a trick. Amid the crowd that throng about Severus is one whose keen searching look and lively cast of countenance bespeak anything but weakness of understanding; he is the celebrated teacher of oratory, a heretic, Austin by name, and this distinguished man shouts out aloud that it is the work of God—a miracle obtained by the prayers of the saints. Another moment, and again imagination shadows to us that same Austin, melted to tears by the sweetness of the music as he stands outside that large open doorway with a curtain hanging over it, hearkening to the singing of the choir. Though his footsteps falter, deeming as he does that there cannot be truth in Catholicism, a something draws him in, and he leans against one of those pillars out of sight of the increasing crowd. Shortly Ambrose the bishop is seen to come from that large marble chair at the furthest end of the presbytery, and go up into the ambo, or as some then called it, the 'tribunal,' to preach. Austin listens, eye and ear, not so much to learn as to criticise; every moment, however, he is more and more overpowered by the speaker's strength and fitness of argument, and delighted with the beauty of his language; but still he thinks, or strives to think, that his friend Faustus, the Manichean, has a more graceful utterance, a much more sonorous delivery. A few more sermons and Austin ceases to be a Manichean, yet does not become a Catholic. Two years creep away, when early one bright September morning in A.D. 386, Ambrose the bishop, surrounded by a few of his clergy, is seen walking from the baptistery to the cathedral, hand in hand with a neophyte clad all in white; that convert is Austin, who, like his teacher, will be a great bishop and learned doctor in God's Church, and a most powerful and successful opponent of heretics and heresy in different ages. Again imagination brings other personages before us, and we behold S. Ambrose clad for mass in wide majestic chasuble and long broad pall twined with such seemliness about his shoulders, and before him in some church's vestibule a glittering array—an emperor robed in imperial purple and a crowd of courtiers as grand as golden bravery of dress can make them. Nothing dazed, and heedless alike of royal frowns or ministerial threats, the undaunted man of God, with the same right hand that led the reclaimed Austin across the church's threshold, now uplifted in mild sternness, bars the entrance there of a master of the earth, the blood-stained Theodosius. As the present cathedral stands where stood the ancient mother church of Milan, and as the then one sole baptistery for the city, as well as the imperial palace, were both close to it, the Ambrosian basilic could not have been the scene of these two thrilling events.

Go we now to look well at that beautiful and curious altar; and we shall find it worthy of most minute examination, as a witness to many liturgical practices of the olden times, and so valuable as a work of early mediæval art. An oblong cube in shape, it stands perfectly detached; on three of its sides it is sheathed in silver parcel-gilt, on the west side, all in purest gold, but everywhere sprinkled with precious stones, and ornamented with bands of elaborate enamel. A ciborium or hollow hemisphere resting upon four porphyry columns overshadows it. Deemed by the people as well as by the priesthood the throne upon which the King of kings, the Word made flesh, the God-man, comes down in all his majesty, though hidden beneath sacramental veils, and occupies as often as the words of consecration at mass are uttered, the altar had given to it that peculiar mark—that emblem from the earliest ages of a ruling prince, the canopy—which distinguished, as it yet distinguishes, after many fashions, the sovereign, or kingly, or imperial chair, from every other seat of state. Even when there were more altars than one, each had its own dome-like covering, as may yet be seen in the three old altars, standing in a row within the presbytery in that curious but overlooked church, the cathedral of Terracina. Those primitive feelings of royal reverence for our Lord in the Eucharist, and for the altar as His throne, still live and show themselves in the umbrella and the canopy borne over the Blessed Sacrament, and in the crimson silk gold-fringed baldacchino found hanging down from the roof over many a high altar in the churches on the Continent. Not merely because gold happened to be the most precious among metals, and porphyry one of the most beautiful and rarest of marbles, was it that these two substances came to be employed upon this altar and its canopy: in the well-known symbolism of the times, gold typified the heavenly wisdom, the divinity of Our Lord; and the purple of the porphyry told of Him as being the King of kings, while its fire-like colour spoke of that glowing warmth of love which made Him pour forth His heart's blood for man's redemption.

The first glance, however hasty, at this altar-covering of gold and silver, will be enough to show how strong, in the mind of its designer, was the wish to set before the beholders' eyes the token of the great Atonement, and all the mysteries connected with it; for the cross is the grand leading ornament spread out all over three of its four sides; and in each place, upon the cross is lavished, always the most beautiful, often by far the greater number, of the precious stones there. This earnestness in associating the table for the Eucharistic sacrifice, and the emblem of the sacrifice at Calvary, so closely with one another—so as to teach the people that they were, in reality, but the one same sacrifice— was, in those times, carried so far, that there may be found in some illuminated codices of the liturgy the altar figured as overspread by a cloth marked all its length with one large wide cross.

Between the limbs of the large cross on the western front of the altar facing the people are wrought, in low relief, the chief events in the life, death, and resurrection of Our Lord, all in purest gold. On the eastern side, the subjects are taken from the life of S. Ambrose, done in silver parcel-gilt. This distinction between the precious metals—of gold for Our Lord, of silver for one of His saints—is not without a strongly emphasised symbolic meaning. Gold, being understood as the emblem of the Godhead, is here given as the especial material for setting forth the life, death, and uprising of Our Saviour; while the far lower, less costly metal, silver, is purposely allotted for showing the doings of the saints, all of whose strength for what is good and holy is not their own, but the free gift of Heaven, shed like rays of light upon them from on high, so happily expressed by those partial streaks of gold or parcel-gilding, that gleam so thickly all about this eastern portion of the frontal. To this side of the altar, wrought with some of the events in the life of S. Ambrose, we will now confine ourselves; for several of them are highly interesting in a ritual point of view, as affording, in one instance, unmistakeable evidence upon a question which has hitherto been misunderstood by all writers on the liturgy, and throwing an equally strong light upon another matter lately much discussed among ecclesiastical antiquaries and secular archæologists.

On one of the panels S. Ambrose is figured standing at the altar, but in a state of trance: a deacon and a subdeacon are with him. The saint wears a large chasuble reaching well down upon his arms, and from his shoulders falls, before and behind, a long broad pall. Though made in such graceful fullness, the chasuble is not an atom wider than that vestment would now be, were it allowed the same ample dimensions assigned it by S. Charles Borromeo in his Acta Ecclesiæ Mediolanensis. The deacon's dalmatic shows very full sleeves, and he bears his stole outwards hanging on his left shoulder. Such, to this day, is the practice followed both in the Ambrosian and the Greek rite, as well as in the Armenian. The subdeacon's tunicle sits somewhat closer to the person, and its sleeves are narrow when seen along with those of the deacon's dalmatic. This subdeacon is reading the epistle, in an elevated position—in an ambo—shown by an ornamented kind of stool upon which he is standing. The old ambones are still happily left in many churches through Italy, and in some places are even yet used, for their original purposes, at high mass; for instance at Narni, not far from Rome, as I was assured by the parish priest there, A.D. 1853. This I witnessed myself, the same year, at Milan in the cathedral, where they sang the epistle and gospel, at high mass, in the same ambo—that on the north side—and the sermon was preached in the one on the south. On that occasion the epistle was chanted by a cleric in a surplice; but lights, incense, subdeacon, deacon—all went up into the ambo for the gospel. The deacon had his stole outside his dalmatic, but crossed, like a belt, from left to right;* and priest, deacon, and subdeacon wore an apparel about the neck, just as I had observed to be the custom in the south of Spain,

* In a fine oil painting by Macrino d'Alba, of S. Lawrence, now, A. D. 1864, possessed by the Marchese d'Azeglio, Sardinian minister in England, the holy martyred deacon wears his stole after the usage of the Ambrosian rite, that is over, not under, his dalmatic, and beltwise. By this I should think Macrino had studied or lived some time at Milan.

A.D. 1836. But to get back to the bas-reliefs figured on this ancient frontal.

There is neither candlestick nor crucifix shown upon the altar, but right over it hangs a small crown, the appearance of which, in such a position, will help us in clearing up a controversy which has been, and is still agitating, odd enough to say, some diplomatic circles, as well as the antiquarian world in England and abroad. Towards the beginning of 1859, at Fuente de Guarrazza, two leagues from Toledo, was found, in an old burial-ground, a hoard of no less than eight golden crowns of different sizes, all of them having beautifully wrought chains for hanging them up, and several were gorgeously jewelled. As mere metal they were valued to be worth 2,000*l.*, without estimating the fine pearls, oriental sapphires, and precious stones with which they were studded, and of which the value doubled the above amount. From the name of Reccesvinthus thus occurring upon the best and largest, it was immediately assumed that this was nothing less than the very regal crown once worn by that prince, one of the last Gothic kings of Spain; the others, those of his queen and several children; and that the royal family, while flying before the invader Tarick and his Arabs, had buried them at Guarrazza, twelve hundred years ago. The whole of this find was stealthily carried off to Paris, sold to the French Government for a high sum, and may now be seen in the museum at the Hôtel Cluny. On both sides the Pyrenees, they were unhesitatingly pronounced to have been the crowns of the Gothic rulers of Spain—in fact, the olden regalia of that country. As rightly belonging to herself as such, Spain naturally sought to recover all these crowns, and instructed her minister at Paris to ask them from France; and a diplomatic controversy began, which, under some circumstances, might have grown into a pretty quarrel between two great nations.* At one of the meetings in 1859 of the Archæological Institute, I was the first individual to deny that these Spanish crowns were royal ones at all, or that any of them had ever been worn as such, and to assert that they were no other than liturgical crowns for hanging over altars and about the walls in churches, and had all been made and given to some sacred edifice for such ritual purpose. This shows how the knowledge of ecclesiastical antiquities may, sometimes, stand in useful stead even to those who are, or are likely to be, employed in diplomacy.

If, but a few years ago, Spaniards fell into such a mistake about crowns, Frenchmen, at the beginning of this same nineteenth century, were betrayed into a much more egregious blunder concerning sceptres. For the coronation of the First Napoleon, it was wished that, of the several appliances needed on the occasion by the ritual, as many as possible which had a dynastic antiquity about them, should be sought out and used at the function. Something of Charlemagne's was much wanted; and a silver-gilt wand with the figure of that great man at top of it, in the sacristy of S. Denis's, was thought of and brought to Paris to do

* Since this first discovery, other and more splendid liturgical crowns of the like kind have been found at the same spot, and are now to be seen at Madrid.

duty as a sceptre—Charlemagne's own sceptre—for the important occasion. With regard to age and ownership, this staff had its own and quite another tale to tell, for it bore inscribed upon it its pedigree, in these verses:—

D'argent fist faire ce baston
Lan MCCC quatre vins
Quatorze ne plus ne moins
Ceux qui le tiendront en leurs mains
Veuillent prier après la vie
Que same soit es cieux ravie
. . . Qu'il fust gardé
Et en grans festes regardé
Car pour loyaulté maintenir
Le doibt chantre en la main tenir.

Or in other words, the giver—but his name is lost—to get prayers for his soul after death—had this silver staff made in the year 1394, on purpose for the precentor's use on great solemnities: it is, in fact, nothing but a ruler of the choir's staff, then always, and even now in some places still, borne about, in hand, by the precentor, on high festivals. To hinder the cheat from being found out, the inscription was scratched off, and instead of the illustrious Charlemagne's sceptre, Buonaparte swayed, on his coronation day, the choir staff of the monk precentor of S. Denis's abbey. Mediæval archæology was at a very low ebb in Paris towards the beginning of the century, and not knowing enough then to see the glaring discrepance between an artistic work said to be of A. D. 800, and the one wrought in 1394, with the gap of six hundred years intervening. But, worse still, though French antiquaries were for the time successfully deluded, more recent ones have ably exposed the trick; yet this supposititious relic of Charlemagne's regalia is still left to carry on the falsehood in the museum at the Louvre, where whatever had once belonged to the regal or imperial families of France, that could be brought from far or near, is shown; or as Didron expresses it, 'Aujourd'hui cet heureux bâton se pavane dans le Musée des Souverains, au Louvre, au milieu des pièces les plus authentiques.'—Annales Archéologiques, t. xix. p. 127.

Of those various rich and beautiful adornments that, at the remotest periods, were everywhere employed for the ornamentation of the church, but more especially the altar, there is a distinguished one—the crown—which, singularly enough, has been either quite overlooked, or, at best, but slightly glanced at, by everyone who has written upon the architecture or the ritual of the early ages: a few words, then, to fill up such a gap, may not be out of place on this occasion.

Those sayings of the Psalmist, 'Thou hast crowned him with glory and honour' (Ps. viii. 6); 'Thou hast set on his head a crown of precious stones' (xx. 4); as well as that of S. Paul to Timothy (2 Tim. iv. 8), 'There is laid up for me a crown of justice,' that have been so strongly set forth in all the liturgies of the Greek as well as Latin quarters of the Church, no doubt made a deep impression upon the earliest ritualists no less than the framers of Christian symbolism. S. Eucharius, made Archbishop of Lyons A.D. 412, looked upon the crown as the emblem of everlasting glory—

corona, æterna gloria; and our own countryman, the unnamed Cistercian monk, who, at the end of the twelfth or beginning of the thirteenth century, wrote his valuable 'Distinctiones,' first given in print to the world by Dom (now Cardinal) Pitra, utters at his day the same sentiment:—'Corona significat præmium vitæ æternæ; unde: "Esto fidelis usque ad mortem, et dabo tibi coronam vitæ"' (Apoc. ii. 10)—Spicilegium Solesmense, t. iii. 402, 461. That at a very early epoch sprang up the custom of hanging crowns wrought of gold, and silver richly gemmed, at various spots about the church and for different symbolic purposes, we know from the best authorities. The wise economy exercised by the Church in introducing into public use the crucifix—that is, a full-length figure of Our Lord nailed to a cross—I have hinted at elsewhere ('Hierurgia,' p. 360, 2nd edition); and how praiseworthy was her sagacious precaution, in this instance, is well shown us by that blasphemous crucifix, with an ass's instead of Our Saviour's head, found scrawled in charcoal on the wall of a vault on the Palatine hill at Rome not long ago, and affording an illustration of the scoff which the heathen tried to fasten on our holy belief by calling its followers by the nickname of 'Ononychites.' Among the Church's first endeavours to strip the emblem of redemption of ethnic opprobrium, one was to wreathe it with the victor's floral garland, and encircle it with the mark of regal honour, at the same time that she sought to convey a salutary teaching through this symbolism. Telling his friend Severus all about the church he had just built at Nola, the learned bishop of that city, S. Paulinus, A.D. 394, speaks first of the crosses in the vestibule:—'Item dextra lævaque crucibus minio superpictis, hæc epigrammata sunt—

> Ardua floriferæ crux cingitur orbe coronæ,
> Et Domini fuso tincta cruore rubet, &c.
> *Epist. ad Severum.*

having before that told him—

> Cerne coronatam Domini super atria Christi
> Stare crucem, duro spondentem celsa labori
> Præmia: tolle crucem qui vis auferre coronam.

Inside the church walls the same principle, but after a more costly manner, was acted on. All about the sacred building, but more especially over the altar and within the ciborium or domed canopy resting upon four columns which overshadowed it, hung, by three chains, a narrow but often richly-gemmed golden crown, having within it and hanging still lower down, but much more jewelled, a figureless cross: the olden mark, in heathens' eyes of ignominy, by being thus honoured, became in due time, even to their thinking, a token free from shame—nay, honourable. Of such liturgical crowns with crosses, one of the earliest and most noteworthy is that which S. Aredius, who died in the latter half of the sixth century, bequeathed in his will to a favourite church:—'Similiter in oratorio sancti Hilarii corona cum cruce argentea deaurata cum gemmis pretiosis plena reliquiis sanctorum Domnorum, et suo ornatu—habens corona illa in se pendentes (*sic*) folia ex auro et gemmis facta numero viii. et in illa cruce similes factæ duæ, et mimitatæ gemma grande circumcirca auro, et subtus crucicula ex auro et gemmulenas viii.' (S. Gregorii

Turon. App. ed. Ruinart, p. 1313.) Of this kind of crown, sometimes called 'regnum,' mention is often made by Anastasius Bibliothecarius, while enumerating the precious gifts bestowed by the Roman Pontiffs and royal personages upon the churches at Rome. In that writer's list of all those costly presents made to S. Peter's and the other basilicæ, by the untiring Leo III., A.D. 795–816, we are struck by the astonishing number of these coronæ, not merely of silver but oftener of gold, far beyond a hundred; and as so near to our purpose, we may aptly instance the 'regnum panoclystum, ex auro purissimo cum cruce in medio pendens super ipsum altare, pensans libram unam et uncias XI.,' which that Pontiff bestowed upon the oratory of the Holy Cross in S. Peter's. (Liber Pontificalis, ed. Vignolio, t. ii. p. 280.) Of this good and bountiful Pope's immediate successor, another Leo and a Saint, Anastasius tells us:—'Confessionem (in ecclesia Quatuor Coronatorum) cum sacro altari argenteis tabulis pensan. libras nonaginta et tres decoravit Sanctorumque effigiebus perornavit. Super quod etiam obtulit regnum de argento purissimo pretiosissimis gemmis, habens in medio crucem, quod usque nunc super eodem pendere altari conspicitur.' (Lib. Pont. iii. 96); and for the high altar of the same church the same Pontiff provided a still far richer crown:—'Regnum ex auro purissimo unum pendens super altare majus cum catenulis similiter aureis sculptilem habens in medio crucem auream habentem gemmas quatuordecim, ex quibus quinque in eadem cruce fixas, et quæ ibidem pendent, novem; sex quidem albas et hyacinthinas tres, pens. simul libram unam et semis uncias.' (*Ib.* p. 122.) The way in which these jewels were arranged, some set immediately upon the cross, but the greater number drooping from it, will not escape the notice of those curious about the mounting of mediæval jewellery. No less than twelve golden coronæ were given to S. Peter's by Leo. (*Ib.* p. 137.)

Sometimes these same crowns were anciently put to another and important ecclesiastical use, which, although it is not without some weight in helping to support the doctrinal teachings of the Church, is, at the present period, known to a very few. At a very early epoch, perhaps even in the days of Constantine himself, the custom was to hang just over the grave of the holy dead one of these crowns, in signification of the Church's belief that he or she whose body lay entombed there, had won a place in heaven, was living a saint with God in everlasting glory; in fact, to put, in those far-off times, a crown of gold or silver over a sepulchre, was like the Church's present system of a solemn canonisation; and a valuable record of such an instructive practice is afforded us by a contemporary of Anglo-Saxon England's apostle S. Gregory the Great—another S. Gregory—S. Gregory of Tours. Telling, as is his wont, with great and to us most fortunate minuteness, of a theft committed in a church, the illustrious Gaulish prelate says:—'Chunus quidam rabidus instinctu demonis actus, coronam sepulchri quæ Sancti (Martini) meritum declaravit, violenter arripuit,' &c. (De Mirac. S. Martini, ib. i. c. ii. p. 1002 opp. ed. Ruinart.) But this idea was carried out further: such a crowning—the emblem of holiness, and everlasting happiness in the saintly dead—was used as such, over the statues and pictorial effigies of apostles, martyrs, and saints in general, long before the employment of the nimbus or circle of lightsome glory round their heads, and must have given rise to the modern emblem. Keeping this in sight, we more easily understand the introduction into art-works of these crowns. At the Church of S. Apollinaris in Classe near Ravenna, there are figured, in mosaic, all round the apsis, several of the early bishops of that see, and over the head of each one of them is shown hanging, between curtains, a crown suspended by three chains; such a crown then, at the beginning of the sixth century when the church was built by Theodoric, betokened the personage over whom it hung was a saint. Two hundred years later the very same ritual practice was still followed at Rome, where we find that zealous and most munificent Pontiff Leo III., among other splendid gifts in art-work, bestowing the one following upon S. Peter's:—'Salvatorem stantem; dextra lævaque ejus beati apostoli Petrus et Paulus, habentes pariter coronas ex gemmis pretiosis,' &c. (Lib. Pontif. ii. 273.)

Beginning with the early Christian consular ivory diptychs up to the illuminations in service-books of the eleventh century, modifications of such a symbolism may be found in those crowns that are represented about, though rarely over, the head of a consular dignitary or an imperial personage. In one of the illuminations of a beautiful evangeliarium now in the public library at Munich, but brought thither from Bamberg, the emperor Henry II., A.D. 1002—1024, is figured wearing his imperial diadem and throned between two of these liturgical coronæ, which have drops all about them like the Guarrazza ones, but without a cross hanging down within. The Emperor's crown, as well as those of the four angels hovering around him, are quite different from the Church-crowns, as may be seen in a curious recent publication (Föster, Denkmale Deutscher Baukunst Bilduerei, t. ii.). The indication of such crowns upon the ivory diptych, and in the illuminated page, may have been a piece of delicate courtier flattery, or perhaps, as then understood, a gentle hint to the consul or the emperor to lead a life of holiness here if he wished to win for the hereafter the guerdon of the upright and the good—a crown of everlasting glory.

The liturgical usages of Rome were followed in other parts of Christendom, and in Spain, as elsewhere, these crowns were abundantly supplied for the embellishment of churches. Of this the 'Coronica General de la Orden de San Benito,' by Yepez, will yield us many proofs. 'Confero'—says a prince living A.D. 759—'ibidem sacrosanctis altaribus suis in ornamentorum esse—tres coroneas argenteas,'&c. (t. iii. p.20. b. opp.)—'Offero —coronas argenteas—ecclesiæ S. Andreæ,—Testamentum S. Genadii Ep. Astorgensis, A.D. 953.' (*Ib.* t. iv. p. 447.)—'Ministeria ecclesiæ—coronas argenteas tres, ex quibus unam gemmis et auro comptam,' &c. (Test. Rudesindi Ep. Dumiensis, A.D. 930; *ib.* t. v. p. 424 a.) In a deed as late as A.D. 1101 the Spanish King Ferdinand makes over to a church, among other ritual appliances,—'coronas tres aureas una ex his cum sex alphas (unionibus) in gyro—tertia vero est diadema capitis mei aureum,' &c. (*Ib.* t. vi.)

Up then to the end of the tenth century, and even later, almost every altar had hanging over it a crown either of gold, silver, or of the baser metals, doing worship, as it were, to the cross which, though not always, very often, it encircled; and this same cross that, when there, came from the middle and hung somewhat lower and out of the crown so as to be well seen—like the Spanish ones, and the one given by Queen Theodolinda to the Church at Monza, where it may yet be found—was usually covered with pearls and jewels, out of love for Him who died upon a cross, and to honour, in the most conspicuous way, this token of redemption; in fact these crowns served all the ritual purposes of the crucifix which superseded them, and began in general to be put upon the altar itself, about the end of the tenth century. Of the several altars shown in this gold and silver frontal, almost every one has over it a suspended crown. There may be, though I do not know, another work of art in any kind which so unmistakeably lets us see the ancient use of these liturgical crowns, of which such frequent mention is made by writers of the early mediæval period, and that, as offerings, were so often carried from this country to Rome, by our Anglo-Saxon kings, nobles, and wealthy churchmen when they went on pilgrimage to the cradle of their faith, and to pray at the shrine of the Apostles.

More interesting still—indeed of the utmost value in a ritual point of view—is another panel where the saint is figured with the same sort of square altar in front of him, and where the artist has handed down to us the key for unlocking what has hitherto been a puzzle to every writer who has tried the solution of that curious and much-debated canon of the council of Tours held A.D. 570. 'Ut corpus Domini in altario, non in imaginario ordine, sed sub crucis titulo componatur.' Eminent canonists, the greatest liturgical scholars, are divided on the meaning of this ordinance. In it some behold a prohibition to place the holy Eucharist—when kept as a viaticum for the dying—among the images that stand upon the altar; others see in it a command to bake the altar-breads with a sign of the cross impressed upon them; one imagines that by it the host and chalice were directed to be put on the centre of the altar; and Mabillon, after noticing these variations of opinion, puts forth another of his own, and thinks the canon refers to keeping the Eucharist not among the sacred vessels in the sacristy, but hung up over the altar, from the cross on the canopy. Mabillon, Lit. Gallic. pp. 92 &c. Gavanti, following Baronius, understood it as referring to the way in which the Blessed Sacrament should be continually reserved within a tabernacle fixed upon the altar.—T. i. p. 127. At first sight, this seems by far the most plausible interpretation of the canon: such I took it, in 1833, rendering it to mean, 'That the Body of the Lord should be placed upon the altar, not amid the row of images, but beneath the figure of the cross,' that is, 'upon the altar itself, within an ark or tabernacle which was surmounted by the cross.'—Hierurgia, 1st ed. p. 283. Soon afterwards, however,

I saw reason to doubt of this interpretation: I remembered that for centuries after the holding of that council, the altar was left to stand alone, quite away from the wall, and without cross or crucifix, or image of any kind resting immediately upon its table; bearing also in mind that in the Mozarabic and the Gaulish rituals—perhaps, too, in all the other liturgies then in use in the other Western parts of the Church, the many particles into which the host was broken, were directed to be so arranged—'Corpus Domini . . . componatur'—upon the altar, as to form a cross, it therefore seemed to me that this canon had nothing to do with how the Blessed Sacrament was to be kept night and day at the altar, but that it meant to say that the particles into which the host, after consecration, is broken at mass, should be arranged—'componatur'—not in any way that individual caprice or imagination might suggest—'imaginario ordine'—but invariably in the form of a cross—'sub crucis titulo.' Being at Milan in 1853, I had an opportunity of often seeing, and minutely studying, the Ambrosian high altar. I had beheld it many years before, when I was young and did not know how to read its liturgical teachings, or understand its worth as a sample of mediæval workmanship. Now was it that a view of that precious ornament strengthened my conviction that this latter way I had adopted, and put forth four years before—in 1849—of interpreting the canon of the council of Tours, was the true one.—'Church of our Fathers,' i. 106. As said just now, S. Ambrose is figured standing, in his mass vestments, at an altar in front of him. The words of consecration have evidently been uttered, and a deacon is holding a large two-handled chalice, called a ministerial chalice because it served for the ministration or communion to the people under both kinds. Right before the holy bishop are four round particles, each marked with a cross; and they are so put out upon the altar as to form among themselves a cross, thus: ⊕ ⊕ ⊕ ⊕. Whether the intention of the artist were to signify many entire hosts piled up into four heaps, or to express the particles only of one large host broken in four, and each fragment represented, for the sake of identification and symmetry, quite round and with a cross upon it, matters not; for, from the way in which they are so carefully placed, that they should form by themselves an exact cross upon the altar, it is quite evident his wish was to represent some well-known rubric of those times: that is, 'ut corpus Domini in altario, non in imaginario ordine, sed sub crucis titulo componatur.' Thus, to my thinking, we get from art-work, from a figured monument, a most trustworthy, nay, the only true explanation, of a written monument of ecclesiastical antiquity which has hitherto baffled many eminent and learned men; furthermore, from this placing of the particles crosswise, we gather another proof of how the Church sought to teach then, as she teaches now, that the body of Christ crucified at Jerusalem is the very same as the one present before the priest, upon the altar. The rubrician, too, will not overlook the fact that, when this frontal was designed, altar-breads were made round, thin, and stamped with the sign of the cross.

The love, the reverence, the warm devotion then cherished for our Blessed Lady, are well signified by the way in which she is figured upon this altar. In one of the panels on the western or golden side the subject of the Annunciation is treated. Here we behold her, not in the posture of an equal or inferior—standing—but like some higher being, one above even an archangel—seated, and seated, too, not in an ordinary chair, but on a royal throne, with its dome-like canopy upheld by two columns. Exactly after such a manner is the Mother of God represented in the splendid Anglo-Saxon Benedictional, once Æthelwold's, now belonging to the Duke of Devonshire; in that MS., so beautifully written and so gorgeously illuminated by the hand of Godeman the monk of Winchester, Gabriel stands, as a token of respect, while telling his message to her who was full of grace; and Christ's future Mother listens to the errand—seated, queen-like, upon a domed and pillared throne. This same feeling for sweet S. Mary was proclaimed in works of art, all through the middle ages, by a throne and crown, and in paintings by that ensign of royalty called the cloth of estate, or piece of richly brocaded stuff hung behind her, or spread out over her head like an extemporised canopy or royal throne, as we find in every work of art belonging to that period. Moreover, in the abovenamed Anglo-Saxon MS., the archangel, while calling the Virgin 'blessed,' suits, after a certain manner, his action to his words by outstretching the first three fingers, the thumb being one, of his right hand, according to the Latin way of holding the hand the while the words of blessing were being said by pope or bishop, by abbot or simple priest.

In the middle of the east or silver side of this frontal, its artist has figured himself holding this very altar in his hands, and bending down his head for a blessing which he has asked, and is getting from S. Ambrose, who stands, not upon the same level upon earth, but on a higher one in heaven. The inscription hard by—'Wolvinus magister phaber'—tell us his name was Wolvin. The word 'faber' is written with 'ph' instead of 'f,' being phaber, a peculiarity in spelling upon which I shall soon have to lay some stress. Now comes the question;—what countryman was Wolvin? However wishful to make him out an Italian, Ferrario, Cicognara, and other Italian writers, have failed in all their endeavours. The name itself, with its stubborn foreign W., while so very un-Italian, is quite Teutonic—just such a one in fact which might have been, as in reality it was—still is, common in this island. That its bearer, the artist of this precious altar, was, by birth as well as education, an Anglo-Saxon, I have not the slightest doubt. Then, as now, the names of people were very generally compounded of two words, and had a signification. In Anglo-Saxon 'Wol' means 'wretched,' 'miserable,' 'lowly,' and 'Win,' a 'scholar,' a 'follower;' thus Wolvin, put into modern English, would be 'Lowly-follower,' which, to our forefathers' ears, ten centuries ago, must have sounded as natural and unsingular a name as does Lowman, Slowman, Trotman, or Longfellow, or Stringfellow, to ourselves at the present day.

Wolvin, as a name, never died out here: it lived all through the middle ages, and families still bearing it are to be met with in this country, and as far as I know, in this country alone. Among the lands that in Saxon times belonged to the monks of Ely were: apud Gyllinges v hýdas quas Wlwinus cocus et uxor ejus Ælfsneth—per transgressionem amiserunt. Hist. Eliensis, lib. secund. p. 116, ed. Stewart, for the 'Anglia Christiana.' The precious 'Liber Vitæ' which once used to lie upon the high altar at Durham cathedral, and was lately printed by that most useful society—the Surtees—gives, among the names of its Anglo-Saxon benefactors, that of one Walewein, p. 84.

In the year 1316, the Earl of Hereford warmly besought the monks of Durham, at a vacancy of that see, to elect as its bishop one of the clerics belonging to his household, one John Walwyn. *Historiæ Dunel. Scriptores Tres*, ed. Surtees, p. 98. Among the many beautiful stained glass windows which once adorned the fine priory church at Great Malvern, one there was which had been given by a man and his wife, bearing this name, as under it was written :—'Willielmus Walwein et Jana uxor ejus—Christe nos adjuva—Omnes vos qui ituri estis istam per fenestellam pro animabus orate nostris ut det Deus' . . . . . as we learn from that distinguished Catholic antiquary, the unjustly treated Mr. Abingdon, Mon. Ang. iii. 446. Of the three who bore witness to the good state of the parish, at a visitation of the church of Merington, in the diocese of Durham, A.D. 1501, one was Robert Wolwen. Ecclesiastical Proceedings of Bp. Barnes, ed. Surtees, Appendix, p.

xxviii. 'The morowe after the day of coronation of (Tudor Mary)—at the palys of Wystmister, were dobyd the knightes of the carpet foloinge, in the presence of the quenes majestie in her chamber of presens under the clothe of estate, by therl of Arundell.' Of these many gentlemen, the last was Sir Rychard Wallwine. Diary of H. Machyn, ed. J. G. Nichols for the Camden Society, p. 335. H. Walwyn, a citizen of London, A.D. 1612, bequeathed various sums of money for charities. Hibbert's 'Livery Companies,' t. i. p. 353. Myself, when living in Staffordshire, twenty-odd years ago, I knew a labourer's family named Wolwin in the neighbourhood of Alton; and people bearing that patronymic are yet common in Herefordshire. True, indeed, is it that in every one of the instances just now given, this name of Wolvin is written differently. That, however, with those who know what ancient documents are, will make nothing against the argument. Until lately people spelt their words more to the ear than the eye, and in drawing up a deed, or while framing his will, a man would spell his own name, even in as many ways as he had occasions for writing it. This happened not only here but elsewhere. Among our French neighbours, not the least remarkable instance of this variation of spelling a proper name is the one furnished by the family of Nouailher, which had, through several generations, given to Limoges some of its best workmen in enamel. Speaking of the last members of that race, in the eighteenth century, the late Abbé Texier, whose death was such a loss to ecclesiastical archæology, says:—'A peine savent-ils leur nom; ils signent indistinctement Noalher, Noualher, Nouailher, Nouailliher, Nouaillier, Noualhier, et Noaillé.' 'Essai Historique et Descriptif sur les Argentiers et les Emailleurs de Limoges, Mémoires de la Société des Antiquaires de l'Ouest, année, 1842,' p. 512. But a very few months ago, the short inscription on the Guards' Crimean monument in Pall Mall, had to be amended in its bad spelling; and lately only, in the papers given in at a competitive examination, the word 'Mediterranean,' as I was told by a credible individual, was spelt seventeen various ways. As far then, as mere name goes, we may fairly claim Wolvin, the artist of the beautifully wrought altar at Milan, as an Anglo-Saxon countryman. Whether written W*o*lwin or W*a*lwin, that is, with 'o' or with 'a,' the sound from an English mouth would be the very same.

No Italian would ever think of writing 'Phaber' for 'Faber;' so thoroughly does he dislike this 'ph,' that instead of putting it in where it should not be, he invariably leaves it out wherein it ought to come; for example, Philippus and Photius he spells Filippus and Fotius with F for Ph, and 'filosofia' for 'philosophia.' I do not know whether a Teuton of Germany Proper would have in the ninth century substituted 'ph' for 'f' in a Latin word; but the Anglo-Saxons would, and did so. To give an instance: in that valuable work the 'Pontifical of Ecgberht Abp. of York, from A.D. 732 till 766,' 'proferatur' is written with 'ph' for 'f.' Ed. Surtees Society, p. 122. For such an affectation of a Grecism it is easy to account. Theodore, born at Tharsus in Cilicia, and sent by Pope Vitalian to Britain as archbishop of Canterbury, after having been consecrated by that Roman Pontiff himself, A.D. 668, was very learned in the Greek tongue, and ever showed his eagerness in spreading the knowledge of it through this land. So successful, too, were this primate's labours, in which he had a willing helper in his friend the abbot Hadrian—an African by birth, who came with him from Rome—that Beda says of them, in his own times there were yet living some of their scholars who knew the Greek and Latin languages quite as well as their own mother-tongue:—'Usque hodie supersunt de eorum discipulis qui Latinam Græcamque linguam æque ut propriam in qua nati sunt norunt.' *Hist. Eccl. lib. iv. cap. ii.* While Wolwin's 'ph' for 'f' cannot make us wonder, it leads us to believe that he was born and bred in this country, where this peculiar way of spelling was followed through many centuries afterwards. At the beginning of the history of Ely monastery, where its writer evidently keeps to the Anglo-Saxon spelling of the original documents which he is transcribing, the word 'multifaria' is written 'multi*ph*aria.' Hist. Elien. lib. i. p. 46; again, 'ph' for 'f' may be read in one of the Close Rolls of Henry III.'s reign, in the expenses 'ad operationem *ph*eretri beati Edmundi,' in Westminster Abbey; and at the threshold of the chapter-house at York Cathedral, these two Leonine verses, blazoned in letters of gold, thus set forth in flowery yet fitting praises, the beauty of perhaps the most beautiful building of the kind that the world ever saw:—

Ut Rosa phlos phlorum,
Sic est Domus ista domorum.

Wolvin's spelling, then, leads to the belief that he was born and bred in this country.

Hardly ever did an Anglo-Saxon sovereign send messengers, or Anglo-Saxon churchmen go to Rome, but they carried with them, as presents for the Pontiff, vessels made of gold or silver. Thus, when Vighard the priest went thither to be consecrated Archbishop of Canterbury, A.D. 664, he took along with him as gifts to Pope Vitalian from Egberct II. of Kent, and Osvio, King of the Northumbrians, gold and silver vessels not a few: 'Missis pariter apostolico papæ donariis, et aureis atque argenteis vasis non paucis.' Beda, Hist. Ecc. lib. iv. c. i. Hence not only at Wolvin's time, but very long before, we easily understand how Anglo-Saxon skill in every sort of nice work in gold and silver, stood so high in the estimation of Italy, that certain kinds of church-lamps made in this island were much sought for, and became known at Rome itself by the distinctive name of Saxon vessels—'gabatæ Saxicæ'—as we find from so many passages in the curious 'Liber Pontificalis.' That these lamps or *gabatæ* were beautiful, not merely as specimens of handicraft, but also as works of art, and admirable for the sculptures on them, we gather from that epithet, 'interrasiles,' bestowed upon them: 'Obtulit (Gregorius IV. A.D. 827) in ecclesia beati Marci—gabatas interrasiles de argento xii. Anglorum opere constructas' (Lib. Pon. iii. 13). The meaning of 'interrasiles' is shown by these lines:—

> Quod nunc sculpturis, quod nunc planitia variatur,
> Hoc et non aliud opus interrasile dicas.

In the printed Anastatius here quoted, its editor,

Vignoli, instead of 'Anglorum opere,' gives us 'Angelorum opere.' Were this the true reading, such angels' work would have had bestowed upon it, as it merited, other and far more conspicuous notices and from other pens besides that of the writer of the 'Liber Pontificalis.' Such notices are, however, all wanting. To those who have had to look into old codices, it is well known that those MSS. are crowded with contractions. Now, it so happens that the words 'Angelorum' and 'Anglorum' are shortened by the selfsame form of contraction, written thus, 'Anglor.' Forgetting this, Vignoli was easily led into his mistake of transcribing 'Angelorum,' instead of the true reading, 'Anglorum.' In most glowing terms does Leo, cardinal bishop of Ostia, speak of the magnificent shrine of Anglo-Saxon workmanship standing in the abbey church of Monte Cassino :—'Loculus ille mirificus—argento et auro gemmisque Anglico opere subtiliter et pulcherrime decoratus.' Chron. SM. Cassin. lii. c. xxxiii. A short hundred years after the death of S. Gregory the Great, the arts throughout Italy fell into decay amid the din of war raised by the uncouth Northmen as they rushed down upon and swarmed all over that beautiful but unhappy land. By Leo the Isaurian, Constantine Copronymus, and several of the other Greek emperors who reigned in the seventh and next two centuries, not only were all sacred art works torn or broken, but the makers of them, the unfortunate artists themselves, were driven from their native land, or put to death, if they stayed to work there. Thus, as the Church has ever been and always will be the great support of art-labour, the arts themselves fell headlong into barbarism at Constantinople and all over the East wherever the wrathful ill-will of iconoclasm might follow them. Not so here in this our island. From the eighth till the end of the thirteenth century England stood far above Greece and Italy in the successful cultivation of the fine arts. Objects of Anglo-Saxon workmanship won admiration at Rome and in other places in Italy, and our workmen themselves were sought for, and going thither found wide employment among the Italians. While recording the events in the pontificate of Pope Nicholaus I., A.D. 858, the Liber Pontificalis tells us that 'quidam de Anglorum gente Romam venerunt, qui in oratorio beati Gregorii papæ et confessoris Christi, in principis Apostolorum æde Frascatæ constructa, unam tabulam argenteam posuerunt habentem lib . . .'—T. iii. p. 203. Of this body of Anglo-Saxon pilgrims then at Rome, some, as it seems to me, were goldsmiths working there, where, at the common expense, they wrought this silver altar-frontal, which was given as the united offering of all to the church at Frascate. Be that as it may, proof positive we have that Anglo-Saxon artists were employed in the neighbourhood of Rome, since Leo Ostiensis, telling of an awful thunderstorm that rolled over Monte Cassino, mentions how an English goldsmith, while busy about some work in the church at the time, happened to be killed upon the spot by a flash of lightning :—'cum Anglo quodam aurifice duos alios longe distantes uno ictu ad portam majorem cecidisse.' Chron. S. Mon. Cassin. lib. iii. c. xxii.

The great quantity of fine enamel work, in the shape

of long bands and many small medallions of saints' heads, upon the work at Milan of Wolvin's, makes this jewelled gold and silver altar still more precious as an art production. The enamelling is done in that early style known as framed enamel, called by the French *cloissonnée*, now become so rare, and so eagerly sought for by collectors. One of the oldest, as well as finest samples, is the jewel made by order, as its Anglo-Saxon inscription says, of Alfred, which was found at one of the hiding-places of that great good man, in Somersetshire, and now is in the Ashmolean Museum, Oxford. The heads on the Ambrosian altar are of the framed enamel identically the same in workmanship with this Anglo-Saxon piece of work wrought in the same century in this country. The Italians of that period were totally unacquainted with the process. Enamelling, as an art, entirely unknown either to the Greeks and Romans, was found out and exclusively followed by the barbarians in the ocean, as we are told by Philostratus, a Greek, who was brought to Rome by Septimius Severus (third century), with whom he lived amid all that was most beautiful or curious in art that imperial rapacity could bring together from a plundered world. Of a certainty these ocean barbarians were no other than our ancient Britons, and sure enough, while enamelled ornaments are found in graves in this island, on the opposite coast of France, and in some parts of north-west Germany, whither trade could have easily carried them, never are they turned up from tombs of an early date in Italy. If the Anglo-Saxons were ignorant of enamelling before their coming hither, very soon afterwards they learned to become great proficients in that art, as the ornaments lately brought to light from Anglo-Saxon burial-grounds sufficiently declare. By themselves, therefore, these framed enamels, set like gems upon the altar, afford an additional argument in our favour.

Knowing then that Wolvin's is an Anglo-Saxon—nay, even now an English name, and that his spelling of Latin was so un-Italian and so very Anglo-Saxon; remembering, too, that while at a time that the Greeks and Italians had no good artists in the goldsmiths' craft, then precisely was it the Anglo-Saxons were famous in that art, their works so admired, so sought for, and Anglo-Saxon workmen employed by the Italians themselves even in and about Rome, we are fully justified, methinks, in saying that Wolvin was, as well by artistic education as by birth, an Anglo-Saxon. Very likely, in going to or coming back from Rome, he found work at Milan. Whether so or not, his frontal is an admirable proof of the widely felt and healthy action exercised by the Church upon arts and artists, making them, in a manner, her mouthpiece for her teachings to the people. Her principles on that matter are well set forth by S. Gregory the Great, in two of his letters to Serenus:—'Idcirco enim pictura in ecclesia adhibetur, ut hi, qui literas nesciunt, saltem in parietibus videndo legant, quæ legere in codicibus non valent.' Lib. vii. Ep. 110. 'Nam quod legentibus scriptura, hoc idiotis præstat pictura cernentibus, quia in ipsa etiam ignorantes vident quod sequi debeant, in ipsa legunt qui litteras nesciunt.' L. ix. Ep. 9. Besides its general æsthetic excellence, Wolvin's work is very instructive on several particulars; for instance—

1st. Those crowns wreathing with royal—with imperial—dignity, as it were, a richly jewelled cross, figured hanging over altars, are valuable among those other proofs furnished by the arts—not forgetting the heathen's gibe, the 'Deus Christianorum ononychites,' or blasphemous crucifix of the Palatine—of that honour and reverence shown from early times by the Church to the sign of our redemption, and how a cross was present near the altar, to identify it as the spot whereon the one same great sacrifice of Calvary is offered in the mass.

2nd. Hung over a grave, it told the Church's belief that the soul of the saint buried there is even now reigning with God, wearing its crown of everlasting brightness; or, as the Anglo-Saxon ritual then said: 'Magnificavit eum (Deus) in conspectu regum, et dedit illi coronam gloriæ,' &c. Ritual. Ecc. Dunelm. ed. Surtees Society, p. 88. 'Accipient sancti regnum decoris et diadema speciei de manu Domini.' *Ib.* p. 92. And as the Anglo-Saxon hymn-book sang:—

> Spiritum sumpsit chorus angelorum
> Intulit cœlo pie laureandum.—Ed. Surtees Society.

3rd. In that ritual distribution of the particles of the consecrated host, so as to form with them a cross, we behold how the Church sought to teach by her liturgy that the sacrifice in the mass, and that on Calvary, was one; that the body of Christ, crucified by the Jews at Jerusalem, was the very same as the one there stretched out in a cross before the priest upon the mount-like altar.

4th. The suppliant position of Wolvin, so lowly

bending down before S. Ambrose, whose head has about it the nimbus, is a further evidence of the belief of those times, and announces that the invocation and intercession of the saints in heaven were among its articles.

5th. And the way in which the Annunciation is represented proclaims to us that she, whom all generations are to call 'blessed,' was then, as now, looked upon, and loved, and honoured, though a creature, as the best, the first, the highest of created beings, the queen of men, the queen of angels.

To conclude, this altar is but one amid a thousand examples that might be brought to show what powerful help art-work often lends to ecclesiastical studies in their widest range, proving, in fact, how instances may be found in which figured are better even than lettered documents, and that the pen of the writer is not sometimes so able to tell his meaning as is the pencil or the chisel of the artist, realising the poet's words:—

> Segnius irritant animos demissa per aurem,
> Quam quæ sunt oculis subjecta fidelibus, et quæ
> Ipse sibi tradit spectator.

The fair inference from this is that the keenest theologian, the clearest liturgist, the readiest polemic must be he who knows, not merely the Church's writings, but also the Church's works of art, and therefore, that the study of ecclesiastical antiquities in architecture, sculpture, painting, and all the sister arts, is to be earnestly recommended; and instead of being, as unhappily it oftener is, lost sight of, ought to be untiringly followed by every good churchman, not merely as affording him a seemly recreation after higher and more urgent duties have been fulfilled, but as yielding a help so mighty for upholding against the unbeliever God's revealed truths and articles of faith, and for showing how the teachings of them by His Church has been, through various ages, at different places, the same unvarying one, though uttered after several ways, at sundry times and different ages, and by men unlike each other in laws, in language, and in country.

Before ending this paper, I ask to say a few words, which, though not immediately belonging to the subject, are not unfitting this occasion.

From the earliest times, amid the bishops whom God has set to watch over that part of His Church existing in this island, always have there been those who learned themselves, or, loving learning, were anxious to further its advance among their fellow-countrymen. The results of such a zeal were happy; Religion left her mark upon all the civil institutions of the land, and stamped her character on all the arts of civilised life. Among the Britons, S. Dubritius and S. Iltute are renowned as having founded colleges; and the names of Gildas, Nennius, and Mark the hermit are, or ought to be, known to every Englishman. Theodore, S. Aldhelm, Ecgberht, Ælfric, S. Æthelwold, and S. Dunstan among our Anglo-Saxon archbishops and bishops, with Eddi, Benet Biscop, Venerable Beda, Alcuin, Wolstan and other monks, besides a crowd of lesser worthies belonging to the secular clergy, are examples of that high state to which learning was carried in their days. After them came Lanfranc, S. Anselm, S. Thomas—whose life and martyrdom have been so admirably written lately by Canon Morris—Lancton, Peckham, Bradwardine, Chicheley and Pole, all English primates—Bury, Wykeham, Waynflete, Fox, and Wolsey, English bishops and all learned or promoting learning. Without a thought on our fine old cathedrals and parish churches, Oxford, the best endowed, the most beautiful of all scholastic cities in the world, is by itself a sufficient standing witness to the religious zeal, the pious munificence, of our old Catholic churchmen, and of their wishfulness to spread around them the influence of all the elegant and intellectual arts of peace. In these our own times some among us have known a Milner, an Oliver, a Lingard—all have read the works of a Challoner, an Alban Butler, each of them, by far, the foremost in his own path of literature during his day. Though the last in his order of sitting upon England's primatial chair, by no means the least in multifarious learning is the highly gifted prelate, the Cardinal Archbishop of Westminster, whom we have the happiness to see presiding over a young institution so needed at the present time, and of which his Eminence is the originator. Had we not already those several productions of his learned and varied pen that have won for him a lofty place in the Catholic literature of this country, the establishment of the present branch of the Academy would have been quite enough to show how the zeal for learning had come down to him as an inheritance from the earliest through the latest bishops and churchmen of this land; and how, like them, he had striven to cleanse the gold from dross, and stamp it with the true effigy, by letting Religion assay and make her impress on it.

While, then, we all thank the Cardinal Archbishop most heartily for providing God's Church in England with such a useful appliance for upholding and defending her truths; and for gathering together, churchmen and laymen—the divine, the historian, the herald, the antiquary, the botanist, the painter, the naturalist, the poet, the geologist, the sculptor, the linguist, each strong in wielding his own peculiar weapon, and ready at the call of Faith to do battle for her sake—let us cherish the hope that our Primate may long be spared to witness the happy growth and energetic action of this his own good work.

ON

THE BIRTHPLACE OF SAINT PATRICK.

BY J. CASHEL HOEY.

THE question of the birthplace of S. Patrick—a question which has been debated with considerable learning and acrimony for several centuries—has always seemed to me to have an interest far beyond the rival claims of clans and the jealous litigation of the antiquary. It is interesting not merely because it is in reality a curious archæological problem, but also because it may in some measure afford a clue to the character of one of the greatest saints and greatest men of his own age or of any other—a saint who was the apostle of a nation which he found all heathen and left all Christian: who succeeded in planting the Catholic faith without a single act of martyrdom, but planted it so firmly that it has never failed for now 1,400 years, though tried in what various processes of martyrdom God and man too well know; a saint whose apostolate was the mainspring of an endless succession of missionary enterprises, prosecuted with the same untiring zeal in the nineteenth century as in the fifth, wherever the vanguard of Christendom may happen to be found, whether in Austria, in Gaul, in Switzerland, or in

Iceland, as now at the farthest confines of America and of Australasia. Add to these ordinary evidences of the supernatural efficacy of S. Patrick's mission, the testimony which is derived from the peculiar spiritual character of the people that he converted. The Irish nation retains the impress which it received from the hands of S. Patrick in a way that I believe no other Christian nation has preserved the mould of its apostle. If that nation has never even dreamed of heresy or schism, it is because in terms as positive as an Ultramontane of our own days could devise,* S. Patrick established the supreme authority of the Roman Pontiff as a chief canon of the Irish Church. Patience in poverty, an innate love of purity, prodigal alms-giving, and mutual charities, the practice of heavy penances and of long fasts, a peculiarly vivid sense of purgatory, and a strong devotion to the doctrine of the Trinity, which the Saint taught in the figure of the shamrock—these have always been the distinguishing characteristics of Irish piety. They were the peculiar characteristics of the Christian of the fourth

* 'Quæcunque causa valde difficilis exorta fuerit atque ignota cunctis Scotorum gentis judiciis, ad cathedram archiepiscopi Hibernensium, atque hujus antistitis examinationem recte referenda. Si vero in illa, cum suis sapientibus, facile sanari non poterit talis causa prædictæ negotiationis, ad Sedem Apostolicam decrevimus esse mittendam; id est, ad Petri Apostoli cathedram, auctoritatem Romæ urbis habentem.' This canon of S. Patrick is contained in the Book of Armagh, the antiquity of which is instanced in the text of the present paper. The canon is of a date early in the fifth century; and it would be difficult to show so early, so emphatic, and so complete a recognition of the Papal authority in the ecclesiastical legislation of any other national church.

century, who had not yet learned to live at peace with the world—who felt that as yet Christians were in the strictest sense one family community—who practised mortification, as if the untamed Pagan blood were still burning in his veins, and the great temptation to whose faith was the heresy of Arius, and the question of the relations of the Three Divine Persons. But S. Patrick was not only a great saint—was not merely and simply the apostle of the Irish; he was their teacher and their lawgiver, their Cadmus and Lycurgus as well. The school of letters, which he founded in Ireland, so well preserved the learning which had become all but extinguished throughout Western Europe, that your own Alfred, following a host of your nobles and clerics, went thither to be taught, and the Universities of Paris and Pavia owe their earliest lights to Irish scholars. The Brehon laws, which are at last to be published, by order of Parliament, a complete code of the most minute and comprehensive character, were, according to the evidence of our annalists, carefully revised and remodelled by S. Patrick, with the consent of the different Estates of the Kingdom of Ireland; and there is good reason to believe that this revision, of which there is abundant intrinsic evidence, had reference, not merely to the Christian doctrine and the canons of the Church, but to the Body of the Roman civil law.

It would throw a certain light upon the character of a saint whose works were so various and so full of vitality, if we could arrive at any solid conclusion as to the place of his nativity, the quality of his parentage, and the sources of his education. The theory most generally accepted, and which certainly has the greatest weight of authority in its favour, is that which assumes that S. Patrick was born in Scotland, at Dumbarton, on the Clyde—the son, as we may suppose, of a French or British official employed in the Roman service at that extreme outpost of their settlements in this island, where he would have spent his youth surrounded by a perpetual clangour of barbarous battle, amid clans of Picts and Celts swarming across the barriers of the Lowlands. The opinion that S. Patrick was a Scotchman has the unanimous assent of all the antiquaries of Scotland; but I am not aware that any of them has succeeded in identifying any single locality named in the original documents with any place of sufficient antiquity in or near Dumbarton; nor could I, in the course of a careful examination of the district and the recognised authorities concerning its topography, arrive at any acceptable evidence on the subject. I have to add to the Scotch authorities and pleadings, however, all the best of the Irish. That S. Patrick was born in Scotland is the opinion of Colgan,* a writer whose services to the history of the Irish Church cannot be excelled and have not been equalled. The opinion of Colgan has overborne almost every other authority which intervened between his time and the present. The Bollandists † accepted it without hesitation; and I hasten to add to their great sanction that of the two most learned

* Colganus, R. P. F. Joannes, *Triadis Thaumaturgæ, seu Divorum Patricii, Columbæ, et Brigidæ, trium Hiberniæ Patronorum, Acta.* Lovanii, 1647.

† *Acta Sanctorum Martii* a Joanne Bollando, tom. ii. Antverpiæ, 1668.

antiquaries of the latter days of Ireland, Dr. John O'Donovan and Professor Eugene O'Curry. They, I am aware, were also of Colgan's opinion; and so, I believe, are Dr. Reeves and Dr. Todd, whose views on most points of ecclesiastical antiquities connected with Ireland are entitled to be named with every respect.

Still it is to be said, on the other hand, that the opinion that S. Patrick was born in France has always had a traditional establishment in Ireland. It is asserted in one of the oldest of his Lives, that of S. Eleran, and indicated in another, that of Probus. Don Philip O'Sullivan Bearre * is not the first nor the last of the more modern biographers of the Saint who has held that he was of French birth, though of British blood. But before the time of Dr. Lanigan, the most acute, the most conscientious, and perhaps the most generally learned of Irish historians, there appears to have been no really candid and scientific examination of the original documents and evidences. Irish scholars were too angrily engaged in the controversy of Scotia Major and Scotia Minor to be seriously regarded when they proposed to remove S. Patrick's birthplace from the neighbourhood of Glasgow to the neighbourhood of Nantes. Until Dr. Lanigan published his Ecclesiastical History,† no one seems to have even attempted to identify the localities named in the various original documents which concern the Saint. Dr. Lanigan came

* D. Philippi O'Sullevani Bearri Iberni, *Patritiana Decas*. Madrid, 1629.

† Lanigan, John, D.D., *An Ecclesiastical History of Ireland* Dublin, 1829.

to the conclusion that he was born not at Dumbarton but in France, at or in the neighbourhood of Boulogne-sur-Mer. I am able, I hope, to perfect the proof which Dr. Lanigan commenced, and which, if he had been enabled to follow it up by local research and by the light lately cast on the geography of Roman Gaul, would, I am sure, have come far more complete from his hands.

I hold, then, with Doctor Lanigan, and with a tradition which has long existed in Ireland, and also in France, that S. Patrick was born on the coast of Armoric Gaul; and that Roman in one sense by descent—by his education in a province where Roman civilisation had long prevailed, where the Latin language was spoken, and the privileges of the Empire fully possessed—Roman too by the possession of nobility, which he himself declares, and of which his name was a curious commemoration*—Roman, in fine, in the connection of his family which he testifies with the Roman government and with the Church, S. Patrick was a Celt of Gaul by blood. The fact that the district between Boulogne and Amiens was at that time inhabited by a clan called Britanni has misled both those who supposed he must have been born in the island of Britain, and those who held that, if born in

* Gibbon says (*Decline and Fall of the Roman Empire*, v. vi.), 'At this period the meanest subjects of the Roman Empire assumed the illustrious name of Patricius, which by the conversion of Ireland has been communicated to a whole nation.' It is supposed that the name was conferred on S. Patrick in consideration of his parting with his nobility for a motive of charity, as he mentions in his Epistle to Coroticus. But he was certainly not the first of the name. Patricius was also the name of S. Augustine's father, born fully a century before.

France, he must have been born in that part of it which was subsequently called Brittany.

The original documents which bear on the point are only two in number—the Confession of S. Patrick himself, and the hymn in his honour, composed by his disciple S. Fiech. Of the antiquity of these documents, we have evidence the most complete that can be conceived. Not merely does written history certify the record of their age—they have borne much more delicate tests. The hymn of S. Fiech is written in a dialect of Irish that is to the Irish of the Four Masters as the English of Chaucer is to the English of Lord Macaulay. The quotations of Scripture, which are given in the Confession of S. Patrick, are taken from the version according to the interpretation of the Septuagint, and not according to the recent version of S. Jerome, which had indeed been just executed in S. Patrick's time, but had not yet been publicly received. At the same time, the 'Liber Armachanus,' which contains the original copy of the Confession, contains also S. Jerome's translation of the New Testament—thus curiously marking the fact, that the date of the one document by a little preceded the date of the other. The manuscript itself has been subjected to a most curious and rigorous examination. The authentic signature of Brian, Imperator Hibernorum, commonly called Brian Boroimhe, on the occasion of his visit to Armagh, carries us back at a bound eight hundred years in its history; but the scholar who is expert in the hue of vellum and the style of the scribe, will tell us that the Book of Armagh was evidently a book of venerable age even then. The

Rev. Charles Graves,* a Fellow of the University of Dublin, and a scholar specially skilled in the study of the Irish manuscripts and hieroglyphs, published a paper some years ago in the 'Proceedings of the Royal Irish Academy' on the question of the age of the Book of Armagh. That the version at present preserved in the library of Trinity College, is a copy from a far older version, he says there can be no doubt. The marginal notes of the scribe show that he found it difficult in many places to read the manuscript from which he was transcribing. But the same notes, the character of his writing, and a reference to the Irish Primate of the time, under whose authority the work was undertaken, leave no doubt that the transcript was executed by a scribe named Ferdomnach, during the primacy of Archbishop Torbach, at a date not later than the year of Our Lord 807.

Of the Confession, besides the original copy in the Book of Armagh, there are several manuscript versions of great age in England: two at Salisbury; two in the Cotton Library; one, I believe, at Cambridge; another very interesting and valuable copy, that which was used by the Bollandists in printing their edition of the Confession, existed until the time of the Revolution in the famous French monastery of S. Vedastus. Fragments of the precious manuscripts of that learned congregation are scattered among the libraries of Arras, of Saint Omer, of Boulogne, and of Douai; but among them I could not find any trace of the missing manuscript of

* Graves, Rev. C., *On the Age of the Book of Armagh; Proceedings of the Royal Irish Academy*, vol. iii. p. 316.

S. Patrick's Confession; nor could the present learned representatives of Bollandus, who were good enough to interest themselves in my enquiry, give me any room to hope that it still exists. It would have been of much importance to have been able to compare the style and the text of the only existing French copy with the original in Ireland—especially as that French copy belonged to the very district from which S. Patrick originally came.

There are four localities designated in these documents; three of them in the Confession of S. Patrick, and one in the hymn of S. Fiech. In the Confession, S. Patrick says of himself, 'Patrem habui Calphurnium Diaconum (or Diacurionem) qui fuit e vico Bonaven-Taberniæ; villam Enon prope habuit, ubi ego in capturam decidi.' The hymn of S. Fiech adds that the Saint was born at a place called Nem-tur.

The ancient Lives of S. Patrick cite these localities with little variation.

The first Life given in Colgan's collection, and ascribed to S. Patrick Junior, says, 'Natus est igitur in illo oppido, Nempthur nomine. Patricius natus est in campo Taburnæ.'

The second Life, which is ascribed to S. Benignus, is word for word the same with the first on this point.

The third, supposed to be by S. Elcran, suggests that he was of Irish descent through a colony allowed by the Romans to settle in Armorica; but that his parents were of Strato Cludi (Strath Clyde); that he was born, however, 'in oppido Nempthur, quod oppidum in campo Taburniæ est.' This Life is of very ancient date, and shows clearly enough how old is the Irish tradition concerning the Saint's birth in France.

The fourth Life, by Probus, says: 'Brito fuit natione . . . de vico Bannave Tiburniæ regionis, haud procul a mare occidentali—quem vicum indubitanter comperimus esse Neustriæ provinciæ, in qua olim gigantes.' Here, again, we observe the same confused tradition of the Saint's French origin; for Neustria was the name in the Merovingian period of the whole district comprised between the Meuse and the Loire.

The fifth and best known Life, by Jocelyn, has it, 'Brito fuit natione in pago Taburniæ—eo quod Romanus exercitus tabernacula fixerant ibidem, secus oppidum Nempthor degens, mare Hibernico collimitans habitatione.'

The sixth Life, by S. Evin, declares that he was 'De Brittanis Alcluidensibus, natus in Nempthur.'

The Breviaries repeat the same names with as little attempt to fix the actual localities.

The Breviary of Paris says: 'In Brittania natus, oppido Empthoria.' The Breviary of Armagh: 'In illo Brittaniæ oppido nomine Emptor.' The old Roman Breviary says simply: 'Genere Brito.' The Breviary of Rheims: 'In maritimo Brittaniæ territorio.' The Breviary of Rouen: 'In Brittania Gallicana.' The Breviary of the Canons of S. John of Lateran: 'Ex Brittania magna insula.'

It will be observed that in the principal of these authorities, there is a concurrence in accepting the locality called so variously Nemthur and Empthoria, as well as the second of the localities, the Taberniæ, named by S. Patrick himself; and also that there is no appearance of certainty in the minds of the writers as to the exact sites of the places of which they speak. None of them ventures to name the exact district or diocese where Empthoria or the Taberniæ are to be found.

But certain scholia upon the Hymn of S. Fiech, which were for the first time published by Colgan in the 'Triadis Thaumaturgæ,' boldly lay down the proposition that 'Nemthur est civitas in Brittania Septentrionali, nempe Alcluida;' and the name is also translated as meaning 'Holy Tower.' The same writer, however, adds in another note that S. Patrick was not carried into his Irish captivity from Dumbarton, but from Boulogne, where he and his family were visiting some of their friends at the time when the Irish pirates swept down upon the coast of Gaul. The Irish annals say that about the period of S. Patrick's captivity, Nial of the Nine Hostages lost his life on the Sea of Iccius between France and England. These long piratical forays were not uncommon at the time.* A little later, the last of our Pagan kings, Dathy, was killed by lightning near the Rhætian Alps.

Colgan with a curious credulity accepted this improbable solution of the scholiast, of which it may in the first place be said that it is incompatible with the statement of S. Patrick himself, who declares distinctly that he was captured at a country house belonging to his father, near the town to which his family belonged.

Usher, however, who had equal opportunities of

* Totum cum Scotus Iernen
Movit, et infesto spumavit remige Tethys.—CLAUDIAN.

studying the original documents, also adopted this explanation. Several Irish writers, and especially Don Philip O'Sullivan, vaguely conscious of the tradition of S. Patrick's French origin, attempted to reconcile the fact of his being a Briton with the fact of his birth in France by the supposition that he was a Breton of Brittany. This theory, however, falls summarily to the ground, when it is opposed to the fact that the province now known by the name of Brittany, was not inhabited by any tribe which bore the name in the time of S. Patrick. 'The year 458,' says the Benedictine Lobineau* in his learned History of Brittany, 'is about the epoch of the establishment of the Bretons in that part of ancient Armorica which at present bears the name of Bretagne.' There was, however, a clan called Brittani, farther towards the north of France, a clan whose territory Pliny and the Greek Dionysius Periegetes had long before designated with accuracy: Pliny in these words, 'Deinde Menapii, Morini, Oromansaci juncti pago, qui Gessoriacus vocatur; Brittani, Ambiani, Bellovaci.'† The

* Lobineau, D. Gui Alexis, *Histoire de Bretagne*, Paris, 1707.

† Plinii Secundi *Historia Naturalis; de Gallia*, l. iv. The editors of the Dauphin's edition have a note on the word Brittani, which is worth quotation. 'Ita libri omnes. Hi inter Gessoriacenses Ambianosque medii, in ora similiter positi, ea loca tenuere certè, ubi nunc oppida Stapulæ, Monstrolium, Hesdinium, et adjacentem agrum, Ponticum ad Somonam amnem. Cluverius hic Briannos legi mavult.' See also the learned essay on the Britons of Armorica in the *Acta Sanctorum, Vitâ S. Ursulæ*; Octobris, vol. ix. p. 108. A glance at the map will show the close relation of the district marked by the present towns of Etaples, Montreuil, Hesdin, and Ponthieu to the localities named a little farther on. That the Britons of Great Britain originally came from this district is declared in the Welsh Triads: thus—'The three beneficent tribes of the Isle of Britain.

Brittani of the time of S. Patrick are to be found in the country that lies between Boulogne and Amiens. It is there that Lanigan came upon the first authentic traces of the origin of our Apostle.

He was guided to his conclusion, mainly, I think, by the History of the Morini, published in the year 1639 by the Jesuit Malbrancq,* and which seems strangely to have escaped the notice of every earlier Irish writer. In this work, there are two chapters devoted to the tradition of the connection of S. Patrick with the see of Boulogne. Malbrancq relates this tradition, which states that previous to his departure for the Irish mission, S. Patrick remained for some time at Boulogne, occupied in preaching against the Pelagian heresy, to contend with which Saints Germanus and Lupus had crossed over to Britain. Malbrancq refers, in proof of this fact, to the 'Chronicon Morinense,' to the Catalogue of the Bishops of Boulogne, and to the Life of S.

The first was the nation of the Cymmry who came with Hu the mighty to the Isle of Britain, who would not possess nor country nor lands through fighting and persecution, but of equity and in peace; the second was the stock of the Lloegrians, who came from the land of Gwasgwyn (Gascoigne), and were descended from the primitive stock of the Cymmry; the third were the Brython, and from the land of Llydaw they came, having their descent from the primary stock of the Cymmry.' And again, Cynan is spoken of as lord of Meirion (probably a Celtic form of the word *Morini*) in Llydaw. Taliessin also mentions the *Morini Brython* in his *Prif Gyfarch*. Lydaw, Latinised Letavia, is one of the early Celtic names of the country of the Morini, as Neustria, in the Life by Probus, was that given in the Merovingian period to the whole province between the Meuse and Loire, including Boulogne of course. Pliny mentions Boulogne itself as the *Portus Morinorum Brittanicus*.

* Malbrancq, Jacobus, *De Morinis et Morinorum rebus*. Tornaci Nerviorum, 1639—1654.

Arnulphus of Soissons. This tradition is to a certain extent a clue in tracing the early and intimate connection of S. Patrick with this country—but as yet it is nothing more.

The critical question is, whether the four names given by S. Patrick himself, and by S. Fiech, can be identified with any localities now known either in the district of Boulogne or any other district in which, towards the close of the fourth century, it is possible to find the conditions of Roman government and British blood combined. Before Lanigan there was, it seems to me, no serious attempt made to solve this question. The scholiast whose authority was so unhesitatingly adopted by Colgan and Usher, simply says, 'Nempthur est civitas in Brittania Septentrionali, nempe Alcluid.' There is not a word more. He does not attempt to show how Nempthur and Alcluid are to be considered as convertible terms. Nor does he attempt to interpret the names of the three localities stated by S. Patrick himself. The same may be said, in the most sweeping way, of the biographies and the Breviaries.

I will now read the reasons which Lanigan gives for identifying Bonaven with Boulogne, and Taberniæ with a city very famous in the wars of the middle ages, long before Arras had been fortified by Vauban or defended by General Owen Roe O'Neill. It will be observed that Lanigan does not attempt to identify the two other localities Enon and Nempthur. The former he regarded as too insignificant, the latter he did not believe had any existence. I will not say that his proof with regard to the identity of Boulogne with Bonaven is conclusive;

but if the whole of his proof rested on as strong presumptive grounds, little would remain to be said on the subject. The second part of it is, however, in my humble opinion, wholly erroneous. He says:—

'Colgan acknowledges that there is an ancient tradition among the inhabitants of Armoric Britain that S. Patrick was born in their country, and that some Irishmen were of the same opinion. He quotes some passages from Probus and others, whence they argued in proof of their position, but omits, through want of attention to that most valuable document, the following passage of S. Patrick's Confession: "My father was Calpurnius, a deacon, son of Potitus, a priest of the town Bonavem Taberniæ. He had near the town a small villa Enon, where I became a captive." Here we have neither a town Nemthor, nor Aleluit. Nor will any British antiquary be able to find out a place in Great Britain to which the names Bonavem Taberniæ can be applied. Usher, although he had quoted these words, has not attempted to give any explanation of them, or to reconcile them with Nemthur.

'The word Taberniæ has puzzled not only Colgan, but some of the authors of the Lives which he chose to follow; for while they left out *Bonavem* as not agreeing with *Nemthur*, they retained Taberniæ, or, as they were pleased to write it, *Taburniæ*, which they endeavoured to account for by making it a district that got its name from having been the site of a Roman camp in which there were tents or tabernacles. Colgan, who swallowed all this stuff, quotes Jocelin as his authority for Taburnia being situated near the Clyde, at the South Bank. Great authority, indeed! It is, however, odd that such a place should be unnoticed by all those who have undertaken to elucidate the ancient topography of Great Britain. The places of Roman camps in that country were usually designated by the adjunct *castra*, whence *chester*, or *cester*, in which the names of so many cities and towns in England terminate.

'Bonavem, or Bonaven, was in Armoric Gaul, being the same town as Boulogne-sur-Mer in Picardy. That town was well known to the Romans under the name of Gessoriacum; but about the reign of Constantine the Great, the Celtic name Bonaven or Bonaun, alias Bonon, which was Latinised into Bononia, became more general. According to Bullet, who informs us that Am, Aven, On, signify a river in the Celtic language, the town was so called from its being at the mouth of a river; *Bon*, mouth, *on* or *avon*, river. Baxter also observes that Bononia is no other than *Bonavon* or *Bonaun*, for *aven*, *avem*, *avon*, *aun*, are pronounced in the same manner. The addition of *Taberniæ* marks its having been in the district of Tarvanna or Tarvenna, alias Tarabanna, a celebrated city not far from Boulogne, the ruins of which still remain under the modern name of Terouanne. The name of this city was extended to a considerable district around it, thence called *pagus Tarbannensis*, or *Tarvanensis regio*. Gregory of Tours calls the inhabitants Tarabannenses. It is often mentioned under the name of *Civitas Morinorum*, having been the principal city of the Morini, in which Boulogne was also situated. Boulogne was so connected with Tarvanna that both places anciently formed but one episcopal see. Thus Jonas, in his "Life of the Abbot Eustatius," written near twelve hundred years ago, calls Audomarus Bishop of Boulogne and Tarvana. It is probable that S. Patrick's reason for designating Bonaven by the adjunct *Taberniæ* was lest it might be confounded with the Bononia of Italy, now Bologna, or with a Bononia in Aquitain, in the same manner that, to avoid a similar confusion, the French call it at present Boulogne-sur-Mer. Perhaps it will be objected that *Tabernia* is a different name from *Tarvenna.* In the first place, it may be observed that, owing to the usual commutation of *b* for *v*, and vice versâ, we might read *Tavernia.* Thus we have seen that Tarvenna was called by some *Tarabanna.* To account for the further difference of the names, nothing more is required than to admit the transposition of a syllable or a letter, which has frequently occurred in old words, and particularly names of places. Nogesia, the name of a town, became Genosia. Dunbritton has been modified into Dunbertane, Dunbarton, Dumbarton. Probus agrees with the Confession, except that, according to Colgan's edition, for Bonavem Taberniæ he has "Bannave Tyburniæ regionis," and adds that it was not far from the Western Sea or Atlantic Ocean. Although we may easily suppose that some errors of transcription have crept into the text of Probus, yet as to Bannave there is no material difference between it and Bonavem. *Ban* might be used for *Bon*; and the final *m*, which was a sort of nasal termination, as it is still with the Portuguese, could be omitted so as to write for Bonavem, or Bonauem (*v* and *u* being the same letter), Bonaue. Probus's addition of *regionis* is worth noticing, as it corresponds with what has been said concerning the *Tarvanensis regio.*'

I think the proof in this passage with regard to the word Bonaven is very strong. The passage which Lanigan cites from Baxter distinctly says, 'Gallorum Bononia eodem pene est etymo; quasi dicas Bon-avon sive Bonaun.' The derivation of the word is clear enough. Avon even in England retains its Celtic signification of a river. But the passage identifying the *Taberniæ* of Boulogne with Therouanne is in my opinion altogether incorrect. Where he accounts for the change in the structure of the word by the usual transmutation of *b* and *v*, he overlooks the letter *r*—a letter which does not melt into the music of patois by any means so easily. Again, he hardly lays sufficient stress on the fact that the word *Taberniæ* is invariably understood in all the scholia, and in all the Lives, to mean the *Campus tabernaculorum*—the barracks and district occupied by a Roman army. In fine, he confuses Therouanne, which is at a distance of thirty miles from Boulogne, and certainly did not stand in the relation he supposes to it, with another city some twenty miles still farther away. But Malbrancq, who was his chief authority, does not omit to mention that Tervanna and Taruanna are two absolutely distinct places: Tervanna was the old Roman name of the town now known as Saint Pol *—Taruanna that of Therouenne.

It is very possible—I may add to the proof concerning the word Bonaven—that it may have been written

* *Comitum Terranensium Annales Historici*, Collectore Th. Turpin Paulinati. Ord. Predicat. 1731.

originally Bononen, for Bononenses Taberniæ. Anyone familiar with the form of the letters of the early Irish alphabet, indeed of almost all early manuscript, will readily comprehend how easily an *o* might be written for an *a*, an *n* for a *r*, and vice versâ, by a scribe ignorant of the exact locality, and copying from a half-defaced document. Anyone who looks at the form of the letters in the alphabet of the Book of Kells, given in Dr. O'Donovan's Grammar, will conceive at a glance how this might have happened.

Assuming, however, that Lanigan is correct in his conjecture as to Boulogne, I have endeavoured to discover whether the other localities named in the Confession and Hymn can be identified with localities now existing within the proper circumscription of the Roman military occupation around that city, and of a certain and unquestionable antiquity. I need not inform the Academy of the great military importance of Boulogne at the time of which we treat. It was the point from which England had been invaded. It was the principal military settlement of the Romans in Northern Gaul. Julian the Apostate had held his head-quarters there shortly before S. Patrick's birth. The country all around is marked by roads and mounds, which exhibit the rigid lines and stern solidity of Roman construction. I learn from a recent essay by M. Quenson, an accomplished scholar of Saint Omer, that eighty-eight different works have been written to settle the site of the Portus Itius, whence Cæsar embarked to invade Britain, and nineteen different localities assigned. Since M. Quenson wrote,

M. de Saulcy has again opened, and this time I think finally determined, that controversy. Perhaps I am so far fortunate that the absorbing zeal with which this difficult problem has been pursued, in a country of such zealous scholars, still leaves to a stranger somewhat to glean, in places far inland from the famous Port which they have so long laboured to identify.

The localities to which S. Patrick refers have, I find, all been preserved with the least alteration of their etymology that it is possible to conceive in the space of so many centuries; and this, I may add, is peculiarly wonderful in a country where so many Roman names have, by the friction of the much mixed dialects of Northern France, been almost frayed out of recognition. Who would suppose, for example, taking some of the familiar names of the Department, that Fampoux was the *Fanum Pollucis*, Dainville *Dianæ villa*, Lens *Elena*, Etaples *Stapulæ*, Hermaville *Hermetis villa*, Hesdin *Helenum*, Souchez *Sabucetum*, Surques *Surcæ*, Ervillers *Herivilla*, Tingry *Tingriacum?** And yet regarding these names there is no doubt that the modern French is a corruption of the old Latin form. Of the localities, which I proceed to designate, I submit that each has kept its original name with far less violation of the ancient word. The *Enon*, the *Nemthur*, the *Taberniæ* of S. Patrick are, to my mind, manifest in comparison with the majority of a hundred other localities in the Boulonnais which undoubtedly derive their titles from a Roman source.

* The name of the neighbouring village of Ardres has run through the following traceable variations since the Roman period: Horda, Ardra, Arda, Ardrea, Ardes, Ardres.

In the first place, let us take the word Enon. The river Liane, which runs into the sea at Boulogne, was known to the Romans as the Fluvius Enna. It is so marked on the most ancient maps of Northern Gaul. It is so written in Latin by Malbrancq. Near Desvres—once called Desurennes, or Desvres-sur-Ennes—there is marked a little village of the same name, called also Enna. I will not be said to strain language, which has survived so many centuries, very severely when I venture to identify S. Patrick's Enon with this undoubtedly Roman Enna.

Lanigan totally disbelieved in the existence of the town called Nempthor. I could not do so; nor underrate the importance of identifying it, if possible, in such an enquiry as this. But the difficulty of discovering this place was hitherto greatly increased by a mistranslation of its meaning, for which I believe Colgan is responsible. The word was always supposed to mean 'Holy Tower'—*Neim* holy, and *Tur* tower—until Professor Eugene O'Curry, when compiling, some years ago, his valuable Catalogue of the Irish MSS. of the British Museum, after a minute examination of the manuscript, which is the oldest copy of the Hymn in existence, came to the conclusion that the word should really be written 'Emtur,' as it is indeed, though by accident I take it, in some of the Breviaries. 'The place of Saint Patrick's birth,' he says, 'is generally written Nemtur; but there is clear evidence that the N is but a prefix introduced to fill the hiatus in the text, and that Emtur is the proper form of the word.' The word, then, means not Holy Tower, but the tower of some place or person indicated by the word Em. Some eight miles distant from Desvres, towards the north, still within the military circumscription of which it is the centre, there is such a place. The River Em, or Hem, flows past a village of so great an antiquity, that even in the ordinary geographical dictionaries, the record is preserved that Julius Cæsar slept there on his way to embark for the invasion of Britain.* The town contains a Roman

* 'Ce lieu existait lorsque les légions romaines pénétrèrent dans la Morinie, l'an de Rome 697, ou 57 ans avant l'ère vulgaire, et consistait alors en un château fort garni de tours, d'où est venu, selon Malbrancq, la dénomination de *Tournehem*, du latin *à Turribus.* César s'empara de ce château et y fit quelque séjour pour l'avantage de sa cavalerie. Environ deux siècles et demi après, c'est à dire en 218, Septime-Sévère, autre empereur romain, fit camper dans le voisinage de Tournehem (sur la montagne de Saint Louis) une partie de son armée destinée pour une expédition contre la Grande Bretagne, qu'il effectua glorieusement la même année.'—P. Collet, *Notice Historique de Saint Omer, suivi de celles de Therouanne et de Tournehem*, Saint Omer, 1830. Both M. Collet and Père Malbrancq, however, overlook the obvious derivation of the word—though both note the name of the river, which flows through the town, and which M. Collet calls 'la rivière de *Hem* ou de *Saint Louis.*' Again, M. H. Piers, in the *Mémoires de la Société des Antiquaires de la Morinie* (Saint Omer, 1834), says, 'César après s'être emparé des forteresses de la contrée s'y rendit de Therouanne, Sithieu et Tournehem, l'an 55 ou 56 avant l'ère vulgaire, pour subjuguer la Grande Bretagne.' In the same volume there is an interesting paper by M. Pigault de Beaupré on the castle of Tournehem, which, he says, was partially rebuilt by Baldwin II., Count of Guines, in 1174, and continued to be a principal residence of the Dukes of Burgundy at so late a date as 1435. But the vastness and solidity of the works which he describes, some of them subterranean roads evidently used for communication with other fortified works, clearly indicate their Roman character. Baldwin, indeed, a prince far in advance of his age, seems to have attempted to revive Roman ideas, and rebuild Roman works wherever he found them within his dominions. The castle of Hâmes, near Calais, which he likewise rebuilt, and which he ceded to the English as part of the ransom of King John

arch and the ruins of a Roman tower, from which the village derives its name. The name is Tournehem, or, as it was written in Malbrancq's time, Tur-n-hem. The tower and the river show the derivation of the word at a glance. The exigencies of Irish verse simply caused their transposition. I have only to add to Mr. O'Curry's ingenious note on the subject the remark, that the *n* was not, as he supposes, merely inserted to fill up a hiatus in the line, but was obviously a part of it. It is a copulative as common in Celtic words as *de* in modern French, and has precisely the same meaning. Ballynamuck, for example, means the town of, or on, the river Muck. Tulloch na Daly (whose swelling dimensions the French afterwards curbed into the famous name of Tollendall) is a more apposite instance.

I have yet to identify the *Tabernicæ.* To the eye, and on the old maps, they almost identify themselves. Desvres has all the characters of a great Roman military position—a vast place of arms, the tracings of fortified walls, the fosse, lines of circumvallation, and hard by on the forest edge the *Sept Voies*, or *Septemvium*, the meeting of the seven great military roads leading from and to the other principal strongholds of the Imperial power in Northern and Western Europe. Any one who examines in particular the 'Carte des Voies Romaines du Département du Pas de Calais,' published by the Commission of Departmental Antiquities,* cannot fail

of France, was also, as M. Pigault de Beaupré shows, of Roman construction.

* *Statistique Monumentale du Département du Pas de Calais. Publiée par la Commission des Antiquités Départementales.* Arras: chez Topino, Libraire, 1840.

to perceive that this now obscure village, which certainly never was raised to the rank of a Roman city, was nevertheless once a great nucleus of Roman power. The fragment of an ancient bridge is still known as the *Pont de Cæsar.* The *Septemvium,* with its remarkable concentration of roads, is alone sufficient to indicate the importance of the place. There is one road leading straight to Amiens; one that reaches the sea by the mouth of the Canche; another that runs to the harbour of Boulogne; another that joins the roads from Saint Omer and from Tournehem, and carries them on to Wissant and Sangate, the supposed Portus Itius and Portus Inferior; the fifth road was to Tervanna and Arras; the sixth to Taruanna; the seventh to Saint Omer. Would so many roads, communicating with places of such military importance, have been concentrated by a race of such a centralising talent as the Romans, anywhere except at the site of a great city or a great camp? On the ancient maps, indeed, the country which lies between Desvres and Boulogne, along the Liane, is simply marked *Castrum.*

I now approach, not unconscious of its difficulties, the etymology of the word. In the lax Latin of the middle ages, we first find Desvres spoken of as *Divernia Bononiensis.* There is the epitaph of a churchman, born in the place, which says on his behalf:—

'Me Molinet peperit Divernia Bononiensis.'

The local historian, Baron d'Ordre, speaks of the place as 'Désurène, *Divernia,* aujourd'hui Desvres.'* The

* *Notice historique sur la ville de Désurène, Divernia, aujourd'hui Desvres.* Par M. d'Ordre. Boulogne, 1811.

name Desvres itself evidently has undergone strange, yet traceable, variations and modifications.* Its first appearance as a French word is 'Desnrennes,' and this is derived from Desvres sur Enna, or Desvres upon the Enna or Liane, which, as I have said, flows past the place, giving its name to a little village near the forest. By this derivation, however, only the first two letters of the original word Desvres are left. How do they disappear, why do they reappear in the modern form of the word, and what is its original derivation?

It is a very curious fact, that in England the Roman camps seem to have been always known as 'Castra,' while in Gaul the Tabernæ is the name which generally adhered to them. Lanigan says, and correctly, so far as I have been able to discover, that there is no trace of a Roman station called *Tabernæ* in England, while the affix *chester* is the most common in its topography. In England, it may be said the Romans encamped; in France, the *Tabernæ* meant a more settled and familiar residence, as familiar as the Caserne of the Empire. It would be interesting to inquire whether as many cities in France do not derive their origin from these military stations, as England has of Chesters. But the student who attempts this task will be sure to find the Latin word almost defaced beyond power of recognition by the etymological maltreatment which it has sustained

* 'Il n'y pas 50 ans que le nom de Desvres a prévalu sur celui de Desuremne que cette ville avait toujours porté auparavant.'—M. L. Cousin, *Mémoires de la Société des Antiquaires de la Morinie*, vol. iv. p. 239. M. Cousin's papers on Monthulin and Tingry, in the Transactions of this society, are in general accord with what I have said of the ancient military importance of the whole district of Desvres.

in that conflict of consonants which has resulted in the present high polish of Academic French. I may mention one or two instances to show how little violence I do to French philology in identifying the *Divernia Bononiensis* of the middle ages with the Tabernæ of Boulogne. Saverne in Lorraine is well known to be the *Tabernæ Triborocorum.* It was known in a semi-Germanic form as *Elsas Tabern.* Gradually the sibilant *ss* of the first word invaded the second; and it has long settled down into one word in the form of Saverne. The *Tabernæ Rhenanæ*, on the other hand, retained the hard *b* instead of converting it into *v*, as inevitably happened in the South, and instead changed the T into Z, Rhein-Zabren. In ages which had no hesitation in changing the pure dental T into the sibilant dentals S or Z, it will not be considered surprising that it was sometimes changed into D—the only other pure dental sound. Indeed, of all the transmutations of letters, those of *d* and *t*, and those of *v* and *b*, are notoriously the most common. 'The Irish *d*,' says O'Donovan, 'never has such a hard sound as the English *d*.' Again, 'in ancient writings, *t* is frequently substituted for *d*.' Again, 'it should be remarked that in ancient Irish MSS. consonants of the same organ are very frequently substituted for each other, and that where the ancients usually wrote *p*, *c*, *t*, the moderns write *b*, *q*, *d*.'* Decline the Irish word *Tâd*, father. It becomes *Ei dâd*, his father; *Ei thâd*, her father; *by nhâd*, my father. We carry the tendency into English. The mistake is one from which certain parts

* O'Donovan, John, LL.D., *A Grammar of the Irish Language.* Dublin, 1845.

of Ireland, as well as certain parts of France, are not exempt even to the present day; and in Munster one may still hear, as in the times when the ballad of 'Lillibullero' was written, the letter *d* occasionally used where the tongue intended *t* or *th*. Nor is this vagary of speech confined to the Irish. Why do the Welsh say Tafyd for David? It is the most frequently recurring of that systematic permutation of consonants, which is one of the chief difficulties of the Cymric tongue. The Welsh *d* and *t* turn about and wheel about in their mysterious alphabet without the slightest scruple. In German, the convertibility of the same letters is also very marked. The German says *das* for that, *Dank* for thanks, *Durst* for thirst; and again, *Teufel* for Devil, *Tanz* for Dance, *Theil* for dial. As to the same abuse in France, the Dictionary of the Academy and that of Bescherelle* lay down the principle very plainly:—'Le *t* est une lettre à la fois linguale et dentale, comme le *d* son correlatif, plus faible, plus doux, avec lequel il est fréquemment confondu, non-seulement dans les langues germaniques, mais dans la plupart des langues. En latin, cette lettre se permute fréquemment avec le *d*: *attulit* pour *adtulit*. On écrivit primitivement set, aput, quot, haut, au lieu de sed, apud, quod, haud.'

So far as to the permutation of T and D. I will not waste the time of the Academy in order to show that the conversion of *v* into *b* is even more common. We find a familiar illustration of it in the old Latin name of

* *Dictionnaire de l'Académie Française.* Bescherelle, *Dictionnaire National.* Paris, 1857.

Ireland, which, as every one knows, is variously written Ibernia, Ivernia, Hibernia, Juvernia, and Iernia. But the English word Tavern, which is exactly derived from the Latin Tabernæ, is a still more apposite illustration in the present case. In this word, finally, the intermediate vowel swayed in sound with the consonants which enclosed it. As the primary Latin T changed into the softer and feebler D, and the *b* into *v*, the intermediate *a* lost its full force. The mediæval Latin melts it into an *i* in Divernia. The modern French form, Desvres, brings it halfway back towards its place at the head of the alphabet. It does not run the whole gamut of the vowels, as from Ibernia to Juvernia.

This *Divernia Bononiensis*, then, I claim to identify with the *Taberniæ Bononienses*, Tournehem with Nemtur or Emtor, Enna with Enon. If it were necessary even to push the proof a step further, there is the district called *Le Wicquet*, which M. Jean Scoti, who was *Lieutenant particulier de la Sennechaussée de Boulogne*, tells us is undoubtedly derived from the Latin Vicus, and which might naturally be the *vico Bonaven Taberniæ* of which the Confession speaks; but the historian of Desvres, Baron d'Ordre, whom I have already cited, disputes this derivation, and says the word is Celtic, and comes from *Wic*, Celtic for wood, like our word wicket. Both may be right, for Vicus may be a Latin form of the same word.* But the point is not material.

Let me now add to the etymological evidence a few historical illustrations.

* Among the names of villages in this district of whose history I could find no trace, is one called Erin, the place where Blessed Benedict Joseph Labre was born.

S. Patrick is stated in almost all his biographies to have been a nephew of S. Martin of Tours. S. Martin, though said to be a Celt of Pannonia, was during his military and early ecclesiastical career stationed in this identical district. The well-known legend of his division of his cloak with the beggar, who proved to be Our Lord Himself, is alleged to have taken place at Amiens. It is recorded that he was baptised at Therouanne. The first church raised to his honour was built there. The principal missionaries of the district are said to have been his disciples, and evidently entertained a deep devotion to him, of which there are still abundant evidences.*

S. Patrick, while in captivity at Slemish in Ireland, lived within sight of Scotland. A few miles only separate the coasts at Antrim. But when he escaped, he did not attempt to pass into Scotland. He made his way south, and passed through England to France. He says he was received among the Britons as if (*quasi*) among his own clan and kin. Doubtless there was close relationship of race and language between the Britons of the island and of the continent. There were Britons and there were Atrebates on both sides of the sea.† But

* Of the 420 churches comprised in the ancient diocese of Boulogne, 82 had S. Martin for patron. I also find several dedicated to the Irish S. Maclou and S. Kilian; but, strange to say, not one to S. Victricius.—V. *Histoire des Évêques de Boulogne*, par M. l'Abbé E. Van Drival. Boulogne, 1852.

† M. Piers, in the paper already cited, quotes M. Amédée Thierry as saying: 'Les *Brittani* furent les premiers qui s'y fixèrent; ils habitaient une partie de la Morinie; peut-être par un pieux souvenir ont-ils appelé leur nouvelle patrie la Grande Bretagne. Les *Atrebates* anglais, originaires de Belgium, résidaient à *Calera* ou *Galena Atrebatum*, à 22 milles de *Venta Belgarum* dans le canton où est

Britain was not the Saint's native place nor his resting-place. He went on, and abode with those whom he calls his brethren of Gaul, 'seeing again the familiar faces of the saints of the Lord,' until he was summoned to undertake his mission to Ireland.

In his own account of the vision, which induced him to undertake the apostolate of Ireland, he says he was called to do so by a man, whose name is variously written, Victor, Victoricius, and Victricius. The real name is in all probability Victricius; but if it were Victor or Victoricius, it would be equally easy (were it not for the fear of failing by essaying to prove too much) to identify the source of the Saint's inspiration with the same district. Saint Victricius was the great missionary of the Morini at the end of the fourth century; but he had been preceded in that capacity by S. Victoricius, who suffered martyrdom with SS. Fuscien and Firmin, at Amiens in A.D. 286. Again, the name Victor is that of a favourite disciple of S. Martin, whom Sulpicius Severus sent to S. Paulinus of Nola,* and of whom they both write in terms of extraordinary encomium. But the person

aujourd'hui Windsor.' M. Piers adds, that there is a tradition that a colony of the Morini had given their name to a distant country of islands which they discovered; but that he has found it impossible to discover the name in any ancient atlas. Perhaps the district of Mourne, on the north-east coast of Ireland, is that indicated. The Irish derivation of the name is at all events identical with the French.

* S. Paulini Nolani *Opera. Epistola* xxiii. in the *Patrologiæ Cursus Completus* of J. P. Migne, vol. lxi. Paris, 1847. See also the two epistles to S. Victricius, who with S. Martin persuaded Paulinus to withdraw from the world. I have a suspicion that the disciple of S. Victricius, named in these epistles now as Paschasius, now as Tytichus or Tytius (the name being evidently misprinted, but there being no doubt, as the Bollandists say, that the two names

referred to in the Confession is far more probably S. Victricius,* who was an exact contemporary of S. Patrick, who was engaged on the mission of Boulogne at the time of his escape, and who is said to have been a French Briton himself. Malbrancq's 'Annals of the See of Boulogne' aver that in the year 390 the 'Morini a Domino Victricio exculti sunt,' and that in the year 400 he dedicated their principal church to S. Martin.†

When S. Patrick was on his way to Ireland, with full powers from Pope Celestine, it is recorded that he was detained at Boulogne by the request of SS. Germanus and Lupus, who were proceeding into Britain in order to preach against the Pelagian heresy; and that during their absence, he temporarily exercised episcopal functions at Boulogne, and so came to be included in the list of its Bishops. If S. Patrick were a native of the island, is it not probable that Germanus and Lupus would rather have invited him to join their mission? But their object in asking him to interrupt his own special enterprise for a time, in order to remain among the Boulonnais, was, it is said, to guard against the spread of this heresy on the Continent. And it is very natural that

refer to one and the same person), may have been in reality S. Patrick. In his 17th Epistle, S. Paulinus refers to the accounts he had heard from this young priest of the anxiety of S. Victricius for the evangelisation of the most remote parts of the globe, and speaks of him as a disciple in every way worthy of his master: 'In cujus gratia et humanitate, quasi quasdam virtutum gratiarumque tuarum lineas velut speculo reddente collegimus.'

* Franciscus Pommeræus, O.S.B., in his *History of the Bishops of Rouen*, says S. Victricius was also sometimes called Victoricus and Victoricius.

† See also *Acta Sanctorum Augusti*, tom. ii. p. 193. Antverpiæ, 1735.

they should have asked him to stay for such an object, and that he should have consented, if this were indeed his native district, in which his intimacies were calculated to give him a special degree of influence; but not otherwise, hastening as he was under the sense of a Divine call to the conversion of a whole nation plunged in Paganism.

And, as I began by saying, all this proof is important mainly because it tends in some degree to elucidate the spirit and the work of the Saint. We begin to see how with the Celtic character of a French Briton, which made him easily akin to the Irish, he combined the Roman culture and civilisation, which added to his mission a peculiar literary and political energy, that long remained. We see in him the friend and comrade of the great saints of a great but anxious age. We see how he connects the young Church of Ireland, not with Rome alone, but with the great militant Christian communities of Gaul—a connection which his disciples were destined so to develope and extend in the three following centuries; and we cease to wonder that both Ireland and France have clung so fondly to a tradition, which linked together in their earliest days two Churches whose mutual services and sympathies have ever since been of the closest kind.

THE POSITION OF A CATHOLIC MINORITY IN A NON-CATHOLIC COUNTRY.

BY FREDERICK OAKELEY.

THE position of Catholics forming a minority in a nation whose institutions and instincts are diametrically opposed to the genius and habits of their religion, is a state of circumstances too well known to most of us by experience to require any laboured elucidation. Its anomalies, its drawbacks, its complications, and its trials, are painfully familiar to all classes of Catholics in this country with two only exceptions; the exception, first, of those (if such there be) who have so deeply imbibed the national spirit as to have lost their Catholic susceptibilities; and the exception, secondly, of those favoured children of the Church who have been withdrawn under the shelter of the Religious Life from the stormy atmosphere of the world, and are winning by their prayers, and earning by their sacrifices, those victories of faith over heresy, and of right over oppression, which their brethren whom they have left behind must slowly work up to with dizzy eyes, and feeble hands, and fainting hearts. But, between these extreme points in the horizon, there lies a wide field of labour and enterprise, with many to occupy it. Every class, order, and rank, of Catholics in these islands, but especially in our own, whose calling is carried out in the world, is brought into situations of difficulty, because into practical relations of some kind or other with the great non-Catholic majority; and is thwarted, or embarrassed, or tempted, or tried, in consequence, according to its characteristic liabilities. Around one class the majority weaves the scarcely perceptible, and therefore all the more dangerous, web of worldly sophistry. Others it entangles in the silver meshes of fashion; while those of a lower grade it assails with weapons of a ruder temperament and a more cruel contrivance—the armoury of petty persecution—the instruments of that domestic and purely moral warfare which involves no sacrifice in the wagers, and brings no renown to the conquerors, but which threatens a more terrible retribution to the one in proportion as it entails no earthly punishment, and promises a more exalted glory to the other in proportion as it enlists no human sympathy. But nowhere is the experience of these difficulties more frequent or more acute than in the great arena of politics. For there it is that the dominant and domineering majority is most at home, and the Catholic minority most defenceless. There it is that the incompatible principles, and inconsistent aims, of the two contending parties are brought into the closest juxtaposition and the most active conflict; and that compromise, greater or less, becomes the absolutely essential condition of practical success. Catholics, even the most valiant and ingenuous, must there be prepared to act a part and sustain a character in that dignified drama, in which there is no duplicity but such as is common to all, and no deception, because deception, like injury, presupposes, as a general rule, an unwilling subject. We are all, in fact, thrown, against our inclination, upon a discipline of economy or management; we must adapt our sentiments, so far as it may be safely and rightly done, to the popular standard of acceptance; adjust our claims to the measure of probable recognition, and shape our language by the rule of the public intelligence. This, then, is our position; and to state and describe it is to denote its intricacy, imply its arduousness, and shadow forth its moral dangers.

Even we, the clergy, whose comparative immunity from the occasions of these temptations might seem to render us safe from their approaches, have many of the same perils to face, and the same questions to solve. The clergy of Catholic countries have some trials from which we are happily exempt; but those under consideration are (at least in their actual extent) peculiarly our own. We cannot help being brought into constant relations, special to ourselves, with this alien and powerful majority; and the conditions of trial and difficulty thus introduced are such as might well justify a new chapter in our practical theology. Protestants frequent our churches from curiosity, and even resort to our presbyteries for advice. How are they to be dealt with, counselled, and converted? Protestants cross our path in the transactions of business, or are found at our side in the intercourse of society. How are they to be met with a dignity which involves no breach of humility, with a tact which is consistent with Christian simplicity, with a kindness which implies no recognition of their error? Where may controversy be safely employed; where may it more safely be suspended; what is to be its character and what its conditions? But of all the exigencies which this anomaly entails upon the same order, those perhaps are the hardest to encounter with firmness, with judgement, and with charity, which result from our official connection with Protestant institutions; and for this, among other reasons, that such difficulties are generally of the nature of emergencies, sudden in their origin, yet critical in their result, and requiring therefore to be met rather by instinct than by calculation.

We receive all these trials as the merciful counterpoise of our present especial consolations. They do not belong to a crushed Church, such as the Roman under the persecuting Emperors, or our own in the time of the Penal Laws; still less, of course, to a Church in the ascendant. They are the natural and necessary accompaniments of a state of progress towards recovery. They are not the sharp pangs of martyrdom, nor the inert throes of helpless prostration; neither are they, on the other hand, the temptations of confirmed health and restored vigour, but the drawbacks on a state of convalescence. They are not much more than half a century old, and they have made marvellous strides towards maturity in the last few years. It is far easier to note the date of their origin, and the steps of their progress, than to foresee the term of their continuance. Certain only it is, that other troubles will be ready to take their place whenever they shall pass away. But they constitute, for the time being, the problem of our day, and as such it may be interesting to discuss them. I hope that, in presuming to do so, I may obtain credit for sincerity when I say that my object is not to teach, still less to dogmatise, but to enquire, consult, and suggest. Perhaps, indeed, I am not quite free from the pardonable selfishness of a desire to clear my own views and ascertain my own duty through an interchange of thought, and a comparison of difficulties, with the representatives of so many Catholic interests, the subjects of so much varied experience, and the victors in so many critical combats.

The position, then, to be realised is this: we Catholics are, by the grace of God, children, whether by inheritance or adoption, of the Church which is the sole and exclusive depository on earth of eternal and immutable Truth; nor alone the passive receptacle of that Truth, but its ordained guardian and active dispenser. We neither share our treasure, nor divide our claims, with any other religious body whatever. The most imposing of the pretensions of other bodies does not even approach the limits, far less invade the province and threaten the majesty of our prerogative; the most orthodox of their opinions does not, in one and that a most important sense, come a whit nearer to our Truth, than the wildest and most fanatical of their doctrinal innovations. We claim their agreement as an impressive coincidence, we appreciate it as an independent testimony; but we utterly discard it as a point of ecclesiastical assimilation.

I am bound to apologise for the enunciation of truisms so obvious; I produce them, of course, merely in order to illustrate, in the strongest manner, the opposition which exists between the very rudimental principles of our religion and those with which we are called upon at every step to contend. Far from having conceded to us the exclusive possession of religious truth, we are extensively believed to lie in the depths of extreme and most pernicious error. Far from being accredited with our claims as Catholics, we have to battle every inch of our way in order to secure our rights as citizens. Far from being accorded an external position in this country which is any fit representation, or sufficient public exponent, of our true place in the world, we are doomed to the humiliation of seeing the upstart sects of yesterday preferred to us in the race of privilege or the scale of power. Far from being permitted to assert our ascendency as a prerogative, we are treated to scant measures of the barest right with a smile of patronage or a bow of condescension.

I hope that I shall sufficiently clear myself, as I proceed, from being supposed to note such facts in any tone of complaint and expostulation, or indeed any otherwise than as the illustration of an argument. They are the phenomena, neither strange nor inexplicable, of our position as a Catholic minority in a non-Catholic nation. Thanks to a merciful Providence, things are much better than they might have been, than they have been, and than elsewhere they are; and, thanks, under the same gracious superintendence, to the zeal, perseverance, and good judgment of those who stand foremost in the battle, our difficulties are every day diminishing in number and weakening in force. My present concern with them is chiefly in their bearing upon our own personal characters. The problem which they bring before us is that of adjusting the greatest amount of practical gain with the least surrender of characteristic principle. This problem, I need not add, is both soluble and solved. But its tendency is to throw us into one of two extreme attitudes; that of unpractical theorists, on the one hand, or that of practical laxists on the other; those who stand upon abstract principles with too little regard to great practical results, and those who pursue such results at some cost or other of essential principle.

For, no matter how severe the sacrifice of feeling, we must make up our minds either to understate our claims, economise our principles, and resort to a phraseology utterly inadequate to the true facts of the case, or withdraw altogether from the arena of public usefulness. But of this course the present line of our duty does not admit. It is not now either solely or chiefly some object of personal aggrandisement, or political exemption, which claims our interest and invites our exertion. It is the training of the youthful members of Christ's family; it is the protection of God's poor; the nurturing of His orphans; the emancipation of the helpless inmates of the workhouse or of the gaol* from a far tighter bond than either human art can forge or human mercy snap asunder. With interests such as these at stake, it becomes our duty to ascertain the conditions of essential principle and the limits of lawful concession; how far we may

* Since this address was delivered, a most important step has been gained in this department of our claims by the 'Prison Ministers' Act,' as well as by the regulations made for the improvement of the religious condition of Catholics in the Government prisons.

relax abstract rules of duty in the presence of an overpowering necessity; how far descend from our true place without abandoning it, or derogate from our just rights without surrendering them; and lop off from our vocabulary some of those luxuriant shoots which, while they minister to its beautiful efflorescence, are not necessary to its vital integrity.

It cannot, however, be denied that the process, needful as it is, has its attendant dangers. It is a misfortune when our best argument with an opponent is the *argumentum ad hominem.* The position of standing upon rights and stickling for prerogatives, is anything rather than one which the humble and retiring Catholic would choose if he had the option. But it is peculiarly painful to his best instincts, when even the rights for which he is compelled to battle are but the phantoms of his true claims. Here are we, in this country, the treasurers and guardians of the eternal Truth, the inheritors of the original Religion, the members of that Church whose ancestry alone is royal, whose pedigree alone untarnished, and whose relations with the world she has to conquer are alone unfettered by the boundaries of human empire, and independent of the fluctuations of human caprice—here are we, I say, through the effects of that misery which is proverbially the parent of unnatural coalitions, compelled to cast in our lot with those separatists of yesterday, even in their largest comprehension and minutest intersection; with the rejected of the rejected, the offshoots of the dissevered branch; with the fautors, however unconscious, of heresy doubly distilled, and the victims of schism twice divided; and compelled to think it gain if we can get anywise into port by the aid of a towage so rude, or under a convoy so shabby. Certainly it is an abject position for the Queen of the nations and the Bride of the Lamb.

The bare mention of such exalted titles, lighting up as they do in our minds the vision of that illustrious Church whose fortunes were the theme of prophets, and whose glories the consolation of saints, is enough to throw into a contrast, which would be ludicrous if it were not melancholy, the forms of expression into which one and all of us are driven, by the necessities of our position, to cast our Catholic ideas. Thus, while forced to apply the venerable name of a Church to that great religious society, the queen of all the sects, though but a sect, which in this nation and its dependencies usurps the place, assumes the titles, affects the privileges, and appropriates the revenues, of the ancient and rightful Church of England, we are precluded from applying to ourselves in popular parlance any loftier appellation than that of 'the Catholic body.' While using, in a certain sense correctly, of heretics and schismatics, who are our fellow-citizens and companions in distress, the amiable and endearing title of 'brethren,' we are obliged so far to fall in with the very defective notions of religious brotherhood which prevail around us as to call our own true brethren, and the fellow-heirs with ourselves of the Christian promises, by so cold a title as that of our 'co-religionists.' While complimenting those motley forms of heterogeneous error which prevail outside with the magnificent appellation of 'creeds,' we must needs hear without protest the faith of the saints designated as a 'denomination' or a 'persuasion.'

All this is a simple matter of necessity. But it cannot be denied that the habit is full of danger to ourselves—of danger which can be obviated by nothing but by habitual acts of faith and renewals of intention, by frequentation of the sacraments, and occasional retreats from the world. Our minds and characters are the creatures of our lips. If it be true that we may talk ourselves into the belief of a known fiction; if professors of the histrionic art, through constant use of elevated language, can scarcely help falling into the use of blank verse in ordinary conversation, then conversely the habit of applying to Catholic subjects a language which, if not absolutely false, is at any rate equivocal, and which, if not wholly unsuitable, is at any rate miserably inadequate to the matter in hand, must be likely to react dangerously upon our own minds, and tempt us to impute exaggeration and eccentricity to those who speak of the Church of God in terms strictly accurate, though now grown by long desuetude unfamiliar to our ears.

But more perilous still than the constant use of extenuating and apologetic language, is the temptation to defend Catholic Truth, or promote Catholic objects, by un-Catholic means. I do not forget that it is quite as easy to exaggerate this danger as to undervalue it; it is indeed of the utmost importance, in endeavouring to steer clear of those twin rocks which beset our course, that we should beware of mistaking for that which is essentially Catholic some personal taste, or private fancy, or favourite crotchet of our own. But, with full allowance for this exception, there can be no doubt that the temptation in question is peculiarly the danger of zeal; though I must also add, that the disposition to impute it is sometimes the attribute of lukewarmness. However, at any rate, it is necessary that we should all clear up our principles and make up our minds as to what may, and what may not, be done with a safe conscience; and for this, among many better reasons, that there is absolutely no point upon which our enemies, whether religious or political, are more keenly vigilant, or more conspicuously unfair, than upon the least appearance of inconsistency between our supposed principles and our actual exhibition. We ought, I think, to have a reason to give them for this apparent inconsistency, such as even they may be able to understand, however incapable of appreciating it. Such a reason, I cannot help thinking, would often be found in the plea of the argument *ad hominem*. Thus, when we are charged with advocating principles highly favourable to toleration in one country, and apparently at variance with it in another, to this charge we have a complete and satisfactory answer at hand. But as it is one which our opponents are quite incapable of appreciating, we may therefore well waive the abstract question and refer them to those principles of religious equality which in this country are so ostentatiously professed, and often so partially applied.

It is a trite, but all the truer observation, that this kind of inconsistency (where really such) has a peculiar habit of avenging itself in the failure of the objects it seeks to compass. The policy of that ill-starred sovereign James the Second will suggest itself to every reader of English history as a case in point. James, to his honour, had one grand object at heart—the restoration of religion in England. But he made the mistake of trying to effect in a trice what was the work, at least, of a generation; hence, like a desperate gambler, or a drowning man, with a great cause at stake, and but feeble human resources at his call, he caught at the first relief which offered itself, with more of eagerness in the pursuit than of care in the selection. Two expedients presented themselves to his short-sighted zeal: the one to conciliate the High Church party on the ground of religious approximation; the other, to buy over the Dissenters by a liberal act of amnesty. Either course was feasible by itself, but the two together were self-contradictory and mutually destructive. However, he tried first one and then the other. What was the consequence? He was reproached by his natural allies with ingratitude, and by his natural enemies with hypocrisy. He managed, with an infelicity which knows no parallel, to help every cause except his own, and to make everybody friends with everybody except himself. He effected what were, in their own way, little less than miracles of policy. He reconciled regicides with cavaliers, and made Puritanism shake hands with Prelacy. More wonderful than all, he raised a complete furore of romantic interest and chivalrous enthusiasm in favour of that most prosaic of causes, the cause of the Church Establishment. He raised the arms of seven zealous and conscientious Anglican prelates into the unwonted attitude of benediction, and bowed the knees of myriads of their delighted followers into the still more unwonted attitude of genuflection. But this most unexpected and unintentional of victories was the prelude of his speedy ruin. An ungrateful posterity has forgotten his sincerity in his ill success, and his zeal in his maladroitness; and with the same power of amalgamating the most heterogeneous elements, and uniting the most opposite parties in common hostility to himself, which he manifested when alive, he has blended in a chorus of adverse criticism so discordant a triad of historians as the infidel Hume, the liberal Macaulay, and the Catholic Lingard.

It will not, I hope, be considered as at variance with the undidactic and interlocutory tone which I feel to be the only suitable expression of my relations with an assembly like the present, if I submit to your better judgment some few very general thoughts on the mode by which we may hope to thread, without unlawful concession on the one hand or needless offence on the other, the singularly arduous course upon which we are thrown as a handful of Catholics in the midst of a population deeply imbued with prejudices, whether natural or simply gratuitous, against our religion. When I add my sincere conviction that the mean to be hit is as delicate as the needle's point, upon which it is said that angels alone can poise their steps, I shall make it evident how little I feel that any general directions can avail in a case where so much must be left to the conditions of individual trial, and so much more to the powers of a well-trained spiritual instinct. It is the reproach of human philosophy, though it is the consolation of Divine faith, that there are sons and daughters of Catholic Ireland in this wild and wicked metropolis, who, with little of worldly knowledge, are practically solving this great problem with an accuracy and precision which education cannot teach, nor rules supply. With this qualification I proceed.

We shall all, I am sure, agree in this conclusion, that those understatements of Catholic truth which our position entails should be strictly limited to cases of overpowering necessity, or the most obvious expediency. They come, indeed, under the head of those studied ambiguities of phrase which our theology rather permits than encourages. Nor can I conceive but that a Catholic must ever use such phrases with regret, and escape from them with pleasure. He must regard them as a kind of condescension, the only sort of condescension which is consistent with Christian humility; and the sense of relief with which he must exchange the society to whose dwarfish standard of moral and spiritual attainment they are accommodated, for the company of like-minded friends, and for the House of Prayer where Catholics breathe most freely, and things are called by their right names, is but faintly paralleled by that with which the recovering patient exchanges, for the first time, the closeness of the sick-room for the fresh air of the early summer, or with which the monarch passes from his levée, where for several hours he has been receiving strangers in an uncomfortable position, and with forced civilities, for the solitude of his private apartment, and the conversation of his intimate friends.

The course of my argument has hitherto led me to dwell chiefly on dangers to faith. But I must not for a moment be understood to mean that the dangers to charity are either fewer or less momentous. It is a pleasant thought that faith and charity are but different sides of the same truth, and that by harbouring thoughts of kindness, and multiplying inventions of love, towards our estranged fellow-countrymen, we are not deviating from our Catholic path, but advancing in it; not raising obstacles in the way of our faith, but regulating, and so deepening it.

1. The first suggestion of such a policy must surely be, that we habitually abstract the error from its maintainer, and accompany our needful severity against the one by even an excess of kindness and tenderness towards the other. Another, that we should never meditate on our own superior privileges, but as a motive to increased humility and superior virtue; using the lesser responsibility of the heretic (where his heresy is not self-chosen) as a set-off against his inferior attainments, and the greater responsibility of the Catholic as a counterpoise to his more exalted privilege. Another, that we should make the largest allowance which our theology permits for the possibilities of an exculpating ignorance; bearing especially in mind, that the ground of excuse is not alone the privation of knowledge, but some such incapacity of receiving that knowledge in its practical consequences as God sees to be independent of any fatal obliquity of the will.

And here I may take occasion, by the way, to remark that one of the misfortunes of our position is the temptation it creates to think better of 'liberal Protestants' than of what are called 'bigots.' Of course, in this judgement we are not entering into a comparison between the spiritual state of these several classes, but on their respective relations towards ourselves. Nor can it be denied that, *cæteris paribus*, it is in favour of any Protestant, and even suggests a well-grounded hope of his conversion, that he should be kindly disposed towards the Church. But we all know that our theology gives a preference to those who are faithfully acting upon the dictates of an erroneous conscience over those who renounce, in practice, the conclusions of their better knowiedge, and treat the question between themselves and us under any other point of view than as one of the gravest personal import; and since we ought to seek out the motives to charity most of all in those cases which present the most provoking temptations to a breach of it, we may do well to rest occasionally in a consideration which invests even our bitterest opponents with a softening and attractive light.

One or two additional reflections on this more inviting side of my subject, and I will release you.

There is no duty more eminently Christian, and therefore more characteristically Catholic, than that of habitually putting ourselves in the place of others, looking at things through their medium, and making their trials our own. The great moral philosopher of antiquity, if my memory do not fail me, gives to this quality of fellow-feeling a place in his system intermediate between selfishness and active sympathy. Then only would such a habit become dangerous, when, in eliciting our forbearance, it should stifle our zeal, and pass from the character of an indulgent allowance, or an equitable judgement, into a surrender of principle and a contented toleration of error. There is one class of Catholics among us, at all events, who should find no difficulty in this exercise—the converts. One of the most beautiful features in the character of S. Paul, is the tenderness of his bearing towards those who, having been once his companions in error, afterwards became the objects of his converting zeal.

Just in proportion to the extent and gravity of our moral and theological differences with our heretical fellow-countrymen, must be our eagerness to seize upon points of accidental agreement, and even occasions of lawful cooperation with them. There is, happily, a vast neutral territory of benevolence, involving no compromise, upon which our theology, with characteristic largeness and tenderness of spirit, permits us to unite even with those who are most opposed to us; and the liberty is one of which no Catholics are more ready to avail themselves than those who are proved to be the most unflinching champions of the Faith.

Nor is it on the broad platform of active benevolence only, that we may find a point of contact with our religious opponents, and reciprocate those friendly offices which, in justice to them it must be said, they are so generally disposed to extend to us. We have often the power, and should never want the will, to render them essential service in the common cause of public morality. The question, for instance, is now frequently mooted, of removing one or other of those venerable landmarks of purity or decorum, which are among the last surviving remnants of the ancient religion of England. The controversy on the subject of divorce which terminated so fatally for the interests of wedded sanctity, will occur to every mind as an illustration of this remark. The unrestricted allowance of marriage in cases of close affinity is another. This class of political questions seems to be peculiarly our own property; and, to aid in their adjustment on terms the most favourable to national virtue, seems no less the act of true Christian citizenship than the obvious dictate of a wise and enlarged Catholic policy.

In contrast to the line of duty which I have here attempted to sketch, are the attributes of what I may call the sectarian spirit. A few words will suffice to explain my meaning. The more truly we realise our position as the Church of the whole world, the stronger our faith in the promises which guarantee our indefectibility, and the principles which should regulate our course, the less shall we manifest of that sensitiveness to reproach, and craving after popularity, which are rather the characteristics of sectarian mistrust than of Catholic confidence. These nervous sensibilities, the effect of conscious weakness, so far as they enter into our temptations, are the natural relics of a state of obscurity and depression. If I might sum up in a single item the gains of the Catholic Church during the eventful quarter of a century in which our lot has been cast, I think I should select our advances, under high guidance, to a truer estimate of our place and character, as the most accurate exponent of the great result. But to dwell for an instant upon the topic from which I have thus digressed: I know of no more miserable feature in the spirit which I have called sectarian, than the readiness to make what may be called 'controversial capital' out of the mistakes or humiliations of those who are divided off from us. To dwell with complacency, or rather without shame and sorrow, upon the lapses and reverses of others, even though it make for ourselves, is to reduce the great contest between truth and error to a game of mere mechanical balance in which the elevation of the one side is due, not so much to its own skill or prowess, as to the accidental depression of the opposite. Where, indeed, the fall or failure is the direct consequence of some specially heretical tenet, or the *reductio ad absurdum* of some vaunted but baseless theory, I grant not only that the temptation in question is strong, but that the opportunity may lawfully, if guardedly, be turned to our account. Yet I cannot but feel that such cases are often too sad for triumph, and that the evil of the common scandal generally outweighs the benefit of the controversial advantage. The recent opening of the feeble flood-gates which have heretofore secured the Established Church from the influx of scepticism and infidelity, will probably occur to everyone here present as a case directly in point; and I cannot but think that the instinct of self-preservation, no less than of charity, is enlisted on the side of sympathy with those of our unhappily separated brethren, who are endeavouring, by whatever means at their command, to put down a movement which, although it confirm our anticipations and illustrate our theories, is of too subtle and elastic a character to be confined within the limits of the particular sphere in which it happens, in this country, to have originated.

> Tua res agitur, cum proximus ardet
> Ucalegon.

I had intended to illustrate this whole subject, with the assistance of a learned friend, by some passages from the New Testament, and from the Fathers of the Church, bearing upon the relations of its members with those who are without. But my limits are already reached. With two extracts from S. Augustine, which occur in the course of his controversy with the Donatists, I will bring this essay to a close :—

'O si eos charitas potius quam animositas superaret; inde victores fierent, unde victi essent. Nos autem Ecclesiam Catholicam, ad cujus pacem et concordiam et reconciliationem invitamus inimicos ejus, non humanis opinionibus, sed divinis testimoniis, amamus, tenemus, et defendimus.'

The Saint concludes the same discourse with these noble words, which I cannot do better than make my own :—

'Illum pro nobis rogetis, in quo spem ponimus ut de nostra disputatione gaudeatis. Tenete ista, fratres, obsecramus vos : per nomen ipsius Domini, per auctorem pacis, plantatorem pacis, dilectorem pacis, oramus vos, ut Eum pacifice oretis, pacifice deprecemini ; et memineritis esse filii Ejus, a quo dictum est, *Beati pacifici, quoniam filii Dei vocabuntur.*' *

* S. Aug. Serm. ccclviii.

NOTE.—The above paper was prepared, on a very short notice, to supply the place of one which its author was unavoidably prevented from completing. I have not felt myself justified in making any material additions to my own essay, but have let it remain exactly in its original shape. These facts will account for its insufficiency as an exposition of the whole subject on which it is employed.

F. O.

ON

BISHOP COLENSO'S OBJECTIONS TO THE VERACITY OF HOLY WRIT.

BY FRANCIS HENRY LAING.

On Dr. Colenso's chief objection concerning the name 'Jehovah'; as being asserted in Ex. vi. 3 not *to have been known before, in contradiction to the fact that, before, habitual use is well known to have been made of it.*

Of the objections that Dr. Colenso has brought forward in his now notorious book, some are but mere cavils on words, which criticism revolts at; others are made out of obscurities, which, capable themselves of satisfactory explanation, are nevertheless such as, considering the amount of knowledge—that is, the ignorance—which our distant age, and, along with it, Dr. Colenso himself, has of the Hebrew times, a book like the Hebrew Scriptures must, of its own nature, be expected to present. Among these objections, one alone of any such dignity as a really impressive-looking charge of inconsistency could lend to it, is his allegation of falsity against the Scripture for its statement concerning the introduction of the name Jehovah; which is said, in God's revelation of it to Moses, not to have been known before that very occasion. This assertion's seeming incompatibility with the undoubted fact of the word's previous customary use, forms the grounds of his accusation, which the grounds themselves are of a sort to make very specious. And it has accordingly received at the objector's hand a greater amount of handling than most others, occupying in his Second Part, of almost four hundred pages, the principal place, as culminating point of the whole argument. It is founded on Ex. vi. 3, where, notwithstanding the commonness of the Name in the mouths of the Patriarchs, a distinct statement is yet made that it was not known to them. 'By My name Jehovah was I not known to them.' The passage it is worth while to quote at length, as given by Dr. Colenso. His words are these:—

'In the story of the Exodus we read as follows:—

'"Then the Lord said unto Moses, Now shalt thou see what I will do to Pharaoh: for with a strong hand shall he drive them out of his land. And God spake unto Moses and said unto him, I am Jehovah: and I appeared unto Abraham, unto Isaac, and unto Jacob, by the name of God Almighty, but by My Name Jehovah was I not known to them. And I have also established My covenant with them, to give them the land of Canaan, the land of their pilgrimage, wherein they were strangers. And I have also heard the groaning of the children of Israel, whom the Egyptians keep in bondage; and I have remembered my covenant. Wherefore say unto the children of Israel, I am Jehovah, and I will bring you out from under the burdens of the Egyptians, and I will redeem you with a stretched-out arm, and with great judgements, and I will take you to Me for a people, and I will be to you a God, and ye shall know that I am Jehovah your God which bringeth you out from under the burdens of the Egyptians. And I will bring you in unto the land concerning the which I did swear to give it to Abraham, to Isaac, and to Jacob; and I will give it to you for a heritage. I am Jehovah."

'The above passage,' he continues, 'cannot, as it seems to me, without a perversion of its obvious meaning—the meaning which would be ascribed to it by the great body of simple-minded readers, who had never had their attention awakened to the difficulties in which the whole narrative becomes involved thereby, be explained to say anything else than this: that the name Jehovah was not known at all to the Patriarchs, but was now for the first time revealed as the name by which the God of Israel would be henceforth distinguished from all other gods.'

After a few more lines, he goes on:—

'But then we come at once upon the contradictory fact, that the name Jehovah is repeatedly used in the earlier parts of the story, throughout the whole Book of Genesis. And it is not merely employed by the writer, when relating simply as an historian, in his own person, events of a more ancient date, in which case he might be supposed to have introduced the word as having become in his own day, after having been thus revealed, familiar to himself and his readers, but it is put into the mouth of the Patriarchs themselves, as Abraham (xiv. 22), Isaac (xxvi. 22), Jacob (xxviii. 16).

Nay, according to the story, it was not only known to these, but to a multitude of others: to Eve (iv. 1), and Lemech (v. 22), before the Flood; and to Noah after it (ix. 26), to Sarai (xvi. 2), Rebekah (xxvii. 7), Leah (xxix. 31), Rachel (xxx. 24), to Laban also (xxiv. 3), and Bethuel (xxiv. 30), Abraham's servant (xxiv. 27); even to heathens, as Abimelech the Philistine, king of Gerar, his friend and his chief captain (xxvi. 28), and generally we are told that as early as the time of Enos, the son of Seth, there began men to call upon the name of Jehovah (iv. 26), though the name was known to Eve according to the narrative more than two centuries before.' It may be said to occur about one hundred and sixty times.

A very tangible objection, and fairly enough put—against which it is of little use to say, as is so often superciliously said against these difficulties, that 'it is all an old story; we have heard it all before.' True, the objection is old, and common enough too—treated by many men before for centuries, and one which every attentive reader himself meets without further suggestive aid than his own recollection of the preceding part of the Scripture narrative. But neither is it put forward, as we must admit, by Dr. Colenso as being new, but as being invincible: upon which therefore but little advance is to be gained out of the fact that his meeting with it has been in common with many others before him: for, that a difficulty has presented itself to many minds is nothing to allege in the way of its solution; rather, perhaps, the objection is advantaged by it, unless equal familiarity attend its satisfying reproof. To be content, therefore, as is perhaps too often the custom, with throwing the imputation of oldness or commonness upon the objection, is only letting the thing grow still older or more common in its strength. It must be allowed, then, that, for bringing forward this well-known difficulty, there is as much right to standing-room for Dr. Colenso as for any one else, either before or contemporary with him, whether German or English. Instead, then, of calling it stale, which it will not be, until it has been upset, I would confine myself to—what, for once in his objecting career, a certain prestige in the objection itself seems really to deserve—the task of making one more attempt at its solution : which can hardly be said to be superfluous yet. For whatever satisfactory answer to it has been given, if there be any such, has not at least had the good fortune to make its way into easily accessible books, amongst the ones which are commonly assigned. What these answers are, we may very fairly presume to be able to gather from an able article on the word 'Jehovah' in Smith's Biblical Dictionary; which, at the end, gives an account of those ones that have been considered to be the most deserving. Of these solutions, the first one is that which supposes the previous use of the word Jehovah to be by 'anticipation.' This is that of Le Clerc. What sort of elucidating meaning this account may carry to the minds of some, I do not know; but I will own, that, for myself, it seems not so much an explaining answer, as a feebler way of stating the difficulty itself; which is founded upon the appearance of that very anticipation which is given to solve it. Another one is that which supposes the first making known of the Name, which is attributed to this revelation to Moses, to consist in a greater fulness of knowledge than was possessed of it before by the Patriarchs: this is the gist of many answers couched in various forms, as for instance that it contained a recognition of God's glory and majesty; again, that it revealed a greater depth of fulness of the Divine nature, which 'had not been yet understood in its essence and depth.' Another one is, that it presented to the mind His personality and essential being:—not as it is incomprehensible or unknown, but in its manifestations. This last excepted, these explanations, from many different authors, are pretty much alike in meaning, and sometimes similar even in expressions. Kurtz and Kalisch, as quoted by Dr. Colenso in this place, give answers of the same character. Their adopted explanation from fulness of meaning as to attributes &c. will not, however, as I think would even be felt by those who allege it, meet the question exactly, with whatever justice a very near concern with the question may be allowed for it. And it certainly has that, in spite of its contemptuous rejection by Dr. Colenso: who, after his usual manner, with no more ado than a line, dispatches it, as he thinks, by calling it 'a mere assumption made to get over a difficulty;' which, however, it certainly is not, from evidence the most obvious. Even the simple-minded reader whom he supposes, if he has any sense, must immediately feel, on reading the 3rd and 6th chapters, that a new explicitness, which the Patriarchs are not known to have enjoyed, is given to the Name by God Himself in His making it particularly a matter for His own interpretation, as He does, when, in His answer to Moses' question, 'If they' (the Israelites) 'say to me, What is His name? what shall I say to them?' He replies, 'I Am Who Am. Thus shalt thou say to the children of Israel, I Am hath sent thee.' This interpretation certainly conveyed something like what the before-cited authors speak of as the attribute of self-existence—essence, essential being—which was really the notion of God as the Being of beings—being itself in the absolute sense of the word. This majestic idea presents the name of God in a light, as all must feel, beautifully apt for it as about to be made the established object for the Church's enlightened worship. This view of it, as given by the mouth of God Himself, is evidently something which indicated an intention on His part to put the name in a light more fit for His people's contemplation than had been done for their ancestors; which was at least, in order to some more special impartment of the Name. And such an evidently serious purpose in this Divine declaration, should make the attempted explanation which assigns it, deserving of something better than Dr. Colenso's contemptuous treatment. At the same time, intimately associated with the knowledge of Jehovah as is the sublime idea of absolute being, declared to be the word's own meaning—this being a pure theological notion of God, is not itself precisely what the Scriptural language intends to signify by the phrase 'known,' 'knowing the name of,' &c., which does not refer so much to the knowledge of God in the abstract as the one self-existent Being, or in any other absolute attributes, as that knowledge which comes by the *gracious relation* in which He puts Himself to be known to the people to whom He communicates Himself. That it is so, is shown even in the very passage itself; in which Moses, when asking Him, 'If they should say, What is His name? what shall I say to them?' is not enquiring what is the theological notion of God, as signified by His Name, but what was the name, which he might cite to them as a guarantee or record of Him as the God of the Israelites, who on his returning to them might enquire What is His name? What is the title for them to use in designating Him, in contradistinction to the other nations who had names for their gods? And in such sense is it also afforded by God Himself, who after giving the explanation, 'I Am Who Am,' says in reply, 'This is My Name and this is My memorial unto all generations,' which is as much as to say, 'This is the name by which I choose to record Myself amongst them —My proper name for them to call Me by henceforth.' Hence it is, that from this time forward, in the Mosaic dispensation, He is always called Jehovah *thy* God, Jehovah *our* God, the God *of Israel*.

The knowing or being known of Jehovah must, therefore, refer to Him as known in some *new relation*; which is not, however, found precisely in that grand conception, newly developed as it is, of Him in His absolute essence, as the one true Being of beings. This, therefore, only very distantly meets the want of the question. More akin to the real answer, as being founded on the *relational* aspect of God, is another kind, such as is that which states that the name Jehovah as now made known, presented God in His office as Redeemer; and again, that it revealed Him in His several attributes, and in His true character as God of the Covenant, &c. These ideas do, I believe, contain the germ of the true answer, but yet so mixed up with the dross of other elements, or else so faintly presented, and so undecidedly developed, that whatever glimmering of the truth may be in them, as I am inclined to think there is, their hold of it is too feeble to convey to the mind that luminous conviction which would set it free from uncertainty. And as these solutions have deservedly won the greater favour, as being the best, should there be any minds to whom their insufficiency shall be apparent, such persons at least will admit that there is still room for another attempt at solving the question: which in undertaking, we must guard against incurring the imputation of inventing suppositions for clearing the objection. If it has to be solved at all, the answer must be sought by a patient induction from those passages in the Scripture, especially the text itself, which pertain to its subject. And this course will give us a clue, which, I believe, will not fail to change this bulky-looking objection, confidently affirmed as it is by the Doctor, into something of less terrifying dimensions. All that it shrinks to, after undergoing its critical tapping, will be found to be nothing more than simply one of those not uncommon cases, in which the drift of the speaker's language has been totally lost sight of through an entangling word usurping all attention, to the detriment of the general context: to which the critical sight thus partially applied can produce in commentator nothing but strained excuses;

and be to the unscrupulous only ground for cavils. And it is such an unscholar-like way of looking at the text, if I may say so, which has been, in friend and foe, the real origin of this difficulty's strength. What else indeed might be even suspected, when we come to think about it, from the very idea, which the notion carries with it, that the whole object in the name Jehovah being now so solemnly announced to Moses the legislator was simply—what? why, nothing more than just to put a new word of four letters into the Hebrew vocabulary! for such is actually supposed to be the whole purport of the revelation, according to the objection as brought by Dr. Colenso. His argument is this:—'The word Jehovah, as a name for God, was well known and commonly used before for centuries; yet here it is said to have been for the first time given to Moses.' Now, does not this alleged contradiction rest for its whole force upon the assumption, that the grand thing now for the first time announced by revelation in the word Jehovah, was merely a new synonym for the name of God, made current for the Hebrew lips to call Him by? But what a most insignificant object to imagine for an act so professedly solemn as is this—the inauguration of a new dispensation; and might not this disproportion between the revelation and its imagined purpose be sufficient of itself to awaken in us a little circumspection as to the opinion which it is the offspring of;—whether this might not have arisen from what is so usual with infidel objections, some narrow-minded misconception of the speaker's scope, caused likely enough by a salient feature in the passage, drawing off to itself all the attention from the other parts of the text?

And that this sort of thing is the source of the difficulty will be manifest upon the more accurate examination being made. Even its first attempt, when applied to the two ideas, the known previous use of the name Jehovah, and its declared non-use previously, will put to flight (I had almost said before the bodily eye) two-thirds much in the bulk of their imposing contradictoriness, in a better rendering being thereby afforded of one single misleading word—the word '*known*,' as it occurs in the sentence, 'By My name Jehovah was I not known to them.' For this word 'known' it is—making the sentence sound as if to affirm the name Jehovah was altogether unknown to the Patriarchs—which gives the chief force to the objection as put forward by the Doctor. But this ensnaring expression 'known' will be loosed of its power, by being duly straightened from a general meaning into another one more specific—that is, 'made known,' which is the true meaning of the original word, (נוֹדַעְתִּי) for its root יָדַע signifies as often 'to *come* to know' as 'to know,' and its passive or niphal conjugation as often '*to come to be known*,' 'to be *made* known,' as 'to *be* known.' In such a sense it can be translated, and so it *should* be, where the sense requires it. For a possible and customary meaning becomes the certain one where *it* makes sense, and every other would make nonsense: as it almost would in this case. Such a meaning will be taken as the sense of an author by any one, except him whose labour is to make the author talk as much nonsense as possible. The better motive, which supposes him to be most likely consistent, should give undoubting preference to the sense '*made known*,' rather than that of simply 'known.' This rendering of the sentence, then, gives us as the amended sense, that under His name Jehovah, He had not been 'made known' by His own act. For the being made known, which is here denied to have been done in the former manifestations, is the same 'being made known' which is now done to Moses—that is by God Himself. And this gives us to understand this fact only, that previously there had been no making known of Himself under the name Jehovah *by His own revelation*. This making known by God's own manifesting act, is a marking feature which at one cut, and that only the first one, reduces the dimension of that asserted non-acquaintance with His name to such cases as were themselves the acts of God alone. This limitation would be still more expressly drawn by the force of a further very likely emendation, changing the word from its passive to its *reflective* sense—'I *made Myself* known,' which is authorised by many examples, from Ezechiel referring, too, especially to this very sort of making known which is mentioned here. Little difference in effect, of course, exists between 'I was not made known by Myself,' and 'I did not make Myself known,' except that the becoming known in one case is represented as God's own doing, and in the other less pointedly, as done by God. At the same time, the reflective form, which is as probable as the other one, more directly represents the knowledge as coming from the act of God. At the worst, the certain correction from 'known' to 'made known,' disencumbers our question at once of all the long list of cases where it was used before the Flood and after the Flood —of Eve and Noah, Rebekah, Bethuel, Abimelech, Abraham, Isaac, Jacob, and the rest—in fact, all the cases of the use of the word Jehovah outside the ones in which God's own mouth pronounced it.

And these are left the only ones with which we have to deal:—and that not as a doubtful result. For this limitation of the idea 'known' to that which came by God's own previous manifestation of His name, is confirmed by a further consideration of the passage, turning upon another word in it—a word less than the word 'known.' This is the little preposition 'by,' or 'in,' (b'), as supplied in the phrase, 'By My name Jehovah;' for this word 'by' is not found in the original, as in the Protestant translation, written immediately before the word 'My name,' the original gives literally this:—'I appeared to them by or in El Shaddai, but My name Jehovah was I not made known,' &c., so that if the wanting word 'by' or 'in' is to be understood in the second clause, this must be supposed to borrow it from the preceding clause, where it occurs before El Shaddai in the phrase, 'By El Shaddai I appeared.' In this place this one preposition 'by,' then, affords in both the clauses a common service, which shows the two clauses about El Shaddai and Jehovah to be coupled together in sense, as well as in grammar; and this identification of reference adds a still more strongly marked connection between the idea of 'appearing,' which was under

El Shaddai, and that of 'being made known,' or 'making Myself known,' which is said not to have yet been done under the name 'Jehovah;' both of which are thus seen evidently belonging to the idea of the Divine self-manifestation in this sentence. So that when it says, 'I appeared to Abraham, &c. by El Shaddai; but My name Jehovah was I not made known by to them' (as we may translate for the nonce); this is almost the same as if it had been said,—'I appeared by El Shaddai, but by My name Jehovah did I not *appear* to them;' and the making known denied of Jehovah is evidently only that 'making known' such as had been used for exhibiting to the Patriarchs the idea of Himself as El Shaddai, which was by His own action of 'appearing.' The name Jehovah was, then, to hold the same place in this revelation as had been in the previous ones held by El Shaddai; and this making known was nothing less than such a making known as God's own *appearing* was able to effect. Thus, then, there arises a new fence to the limitation, which the idea of 'making known' exhibits, showing that the knowing meant here, was no such knowing as a mere acquaintance with the four-lettered word as a current title for God implied, but such a knowledge only as came about by *official* manifestation, under that title, by God Himself.

But besides this, a still further confirmation of the same limitation, even to a still narrower compass, arises from the pursued examination of the passage: from which it will appear, that even these same communications of the Name by the Divine mouth, selected out from others as they are, have themselves to undergo a sifting, in order to come within the class such as this phrase 'making known' regards.

This is evident from these revelations, which are alluded to in the statement '*I appeared*,' being of an order that we may call *first class.* For such are the ones in which the mode of manifestation is this 'appearing,' as denoted by the introductory phrase 'and God appeared.' This manifestation differs by a high degree from that sort in which it is said, 'and Jehovah *said*,' as to Noah; 'and God *spoke to*;' 'and the word of Jehovah *came in a vision to*'—as to Abraham (Gen. xx.). This distinction, besides being actually found in use in the various manifestations themselves, is formally described (Num. xii. 6), where it is declared by God Himself, that His making Himself known in a dream is the more common mode, which would be vouchsafed to a 'prophet' among them less in dignity than Moses; but to Moses, as a matter of greater honour, the manifestation used was, 'mouth to mouth,' even apparently, 'not in dark speeches;' and, adds He, 'the similitude of Jehovah shall he behold.' Here, then, the Divine declaration itself designates that one which goes by the name of 'appearing,' where the vision of God's presence is made clear, as being the highest sort of manifestation.

Now this distinguishing mark of 'appearing,' shown in the phrase, 'and God appeared,' which alone could entitle the use of the name Jehovah, if found in the manifestation, to be brought on a par with that now made to Moses, is a feature which is not found in every manifestation made to the Patriarchs before Moses

Abraham's experience of it seems to have been three times: once (Gen. xii. 7), promising to give the land to his seed; another time (xvii. 1), in his ninety-ninth year, in commanding circumcision and promising the birth of Isaac; a third time (xxviii. 1), at Mamre, on confirming the promise. Isaac found it twice: once (xxv. 3), at Gerar, to confirm in him the promise made to his father; the second time (xxv. 23), at Beersheba (whether in a vision or not is not quite plain), on giving him assurance of protection. Jacob's experience was once clearly, if any more (xxxv. 9), at Bethel, after his coming from Padan Aram to renew the promise made to Abraham and Isaac. This occasion is the one which Jacob's citing of on his death-bed is in so solemn a manner, as to show to have been the great manifestation made to him.*

These five or six occasions, then, are the only ones which, being distinguished by the fact of the 'appearing,' are of such an order as could exhibit in themselves the name Jehovah in that Divinely communicated dignity, as to clash with the truth of the saying, that it was not made known to Abraham, Isaac, and Jacob;—nay, more, for it could not, even *then*, unless that word Jehovah should also be found holding the same position as that held there by the title El Shaddai. For it is El Shaddai's eminent mode of being made known alone, and no other, that is denied of the name Jehovah in

* This is not to be confounded with the manifestation made to him at Penuel, when he wrestled with the angel, as the blundering hostility to Scripture's consistency makes Dr. Colenso do, who out of his own mistakes, like the generality of sceptics, forges matter to charge for absurdities upon the Scripture.

the passage, 'I appeared to them' by El Shaddai, 'but by My name Jehovah I was not made known to them,' i. e., in a manner comparable with the promulgation of the name El Shaddai. The word Jehovah must find itself like and equal in the part it plays in those 'appearings,' before it can be made to interfere with the verity of the statement, that it was not made known to them. This limiting condition cuts away, therefore, from the class of 'made known' ones, all such cases of the name Jehovah, even when by God's own utterance, as are simply there, for current and already known designations of God. Properly sifted, then, the question, whether the name Jehovah was or was not made 'known' to the Patriarchs, reduces itself to this small compass:—Did the name 'Jehovah,' as *now communicated to Moses*, receive from God any such making known as was equal in kind to that making known which was given to the other name El Shaddai, as communicated to the Patriarchs? If so, it will be quite true to say, that there never was any such making known of it before, such as it has now, when announced to Moses; and the verity of the passage which says it will be fully justified.

Thoroughly solving to the whole difficulty as would be the duly established affirmative to the question—the question happily admits of a very clear answer in the affirmative. We confidently answer, Yes, it did! The making known now implied to have been given to the name Jehovah, was not less in import than that which was in the communication of the name El Shaddai: as might easily be, considering the wide range in the signification of the phrase 'made known:' for, properly understood, to 'make known,' or to 'know' a name, may indicate as many different sorts of footing between the knower and the known, as there are modes for knowing itself to take. Which, as in the case of the Queen, in regard to her subjects, may be very various. It may be that of *hearsay*. In that case it denotes nothing more than a general notoriety on the part of the object, and on the other side, an opportunity of hearing.

It may be by *communication* of the name from one to the other; and even that is very various, according as it is by a mediator, as minister, or servant; or by self, through letter or in person; and that again may be either public or private, official or informal, for business, in friendship, to give validity to a law or treaty, to lend a helping patronage to a charity, or to identify the person simply in report. All these, and plenty more, would of course indicate proportionate degrees of fellowship and good-will.

Would, then, the particular tie of fellowship be assumed, with anything like reasonable accuracy, in a method of proceeding which blindly presupposed the same value for every case of making known alike, whether this came by signing act of parliament, or being mentioned in a newspaper — whether at the foot of a proclamation—by publicly heading a subscription list for bazaar or hospital, or by signing a name in a private letter? Its modes of presentment, so diverse, render the word 'making known' itself, if left undetermined, a most absurd ground for building conclusions upon in any matter whatever. And not the less so in the case of God's making known His name as found in Scripture, especially when we find that the idea of knowing God (which 'knowing *His name*' is equivalent to) is taken with such intensity of meaning; as it is, for example, in Our Lord's own language, when He says, 'To know Thee, O Father, and Jesus Christ, Whom Thou hast sent, is everlasting life:' which was certainly not to be won by baldly knowing that there was, or was said to be, a Father, and His messenger Jesus Christ, as any infidel might know; but to know Him with that salutary knowing, which is the root and representative of trust, obedience, and established terms, through Christ, with God the Father as the giver of eternal life; and still more expressly the phrase 'to know His name:' which is accepted in such breadth and depth as even to denote the being in the highest state of grace, as for example, in Ps. xci. 11, where it is the ground to a person of his deserving all sorts of mercy and honour—a thousand falling by his side and ten thousand at his right hand, no evil befalling him, nor plague coming nigh his dwelling, being placed under charge of angels, so as to be kept in all his ways, that he dash not his foot against a stone, and much more of the same. And why all this? 'Because he hath *known My name*,' which, in the same Psalm, is expressed to be 'having made Jehovah his refuge, even the Most High his habitation.'

Wide, however, as is the sense which knowing the name of Jehovah has in the Scriptures, no discrimination in its value is made at all by Dr. Colenso, who omits altogether any consideration of differences. Not a word is there to indicate in him a thought whether the knowing was such as the more primitive Hebrews had, or that of the heathen; or whether it is a privileged knowledge of a favoured person. It is all one to him: all he sees is the word 'known,' and, starting from this, he goes head foremost to his conclusion of an irreconcileable opposition between the 'not known before' in the text, and the former attested knowing. Confidently, however, as this damning contradiction is deduced by him from the word 'known'—this word, nevertheless, has within its range of meaning one so especial as will amply approve the text's asserting it of the name Jehovah, Whose being 'not made known before' will stand clearly true—in a sense not far-fetched nor difficult, but evidently just. And what is that? It is that according to which the making known attributed now to the name Jehovah signifies the *formal setting of it as the covenant name* under which Almighty God would have Himself understood to be a party to the covenant He is now beginning to make with His newly-chosen people Israel. By a 'covenant name' of God, I understand, of course, the name by which He is officially declared in the covenant. In all human covenants, the likeness of which is observed throughout the Divine transactions with men, there are not only parties—promises on one side, obligations on the other, and a sign in making the agreement, but besides these a *name*, by which the promising party is to be designated, and to be held responsible for its due performance. Thus, with the Christian covenant, not merely does the human side in baptism receive a new name, but God Himself has edited a new name, under which He promises to the other party everlasting life, which is the title of 'Father, Son, and Holy Ghost.' This is the name under which He would be appealed to, and held bound in honour for His promises being performed. This is, therefore, the name in which all other treaties between God and the Christian are signed and sealed—the name with which the Christian habitually arms himself, as with a pledge of faith and hope; and this name occupies in the Christian covenant the same position which El Shaddai did before, and, as we are affirming, Jehovah did afterwards. Such is the meaning attached to the phrase, 'covenant name.' This consecration of the word to the position of the covenant title of God, is a feature in this announcement to Moses which would set the making known here far above the order of any utterances whatever of the name, as were less than that solemn sort of publication which attended the other name, El Shaddai, as given to Abraham; and that even when these manifestations were those of 'appearing'—still more, of course, any such manifestations in which that 'appearing' had no place; and farther still—even below all comparison—all cases of its use by men in merely familiar discourse. Not one of the cases previous to its announcement to Moses is such that it could be pretended there was in them anything like an express intention of making it what I have just described—the covenant name of God to the Patriarchs; notwithstanding what will be readily allowed for the name Jehovah even in its previous customary use (especially when the use of its synonym, Elohim, is contrasted with it); a certain favouredness as a title of God, when manifesting Himself in the supernatural or redeeming order: which is traceable enough to bespeak for it the honour of being adopted as the covenant title of God in any system of worship He might hereafter institute as part of a covenant service. But no official declaration had put such an import into the use of the name Jehovah yet, before the day of Moses. These cases, therefore, can none of them present anything to take away the position of 'first made known' from any announcement of the name, if only that announcement shall really be found fraught with the intent of making it henceforward the covenant name of God.

But as the covenant name of God *it is*, that it is now published to Moses:—the truth of which no difficulty attends in proving, except the embarrassment of too much evidence, puzzling one where to choose one's opening for proof.

Even without any laboured proof attempted, the idea of a first publication of the name Jehovah after the word's being in common use would cease to present any vestige of difficulty to the mind, if it were rightly considered how the religious dispensation entrusted to Moses, in which the name Jehovah established for worship is the grand feature, stood in regard to the religious observances before his time. These compared together present it as a regular practice for customs and usages already in vogue before, to be, nevertheless, taken up by the Mosaic dispensation into a position sufficiently unprecedented to justify the assertion that they were not instituted before.

Such, for example, was the period called 'week,'

which, though not expressly named as being composed of 'days,' in the patriarchal ages, was nevertheless then in use, as may be assumed with certainty enough from the seventh day having been hallowed and blessed —from the fact of such an interval being observed by Noah in sending out the raven and dove—from the use of the word in the still more extended application to *years*, as in Jacob's service to Laban. All these show clearly enough, nor has it been gravely doubted, that there previously did exist in customary use the period of a week as *a seven of days*. Yet, on being taken up into the position of a covenant observance, its previous well-known existence finds no explicit reference to itself made in the Mosaic covenant, either in the Ten Commandments, or any other parts of the Mosaic legislation. All this treats Sabbatical observance with such an originating air, that, without attention, we might easily suppose it to have no existence before its being prescribed as part of the national covenant.

But though the thing itself, 'week,' was known, yet its present form of being known for a lasting national obligation was not in being before it was now prescribed as part of the national covenant law. The same principle explains what we find as a Mosaic institution—the Levirate law; according to which a man was expected to take his deceased brother's wife, that the first issue might be imputed to the former husband, lest his name should become extinct in Israel. Yet this same thing is found in customary observance in the Book of Genesis, in the marriage affair of Judah's children.

So, too, the priesthood itself was an office whose

functions are distinctly seen long before Moses in the action of Noah, Abraham, and Jacob. Yet this previous observance is not the acknowledged foundation of the Levitical priesthood organised by Moses into a settled order of service:—and rightly too, considering what it owes to the Mosaic organisation, which raised up this same priesthood into such a new state as a regular professional department of service for national purposes, with such regulated and prescribed modes of action, succession, and duties, as to make it quite as just as it is natural to think of it and speak of it as owing its origination to no other than Moses' institution.

The same thing may be said with regard to all that belonged to the priesthood, its victims, sacrifices, altars, its mode of offering; the distinction of animals into clean and unclean; the propitiatory idea signified by the 'sweet savour;' nay, even the very *rubrics* of sacrifice, as seen in Abraham's dividing all the victims, but not the birds. All these things are clearly enough in use before. Yet this did not prevent their being counted for laws of Moses, because it was he who made them into regular statutes.

Their adoption into a covenant position was not at all alien to the mission of Moses as legislator. This capacity does not imply necessarily that he was the first inventor of all the observances which pass under his name as his laws. His, indeed, to be called so truly, they ought to be: and so also they will evidently show themselves to be, from their Mosaic structure, to anyone, however much impressed with the fact of their being, as we have just described, in use before Moses' time.

When the narrative of Genesis, containing the evidences of this previous use, on passing under the reader's view, leaves in its stead the next part of the narrative for his perusal, he must, on coming to the Books of Exodus, Leviticus, and Numbers, &c., see in the multifarious and systematised detail of regulations for the Israelite life, a something which is so thoroughly unprecedented as fully to justify our calling its authorship an original one. But yet it must be repeated that this did not consist precisely in first devising the material part of all the observances themselves.

The work which gives to him this real character of original legislator, is the originality of the office he was the first to hold among the Israelite people, of having to constitute ordinances under the permanent form of *public law*, by which the people should be once and for ever moulded into that national order according to which they were to regulate themselves. This had been hitherto impossible before his time, for want of their being in a condition of an independent people: which the office of legislator requires as an opening for his work. For any ordination that he might make for them, to be valid as a law for them to live by, should be capable of being enforced amongst them: which it would not be, if they were in such a condition as to be obliged to conform themselves to some alien dominion, keeping them from being their own masters. This requisite of independence for the reception of law proper, was thus wanting to the Israelites, as long as they were not yet out of the grasp of the Egyptians. But now, when the Egyptian rule, by God's delivering hand, falling off from them, left them a people to themselves, capable of living according to laws of native origin, this was the seasonable occasion for the same Divine Providence which had delivered them into the state of a self-subsisting people, to ordain that their own national laws should be given to them. And for this work Moses was the minister employed. His duty, then, was that of making the nation, what it had never been before, a self-governed people, living according to their own national ordinances, designed expressly for them, under a sanction derived from their own more immediate Governor, which was God Himself. This purpose was fulfilled by him as law-giver, in his delivering to them the ordinances they were to live by, in the form of a systematic body of law, set in language, stamped with the Divine obligation for all the Israelite people for ever. Thus it is that we have in them the system of the Priesthood :—a tabernacle planned, the sacrifices ordered—the priestly succession settled—all the rites detailed; and so on for the whole social existence of the Israelite, to whom he acts as universal legislator. This he is in virtue of the fact, that whatever he ordained at all, was ordained by him not merely as a custom worthy of their acceptance, but in that definite form of an authorised rule which national law requires for its stability. In this new national movement, the uppermost feature of novelty was not so much the appearance of a new religious practice, which, however, was itself new in its extended shape, so much as the public seal of national law, in which the religious observance was constituted by him.

So distinguished in its kind from the work of merely first inventing the fashions of their religious life, was his authorising office, as their national legislator, as to allow, without abatement of his legislative originality, a very great degree of ancientness in many of the national observances themselves, which he constituted into law. And so largely is this admissibility of presence along with Moses' instituting merit enjoyed by the ancient usages of the Hebrews, that all that was practised before we find appearing in what is called the Mosaic dispensation: which contains not only what had been already made covenant matter before—as the precepts of Noah and the Abrahamic rite of circumcision, which are all renewed under Moses' more modern sanction—but all that had *not* been made covenant matter, such as those already mentioned—the priesthood and its affairs, sabbatical observances, &c. And perhaps it would be hardly rash to think, that while there is nothing in the preceding practice which does not find itself put into the form of statute law by Moses' highly developed constitutions, there is little in them which does not point back to something in the Patriarchal customs either plainly, or at least with a reference more recondite. And yet, however much the practices of religious worship were in use before, so thoroughly new and unprecedented is the grand system in which Moses' legislative code presents them stamped to the Israelite people in their new covenant, that it would be no unveracity to say, that as sacredly binding ordinances they had never been made known before.

The same thing, then, 'not made known before,' may

be said with equal right of what the system presents as its chief article, its sun and soul—which along with the rest, God now promulgates—the name Jehovah; which, though so well known, and so much used even with a sort of covenant-like prestige upon it, was now for the first time taken by Divine command for the authentic name under which God would have Himself worshipped as an object of faith by His covenant people the Israelites, who had been delivered by Him out of Egypt, on purpose that they might be consecrated to His service.

And that this idea of a covenant import, dignifying God's act of making known His name, is assigned correctly, finds witness enough in the language of the address itself, in various ways.

1. An implication of it is found in the text's associating with this making known, as fellow to it, the covenantal act of God's appearing, when saying, 'And God spake to Moses and said to him, I Jehovah, and I appeared,' i. e. was seen, 'to Abraham, to Isaac, and to Jacob, by El Shaddai '—God Almighty, 'but My name Jehovah I was not made known by to them.' Now this, 'I appeared by,' which the expression, 'I was made known by,' has as its equivalent, denotes a mode of manifestation which is especially employed by the Divine speaker when revealing Himself under the aspect of the covenant God, or as transacting the weightier affairs of the covenant. A like covenant value will then fairly belong to that other idea, which it has abreast with it in position here, as well as in meaning generally, the '*making known*' which is said concerning the word 'Jehovah.'

2. And what its companionship with a covenantal mode of manifestation would imply, is more visible still in its own announcement here, in the very first word, 'I Jehovah.' These words come in here in the address God is making to Moses, after the same manner as El Shaddai is found in the announcement of the covenant made with Abraham, 'I am El Shaddai: walk before Me; be thou perfect.' This announcement is no other than the form of a preface to the covenant; and such too, by parity, will be the burden of the similar declaration to Moses of Jehovah.

3. This is answerably borne out, too, by the sequel: which is in fact the description of the covenant itself, with an express parallel drawn between it and the covenant which had been introduced by the announcement to Abraham of El Shaddai.

'And I established also,' He continues, 'My covenant with them, to give them the land of their pilgrimage, wherein they were strangers. And I have also heard the groaning of the children of Israel, whom the Egyptians are keeping in bondage; and I have remembered My covenant.'

4. And what this covenant is, that its newly made known name introduced, is immediately described.

'Wherefore,' in pursuance of this covenant, 'say to the children of Israel, I Jehovah, and I will bring you out from under the burdens of the Egyptians, and I will rid you out of their bondage, and I will redeem you with an outstretched arm, and with great judgements.'

5. And how justly the making known of His name Jehovah might have *call* for being new, is seen from

the newness of the covenant itself, which it is introduced to sanction, of which the main feature is God's taking the Israelite nation for the first time for His own people, and His being to them in a new sense their national God.

'And I will be to you a God.'

This was as if God was now rising up after a long silence to put a fresh hand to the covenant work which He had let be for so long a time, since Jacob and Joseph. For, although there had before and all along been a destination of the Abrahamic family or tribe, as the people of God; the formal adoption of the nation had not hitherto been made. And this new and unprecedented display of grace, in adopting the people from amongst the nations of the earth, may well impart its own grounds of novelty also to that publication of the name Jehovah which is here officially announced to celebrate it.

6. So implicated with the new act of God as making alliance with the nation, is their knowing His name Jehovah, as to be here actually described as consisting, *partially* at least, if not *mainly*, in that as yet uncommunicated knowledge, which they were henceforth to have of Him, in those acts of goodness which He would do towards them, in this relation, thus newly contracted under that name.

'And ye shall know that I am Jehovah your God who brought you out from under the burdens of the Egyptians. And I will bring you into the land concerning which I sware to give it to Abraham, to Isaac, and to Jacob; and I will give it now for an heritage.'

It was these future acts of guardian guidance, all bound up in this adoption, which were to afford them that experience of Him, by which they should know Him to be Jehovah, their own national God.

7. And as a last and crowning sanction to this promise, He sets His name again, like a signature, at the end of the whole address, which He had begun by citing it before—'I Jehovah.'

How forcibly the whole address made by God to Moses brings out the special meaning of the clause, 'I was not made known,' will be perhaps more conveniently presented to the reader in the form, inelegant though it be, of a paraphrase; which the preceding comments will enable the reader to justify.

'And God spake to Moses, when preparing to deliver the people from their slavery in Egypt, and to bring them out for His own people, "I am Jehovah." Such is the title under which I now intend to have Myself called in that alliance in which I am going to employ you, Moses, as my chief hand or minister: not as I chose to be called before in the covenant work, or part to which I called your fathers the Patriarchs. For in My covenant promise with *them* I appeared, or was seen, to Abraham, to Isaac, and to Jacob, under the title of El Shaddai—God Almighty. Such was the title under which I subscribed My name, to pledge Myself to perform what I promised. But under the name which I have just announced to you, the name Jehovah, did I not make Myself known to them, as by My official name. And, accordingly, I established with them My covenant, which was not an instituted form of national worship, but such an one as was meet for them as Progenitors of the Holy Seed, and prospectively inheritors of the land, to give them the land of Canaan, the land of their pilgrimage, in which they were strangers—a covenant preparatory to the one I am about to make with you, which is to make you a people ordained to the charge of worshipping Me, with a national service arranged for that purpose, under a name more proper than the name El Shaddai for perpetual worship—the name Jehovah or self-existing Being—the Being of beings. With this intent, as I vouchsafed to have respect to your fathers; so now I have heard the groaning of the children of Israel, whom the Egyptians are holding in bondage, and I have remembered My covenant, in which I promised that the seed of Abraham should inherit the land of Canaan. Wherefore, in pursuance of this intention of performing My promise, give to the children of Israel My newly announced name as a pledge, under which I will be bound to do what I say; and say to them, "I am Jehovah," and I will bring you out from under the burdens of the Egyptians, and I will rid you out of their bondage, and I will redeem you with an outstretched arm and with great judgements;' and with the purpose of bringing about your inheritance of the land, and your being made the covenant people, I will take you to Me for a people, such as you have not been before, except in destination and promise, a people to worship Me—a holy people—a people of priests, and I will be to you, in a more manifest manner than during your captivity, a God; not as of the Hebrews only, but God of Israel, the national God, and you shall know Me, own Me, have My name recorded amongst you as the God of Israel, different from the nations about you, Moab, and Ammon, and Egypt, whose adopted gods are false; and you shall know that I Jehovah, to be henceforth cited and worshipped by you under that title for ever, am your God, Who bring you out from under the burdens of the Egyptians.

'And this name shall be a standard, under which I will have you, Moses, to conduct the redemption of them into the land of safety which I sware to give to Abraham, to Isaac, and to Jacob, and I will give it to you, their representatives, for a heritage. This is My covenant, and as assurance of its certainty, behold I pledge the honour of My name—"I Jehovah."'

In this address the Divine speaker sets forth His holy name Jehovah, bearing upon itself so many covenant-like characters as plainly enough show that its being made known was intended by Him to stamp a higher value on it for the interest of Israel; that thus dignified it might henceforth take its stand as the consecrated title for God, in His alliance with Israel.

This covenant value in the name, which the earlier intimation discloses, is unmistakeably exhibited also in those Divine decrees to Israel, which subsequently Moses, as God's mouth-piece to them, was from time to time instructed to communicate.

In them the manifestations of the name are really its actual applications, that carry out the intention, which in first declaring it to Moses before the Exodus, the Divine Author had in mind. And this intended sense of it therefore will be luminously beheld in *them*, as in its destined employments, according to the mode in which it shall be presented by them.

And how plainly their presentment bespeaks a peculiar covenant value for the name, makes itself apparent from the way in which the taking of the name as the standard name for God in the covenant affairs is practised throughout the course of its delivery.

Here we are everywhere met with tokens, reminding us how the peculiar position of the Israelites as God's allied people, was constituted through the *setting* amongst them of the name Jehovah; by which they were consecrated to Him. This setting is that which gives the covenant character to the covenant's main law, the Ten Commandments; as is seen more clearly under the light of Moses' own account of them in Deuteronomy. There, naming God as 'our God' (after the manner customary from God's first giving Himself to be their God), he begins, 'Jehovah, our God, made a covenant with us in Horeb'—the same covenant that Moses, before the exodus, when keeping Jethro's flock in this very mountain, was called to the prospect of being intrusted with, which was that the people should serve God upon this mountain Horeb.

'Jehovah made not this covenant with our fathers:' the very same thing—'not made with their fathers'—that is said of the publishing of the name; whose connection with the covenant itself has thus a common feature to mark it. 'Jehovah talked with you face to face, in the mount, out of the midst of the fire, saying—' And here follow the covenant Ten Commandments themselves, prefaced by the solemn announcement, 'I am Jehovah thy God, who brought thee out of the land of Egypt, from the house of bondage.'

This heading is here put forth to present Jehovah as the grand object of worship, to Whom, under that name, were to be dedicated all the after-stated duties of avoiding false gods, idolatry, profanation of God's name, murder, adultery, theft, &c. And all these ordinary duties—(bounden as the most ancient law of nature had already made them, and even positive enactment)—are here transformed into services of a new covenant merit, capable of earning God's approbation, by the fact of being dedicated to Him under this appointed name. If this name, thus planted as a sanction, could so consecrate their ordinary human obligations, that these should become invested with a value so new: no less new must have been the setting of the name itself, by which those duties received their fresh consecration. And yet it is this very hallowing of the name in the nation's conscience that formed the peculiar saving knowledge of God, which was His chosen people's privilege. This Israelite knowledge of God, as Jehovah, therefore, consisted not in a bare philological acquaintance with the name of the Deity, but in the fact that His precious name Jehovah had been set in their dutiful sense, as the witnessed presence of their own remunerating God.

It is in this same spirit as of an authorising name, that it is appended as God's own signature to His laws, throughout the series of enactments made, as—'Ye shall keep My sabbaths and reverence My sanctuary, I Jehovah;'—'Ye shall fear every man his mother and his father, and keep My sabbath, I Jehovah;'—'Turn not unto idols, I Jehovah;'—'Ye shall not steal, I Jehovah;'—'Ye shall not swear by My name falsely, &c. I Jehovah;'—and so on throughout the statutes, as if the name subscribed to the command gave it a sanction, as an Israelite rule, valid for their observance.

And how truly this same setting of the name to the obedience of Israel, infused a special worth into their duties as His favoured people, is seen in the way in which all the duties that God Himself could be the object of, are habitually regarded as being paid to His *name*. It is His name that they are to sanctify—the name, not of God simply, but *their* God—His name that they are to swear by, as by a presence now made sacred to all, and not to take in vain, nor to pollute, as too sacred to be called in witness of a falsehood, or to apply profanely. It is His name—the glorious and dreadful name—that they are to fear—His name, which is so admirable, so great, so good, to make mention of, to confess, to declare, to publish, to praise, to glorify. It is His name that they should trust in, glory in, rejoice in, and take as their buckler and shield, in whose strength they should do battle and trust for victory. It is His name that they should call upon, hope in, hallow, love, and bless. A name which, as the audible image of God, they should treat with every affection that God Himself could have from man. And why? Because His publishing of it to Israel had made it *now* to be present with them as His pledged memorial of their being betrothed to Him in holiness.

It is this same *setting*, in the spirit of which the holy

name is *proclaimed* by God Himself in a formal manner according to the promise He gave in answer to Moses' petition, that He would show him His glory: to which He replied, 'I will make all My goodness pass before thee, and I will proclaim the name of Jehovah before thee.' And how connected this proclamation was with assuring the benefits of an alliance, is shown from what follows as its comment. 'And I will be gracious to whom I will be gracious, and I will show mercy to whom I will show mercy.' And what He promised is accordingly done, upon the delivery of the second two tables of stone; when solemnly, as if plighting His own honour, Jehovah descended in a cloud, and stood with him there, and proclaimed the name of Jehovah. And Jehovah passed by before him, and proclaimed 'Jehovah, Jehovah, God, merciful and gracious, long-suffering, and abundant in goodness and truth,' &c. This solemn announcement is of the same institutional character that marks the name's established presence in the people.

This same setting is the mother notion, whose likeness crops up perpetually in the course of the Pentateuch, in various exemplifying varieties of the same idea; in which localised presence is attributed to the Divine Name. Thus it is said to be '*recorded*' in a *place.* The place, the house, the tribe where God shall choose to record His name there, is everywhere found; which evidently attributes to the name an inhabiting mode of existence.

Of the same character is the idea of *residence,* which is attributed to it, as when, speaking of the angel, God says, 'My name is in him,' as a motive for their obeying His directions.

Such again is in the idea of *putting* the name upon the people, as where it is said (Num. vi. 27) and they, i. e. Aaron and his sons, 'shall put My name upon the children of Israel:' which consisted in thrice pronouncing the name Jehovah with benediction—'Jehovah bless thee and keep thee. Jehovah make His face to shine upon thee, and be gracious to thee. Jehovah lift up His countenance upon thee, and give thee peace.'

It is the same localisable faculty that is supposed in the idea of the name's being '*called upon*' one, as a pledge of God's favour—as when Jeremiah prays (xiv. 9), 'Jehovah, Thou art in the midst of us; Thy name is called upon us: leave us not:' as if in the name being called upon one, or one's being called by His name, a claim upon His guardian grace was given. 'Thy name was never called upon them'—the heathen—says Isaiah, as an equivalent to—'Thou never bearest rule over them,' so that they should have a right to expect grace from Thee. In the same spirit of the expression, Jehovah Himself speaks, when in the next chapter He says, 'I am sought by a nation that My name was not called upon,' which is here intended to put to shame the unfaithful Israel, whom His name had been called upon in token of their privileged alliance with Him. These, and many more instances, which, if time permitted, might be cited, all illustrate the fact, that the peculiar knowledge which the Israelites were gifted with, in God's name being made known to them, consisted in nothing less than the name's being given to *abide amongst* them as the covenant pledge of the precious alliance with Jehovah's saving strength. And as this rich weight of covenant meaning, which, all along the covenant's delivery, habitual usage shows the idea of knowing the name Jehovah to convey, casts back the credit of being its original source upon that grand occasion, where the first setting of the name for use took place, in the revelation of it to Moses;—this first making known of it to them will, therefore, like its *continuing* to be known amongst them, imply the giving of it as the name under which God would have His newly adopted people regard Him as now belonging to them, in settled alliance, as their own guardian God. So that for God, to make known His name Jehovah, was to consecrate His name amongst them, as in its chosen dwelling place where He might be worshipped with an acceptable service: and for them to have the name to know Him by, was really to be a people dedicated to Him, under that name, as their indwelling God.

And as such a Divine fellowship with a nation, where, as Moses says, God was 'so nigh' to them, had never been vouchsafed before in the history of the earth, we have in 'covenant name,' an idea which shows the name Jehovah, as now made known to Moses, to be of a signification quite on a par with that eminent signification that attended the publication to Abraham of the name El Shaddai: parity with which, therefore, marks a dignity in the new published name of Jehovah, far above the order of any such uses of the same word, as occasions in previous times could show, in the Book of Genesis, even where God Himself employs it, or the

Patriarchs;—still more where the heathens do. These instances, more than one hundred and sixty in number, many and often solemn as they are, implying at the same time no official knowledge of the name, have, therefore, no such comparable element as could enable them beforehand to preoccupy the honour of priority from the making known to Moses of it, as the name under which Almighty God would henceforth have Himself known to His people Israel as their covenant God. This unprecedented sense, making this publication the first of its kind, offers a light by which the Scripture is fully justified in representing Almighty God saying to Moses, when revealing it, that it 'was not made known to the fathers Abraham, Isaac, and Jacob.'

These words, therefore, are not properly open to such an imputation as that which is cast by Dr. Colenso; who, taking the word, in the most un-Hebrew-like sense, to signify the bald knowledge of the word, has used it as a ground to establish against Scripture a charge of falsehood, which he calls 'unveracity'—in his own eyes sufficient to condemn the whole account as a forgery, piously palmed upon the credulous Israelites by some later writer.

The Pentateuch and Book of Joshua critically examined. By the Right Rev. John William Colenso, D.D., Bishop of Natal (*1st Part*).

After so many replies to Dr. Colenso's First Part, another yet added at this period of the controversy may strike the reader as superfluous. 'We are tired,' he will exclaim, 'of Dr. Colenso, and still more of answers to him. If he has been answered already, why trouble us with more? If, after such a multitude, more are required, it would almost seem to argue such a weakness on the defenders' side as would leave it to be supposed that he must be in the right.'

The reader, however, need not fear that he is going to be dragged over worn-out ground in any long dissertation in this paper. This is occupied, in detail at least, upon *two* only of Dr. Colenso's assertions: which have been purposely selected as yet capable of further treatment, from its seeming to the writer that a thorough refutation had not been given them: these are, the one about Judah's age, and the other, more especially, about the number of the first-born. These are the only ones out of the First Part which now merit any particular notice, as those who have taken up the cause against him have repeatedly sifted and exposed the rest. But though no detailed argument about them is here professedly given, yet, in case any reader who has not had leisure to pursue an investigation of them should wish to get, in a speedy manner, an idea of the true worth of the other objections—he will be enabled to judge how entirely void of any formidable element they are, from a short conspectus thrown in of the alleged difficulties, with indications of the answers appended.

Obj. I. This is about Judah's age, which is treated at length in the end of this paper, to which the reader is referred.

II. That the court of the Tabernacle, which could hold only 5,000 persons at most, is supposed to receive the whole assembly of the congregation: which is impossible—since even the adult males alone, according to the narrative, amounted to 603,500 men, which, therefore, could not all be contained in it.

Ans. It was never intended to contain all. The 'all,' the 'whole,' spoken of is the same sort of 'all' which is such by being *deemed to be* so; as when a proclamation made in a market-place, or demand for a show of hands at the hustings, is deemed to be to *all*, or, to use an example from Scripture, which the objector himself most suicidally quotes, 'the whole congregation' is said to stone the blasphemer with stones; which, according to him, ought to mean that the 603,500 men, with women and children, were to engage themselves in flinging stones at him. The 'all' here is such because *none were expressly excluded*; an 'all' sampled in *some*.

III. That Moses and Joshua are said to have addressed 'all the congregation'—which is impossible; as all the congregation of two million—as much as London—could not have heard them. This is proved by arithmetic.

Ans. The same reason suffices: the 'all' were said to be addressed, because *none were intentionally excluded*—'all' sampled in a representative *some*.

IV. That the priest is said to have to carry out a whole bullock at least three-quarters of a mile, and the people to carry out their refuse to an equal distance; all which is incredible.

Ans. The priest is not said to carry it, but to 'cause to carry' it. And even if it did not say so, nothing could be drawn from the expression, since common usage attributes to the chief agent all that the agent has done through his management, or which is done in his name; as, a man is said to build a house, which is materially built by architect, masons, and carpenters, his employés; or, a company cuts a railway, which is really done by navvies. The same sort of reason suffices for the people carrying their refuse.

V. That the shekel of the sanctuary is spoken of before any sanctuary existed.

Ans. The 'shekel of the sanctuary'—if that be the true rendering, rather than 'the holy shekel'—might be spoken of *in prospect*, just as reasonably as in prospect there could be speech made previous to its existence of the sanctuary itself, or anything else belonging to its order. Of this order, the shekel of the sanctuary was an ingredient. If that could not be spoken of before the sanctuary existed, then neither could the sanctuary's rites and observances, which as yet were only in prospect or plan. There did exist, however, a genuine shekel before this, of twenty gerahs, which seems to have been now adopted under a new sanction by Moses, in the same way as he adopted many other preexisting usages into the covenant economy of which he was the dispenser.

VI. The number of persons, 603,500, who paid this tribute was the same as that which is found in the census some months afterwards, which looks very suspicious.

Ans. The people being counted by families and fifties, naturally yielded in the returns round numbers, ending in hundreds and fifties, as they do here. No one knows exactly—nor Dr. Colenso either—what was precisely the system in making a census of the people. He quotes the right answer from Kurtz, which everyone —and I suspect he himself did—will feel to be the true one.

VII. That they are said to have had tents in coming out of Egypt. This is impossible. They could not have got them; nor, if they had, could they have carried them.

Ans. Dr. Colenso has never proved that they could not have had tents, nor that they had no means of carrying them. The difficulty is entirely out of his own head.

VIII. That they are said to have gone out 'harnessed.' This is impossible: they had no weapons.

Ans. We have a right to demand how he knows they had no weapons. His mere conjecture on the point is worth nothing. The word 'harnessed' is, as he himself well knows, most likely 'in orderly array,' or by fifties.

IX. The Israelites are told in one day to keep the Passover. This is impossible, as no notice could have been given throughout the whole nation.

Ans. They were prepared for the exodus long before, —not for days only, but for weeks, nay months: we may say, from what we see of Moses' constant intercourse with them as their acknowledged guide, that remotely even *years* had been spent in God's preparing the people under him for that event. That they were not so is merely gratuitously asserted.

The same principle of a long preparation liquidates many other objections of the same character; as for instance:—

X. That notice of the exodus is given, according to the narrative, on the very night of its taking place.

Ans. Only the last command, not all the instructions.

XI. That without notice given, they borrow of the Egyptians jewels of gold, &c.

Ans. This we know, even from explicit statements, to be false. It was premeditated even as early as Moses' first call (Ex. iii. 22). It was commanded days before the slaughter of the firstborn (xi. 2).

And the success of the action is specially attributed to a miraculous 'favour,' which God gave the Israelites 'in the eyes of the Egyptians' (xii. 32).

XII. It is said that the children of Israel journeyed from Rameses to Succoth, 600,000 men on foot that were men, besides children, &c.—That this is utterly incredible, and impossible on account of the 'indescribable distress' that would have been caused from so many together, still more when we are required to believe that 'in one day' the order to start was communicated suddenly at midnight to every single family, &c. &c.

Yet 'this is undoubtedly what the story of the exodus requires us to believe.'

Ans. This is what undoubtedly the Scripture does *not* require us to believe. It was not suddenly, except at the last word of order, but the effect of a Divinely arranged organisation under the vigilant hand of Moses. With regard to the wonderful order manifested in the exodus under the extraordinarily unfavourable circumstances of night; if we take the Scripture on its own showing, and not on that of Dr. Colenso, we are relieved from any further burden of explaining the wonder at all, as much as we are from that of explaining Christ's resurrection from the dead. Like that, this act of God's bringing His son out of Egypt, with a high hand and outstretched arm, is uniformly described, and celebrated as a stupendous miracle throughout the whole of the Israelite history. This 'great wonder,' therefore, presents only that sort of difficulty which vanishes into that of believing any other miracle. The difference between this and most others is, that while they are usually worked in the body of one person, this was worked in the body of one whole *nation*, Divinely prepared under the generalship of God Himself, Who led Israel about and instructed him as the apple of His eye, as an eagle fluttereth over her nest. If the eagle can take care of her young, and prepare them for flight in due season, surely God could with equal certainty manage to bring His young child Israel into freedom from captivity at the hour that He appointed for Himself.

If Dr. Colenso does not believe in miracles, let him say so. But let him not object against a declared miracle, that it was not possible by merely unaided natural agency.

The same principle explains the next, viz.:—

XIII. That the narrative implies vast herds of cattle as belonging to the people throughout the forty years. This is impossible, as 'such a multitude of cattle' could not find means of support for such a time, under such circumstances; i. e., as he adds at the end, 'without a special miracle, of which the Bible says nothing.'

Ans. The Bible does not say nothing, at least by direct implication. This is made with the same sufficiency, as that by which the greater contains the less, or the whole its part. It does not indeed say in so many words, 'the cattle were sustained miraculously,' but it more than admits it by describing the whole forty years' wandering as a wonderful work of God, as is declared in many places that might be quoted. Let those suffice which Dr. Colenso has himself referred to; as when it speaks of 'Jehovah thy God, Who led thee through the great and terrible wilderness, wherein were fiery serpents and scorpions, and drought, where there was no water;' and again, 'Jehovah, Who brought thee up out of the land of Egypt, through a land of deserts and of pits, through a land of drought, and of the shadow of death, through a land that no man passed through, and where no man dwelt.' What was done to 'thee,' Israel, was done to all the whole nation, reaching to every part of their social economy, even to 'their raiment,' and 'shoes,' that 'waxed not old,' and to their feet, which did 'not swell.' There was no need of making special mention of the cattle as partaking of the universal providence, any more than of the women and children. Everything belonging to them was under the same guardianship of a supernatural agency, guiding the national welfare. If want of water for the men made the men's life to depend upon a supernatural supply, the like want of water and grass made the cattle's support equally the effect of supernatural succour. Dr. Colenso might have spared himself the trouble of writing, and his readers of reading, the tedious demonstration of a desert being a desert, a wilderness being a wilderness, and of a land without water being waterless, as he does by quotations at great length from Dr. Stanley and others. That the place of the Israelites' journeyings was barren, the Bible teaches us in fewer words, much more strikingly, when it describes the scene of this miraculous guidance as 'a waste howling wilderness,' 'a great and terrible wilderness,' 'wherein was drought and no water.'

XIV. That Jehovah says, 'He would not drive out the Hivite and the Canaanite, &c., from before them in one day, lest the land become desolate, and the beast of the field increase against thee.'

Here Dr. Colenso pretends to find a great difficulty, which he maintains by a pompous array of figures about the acres and population of the Eastern countries. All this is brought up in aid of an aggression upon the above inoffensive text, the simple meaning of which is that the human occupier of the land is a natural barrier against the spirit of desolation and that wildness which is represented by 'the beast of the field.' And such is the sentiment which is brought by him to persuade us that the Pentateuch cannot be believed. He is, I suppose, the first to feel, if he really did feel, any difficulty in the sentiment, and we may safely trust that there will be few others to share it with him. The whole objection is evidently the result of a pruriency, which had been by this time increasing upon him, for difficulty-mongering.

XV. The objection concerning the disproportion of the first-born with the number of adult males at the same time is answered at full length at the end of this paper.

XVI. The next objection, which, though capable of being put in a telling manner, the Doctor lays out in rather a pointless form, comes to this:—That the number of the children of Israel at the time of the exodus was, according to the narrative, at least two millions—a population almost as large as that of London—which is incredible, inasmuch as two million persons could not have been produced in the four generations from the seventy persons who went into Egypt, as must be supposed if the account be received. This he proves by an argument, which, if gathered to a point from its scattered state, amounts to this:—

1. That the progenitors of these two millions were only seventy persons.

2. That between these and the two millions were only four generations.

Ans. In this, the only allowable assertion is, that the population were two millions.

All else in the two propositions is unproved.

1. That the progenitors were only seventy persons, is an assertion for which there is no evidence, except what in Scripture can never be taken for evidence—the absence of any detailed account of the rest. Such a reason, if taken as proof, would force us to the absurd conclusion, that, because no persons are mentioned as accompanying Simeon and Levi in their assault upon Shechem, they had no armed attendants with them, in putting the inhabitants to the sword. The absence of any explicit mention of persons in Israel, besides the race

of Israel proper, the genuine Jacobian breed, is nothing in face of the otherwise certain inference that a very large body of people must have accompanied the family, from the circumstance of Jacob's patriarchal condition.

He was very rich already, and had been for many years, in flocks and herds, man-servants and maid-servants—not of his own family.

He most likely also inherited all the retinue that had belonged to his father Isaac; and the fact of Abraham's having three hundred and eighteen trained men, born in his house, which, however, nothing but a mere incidental mention happens to disclose to us, is quite warrant enough for us to suppose that his heir Jacob, although not explicitly stated to have been possessed of them, was no less furnished with servants trained and shepherds. The contrary would be most violent, and would but little consist with the idea, that his brother Esau could have a company belonging to him of four hundred men. The only probable supposition is, that Jacob had already grown into a small nation out of persons who had, by the rite of circumcision, been incorporated into the body of his family household.

That there were only seventy persons as the real progenitors of the Israelite people who went up from Egypt, may be dismissed as at once unproved and in itself incredible.

2. Then, that there were only four generations between them and the two millions, is only supported by supposing that the generations of Levi and Judah represent the number of the generations in the pedigree of all the rest. That there were seven between Ephraim and Joshua, is clear from 1 Chron. vii., and the difficulty

attending the text which states it has received a most ample explanation in Dr. M'Caul's little book, in a passage which is perhaps the most valuable in the work.

This idea of four generations as being the utmost throughout the pedigree of the Israelite people, may be dismissed, and thus there remains nothing for the pretended difficulty to rest on.

XVII. That it is impossible that the three priests could have performed all that is described to have been their charge—of offering up all the sacrifices, the burnt-offerings, sin-offerings, peace-offerings, &c., which were to be made by them, and then again of eating in the holy place all the trespass-offerings, sin-offerings, meat-offerings, &c., which were their perquisites.

Ans. The three priests proper were not the only persons engaged in discharging the detail of these services. The whole Levitical body were, in some sort, consecrated to Jehovah to a part in the priestly duties.

XVIII. That they could not have performed all the duties enjoined them of sprinkling the blood of the paschal lambs slain in the court of the Tabernacle.

Ans. Even upon the supposition, that the paschal lamb was ever slain in the wilderness at all, Dr. Colenso would still have upon his hands the impossible task of proving that it was slain in the Tabernacle, or its blood sprinkled by the priests. Kurtz's idea of their being slain in the private dwellings of individuals, would still be the more probable. As to its being implicitly enjoined, as he pretends, in Lev. xx. 2-6; this only refers to the burnt-offerings, trespass-offerings, peace-offerings, &c. Amongst these the paschal lamb was not included, being of a different category altogether; so that sprinkling of the blood by the priest would be gratuitously asserted, even upon the supposition of the passover ever being kept in the wilderness. And this is itself unproved, for we have no cogent reason to think that it was intended, in the Divine institution of it, that it should be observed, as long as the manna lasted.

XIX. That it was impossible within six months, between Aaron's death and the conquest of Bashan, for all the events to have occurred which are there recorded to have happened: the march to Moab; Balak's sending for Balaam; Israel's abiding in Shittim; the death of twenty-four thousand by the plague, &c. &c.

Ans. Dr. M'Caul's observation is quite enough to meet all this—that there is no sufficient note of time to ground any reliable objection upon.

Such, then, is the list of the 'palpable contradictions' and 'plain impossibilities' which Dr. Colenso fancies he has so convincingly proved against the Pentateuch, as to warrant his demanding from any man who can add up a sum, that henceforth he should renounce all belief in its truth. After an honest canvassing of the whole array, I will not scruple to assert that he has not substantiated one single point. We may write 'unproved' against every one of them at the very worst, nor do I recollect any that is not open to a clearly dissolving answer. After this summary, brief as it is, I do not think that one is bound to suppress a manifestation of the feeling, which a review of them so naturally excites in the mind, of utmost contempt for the book that puts them forth; as one which a scanty insight into Scripture history will enable one to detect as a congeries of mistakes, cavils, and word-catchings, which the affectation of arithmetical and statistical precision, so largely paraded, does not conceal the emptiness.

We now come to the two chief points, which have been taken for more special consideration in this paper: these are:—First, That one concerning the *impossibility of Judah's becoming a great-grandfather within the twenty-two years* from his marriage, which is supposed by the Bishop to be specified for it: and, secondly, that other one about the *disproportion of the number of the first-born in Israel with the total number of the males at the same time.* A few words concerning each; and, as this second objection is the more interesting of the two, and the one which seems to have most puzzled the defenders, I take that first.

I. It consists in this:—that we find from the 600,000 males, upwards of twenty years old, which was their number, according to the census taken shortly after the exodus from Egypt, that, at a fair estimation, the whole number of males, including those *under* twenty years of age, must have been, at least, nine or ten hundred thousand; yet, at the same time, 22,273 was all that there were of first-born sons amongst them: which, being about 22,000 or 23,000, to 1,000,000, will, roundly we speaking, give one first-born amongst 40 males, or one first-born brother to 39 younger brothers, so that every mother must, on an average, have borne 40 boys; and if we suppose the number of female children to have been equal to that of the males, she will, on an average, have had also 40 girls—in all 80 children; a number which we must agree with Dr. Colenso in thinking much too many for one woman, and still more for each. However, such is the conclusion which the Biblical history justifies, according to Dr. Colenso's interpretation of it.

This, at first sight, is a very formidable-looking difficulty: and various ineffectual attempts have been made to answer it, both before and after the publication of his book. It has been replied:—

1. That there are modifying circumstances not related, which, if they were, would very likely make it look quite consistent. This consideration is one which it is, indeed, wise to bear in mind in almost all cases, for one's individual guidance; but, as the respondent does not state what those modifying circumstances were in this case, it will hardly avail against a public adversary.

2. A second reply places this difficulty, along with many others, under the wide solution of arithmetical errors, possibly crept into the Biblical text. Unfortunately, however, for the answer, the numbers are so checked and corrected, as to render the supposition of clerical error impossible.

3. A third sort assigns, as an accounting reason, Oriental exaggeration in the number of the people, or carelessness. But the numbers are so much the result of a census, and so professedly accurate, that such an apology would make still stronger, and of worse colour, too, the charge of want of historical veracity brought by the adversary.

4. A fourth ascribes, with Dr. M'Caul, the undue proportion of the rest of the children to the first-born,

to the effect of polygamy, saying that those intended to be numbered were those only of the first wife, the first-born of the other wives being excluded. This conjecture is fetched from outside the case, and unwarranted by anything in the history.

5. A fifth is that the number of the first-born had been cruelly thinned by Pharaoh having them cast into the river.

6. And, again, one quoted by Rosenmüller is, that a male first-born was a very rare thing; so that it is no wonder there were so few of them, and, besides, the number of still-born males is much greater than that of females.

7. The editor of the 'Jewish Chronicle' supposes that the first-born numbered, were those only who would be qualified for service in the Tabernacle: an idea which has not even a colour of ground to favour it.

8. Another is, that many first-born would have been sisters, not brothers, thus reducing the number one half. This, however, does but *change* the form of the objection, not answer it, since, if we take the sisters into account, we must also take into account the whole female population, with whom their number is compared. To this, it is added, that of the remainder, many would have died from slavery, and also from the unbelief and neglect of their own parents, in not sprinkling the door-posts with the blood of the paschal lamb.

9. Bunsen, as cited by Dr. Colenso, admits the difficulty existing in the Scripture statement, of which, he says, 'no satisfactory explanation has ever been given.

His own is as follows:—' i.e. that the first-born were numbered 'from a month old and upward' up to *six* or seven years only, which he supposes to be the age at which such children were sacrificed to Moloch, among the Syrian tribes.

All these replies have to be thanked for good intentions; but they will, in the opinion of most, I think, leave as yet master of the field Colenso's objection based on stern arithmetic, which, for anything these replies afford, remains still to be answered.

The answer offered in this paper is one which is referred to by Dr. Colenso as being that of the Rev. T. Scott, who assigns the same idea briefly, but does not give any detailed proof of it. The proof of its truth is, so far as I know, hardly hinted at.

Whether it has been given amongst those more than thirty answers which have already appeared, at all events, it has not won its way into anything like the notoriety of a familiar solution.

This answer is drawn, not like the rest, from sources simply conjectural, but from the consideration of the drift of the history itself.

And from this we find a most satisfactory explanation of the fewness of these first-born, in the fact that, though consisting, as it is said, of *all* the first-born in Israel from a month old and 'upward'—that '*upward*' extends only so far as a few years of infancy could reach. And if no further evidence in the passage were forthcoming for it, it would indeed be quite clear enough even from the very intention of the numbering itself: which consisted in Almighty God's purpose of hallowing to Himself such of the first-born as had been born since the slaughter of the Egyptian first-born—in fact, from the time of the first Passover. This is clear from the express declaration made, when commanding the substitution of the Levite tribe instead of these same first-born :'—

'Behold,' says the Lord, 'all the first-born are Mine; from the day that I smote all the first-born in the land of Egypt I hallowed to Myself all the first-born of Israel, both man and beast: Mine they shall be.' (Numbers iii. 13.)

And what is here commemorated, had been before expressly commanded to Moses in the coming out of Egypt :—

'Sanctify to Me all the first-born, whatsoever openeth the womb among the children of men, both of man and of beast: it is Mine.' (Exodus xiii. 3.)

And to this afterwards He alludes, when taking the Levite tribe for them :—

'On the day that I smote the first-born in the land of Egypt, I sanctified them to Myself.' (Numbers viii. 17.)

The persons of the first-born to be numbered were, therefore, only such as, like the firstlings of the cattle, became dedicated to the Lord, as being born after the slaughter of the Egyptian first-born, at the time of the Passover.

And, as this had happened only a short time previous, it is plain that only infants of a short age could be included in the numbering,

When, then, the Lord says to Moses, 'Number all

the first-born of the males of the children of Israel from a month old and upward' (Numbers iii. 40), the '*upward*' would reach only within the age from the coming out of Egypt: and it is nothing but a gratuitous violation of the explicitly declared intention of the census to pretend, as Bishop Colenso does, by insisting on the words '*all Israel*' and '*upward*,' that it refers to the whole male population in Israel, whether young or old.

This of itself, then, might be enough to save the Scripture from the audacious attempt of fastening upon it such an incredible absurdity as giving forty boys to each mother, and as many girls besides.

But, fortunately, we are not reduced to depend, even for our main support, upon the evident scope of the census. For, consistently with this, we find also a little *fact* recorded, that marks, without danger of mistake, the infant age of the persons numbered: and this is, the *infant rate of the redemption money* fixed for those of them who had to be redeemed, instead of being substituted by the Levites.

The naming of this rate occurs in the account of the substitution of the Levites for the first-born of Israel, made, as we learn, from the following command:—

'And the Lord spake to Moses, saying, And I, behold, I have taken the Levites from among the children of Israel: therefore the Levites shall be Mine.' (Numbers iii. 11.)

And again:—

'And thou shalt take the Levites for Me (I am the Lord) instead of all the first-born among the children of Israel.' (Numbers iii. 40.)

So the Levites were numbered: and the first-born numbered also, and the numbers of each were compared. But it was found, that, while the first-born amounted to 22,273, the Levites only amounted to 22,000; so that there were 273 first-born who were without a Levite substitute.

Accordingly, these were decreed to be redeemed by redemption money instead; now the rate of the redemption money fixed for these 273, was *five shekels* per head, without any distinction.

'And for those that are to be redeemed of the 273 of the first-born of the children of Israel, who were more than the Levites, thou shalt take five shekels a piece by the poll, after the shekel of the sanctuary shalt thou take them: and thou shalt give the money, wherewith the odd number of them is to be redeemed, to Aaron and to his sons.' (Numbers iii. 46.)

Now this five-shekel rate taken for these first-born was precisely the rate fixed for the redemption of children under five years of age, as we find from the rules of redemption, stated in Lev. xxvii. 6; where there is given a graduated scale of rates for redemption from vow of those who had been dedicated to the Lord.

	Years.		Years.		shekels.
From	20	to	60	male	50
				female	30
”	5	”	20	male	20
				female	10
	Month.		Years.		
”	1	”	5	male	5
				female	3

And this same five-shekel rate, fixed at this time

for the 273, was afterwards made ordinary law for all first-born children, according to the statute made for that purpose, in which it is particularly to be remarked that though the objects of the law are professedly *children*, the text does not state, in *terms*, any limit to the age *upward*, but only *from what* age—namely, a month old—the estimation was to be made.

'Everything,' says the Lord to Aaron, 'devoted to the Lord shall be thine '—i. e. Aaron's. 'Everything that openeth the matrix in all flesh, which they bring to the Lord, of man or beasts, shall be thine: nevertheless the first-born of men thou shalt surely redeem, and the firstling of unclean beasts shalt thou redeem: and those that are to be redeemed from a month old shalt thou redeem, according to thy estimation, for the money of five shekels, after the shekel of the sanctuary, which is twenty gerahs.' (Numbers xviii. 16.) This is the same five shekels which is usually supposed to have been given for our Lord at the time of His presentation in the Temple.

In these five shekels, then, we have a mark of the age which belonged to the 273 first-born, and, consequently, of the whole number, 22,273; whose age must have been under five years, suitably to the time which had elapsed since the decree of the first-born's sanctification had been determined. Their fewness is thus accounted for from the text.

If the description of the first-born, as being children born since the Passover, is met with the new difficulty (as Dr. Colenso in answer to Scott objects), that in that case the number 22,273 would be too many to suppose to have been born ; we answer, that this objection only rests upon the assumption, that between that Passover and the numbering there had been only the space of *one year* ; which, however, is evidently unproved from Scripture. The time of the numbering of the first-born is unfixed. It is narrated in a chapter unconnected with those events, which are dated as taking place 'on the first day of the second month in the second year.' (Numbers i. 1.) The only date, if such it can be called, is what may be gathered from the following heading in chap. iii. 1 : 'These also are the generations of Aaron and Moses in the day,' i. e. the season, 'that Jehovah spoke with Moses in Mount Sinai.'

How long this 'day,' which in Hebrew means often, as it does here, not a solar day, but a 'period,' we do not know precisely.

There is, therefore, no limitation of the time of the numbering, except as being within the period that they were still abiding at Sinai, before their first removal. This would allow, therefore, time for the number of first-born since the Passover, to have reached the number stated in the text.

And in this is solved the difficulty brought by the Bishop, about the disproportion of their number with that of all the adults of Israel.

II. The second objection, concerning the impossibility of Judah's becoming a great-grandfather in twenty-two years, important as it is, is one grounded on dry calculations about ages and dates, and its treatment will bring interest only to those who are willing to give an attention to minute details.

It is supported by the objector on the following grounds:—Judah being but three years older than Joseph, married, as appears from the story, after Joseph had reached his seventeenth year; which makes Judah, at the time of his first marriage with Bathshua, at least twenty years old; but yet twenty-two years afterwards, when Joseph was only thirty-nine, we find, in the migration into Egypt, that Judah, then only forty-two years old, had become a great-grandfather, inasmuch as we find the names of his great-grandsons, Hezron and Hamul, amongst those who formed the company of that migration. The way in which the objection is presented by Dr. Colenso is as follows:—

'Now Judah was forty-two years old, according to the story, when he went down with Jacob into Egypt.

'(Note.) Joseph was thirty years old when he stood before Pharaoh, as governor of the land of Egypt, and from that time nine years elapsed—seven of plenty, and two of famine—before Jacob came down to Egypt. At that time, therefore, Joseph was thirty-nine years old. But Judah was about three years older than Joseph; for Judah was born in the fourth year of Jacob's double marriage, and Joseph in the seventh. Hence Judah was forty-two years old when Jacob went down to Egypt. But if we turn to Gen. xxxviii. we shall find that in the course of these forty-two years of Judah's life, the following events are recorded to have happened.

'Judah grows up, marries a wife at that time, viz.,

that is, after Joseph's being sold into Egypt; when he was seventeen years old, and when Judah consequently was at least twenty years old, and has separately three sons by her.

'The eldest of these three sons grows up, is married, and dies.

'The second grows to maturity (suppose in another year), marries his brother's widow, and dies.

'The third grows to maturity (suppose in another year still), but declines to take his brother's widow to wife.

'She then deceives Judah himself, conceives by him, and in due time bears him twins, Pharez and Zarah.

'One of these twins also grows to maturity, and has two sons, Hezron and Hamul, born to him before Jacob goes down into Egypt.

'The above being certainly incredible, we are obliged to conclude that one of the two accounts must be untrue.'

The validity of the objection rests upon *three* different assumptions made concerning the Scriptural statement:—

I. That Judah was only *three years* older than Joseph.

II. That his marriage with Bathshua took place when Joseph was seventeen years old.

III. That his great-grandsons, Hezron and Hamul, are supposed, in Scripture, to have gone down into Egypt at the same time with Jacob.

Of these three assumptions, I shall endeavour to prove:—

1. The first to be demonstrably false.

2. The second unproved and unprovable.

3. The third also unproved, and a misuse of the passage employed for it.

1. That Judah was only three years older than Joseph, though not true, is assumed naturally enough, perhaps, from the apparent fact of Joseph's having been born in the *seventh*, and Judah in the *fourth*, year of that second seven years of Jacob's servitude with Laban, which comprised, as it would seem, the birth-time of all the twelve children (eleven sons and one daughter). For Leah was taken to wife, it would seem, at the end of Jacob's first seven years' servitude; and Rachel given in advance just after: so that they were wives simultaneously, from about the beginning of the eighth year. Now, all the bearing of these twelve children was completed in the fourteenth—the end of the second seven years: so that Judah, Leah's fourth son, could not well be born before the *fourth* year of that seven; and, as Joseph was born in the last, there will, at the utmost, be but three years' difference in the ages. A consideration which looks quite natural; and, I must confess, that formerly, along with many others, misled by the view of these marriages, I felt forced, not without reluctance, to conclude that, improbable as it looked, the births of all these twelve children did take place within the second seven years of Jacob's servitude. But that this is a false conclusion, it is astonishing now to me that one does not immediately see, from a most incontrovertible fact, exhibited in the births of all these twelve children, which are clearly

narrated to have taken place in an order one after the other, the same as if they had been born of one wife. This we have in chaps. xxix. and xxx.; where they are given, seriatim, with sufficient circumstances to indicate the lapse of, at the very *least, twelve years.* In the first place, there is the birth of Leah's four sons, Reuben, Simeon, Levi, and Judah—at least requiring four years; then Leah's non-bearing time, in which Bilhah bears two sons—two years; after Bilhah, Zilpah bears two sons (when Reuben, by-the-by, was old enough to know the look and value of mandrakes)—two years more, in all four years; making the time already elapsed *eight years* at least. Then Leah begins to bear again, in which time three children are born, Issachar, Zebulon, and Dinah—requiring, at least, three years more, making eleven years; after which, Rachel bears Joseph, in, at the very least, the twelfth year. This quite upsets the theory of the *one* seven years alone being the time for the bearing of these twelve children; so that we must conclude the time to have occupied the two seven years, or fourteen years. By this, the true reckoning, we are at liberty to put, at least, ten years seniority to Judah, the fourth son. I do not wish to press upon a further point—viz., that it cannot, I think, be actually disproved, though I do not intend to maintain it, that Joseph's birth was not, as some have thought, even at the end of the twenty years that Jacob stayed in Padanaram. I will be content with the certain ten years.

But now to the obvious objection against all this: how are we to make consistent with it the foregoing history of Jacob's marriage with his wives? For it would appear from that, that Leah was not given to wife until after the first seven years, from the following way of narrating the facts: 'And Jacob served seven years for Rachel, and they seemed to him but a few days, for the love he had to her. And Jacob said, "Give me my wife, for my days are fulfilled, that I may have her as my own."' Then followed the marriage feast, and, on the discovery of Laban's fraud, of putting Leah in the stead of Rachel, amongst other things, Jacob says, 'Did I not serve thee for Rachel: wherefore hast thou beguiled me?' From this, it would look as if Jacob *had* served his seven years before Leah's being given to him; that his days of servitude *had been* fulfilled; and that he appealed, in his expostulation, to these same years, *already completed*: so that the first seven years must have already past. A strong looking case, I must own, at first for the Bishop. However, before attempting to explain these words, so as to make them consist with the fact, it may be as well to call to mind a very important circumstance, that, unluckily for the objection, the very same sort of thing may be urged for the second seven years also, which won Rachel. In *this* it would appear, with equal show of probability, that Rachel, also, was given not in advance, but after the servitude completed. For Laban says, in reply to Jacob, 'Fulfil her' (Rachel's) 'week, and we will give thee this one' (Rachel) 'also, for the service thou shalt serve with me seven other years. And *Jacob did so*, and fulfilled her week, and he gave him Rachel, his daughter, to wife also.'

Would it not seem, from this, that the bargain for Rachel was, that she should be given *after* the second week of seven years; and that, accordingly, Jacob's service, stated in 'he did so,' procured the delivery of Rachel to him, stated in these words, 'and he gave him Rachel?' Simply, then, looking at the sequence in narration, which the objection is grounded upon, there is equal ground for supposing Rachel's marriage to have followed the *second seven* years, as for that of Leah having followed the *first* seven: so that, if this were allowed, we must, at the same time, admit, what has the same foundation, that Rachel's delivery to Jacob was after the second seven years' service. And yet it was not so. For we can pretty clearly prove, that Rachel was a wife, and had been for some time a wife, on Leah's fourth son, Judah's being born in Leah's fourth year of wifehood, as is deducible from Rachel's showing, after Judah's birth, a wife's envy at Leah's fruitfulness.

'And when Rachel,' after Judah's birth, 'saw that she bare no children to Jacob' (of course as a wife), 'Rachel envied her sister.' Nay, more, she was a wife before Leah's *first* son, *Reuben*, from Rachel's barrenness being even *then* an observable fact. For before Leah began to bear, we find:—

'When the Lord saw that Leah was hated, He opened her womb' (the fruit of which was Reuben); 'but Rachel was barren.' So that both were wives at the same time; and, as this time was the beginning of the fourteen years, they must both have been given in advance, at the commencement of the servitude. On this account, we cannot conclude, that because Jacob's loving service, which seemed but 'a few days,' preceded, *in narrative*, Leah's delivery to Jacob, that, therefore, Leah was not given previously to the first seven years. But then, if that be the case, what are you to make of the seven years seeming but 'a few days,' for the love he had for Rachel, unless this contented service of seven years preceded, in point of time, the disappointing substitution of Leah for Rachel? This seems natural enough. But equally natural is another understanding of the words, according to what they will mean, that in the *prospect*, the *idea* of seven years seemed to be only that of a 'few days:' and still more naturally will this present itself from a more literal translation of the language itself, by which it will run thus: 'And they were *in his eyes*,' or, as we should say, *in his view*, 'as single days in his love of her.'

But, then, you will say, Jacob himself refers back to a *completed* servitude, before receiving Leah to wife: 'My days are fulfilled,' says he. These 'days' do not, I answer, necessarily refer to the days of servitude. It is a phrase like 'It is high time,' 'The time is come,' that I should have her, referring, most likely, to the usual days of betrothal, or courtship. You might again reply, that the narrative says he *had* served, 'and he served for Rachel seven years, and they were but a few days;' and, besides that, Jacob himself refers again to *past* time in his words: '*Did* I not serve thee for Rachel?' I answer: in the English it would be so; but, as the word rendered 'to serve' is equally good for 'entering service,' 'becoming a servant,' no very cogent argument can be derived from the words translated 'He served,' 'Did I not serve?' It may be as much as to say, 'Have I not become thy servant?' 'Am I not serving thee for Rachel?'

In this view, the whole passage will pretty much run thus:—

'And Jacob loved Rachel, and said, "I will be servant seven years for Rachel thy younger daughter." And Laban said, "It is better for me to give her to thee, than to another man; stay with me." And Jacob entered service for Rachel for seven years, and they were, in *his eyes*, as single days, in his love of her. And Jacob said to Laban, "Give me my wife, for full is my time, that I should possess her." And afterwards, "What is this thou hast done? Have I not become servant for Rachel?"'

In this reading, there is nothing wanting in sense, and no violence to the language. The words of the narrative of Leah's marriage, then, when taken in conjunction with the counterpart on Rachel's side, need not make us scruple in accepting what the order of the twelve children's birth demonstrates so necessary—that fourteen years, not seven, was the period for their coming into the world. Consequently, Judah was not necessarily only three years older than Joseph, as Bishop Colenso assumes, but at least ten or eleven. And, in that case, at Jacob's migration into Egypt, he will have been not forty-two, but fifty or fifty-one. This addition of seven years to his life will be so much relief to the difficulty, if it will enable us to fix his marriage earlier.

2. 'But it *won't* enable us,' the adversary will, of course, reply. 'For, even supposing him to be ten years or even fifty years older than Joseph, there is a fatal impossibility against his becoming a great-grandfather in the time allowed from his marriage. For this was, in any case, not before Joseph's seventeenth year, and he was already great-grandfather before Jacob's migration into Egypt, in Joseph's thirty-ninth. Now take seventeen from thirty-nine, and twenty-two remain; and this twenty-two is all the space you have for getting Judah into a great-grandfather.'

That twenty-two is all that is left from thirty-nine, minus seventeen, I admit; I admit that Jacob's journey into Egypt was in Joseph's thirty-ninth year; and also, that seventeen years was his age in the chapter previous to the one which narrates Judah's marriage with Bathshua. But that his marriage is, therefore, dated by the seventeenth year of Joseph, as undoubtingly inferred by Bishop Colenso, I boldly deny, for a reason which, when stated, any reader, however little critical of Scripture, will, I think, admit to be valid—viz. that the chapter containing Judah's marriage *is entirely independent* of the narrative about Joseph, in the body of which it is found. And for satisfaction on this point, let any one peruse the 37th, 38th, and 39th chapters, and he will immediately perceive that the account of Judah's marriage interrupts the passage about Joseph's departure into Egypt in a manner such that no writer could, for a moment, intend for consecutive narration, even allowing everything for transitions in history. The thirty-ninth ends with an incident of Joseph's career, saying, that 'the Midianites sold Joseph into Egypt, unto Potiphar, an officer of Pharaoh.' Then, all at once, in the thirty-eighth, we are landed upon the words, 'And it came to pass at that time that Judah went down from his brethren,' then proceeding with his marriage with Bathshua, when we are plunged into a series of details about his and his sons' marriages which must have reached forward to thirty or forty years; and this goes on down to the words about his sons Pharez and Zarah: 'And afterwards came out his brother, with the scarlet thread upon his hand, and his name was called Zarah.'

These words bring us all at once right against the beginning of the next chapter, commencing with the resumed incident of Joseph's journey, thirty or forty years before, into Egypt under the hand of the Ishmaelites: 'And Joseph was brought down into Egypt, and Potiphar, an officer of Pharaoh, &c., bought him, &c. Thus the properly indivisible fact of Joseph's capture, a matter of *days*, being split into two parts, is separated by a massive history, all abruptly wedged in, striding over whole generations. Can any one imagine for a moment that any consecution or relation is intended? This thirty-eighth chapter stands out as a distinct document by itself, as plainly as an article or a letter in the *Times* does from the adjoining articles. A patch of red cloth pinned on to a gown of black silk would not show greater difference of colour, texture, and design, than does this said chapter about Judah, in matter, style, and object, from the consecutive tale of Joseph, in the midst of which it suddenly appears, like a block of stone on a smooth path. If it should be asked, Why, then, is it in this place? I would answer, Because there was no better place for it amongst the 'generations of Jacob.' Yet amongst those 'generations' it ought to come; because the family of Judah, who was his son, was a part of those 'generations;' and if we look on throughout those chapters on to the fiftieth, we should in vain seek for a better place to insert it in than this little time of repose between Joseph's exit from the scene in his native land to reappear afterwards as a slave in Egypt. This is the same sort of reason which evidently has determined the place for other documents, as for instance 'the generations of Adam' in chap. v., that of Esau's generations in chap. xxxvi., the list of names of Israel's sons in chap. xxxv., and that other one to which we shall have to refer immediately, of the people who went into Egypt in chap. xlvi., with many other places that could be cited, especially in Kings and Chronicles, which, though not consecutive, have found their places where they are because such were the most opportune for their insertion. It is true, indeed, that Judah's marriage is commenced with the words 'at that time.' But 'at that time,' 'in those days,' like 'in illo tempore,' inserted by the Church before the Gospels, are often so vague that they cannot be taken as any sufficient date for chronological inference. The writers were not always anxious to insure such precision to the time of the events they are content to record. The chapter, then, dedicated to Judah's descendants, though beginning with 'at that time,' may be taken as a piece of history totally independent of the history of Joseph's life and fortunes, and, consequently, undecided for its exact time by the fact of Joseph's captivity. His seventeenth year therefore cannot be taken for the date of Judah's marriage with Bathshua; and we are at liberty to suppose the time of this marriage at any period which will consist with other parts of the narrative. And this extra seven years of life will give seven years' worth of assistance in the difficulty.

3. But now to the last charge. It may be rejoined, make the marriage *at what time you will*, and make Judah if you will ten years older than Joseph—you are still confronted with the incredible result, that the birth of his great-grandsons took place before the journey into Egypt at *Joseph's thirty-ninth year*, which will not allow a reasonable time for growing into a great-grandfather, as he will then be at the most only forty-nine or fifty years.

To this I reply: Not necessarily, unless you choose with Bishop Colenso to suppose the Scripture to have decided that the births of these children were *before* that journey. Now, I contend that it cannot be supposed from the passage on which he relies for proof, for a like reason to that I have employed in the document about Judah's marriage. This passage in chap. xlvi., which is a list of names, is evidently not intended to give an account of the people actually travelling down with Jacob, the 'women' and the 'children' in 'the waggons.' In that case it would not be an object of such great Scriptural interest as it really is. That the bulk of Jacob's family accompanied him, is likely enough But we need not surely suppose that they had in their company all the persons so precisely enumerated in this catalogue. The object of this list seems naturally enough to state what persons and how many constituted the body of the true Israelite nation, who made this signal migration from their native land into Egypt. This migration, for anything the style of the document forces us to imagine, may have been completed with some disconnection in mode and time. It is quite true, indeed, that the list occurs close to the very passage that relates the journey. But it by no means follows that it therefore forms part of the original context. Its presence in this place is only because the occasion of the journey was a very proper one for inserting such particulars. Where else could it have been put so well? But that it really forms no portion of the story in which it appears is sufficiently discernible. It bears upon its face the stamp of being a document distinct from the narrative. The narrative itself is in its style progressive, picturesque, and flowing, after the manner of an easy tale. The catalogue is dry, formal, square, looking like an extract from a record, as likely enough it is, and of a grain altogether at variance with the narrative. And if you take it all out (from verse 8 to verse 27), the remaining context reads more like a continuation, more uniform and more easy than when accompanied by the register, which is much more like a *note* than any portion of the context. This register, then, may be and ought to be taken as a separate document with a different object from that of the narrative of the mere journey; but placed here, as in its most convenient place, to commemorate the names, members, and maternal parentage of the Israelite people proper, who formed the substance of the grand migration from Canaan to Egypt. Anything further, or anything less, than this is violent, and, to use the expression of one of the late writers, a 'perverse literalness.' It is a senseless adherence to words, without attention to the drift of the writer. To press it, then, into such a service, as to make it give a precise enumeration of the number of persons actually travelling in company with Jacob, is employing it for the purpose of cavil, not of truth. We cannot, therefore, allow the document to be made a means of proof of the actual presence of Hezron and Hamul in that company. Its veracity will be fully justified if we attribute to it the object of registering the important part of the body of the Israelites whose migration eventually took place. This argument may be also supplemented perhaps by the exceptional manner, so often alluded to, in which the names of Judah's descendants, Hezron and Hamul, are introduced into the catalogue. These reasons, then, leave us at full liberty to fix the children's descent into Egypt, as also their birth, at any time that will make them partakers of the general migration; and this is, I think, sufficient to meet Bishop Colenso's third assumption, concerning the birth of the children before Joseph's thirty-ninth year.

On the whole, then, the Bishop's three assumptions about Judah's not having time to become a great-grandfather may be confronted with *three facts:*

1. That Judah was not three, but nine or ten years older than Joseph.

2. That the time of his marriage with Bathshua is not fixed in Scripture at Joseph's seventeenth year.

3. That the birth of his grandsons Hezron and Hamul is not intended to be decided before Joseph's thirty-ninth year, the time of Jacob's travelling into Egypt.

And these facts show, with regard to Bishop Colenso's assumption, that:

1. The first is evidently false.

2. The second unproved and unproveable.

3. The third is a misuse of a family document as being a precise picture descriptive of a travelling cortége.

THE TRUTH OF SUPPOSED LEGENDS AND FABLES.

BY H.E. CARDINAL WISEMAN.

[*Taken by Short-hand.*]

THE subject of the address which I am about to deliver is as follows: Events and things which have been considered legendary, or even fabulous, have been proved by further research to be historical and true.

Before coming directly to the subject which I wish to occupy your attention, I will give a little account of a very extraordinary discovery which may throw some light upon the general character and tendency of our investigation. In the year 1775 Pius VI. laid the foundation of the sacristy of S. Peter's. Of course, as is the case whenever the ground is turned up in Rome, a number of inscriptions came to light; these were carefully put aside, and formed the lining, if I may so say, of the corridor which unites the sacristy with the church. It was observed, however, that a great many of these inscriptions referred to the same subject, and a subject which was totally unknown to antiquarians: they all spoke of certain Arval Brethren—*Fratres Arvales.* Some were mere fragments, others were entire inscriptions.

These, to the number of sixty-seven, were carefully

put together and illustrated by the then librarian of the Vatican, Mgr. Marini. It was an age when in Rome antiquarian learning abounded. There were many, perhaps, who could have undertaken the task, but it naturally belonged to him as being attached to the church near which the inscriptions were found. He put the fragments together, collated them one with another, and with the entire inscriptions. He procured copies at least, when he could not examine the originals, of such other slight fragments as seemed to have reference to the subject, the key having now been found, and the result was two quarto volumes,* giving us the entire history, constitution, and ritual of this singular fraternity. Before this period two brief notices in Varro, one passage in Pliny, and allusions in two later writers, Minutius Felix and Fulgentius, were all that was known concerning it. One merely told the origin of it from the time of the kings, and the others only stated that it had something to do with questions about land; and there the matter ended. Now, out of this ignorance, out of this darkness, there springs, through the researches of Mgr. Marini, perhaps the most complete account or history that we have of any institution of antiquity. So complete was the work, in fact, that only two inscriptions relating to this subject have been found since; one by Melchiorri, who undertook to write an appendix to the work; and the other in 1855 in excavating the Dominican garden at Santa Sabina, which indeed threw great light upon the subject. From

* *Atti e Monumenti dei Fratelli Arvali.* Da Mgr. Marini. 2 tom. Roma, 1795.

these inscriptions we learn that this was one of the most powerful bodies of augurs or priests in Rome. Yet neither Pliny, nor Livy, nor Cicero, when expressly enumerating all the classes of augurs, ever alludes to them. Now, we know how they were elected. On one tablet is an order of Claudius to elect a new member, so to fill up their number of twelve, in consequence of the death of one. They wrote every year and published, at least put up in their gardens, a full and minute account of all the sacrifices and the feasts celebrated by them. They were allied to the imperial family, and all the great families in Rome took part in their assemblies. They had a sacred grove, the site of which was perfectly unknown until the last inscription, found in 1855, revealed it. It was out of Porta Portese, on the road to the English vineyard at La Magliana. There they had sacrifices to the *Dea Dia*, whose name occurs nowhere else among all the writers on ancient mythology. It is supposed to be Ceres. They had magnificent sacrifices at the beginning of the year. There are tablets which say where the meetings will be held, whether at the house of the rector or pro-rector, leaving the date in blank, to be filled in the course of the year. We are told who were at the meetings, especially who among the youths from the first families—four of whom acted somewhat as acolytes; and we are told how they were dressed, which of their two dresses they wore. Then there is a most minute ritual given. We are told how each victim was slain; how the brethren took off the toga prætexta, their crowns and golden ears of corn, then put them on again, and examined the entrails of the sacrifices; all as minutely detailed as the rubrics of any office of unction and coronation could possibly be. Then we are told how many baskets of fruit they carried away, and what distribution there was of sweetmeats at the end, everyone taking a certain quantity. All this is recorded, and with it their song in barbarous Oscan or early Etruscan, perfectly unintelligible, in which their acclamations were made. So that now we know perfectly everything about them. I may mention as an interesting fact, that Marini's own copy of his work on the Arval Brethren, two quarto volumes, having their margins covered with notes for a second edition, which was never published, and filled with slips of paper with annotations and new inscriptions of other sorts, which he subsequently found, is now in the library at Oscott.

What do I wish to draw from this account? It is that history may have remained silent upon points which it seems impossible, in the multiplicity of writers that have been preserved to us, should not have cropped out, not have been mentioned in some way, not even have been made known to us through innumerable anterior discoveries. One fortunate circumstance brought to light the whole history of this body. How unfair, then, is it, on the reticence of history, at once to condemn anything, or to say, 'We should have heard of it; writers who ought to have told us would not have concealed it from us.' For a circumstance may arise which will bring out the whole history of a thing, and make that plain and clear before us, which has been scouted completely by others, or of which we have been kept in the completest ignorance.

I could illustrate this by several other examples which I have collected together, but I foresee that I shall not get anything like through the subject I propose to myself. But here is one such instance bearing on Scripture truth. It was said by infidel writers of the last century, 'How is it that there could have been such a remarkable occurrence as the massacre of the Innocents without a single profane historian ever mentioning it—Josephus, if no one else?' Of course the answer was, 'We do not know why, except that we might give plausible reasons why it should not have been noticed.' That is all we need say. It is our duty to accept the fact. We must not reject things because we cannot find corroboration of them all at once. We may have to wait with patience; the world has had to wait centuries even before some doubted truth has come out clearly.

I. The subject which I wish to bring before you is one of those which, perhaps beyond any other, may be said to be considered thoroughly legendary, and even perhaps worse:—it is the history of S. Ursula and her eleven thousand companions, virgins and martyrs. At first sight it may appear bold to undertake a vindication of that narrative, or to bring it within the compass of history by detaching from it what has been embellishment, what has been perhaps even wilful invention, and bringing out in its perfect completeness a history corroborated on all sides by every variety of research. Such, however, is the object at which

I aim to-day; other instances may occupy us afterwards.

It has, in fact, been treated as fabulous by Protestants, beginning with the Centuriators of Magdeburg down to the present time. There is hardly any story more sneered at than this, that an English lady with eleven thousand companions, all virgins, should have met with martyrdom at Cologne, and should have even gone to Rome on their journey by some route which is very difficult to comprehend; for they are always represented in ships. Hence the whole thing has been treated as a fable. But the more refined Germanism of later times takes what is perhaps meant to be a mitigated view, and treats it as a myth, that is, a sort of mythological tale. Thus the writer of a late work,* entitled the History, or fable, of S. Ursula and the Eleven Thousand Virgins, printed in Hanover, in 1854, consider that S. Ursula is the ancient German goddess Rehalennia, and explains the history by the mythology of that ancient divinity.

But let us come to Catholics. A great number have been staggered completely by this history, and have said, 'It is incredible; it is impossible to believe it; we must reject it: what foundation is there for it?' Some have tried to search one out; and perhaps one of the most ingenious explanations, though the most devoid of any foundation, is that which Sirmondus and Valesius † and several other Catholics have brought forward

* *Die Sage von der heilige Ursula und den* 11,000 *Jungfrauen.* Von Oskar Schade. Hanover, 1854.

† *Acta Sanct.* Bolland, Oct. tom. ix. p. 144.

—that there were only two saints, S. Ursula and S. Undecimilla, and that this last has been turned into the eleven thousand. This name Undecimilla has nowhere been found; there have been some like it, but that name is not known. The explanation is the purest conjecture, and has now been completely rejected. But still many find it very difficult to accept the history. If they were interrogated, and required to answer distinctly the question, 'What do you think about S. Ursula?' there are very few who would venture to face the question and say, 'I believe there is a foundation for it in truth.'—For that is all one might be expected to say about a matter which has come down to us through ages, probably with additions.—'I believe the substance of it; it has been so altered by time as to reach us clogged with difficulties; still I believe there were martyrs in great number who had come from England that were martyred at Cologne.' But there are few who like to talk about it: most say it is a legendary story. Even Butler only gives about two pages of history. He rejects the explanation which I have just mentioned; but he throws the whole narrative into the shade, and passes it over with one of those little sermons which he gives us, to make up for not knowing much about a saint; so that his readers are left quite in the dark.

Then unfortunately while many Catholics have been inclined to look at it as more legendary than historical, they have been badly served by those who have undertaken the defence or explanation of the event.

There may be many here who have gone into what is called the golden chamber in the Church of St. Ursula at Cologne, and have seen that multitude of skulls and bones that line the walls, and have been inclined to give an incredulous shrug and to say, 'How could these martyrs have been got together? where did they come from? how do we know they were martyrs?'

We generally content ourselves with looking at such things through the eyes of Mr. Murray's traveller who tells us about them. Accordingly we look round at these startling objects, and say, 'It is very singular; it is very extraordinary.' But there is very little awe, very little devotion felt by us; while, to a good native of Cologne, it is the most venerable, sacred, and holy place almost in Christendom. He prays earnestly to the virgins of Cologne, and considers that they are his powerful patrons and intercessors.

However, little has been done to help us. Works have been published in favour of the truth of this history, but then they have run into excess. The most celebrated of all is one by a Jesuit named Crombach, who was led to compose it by Bebius, another learned Jesuit, whose papers were unfortunately burned in a conflagration at the college in Cologne. Crombach in 1647 published two large volumes entitled 'S. Ursula vindicata.' In them he has included an immense variety of things. He has accepted with scarce any discrimination works that are entitled to little or no credit—contradictory works; he has mingled them all up; and he insists upon the story or the history being true with all details. The consequence is that the work has been very much thrown aside, or severely attacked.

Yet it is acknowledged that it contains a great deal of valuable information, together with an immense quantity of documents which may be made good use of when properly examined, when the chaff is separated from the wheat. On the whole, however, it has not been favourable to the cause of the martyrs.

Now, however, there has appeared such a vindication, such a wonderful re-examination of the whole history, as it is impossible to resist. It is impossible to read the account of S. Ursula given in the 9th volume for October of the Bollandists, published in 1858, without being perfectly amazed at the quantity of real knowledge that has been gained upon the subject, and still more at the powerful manner in which this knowledge has been handled;—an erudition which, merely glancing over the pages and notes, reminds of the scholars of three hundred years ago, in whom we have often wondered at the learning which they brought to bear on any one point.

This treatise occupies from page 73 to 303, 230 pages of closely printed folio in two columns. I acknowledge that it is not quite a recreation to read it, but still it is very well worth reading. All documents are printed at full length. Now, it so happened, that just after the volume had come out, I was at Brussels, and called at the Library of the Bollandists, and had a most interesting conversation with Father Victor de Buck, the author of this history. He gave me an interesting outline of what he had been enabled to do.

He told me that when they came to October 21, and he had to write a life of S. Ursula and her companions, his Provincial wrote to him from Cologne and said, 'Take care what you say, for the people are tremendously alarmed lest you should knock down all their traditions, and I do not know what will be the case if you do.' He replied, 'Don't be at all afraid; I shall confirm every point, and I am sure they will be pleased with what I have to say.' He was kind enough to put down in a letter the chief points of his vindication for me; but I have lost it, and so there was nothing left but to read through the whole of this great work. But, besides, a very excellent compendium has appeared, which takes pretty nearly the same view on every point, and approves of everything the author has said; indeed some points are perhaps put more popularly in it, though the history is reduced to a much smaller compass. I have the work before me. It is entitled, 'S. Ursula and her Companions: A Critical, Historical Monograph. By John Hubert Kessel. Cologne, 1863.' It is a work which is not too long to be translated and made known. What I have to say, after having gone through this preliminary matter, is, that I lay claim to nothing whatever beyond having been diligent, and having endeavoured to grasp all the points in question, and reduce them to a moderate compass. I have changed the order altogether, taking that which seems to me most suitable to the subject, and co-ordinating the different parts and facts so as to make it popularly intelligible. In this I have the satisfaction to find that in a chapter at the end of the book, in which the history is summed up, exactly the same order is taken which I have adopted here. It will not be necessary to give a reference for every assertion that I shall have occasion to make; but I may say that I have the page carefully noted where the subject is fully drawn out and illustrated.

Now, let me first of all give in a brief sketch what Father de Buck considers the real history, which has been wrapt up in such a quantity of legendary matter—that which comes out from the different documents laid before us, as the kernel or the nucleus of the history, as Kessel calls it. He supposes that this army of martyrs, as we may well call them, was composed of two different bodies: a body of virgins who happened, under circumstances which I shall describe to you, to be at Cologne, and a body of the inhabitants, citizens of Cologne, and others, very probably many religious and other virgins who had there sought safety. It may be asked, how came these English to be there? About the year 446, the Britons began to be immensely annoyed by the incursions of the Picts and Scots, which led to their calling in (after the manner of the old fable, about the man calling in the dogs to hunt the hare in his garden) the Anglo-Saxons, who in return took possession of the country; and the inhabitants that they did not exterminate they made serfs. At this period we know the English were put to sad straits. Having so long lain quiet and undisturbed under the Roman dominion, they had almost lost their natural valour, and were unable to defend themselves. There was, therefore, a natural tendency to emigrate and get away.

They had already done this before; for, as De Buck shows, with extraordinary erudition, the occupation of Brittany or Armorica was a quiet emigration from England, which sought the continent, and also established colonies in Holland and Batavia, and by that means obtained a peace which they could not have at home. We have a very interesting document upon this subject. The celebrated Senator Aëtius was at that time governor of Gaul; the Britons sent to him for help, and this is one passage of a most touching letter which has been preserved by Gildas: 'Repellunt nos barbari ad mare, repellit nos mare ad barbaros; oriuntur duo genera funerum; aut jugulamur aut mergimur.'* They were tossed backwards and forwards by the sea to the barbarians, and by the barbarians to the sea; when they fell upon the barbarians they were cut to pieces, and when they were driven into the sea 'mergimur'—we go to the bottom. It does not mean that they ran into the sea, but that they went to their ships, and many of them perished in the sea by shipwreck or by sinking—'aut jugulamur aut mergimur.' That shows that the English were leaving England to go to the continent. I am only giving you the web of the history, without its proofs; but I quote this passage to show it is not at all unlikely that at that moment, when they were, in a manner, straitened between the barbarians of the north and those coming upon them in the south, a great many of them went out of the country, and that especially being Christians they would wend their way

* *Gildas de Excidio Britanniæ*, pars i. cap. xvii. Ed. Migne: *Patrologia*, tom. lxix. p. 342.

to Catholic countries. Religious and other persons of a like character, we know, in every invasion of barbarians, were the first to suffer a double martyrdom. This is a supposition, therefore, about which there is no improbability, that a certain number, I do not say how many, of Christian ladies of good family, some of them, perhaps, royal, got over to Batavia, or Holland (where there have been always traditions and names of places in confirmation of this), and made their way to Cologne, which was a capital and a seat of the Roman Government, a Christian city, and in every probability considered a stronghold, both on account of its immense fortifications, and on account of the river.

Well, then comes the history, very difficult indeed to reconcile, of a pilgrimage to Rome, which it is said they made; but let us suppose that instead of the whole of them a certain number of them might go there. It is not at all improbable that at that time, as De Buck observes, a deputation, or a certain number of citizens and others, did go to Rome to obtain assistance there, as their only hope, against invasion which I shall describe just now. There is no great difficulty in supposing this; and assuming that some of the English virgins also went, that would be a foundation for the great legendary history, I might say the fabulous history, which has been built upon it. Now, there is a strong confirmation of such a thing being done. S. Gregory of Tours* mentions that at this very time Bishop Servatius did go to Rome to pray the Apostles SS. Peter and Paul to protect his

* S. Greg. Turon. *Hist. Franc.* lib. ii. cap. v. Ed. Migne: *Patrologia*, tom. lxviii. pp. 197, 576.

country and city against the coming invasion, as he saw no other hope of safety. He must have passed through Cologne exactly at that time, and, therefore, there is nothing absurd, or improbable, in supposing that some inhabitants of Cologne went with him as a deputation to Rome, and that some of the English virgins may have accompanied them. In the year following, Attila, the scourge of God, the most cruel of all the leaders of barbaric tribes, who invaded the Roman empire, was marching along the Rhine with the known view of invading Gaul, and not only invading it, but, as he said, of completely conquering and destroying it; for his maxim was, 'Where Attila sets his foot, no more grass shall ever grow'—nothing but destruction and devastation. I will say a little more about the Huns later. In the meantime we leave them, in 450, on their way to cross the Rhine with the intention of invading and occupying France. Attila united great cunning with his barbarity: he pretended to the Goths that he was coming to help them against the Romans, and to the Romans that he was going to help them to expel the Goths. By that means he paralysed both for a time, until it was too well seen that he was the enemy of all. It is most probable, knowing the character as we shall see just now of the Huns, that the inhabitants of the neighbouring towns would seek refuge in the capital, and that all living in the country would get within the strong walls of cities. We have important confirmation, at this very time, in the history of S. Geneviève,* who was a

* Vid. Tillemont, *Hist. des Emp.* vi. p. 151. *Acta Sanct. Boll.* Jan. tom. i. in vit. S. Genovevæ.

virgin living out in the country, but who, upon the approach of the Huns, hastened,we are told, immediately to seek safety in Paris, and was there the means of saving the city by exhorting the inhabitants to build up walls, to close their gates, and to fight. This they did, and so saved themselves. That is just an example. When it is known that throughout his march, Attila destroyed every city, committing incredible barbarities (ruins of some of the places remaining to this day), not sparing man, woman, or child, it is more than probable that there would be a great conflux and influx to the city of Cologne, where the Roman Government still kept its seat, and where, of course, there was something like order, although we have unfortunate proofs in the works of Salvianus,* that the morality of the city had become so very corrupt that it deserved great chastisement. However, so far all is coherent. In 451, after Attila had gone to France, and had been completely defeated, he made his way back, greatly exasperated, burning and destroying everything in his way, sparing no one. Then he appeared before Cologne; and this is the invasion in which it is supposed the martyrdom took place.

Having given you what the Bollandist considers the historical thread, every part of which can be confirmed and made most probable, I will now, before going into proofs of the narrative, direct your attention for a few minutes to what we may call the legendary parts of the history. When we speak of legends we must not con-

* *De Gubernatione Dei*, Ed. Baluzii, Paris, 1864, pp. 140, 141.

found them with fables, that is, with pure inventions. We must not suppose that people sat down to write a lie under the idea that they were edifying the Church or anybody. There have been such cases no doubt; for Tertullian mentions the delinquency of a person's writing false Acts of St. Paul, and being suspended from his office of priest in consequence. Such follies have happened in all times. We have had many instances in our own day of attempts at forging documents, and committing the worst of social crimes; but old legends as we have them, and even the false acts as they were called, were no doubt written without any intention of actually deceiving, or of passing off what was spurious for genuine. The person who first suggested this, was a man certainly no friend of Catholics, Le Clerc, better known by his literary name of Clericus; who observes that school exercises were sometimes drawn from Martyrdoms as in our day from a classical subject, as Juvenal says of Hannibal:—

> I demens et sævas curre per Alpes
> Ut pueris placeas et declamatio fias.

Not that students professed to write a real history, but they gave wonderful descriptions of deeds of valour and marvellous events which had never occurred, and were never intended to be believed. In the same way, at a time when nothing but a religious subject could create interest, that sort of composition came to be applied to acts of saints and martyrs; so that many books and narratives which we have of that description may be thus accounted for. It is much like our historical novels, or the historical plays of Shakspeare, for instance. Nobody imagines that their authors wished to pass them off for history, but they did not contradict history; they kept to history, so that you may find it in them; and you might almost write a history from some of those books which are called historical works of fiction. In early times such compositions were of a religious character. Then came times of greater ignorance, and those works came to be regarded as true historical accounts. But, are we to reject them on that ground altogether? Are we to say, any more than we should with regard to the fictitious works of which I have just spoken, that there is no truth in them? We should proceed in the same way as people do who seek for gold. A man goes to a gold-field, and tries to obtain gold from auriferous sand. Now, suppose he took a sieve full, and said at once, 'It's all rubbish,' and threw it away; he might go on for a long time and never get a grain of gold. But if he knows how to set to work, if he washes what he obtains, picks out grain by grain, and puts by, he gets a small hoard of real genuine gold; and nobody denies that when many such supplies are put together they make a treasure of sterling metal. So it is with these legendary accounts. They are never altogether falsehoods — I will not say never, but rarely. Whenever they have an air of history about them, the chances are that, by examining and sifting them well, we may get out a certain amount of real and solid material for history.

The legendary works upon these virgins are numerous and begin early. The first is one which I shall call, as all our writers do, by its first words, 'Regnante Domino.'

This is an account of traditions, evidently written between the ninth and eleventh centuries. It is impossible to determine more closely than this. But we know that it cannot have been written earlier than the ninth century, nor later than the eleventh. It contains a long history of these virgins while in England, who they were and what they were; of a certain marriage contract that was made with the father of S. Ursula, a very powerful king; how it was arranged that she should have eleven companions, and each of these a thousand followers; how they should embark for three years and amuse themselves with nautical exercises; how the ships went to the other side of the channel. It is an absurd story and full of fable, but there are three or four most important points in it. Geoffrey, of Monmouth, comes next. He gives another history totally different from that of the 'Regnante Domino;' but retains two or three points of identity. His is evidently a British tradition, which, of course, it is most important to compare with the German one; and we shall find how singularly they agree. Then, after these, come a number of legends called *Passiones*, long accounts, filled with a variety of incongruous particulars which may be safely put aside; but in the same way germs or remnants of something good, which have been thus preserved, are found in them all, and when brought together may give us some valuable results. We next meet with what is more difficult to explain—the supposed revelations of S. Elizabeth of Schönau, and of Blessed Hermann of Steinfeld. It is not for us to enter into the discussion, which is a very subtle one, of how persons, who are saints really canonised, and held in immense veneration—one of them, Hermann, singularly so — can be supposed to have been allowed to follow their own imaginations on some points, while at the same time there seems no doubt that they lived in an almost ecstatic state. This question is gone into fully; and the best authorities are quoted by the Bollandist. It would require a long discussion, and it would not be to our purpose to pursue it further. These supposed revelations are rejected altogether. Now, we come to positive forgeries, consisting of inscriptions, or of engraved stones with legends carved upon them. One of these mentions a pope who never existed, and also a bishop of Milan who never lived, besides a number of other imaginary people. From the texture and style of these inscriptions there can be no doubt whatever that they are absolute forgeries, and the author of them is pretty well discovered. He was a sacristan of the name of Theodorus. In order to enhance the glory of these virgins, they are represented, as you see in legendary pictures, as being in a ship accompanied by a pope, bishops, abbots, and persons of high dignity, who are supposed to have come from Rome with them. All this we discard, making out what we can from the sounder traditions.

And this is the result. There are two or three points on which, whether we take the English or the German traditions, all are agreed. First, we have that a great many of these virgins were English: that the Germans all agree upon; the earliest historical documents say the same. Secondly, that they were martyred by the Huns; that we are told both by the English and the German writers. It is singular that they should agree on such a point as this; and you will see how—I do not say corroborated, but absolutely proved it is. The third fact is, that there was a tremendous slaughter at the time, a singular slaughter of people committed at Cologne by these Huns. This comes out from all the legendary histories, which agree upon this point, and we can hardly know how they should do so except through separate traditions; for they evidently have nothing else in common. Their separate narratives we may reject as legendary.

Thus we come to an investigation of the true history, and see how it is proved. And first I must put before you what I may call the foundation-stone of the whole history on which it is based—the inscription now kept in the church of S. Ursula. It had remained very much neglected, though it had been given by different authors; until, when the Bollandists were going to write their history, they took three casts of it: one they gave to the Archbishop of Cologne, another they kept for themselves; the third—I cannot say what became of it, but I think it went to Rome, having been taken by De Rossi. I could not afford to have a cast brought here, but I have had a most accurate tracing made of it. Those of you who are judges of graphic character will see the nature of the letters: they are capital, or uncial, letters. First, you may ask what is the age of this inscription? It is pretty well agreed that it cannot be later than the year 500—that would be fifty years after that assigned to the martyrdom of the virgins. De Buck, who is really almost hypercri-

DIVINISFLAMMEISVISIONIB FREQVENH
ADMONIT ETVIRTVTISMAGNAEMAI
ESTATISMARTYRIICAELESTIVMVIRGIN
MMINENTIVMEXPARTIB ORIENTIS
EXSIBITVSPROVOTOC LEMATIVSVCDI
PROPRIOINLOCOSVOHANCBASILICAM
VOTOQVODDEBEBATAFVNDAMENTIS
RESTITVITSIQVISAVTEMSVPERTANTAM
MAIIESTAEMHVIIVSBASILICAEVBISANC
TAEVIRGINESPRONOMINE XPI SAN
GVINEMSVVMFVDERVNTCORPVSALICVIVS
DEPOSVERITEXCEPTISVIRGINIBSCIATSI
SEMPITERNISTARTARIIGNIBPVNIENDV·

tical in rejecting, says he does not see a single objection to the genuineness of this inscription. There is not a trace of Lombard or later character about it: it is purely Roman. The union of some of the letters is just what we find about that time in Roman inscriptions. It is then, as nearly as one can judge, of the age I have mentioned—about the year 500. De Rossi, passing through Cologne three or four years ago, examined it and pronounced it to be genuine, and said it could not be of a later period than that. Dr. Enner, a layman of Cologne, when writing his 'History of Cologne,' could not bring himself to believe that the inscription was so old, and he sent an exact copy in plaster (perhaps that was the third) to Professor Ritschl, the well-known editor of Plautus, and a Protestant, at Bonn. I have a copy of the Professor's letter here, in which he says that he has minutely examined the inscription, and that he cannot see anything in it to make it more modern than the date assigned to it, and that it contains peculiarities which no forger would ever hit upon, such as the double *i*, and other forms. He says, 'I am not sufficiently acquainted with the history of S. Ursula to connect it in any way; but I have no hesitation in saying that the inscription cannot be later than the beginning of the sixth century;' which, you see, takes us back very nearly to the time when the martyrdom is supposed to have occurred. Then I may mention that the very inscription is copied in the next historical document that we have, as being already in the church. This is the translation of the inscription, of which I present an exact copy:—

'Clematius came from the East; he was terrified by

fiery visions, and by the great majesty and the holiness of these virgins, and, according to a vow that he made, he rebuilt at his own expense, on his own land, this basilica.' Then follows a commination at the end, which is not unusual in such cases. Now, every expression here is to be found in inscriptions of the time. For instance, 'de proprio;' 'votum;' 'loco suo' (sometimes it is 'loco empto'), meaning of course land which one made his own, or which was his own before. There had been then a basilica—not the church that now exists, but a basilica—at the tombs where these saints were buried, which we shall have to describe later. He rebuilt the basilica fifty years after the martyrdom, destroyed no doubt during the constant incursions of barbarians. It was probably a very small one; for we know that at Rome every entrance to the tombs of martyrs had its basilica. De Rossi has been successful in finding one or two. One was built by S. Damasus, who wrote: 'Not daring to put my ashes among so many martyrs, I have built this basilica for myself, my mother, and sister;' and there are three niches at the end for three sarcophagi. It is universally allowed that there never was a catacomb without its basilica. In fact, in that of Pope S. Alexander, and SS. Eventius and Theodulus, found lately, there is a basilica completely standing, and the bodies of these saints were found—one under the altar—and the others near it. Then from the basilica you go into the catacomb. So that nothing is more natural than that in the place where these martyrs were buried, Clematius should re-build their basilica.

After this monument, we proceed to the next genuine document, though one of a later date, and by an unknown author—the 'Sermo in Natali.' This, there is no doubt, was written between the years 751 and 839; and I will give the ingenious argument by which this date is proved. But first it quotes the inscription I have read, with the exception of the threat at the end; in the second place, it mentions that the virgins were probably Britons—that it was not certain, but the general opinion was that they had come from Britain; thirdly, it attributes the martyrdom to the Huns; fourthly, it insinuates what is of great importance in filling up the history, that it is by no means to be supposed that they were all virgins, but that many were widows and married people. The reason for fixing the earliest date at 751 is, that it quotes Bede's Ecclesiastical History, which was written in that year, giving apparently his account of the conversion of Lucius; though one cannot say that it is certainly a copy from Bede, because Bede himself copied from more ancient books, and both may have drawn from the same source. Then it could not have been written after 839 for two reasons. In 834 there was a tremendous incursion of other barbarians—of Normans; and it is plain from our book that there had been no such invasion when it was written; nothing was known of it, because the writer speaks of countries, particularly Holland, as being flourishing, which were completely destroyed by them. There is also this singular circumstance. In speaking of the great devotion to the virgins in Batavia, the writer states that this happened at a time when Batavia was an island formed by the two branches of the Rhine. Now in 839 an inundation completely destroyed it, one of the horns or arms being entirely obliterated. Therefore that gives us a certain compass within which the book was written. The author himself was a native of Cologne—for in referring to the inhabitants he once or twice speaks of 'us'—and he would therefore be familiar with the traditions of the people. He says there was no written history at that time; he defends the traditions, and shows how natural it was that the people should have kept them. I ought to mention that he calls the head of the band of martyrs Pinnosa. He says, 'She is called in her own country Vinosa, in ours Pinnosa;' and there is evidence that this was the name first given to the leader: how, by what transformation, it came to be S. Ursula, we cannot tell; it is certain that up to that time hers was not the name of the leader. Afterwards Pinnosa appears on the list, but not as the chief, S. Ursula being the prominent name.

After that period there comes a mass of historical proofs that one can have no difficulty about. From 852 there are an immense number of diplomas giving grants of land to the nuns of the monastery of S. Ursula, at her place of burial. There is no doubt of the existence of that church, from other documents. Then the martyrologies repeat the whole tradition again and again. Thus, then, we fill up that gap of four hundred years (from A.D. 400 to A.D. 800). There is the inscription; there is the 'Sermo in Natali' which quotes it, and gives old traditions; and afterwards there are diplomas and other testimonies which are abundant.

We now proceed to compare the whole tradition with history, with known history, for after all this is our chief business. When we possess a tradition of a country and people we ask, 'What confirmation, what corroboration have we? what does history tell us?' Let us then see what history does tell. It tells us, in the first place, that in the year 450 Attila was known to be coming to invade and take possession of Gaul, having been ejected from Italy. His army is said by contemporary writers to have been composed of 700,000 men. It was a hostile emigration. They brought their women and children in carts, as the Huns always used to do, and they of course marched but slowly. They went along both sides of the Danube, and got at length into France. De Buck, by a most interesting series of proofs, makes it almost as evident as anything can be that they crossed over at Coblentz, therefore not coming near Cologne. They entered, as I have said, into Gaul, destroying everything in their march. Some of their barbarities and massacres are almost incredible. After devastating nearly the whole of the country, they besieged Orleans. The inhabitants having been encouraged to resist, at last succeeded in obtaining certain terms; that is, Attila and his chiefs went into the city and took what they liked, but left the city standing. After this they were pursued by the general whom I have mentioned—Aëtius, a Gaul, but who got together all the troops he could, Goths, Visigoths, Franks, and others, who saw what the design of these horrible barbarians was.

A most tremendous battle was now fought, that of

Catalaunia (Châlons-sur-Marne), in which cotemporary historians tell us 300,000 men were left on the field; but that number has been reduced to 200,000. Such battles, thank God! we seldom hear of now-a-days. Attila, routed, immediately took to flight, and got clear away from his pursuers. He went through Belgium destroying city after city, leaving nothing standing, and massacring the people in the most barbarous way.

Here comes the most difficult knot of the whole history. Authors agree that Attila now made his way into Thuringia, that is, to the heart of Germany; he must therefore be supposed to have got clear over the Rhine, and marched a long way through the country. On this subject De Buck has one of the most exquisite and beautiful geographical investigations, I should think, that have ever appeared. He proves, so that you can no more doubt it than you can doubt my having this paper before me, that there was a Thuringia which lay on this side of the Rhine; he proves it by a series of documents taken from mediæval writers, and from inscriptions, that there was a Thuringia which stretched from Louvain to the Rhine. Indeed it is impossible to conceive how Attila could have got, as by a leap, into the very midst of Germany. He traces the natural course of march (which you can follow by any map), taking the cities destroyed as landmarks, and brings him to this province; and when there, there was no possible way of crossing the Rhine but by Cologne; there was the only bridge, the only military pass of any sort. So there can be no doubt that the Huns, exasperated by their tremendous losses, and by being driven out of Gaul which they intended to occupy, having revenged themselves as they went on, were obliged to go through Cologne; and if you calculate the date of the victory, and consider the country through which Attila passed, destroying everything as he went, you bring him almost to a certainty to Cologne about the 21st of October, nearly the day of the martyrdom. The 'Regnante Domino,' which attributes the martyrdom to the Huns, corroborates all this account, which is the result of a most painstaking examination, extending over many pages.

Next, we come to another important point. Why attribute this massacre to the Huns? Because there was no other invasion and passage of savages except that one. It accords, then, both with geographical and chronological facts. We have the martyrs at Cologne at the very time when these barbarians came.

But we must need say something about the Huns. There is no question that the Huns were the most frightful, cruel, and licentious barbarians that ever invaded the Roman empire. They were not of a northern race, Germans, or Scandinavians; they were, no doubt, Mongols or Tartars; they came from Tartary, from Scythia, and settled on the Caspian Sea; they then moved on to the mouths of the Danube, and again to Hungary, and rolled on in this way towards the richer countries of the West. There are several authors of that period—Jornandes, Procopius, and others—who describe them to us.* They tell us that when they were

* Ammianus Marcellinus, lib. xxxi. cap. ii.

infants their mothers bound down their noses and flattened them in such a way that they should not come beyond the cheek-bones; that their eyes were so sunk that they looked like two caverns; that they scarified all the lower part of the face with hot irons when young, so that no hair could grow; that they had no beard, and were more hideous than demons; that they wore no dress except a shirt fabricated by the women in the carts in which they entirely lived; it was never changed, but was worn till it dropped off, under a mantle made entirely of wild rat skins. Their chaussure consisted of kid skins round their legs, with most extraordinary shoes or sandals, which had no shape whatever, and did not adapt themselves to the form: the consequence was, that they could not walk, and they fought entirely on their wretched horses. They had no *cuisine* except between the saddle and the back of the horse, where they put their steaks and softened them a little before eating; but as to drink, they could take any amount of it. With regard to their morality, it cannot be described. The writers of that age tell us that no Roman woman would allow herself to be seen by a Hun. They were licentious to a degree, and they carried off all the women they could into captivity; probably they destroyed a great many, which was their custom when they became a burden to them. These, then, were the sort of savages that reached Cologne.

They had another peculiarity: of all the hordes of savages that invaded the Roman empire, they are the only ones that used the bow and arrow. The Germans hardly made any use of the bow, except a few men who mixed in the ranks: as a body their execution was with the sword, the lance, and the pike. The use of the bow was distinctly Tartar, or Scythian. Then we are told that their aim from horseback was infallible; that when flying from a foe they could turn round and shoot with perfect facility; that they rode equally well astride or sitting side-ways like a woman; in fact, that they flew and turned just like the Parthians and Scythians from whom they were descended. In this great battle of Catalaunia they either lost heart or steadiness, and they could not fire upon their enemies, so that they were pursued and tremendously routed. That their mode of fighting was by the bow and arrow, you will see in the representations given in the beautiful shrine of Hamelink, where the martyrs are fired into by the barbarians with bows and arrows. Let us see what this has to do with our question. The 'Regnante Domino,' which we have mentioned as legendary, gives a most beautiful description of the mode of dealing with the bodies. The writer says that when the inhabitants saw that the enemy were gone they came out, and in a field they found this great number of virgins lying on the ground. They collected their blood, got sarcophagi, or made graves and put them in: 'and there they lay, as they were placed,' the writer says, 'as any one can tell who has seen them,' evidently suggesting that he had seen them. Now, in the year 1640, on July 2, Papebroch, an authority beyond all question, and Crombach, whose word may be relied on as that of a most excellent and holy man, were at the opening of the tombs. From all tradition this was no doubt the place of the stone of Clematius; there has always been a convent there; and you remember that part of the inscription which threatens eternal punishment to those who should bury any but virgins there. It is now called 'S. Ursula's Acker,' a sort of sacred field where the basilica was. Here they were buried, and so they remained undisturbed except by some translations of the middle ages, which do not concern us. In 1640 there was a formal exhumation, and eye-witnesses tell us what they saw. A nuncio came afterwards to verify the facts.

I will give you the account of how these bodies were found. Many of them were in graves, in rows, but each body separate, there being a space of a foot between them. In other places there were stone sarcophagi, in which they were laid separately. Then, Crombach describes that there were some large fosses, sixty feet long, eight feet deep, and sixteen wide, containing a large number of bodies. They were placed in a row with a space between them; at their feet was another row; then a quantity of earth was thrown on, and another row was placed, and so on, until you came to the fourth. Every skeleton in the three rows was entire, and they all looked towards the east. They had their arms crossed upon their bosoms, and almost every one had a vessel containing blood, or sand tinged with blood. The fourth, or upper stratum, consisted of disjointed bones, and with these also there were vessels containing blood or coloured sand. In this way, the writer says he saw a hundred bodies. Then there was this remarkable circumstance about their clothes.

Eutychianus,* the pope, had published a decree that no body of a martyr was ever to be buried without ving a dalmatic put upon it; and clothes in abundance were found upon these bodies.

Another important discovery was, that immense quantities of arrows were found mingled with the bones; some sticking in the skull, others in the breast, others in the arms—right in the bones. So it was clear that all these bodies had been put to death by means of arrows, and there was no other tribe but the Huns which made use of the arrow as its instrument of death. I may add that there were no signs of burning, or of any heathen burial about them. This also is most important. I have said that there had been other exhumations in the eleventh and twelfth centuries. There are pictures of these, and there are sarcophagi preserved in which bodies were found. These are laid in exactly the same manner as others were found in 1640. Crombach says the whole had been done most scientifically, that the distances were all arranged by measure, so that there was not a quarter of a foot difference anywhere.

Now, I ask, could those bodies have been put there in consequence of a plague, or an earthquake, or any event of that kind? Putting aside the arrows found in immense quantities, and the vessels containing blood, we know that when people die in a plague to the number of hundreds, a foss is made, they are thrown in, and there is an end of them. This could not have

* *Acta SS.* Bolland. Octob. tom. ix. p. 139. *Constant. Rom. Pont. Epist.* Paris, 1721, p. 299.

been a common cemetery. It contained nothing but the bodies of these women (I will speak of their physical characteristics later), all laid in studied order, with great care, and with such peculiarities, and all evidently buried at the same time. After reading all this, may we not exclaim with S. Ambrose, 'We have found the signs of martyrdom,' and with S. Gaudentius, 'What can you desire more to show that they were all martyred?'* And who does not see here confirmed the history of Clematius? Comparing the whole with traditions, both English and German, it seems to me that you have as much proof as you can reasonably require.

Having given you concisely the facts and corroborations of history, let me now proceed to answer objections.

And, first, there is the question, Were all these martyrs? Well, if they were to be tried by the rules established very justly in the modern church, it would no doubt be difficult to say; because, how can you prove that each of these women laid down her life voluntarily for Christ? The tradition of Cologne is that they would not sacrifice their virtue to those heathens, and that they were surrounded and shot. But in those times, a wider meaning was sometimes attached to the word 'martyr.' There were what are called *martyres improprie dicti*, where there could not be the same kind of evidence as in the case of others; or *martyres latiore sensu*. A person was called a martyr when he was put to death without his will being

* S. Ambros. class. i. epist. xxii. Ed. Ben. tom. iii. p. 927. S. Gaud. *Serm. in Dedic. SS. XL. Martyr.* ap. Migne, tom. xx. col. 963.

consulted, as in the case of our own S. Edmund, and in the case of S. Wenceslaus, who was put to death without being interrogated as to whether he would remain a Christian or not, and many others. De Buck shows that there was nothing more common. We have the remarkable case of the Theban legion—another instance of a large number of men being surrounded and cut down by soldiers without being questioned as to whether they were in a state of grace, or whether they were prepared to die. The deed was done *in odium religionis*, by people who merely looked to the gratification of their own passions and their desire for revenge. In those days the question of such persons being martyrs would be a very simple one, if it were known that they were killed by the Huns in hatred, as was supposed, of their virginity and because of their resistance. We have in martyrologies the account of Nicomedia and its twelve thousand martyrs. De Buck supposes that the number included all the martyrs of the persecution. And the 6,700 of the Theban legion are explained in the same way.

The next question is, Were these persons all virgins? Who can know? It is quite certain that even married persons, when martyred, had sometimes the title of virgins given to them. Many instances are supplied by the martyrologies and offices. S. Sabina,* for instance, is called a virgin martyr, though she was a married person. It was considered that martyrdom raised all women to a higher degree of excellence. There are some curious questions, too, arising, which

* *Acta SS.* Bolland. Octob. tom. ix. p. 143.

would not very well do for a discussion here. It is, however, sufficiently proved that when there was a great number of virgins, and others were mixed with them, the nobler title was given to all. Just as if you have a great many martyrs and some confessors united, the title of martyrs is applied to all, as they are included in one office, each sharing in the glory of martyrdom. The 'Sermo in Natali' expressly tells us that it was not supposed at its early period that all were virgins, but that there were ladies of all ranks and children amongst them. Indeed, some remains of children were found.

Then comes the question, Were there eleven thousand? Certainly not as all one company. It is supposed, and there appears nothing unreasonable in it, that when once the rage of the Huns was excited they would give way to an indiscriminate massacre, and that the eleven thousand most probably included persons who had sought refuge, perhaps their own captives, and probably a great number of the inhabitants of the city.

But does it not seem a frightful number of persons to be massacred? Not by the Huns. In the year 436, these same Huns slaughtered at once in Burgundy 30,000 men. They were of the same race, the same family of men as Tamerlane, who had 70,000 heads cut off in Ispahan. And the Turks, when they took the island of Chios, reduced the population of 120,000 to 8,000. So that those slaughters, which to us seem so fearful, are not to be considered in the same light when occurring in those times. We have a frightful example in the case of Theodosius and the inhabitants of Thessalonica. It is said that 15,000 persons were put to death in the theatre for a simple insult. The most moderate calculation is that by S. Ambrose, who gives the number as 7,000. Human life, of course, was not then regarded as by us, especially by men who devastated whole cities and burned them to the ground. Hence the difficulty as to the number of persons, including among them, not merely the followers of S. Ursula, but the bulk of the female inhabitants, is explained.

Another question arises, were they English, or were there English amongst them? That is answered unhesitatingly, Yes. All the traditions, English and German, agree that these ladies had come from England and sought refuge.

I have mentioned the facilities for emigration, and the way in which many went out of the country; so that there would be nothing wonderful in a certain number of British women being at Cologne at that time. Now there is this curious fact illustrating the subject. Very lately the Golden Chamber, as it is called, adjoining the church, where the chief remains are deposited, was visited by Dr. Braubach and Dr. Gortz of Cologne, Dr. Buschhausen of Ratingen, and others, who examined the skulls and pronounced them to be Celtic, not German. The Celtic characteristics, as given by Blumenbach and other writers, are quite distinct—the chin falls back considerably, the skull is very long, and the vertex of the head goes far behind—quite distinct from the Romans or Germans. Moreover, with the exception of ten or fifteen out of from eighty to a hundred, they were all the bodies of females. Now all the writers—all that I have seen at least—say that there could not have been an emigration of some hundreds of women without some men, some persons to guard them, and these would be with them and would share their martyrdom. Then, in the next place, they were all young people, there was no sign of their having died of a plague or any other casualty, but they appeared to be strong, healthy young women: which, of course, as far as we can judge, verifies the narrative to the utmost.

I now leave you to judge how very different historical research has made this legend, as it is called, appear, and how much we have a right to regard it in a devotional spirit, as the inhabitants of Germany certainly do. I do not say that there have not been many exaggerations, false relics and stories; but critical investigation enables us to put all these aside, and to sift their evidence. But certainly we have a strong historical verification of what has been considered until within the last few years as legendary, not only by real discoveries which have come to light, but also by a right use of evidence, which before had been overlooked and neglected.

The whole of what I have said relates to events. But my subject embraces 'events and things.' The latter part remains untouched, and I have yet to show how things or objects which have been looked upon as fabulous have been proved to be real and genuine.

II. I proceed, therefore, to objects which have been, or may be, easily misrepresented, as if asserted to be what they are not, and involving an imputation of imposture on the part of those who propose them to the notice or veneration of Catholics.

I will begin with a rather singular example, but one which, I trust, will verify the assertion which I have made; and if time permits, I will multiply the examples by giving two or three other instances.

I do not know whether any of you in your foreign travels have visited the cathedral of Chartres: I have not seen it myself, but I believe that it is one of the most noble, most majestic, and most inspiring of all Gothic buildings on the Continent. The French always speak of it as combining the great effects of a mediæval church, more perhaps than any other in their country; and as my address will relate to that cathedral, I think it is necessary to give a little preliminary account of it; at the same time warning you that I do not by any means intend to plunge into the depths of the singular mystery in which the origin of that cathedral is involved. It takes its rise from a Druidical cavern which was for some time the only church or cathedral. Over that the Christians—for the town was early converted to Christianity—built a church, of course, modest, and simple, and poor, as the early churches of the Christians were: but in this was preserved, with the greatest jealousy and with the deepest devotion, what was called a Druidical image of Our Lady, which was always kept in the crypt, for it was over the crypt that the church was built. It was said to have existed there before the building of the church; but into that part of the history it is not necessary to enter. In the year 1020, this poor old church was struck by lightning, was set on fire, and entirely consumed. The bishop at that time was one of the most remarkable men in the French Church—Fulbert, who has left us a full account of what was done in his time there. He immediately set to work to build another church, proposing that it should be perfectly magnificent according to all the ideas of the age; and to enable him to do so, he had recourse to our modern practice of collecting money on all sides. Among others Canute, King of England and Denmark, and Richard, Duke of Normandy, and almost all the sovereigns of the North contributed largely. The result was the beginning of a very magnificent church. The singularity of the building was this, that everybody laboured with his hands, not only men, but women, not only the poor, but the noble. These furnished with their own hands provisions or whatever was necessary for the workmen. However, after Fulbert's death, like most undertakings of that class, the work became more languid; and before it was completed (that was in 1094), the building, in which there was a great quantity of wood used, was again burnt to the ground. Well, this time it was determined that there should be a splendid church, such as had never been seen before; and here, again, that same plan of working with their hands was adopted to an extent which, as stated in an account given us by Haymon and one or two others, seems incredible. The labourers relieved one another day and night, lighting up the whole place with torches; provisions were abundantly furnished to all the workmen without their having to move from their places. In fact, the writer says that you might see noblemen, not a few, but hundreds and thousands, dragging carts or drawing materials and provisions; in fact, not resting until, in 1160, seventy years after the destruction, the church was consecrated; and there it remains, the grand cathedral church of Chartres at this day.

Now, it may be asked, what was there which most particularly made Chartres a place of such great devotion, and so attached the inhabitants to its cathedral that they thus sacrificed their ease and comfort so many years to build a church worthy of their object? It was a relic—a relic which had existed for several hundred years at that time in the church, which made it a place of pilgrimage, and which was considered most venerable. What was this relic? The name which it has always borne in the mouths of the simple, honest, and devoted people of Chartres and its neighbourhood, and in fact of all France, is *La Chemise de la Sainte Vierge*—that is, a tunic which was supposed and believed to have been worn by the Blessed Virgin, her under-clothing, and was of course considered most venerable from having been in contact with her pure virginal flesh. However, you may suppose that you require strong proof of such a relic at all, and you will remember that my object is to show how things which may have been doubtful, and perhaps considered almost incredible, have received great proof and elucidation by research. I do not pretend to say that in all respects you can prove the relic: the research to which I allude is modern, but it may guide us back, may confirm a tradition, may give us strong reasons in its favour, showing that it has not been received without good ground, though it may not be able to penetrate the darkness which sometimes surrounds the beginning of anything in very remote antiquity. I am not going, then, to prove the relic, but I am going to show you the grounds on which it had been accepted, and then come to the modern verification of it.

The history is this. A Byzantine writer of the fourteenth century, Nicephorus Calixtus,* tells us that this very relic was in the possession of persons in Judæa, to whom it was left by Our Blessed Lady before her death; that it fell, in the course of time, into the hands of a Jew in Galilee; that two patricians of Constantinople, Galbius and Candidus, traced it, purchased it, and took it to Constantinople, where, considering themselves in possession of a great treasure, they concealed it, and would not let it be known (this was in the middle of the fifth century); that the Emperor Leo, in consequence of the miracles which were wrought, and by which this relic was discovered, in spite of those who possessed it, immediately entered into negotiations, obtained it, and built a splendid church in Constantinople expressly to keep it; and that the church so built was considered as the safety, the palladium as it were, of the city of Constantinople. He mentions another fact which is important; that is, that there were at that time in Constantinople three other churches, each built expressly for the preservation of one relic of Our Lady. I mention these facts for this purpose: there is a very prevalent idea, I believe among Catholics as well as

* *Hist. Eccles.* lib. xv. cap. xxiv.

certainly among Protestants, that what may be called the great tide of relics came into Europe through the Crusades; that the poor ignorant Crusaders, who were more able to handle a sword than to use their discretion, were imposed upon, and bought anything that was offered to them at any price, and so deluged Europe with spurious and false relics. Now, you will observe, that all that I have been relating is referred to an age quite anterior to the Crusades, or to any movement of the West into the East. It is true that Nicephorus Calixtus is a comparatively modern writer, but he could bear testimony to churches that were existing, and tell by whom they were built. The mere writer of a hand-book can trace out the history of a church or any other public monument which is before the eyes of all: but he was not of that character: he was a historian, and he tells us that there were * three churches in Constantinople, just as we might say that in Rome there is the church of Santa Croce, built by Constantine to preserve the relics of the cross. Nobody can doubt that the church was built for the relic, that the relic was deposited there, and that earth from the Holy Land was put into its chapel. Monuments like that preserve their own history. Therefore, when this writer tells us that these churches existed from that period, we can hardly doubt that he could arrive at a knowledge of such facts; and at any rate it removes the impression that these wonderful relics were merely the sweepings, as it were, of Palestine during a fervent

* *Hist. Eccles.* lib. xv. capp. xxv. xxvi.

and pious, but at the same time ignorant and unenlightened age.

Thus, we get the history so far. Now, we know that there was no one who valued relics to such an extent as Charlemagne. We see, by Aix-la-Chapelle and other places, what exceedingly curious relics he collected. I am not here to defend them individually, because I do not know their history; nor is it to our purpose. He was in close correspondence with the East, from which he received large presents; for it was very well known what he valued most. There was a particular reason for this. The Empress Irene at that time (Charlemagne died in 814) wished to have his daughter Rothrude in marriage for her son Porphyrogenitus, and later offered her own hand to himself.

Many relics existed at the time of this correspondence; and as presents are now made of Arab horses and China services, so were they then made of relics, which, if true, monarchs preferred to anything else. Now, there is every reason to suppose that among the presents sent by Irene to Charlemagne was this veil or tunic.* There is in the cathedral of Chartres a window expressly commemorating the passage of this relic from the East to Chartres. Secondly, the relic, as you will see later, was, up to a few years ago, wrapped in a veil of gauze, which was entirely covered with Byzantine work in gold and in silk; which had never been taken off, and it was wrapped up in it till the last time it was verified. We have every reason to suppose that it had come from Constantinople, and that it was delivered at Chartres in

* See note at p. 286.

that covering. In the third place, it is historical—there is no question about it, for all chronicles and authorities agree upon the point—that Charles the Bald, the grandson of Charlemagne, being obliged to leave Aix-la-Chapelle, in consequence of going to settle in France, which was the portion of the empire allotted to him, took the relic away, and deposited it in the cathedral of Chartres. So that, as far as we can trace a transaction of this sort, there seems to be as much evidence as would be accepted in respect to the transmission of any object of a profane character from one country to another. There is the correspondence of the workmanship; there are the records of the place; and there is the fact that the relics were brought from Aix-la-Chapelle, where Charlemagne had collected so many relics that he had received from Constantinople. Mabillon, who certainly is an authority in matters of ecclesiastical history, says it would be the greatest rashness to deny the genuineness of this relic. 'Who will presume to deny that it is real and genuine?' This is in a letter to the Bishop of Blois, in which he is expressly treating the subject of discerning true relics. Everything so far, therefore, helps to give authenticity to this extraordinary relic which made Chartres a place of immense pilgrimage.

Bringing it down so far, we may ask, what was the common, and we may say the vulgar, opinion of the people regarding it? It had never been opened, and was never seen until the end of the last century. The consequence was, that it was called by the name I have mentioned. It was represented as a sort of tunic. It was the custom to make tunics of that form, which were laid upon the shrine and worn in devotion; they were sent specially to ladies of great rank, and were so held in veneration that it was the rule, that if any person going to fight a duel had on one of these chemisettes, as they were called, he must take it off; as it was supposed his rival had not fair play so long as he carried it upon him. In giving an account of the building I forgot to mention the wonderful miracles in connection with the relic there, which are believed by everybody to have taken place. It is even on record that the *Chevalier sans peur et sans reproche* went to Chartres *pour se faire enchemiser* before he went to war.

In 1712 we find that the relic was in a cedar case richly ornamented with gold and jewels—the original case in which it had arrived. The wood being worm-eaten and crumbling, it was thought proper to remove and clean it, and put it in some better place. The cedar case had no opening by which it could in any way be examined, and the Bishop of the time, Mgr. de Merinville, proposed to open it. He chose a jury of the most respectable inhabitants of the town, clergy and laity, to assist. The box was unclosed, and the relic was found wrapped up, as I have said, in the veil of Byzantine work. The veil was not unclosed, so that they did not see the relic itself. The débris of the box was swept away, and the relic as it was was put into a silver case that had been prepared; this was locked up, and then deposited in a larger shrine distinct from all the other relics. The procès verbal still exists in the archives of Chartres giving an account of all that took place, from which the account I have given you is taken.

Infidelity was then spreading in France, and, as you may know, a great deal of ridicule was thrown on this relic. It was said that such a garment was not worn in those days, that the system of dress was quite different, and that it was absurd to imagine any article like this. Now as no one had seen the relic, there was no way of answering these reproaches. In 1793 three commissioners came from the French Government, went into the sacristy, and imperiously desired to look at the relic: it was very richly enshrined, and they intended to carry it off. The shrine was brought to them, as the procès verbal of the second examination relates, when they seemed to be seized with a certain awe, and said, 'We will not touch it; let it be opened by priests.' Two priests were ordered to open the box, and they did so. These men had come prepared to have a good laugh, and scoffing at this wonderful relic. For antiquarians had been saying that such inward clothing was not known so early as the first century, but that instead a long veil used to be wrapped round the body.

Well, they found a long piece of cloth $4\frac{1}{2}$ ells in length—exactly what had been said should be the proper garment. The commissioners were startled and amazed, and said, 'It is clear that this is not the relic the people have imagined; perhaps it is all an imposture.' They then cut off a considerable piece and sent it to the Abbé Barthélemy, author of the 'Travels of Anacharsis,' and member of the Institute—a man who had made the customs and usages of antiquity his study; they did not tell him where it came from, but desired him to give an opinion of what it might be. He returned this answer; that it must be about 2,000 years old, and that from the description given him it appeared to be exactly like what the ladies in the East wear at this day, and always have worn—that is, a veil which went over the head, across the chest, and then involved the whole body, being the first dress worn. I ask, could a verification be more complete than this? And, recollect, it comes entirely from enemies. It was not the bishop or clergy that sought it. The relic was in the hands of those three infidel commissioners, who sent a portion to Paris without saying or giving any hint of what it was (they wanted to make out that the whole was an imposture), and the answer was returned which I have mentioned, and which is contained in the procès in the archives of the episcopal palace at Chartres. If any one wants to read the whole history, I refer him to a most interesting book just published by the curé of S. Sulpice (Abbé Hamon), entitled, 'Notre Dame de France, ou Histoire du Culte de la Sainte Vierge en France.' The first volume, the only one out, contains the history of the dioceses of the province of Paris.

I will proceed to a second popular charge, and it is one the opportunity of easily verifying which may never occur again. It refers to the head of S. John the Baptist, or shall I say, to the three heads of S. John the Baptist? Because, if you read English travellers of the old stamp like Forsyth, you will find that they make coarse jokes about it. Forsyth, I think, says something about Cerberus; but more gravely it has been said, that S. John must have had three heads—one being at Amiens, one at Genoa, and another at Rome; that at each place they are equally positive in their claims; and that there is no way of explaining this but by supposing that S. John was a triceps.

When we speak of a body you can easily imagine that one piece may be in one place, another in another, a third elsewhere, and so on. That is the common way in which we say that the bodies of saints are multiplied; because the Church considers that the place which contains the head or one of the larger limbs of a saint, or the part in which, if a martyr, he was killed or received his death-wound, has the right of keeping his festival and honouring him just as if it had the whole body. Therefore in cathedrals and places where festivals are held in honour of a particular saint, where they have relics, which have perhaps been sealed up for years, and never examined, they often speak as if they have the entire body. This is a common practice, and if I had time I might give you an interesting exemplification of it.* Suffice it to say, that according to travellers there are three heads of S. John. Now as I have said, a body can be divided, but you can hardly imagine this to be the case with a head.

A very interesting old English traveller—Sir John Mandeville—went into the East very early, and returned in 1366; soon after which, almost as soon as any books were published, his travels appeared. He is a very well known writer. Of course you must not expect that accuracy in his works which a person would now

* Since published in *The Month*, 'Story of a French Officer.'

exhibit who has books at his command and all the conveniences for travelling. He was not a profound scholar: he believes almost whatever is told him, so what we must do is to let him guide us as well as he can, and endeavour to judge how far he is right. I will read you an extract, then, from Sir John Mandeville:*—

'From thence we go up to Samaria, which is now called Sebaste; it is the chief city of that country. There was wont to be the head of S. John the Baptist inclosed in the wall; but the Emperor Theodosius had it drawn out, and found it wrapped in a little cloth, all bloody; and so he carried it to Constantinople; and the hinder part of the head is still at Constantinople; and the fore part of the head to under the chin, under the church of S. Silvester, where are nuns; and it is yet all broiled, as though it were half burnt; for the Emperor Julian above mentioned, of his wickedness and malice, burned that part with the other bones, as may still be seen; and this thing hath been proved both by popes and emperors. And the jaws beneath which hold to the chin, and a part of the ashes, and the platter on which the head was laid when it was smitten off, are at Genoa; and the Genoese make a great feast in honour of it, and so do the Saracens also. And some men say that the head of S. John is at Amiens in Picardy; and other men say that it is the head of S. John the bishop. I know not which is correct, but God knows; but however men worship it, the blessed S. John is satisfied.'

This is a true Catholic sentiment. Right or wrong,

* *Travels*, chap. ix. p. 182. Ed. Bohn.

all mean to honour S. John, and there is an end of it. We could not expect a traveller going through the country like Sir John, not visiting every place, but hearing one thing from one and another from another, to tell us the exact full truth. But we have here two very important points gained. First, we have the singular fact of the division of the head at all. We occasionally hear of the head of a saint being at a particular place, but seldom of a part of a head being in one place and a part in another. Here we have an unprejudiced traveller going into the East; he comes to the place where the head of S. John used to be kept, and he finds there the tradition that it was divided into three parts, one of which was at Constantinople, one at Genoa, and another at Rome. Then he adds, 'Other people say that the head is at Amiens.' So much Sir John Mandeville further informs us: he mentions the places where it was reported the head was, telling us that it was divided into three.

This is a statement worthy of being verified. It was made a long time ago, and yet the tradition remains the same. It was as well believed in the thirteenth century in the East, at Sebaste, as it is in Europe at the present moment.

The church of S. Silvestro in Capite, which many of you remember, is a small church on the east side of the Corso, entered by a sort of vestibule: it has an atrium or court, with arches round, and dwellings for the chaplains; the outer gates can be shut at night so as to prevent completely any access to the church. The rest is an immense building, belonging to the nuns, running out towards the Propaganda. When the Republicans in the late invasion got hold of Rome, the first thing, of course, which they did was to turn out the monks and nuns right and left, to make barracks; and the poor nuns of S. Silvestro were ordered to move. The head of S. John is in a shrine which looks very brilliant, but is poor in reality. I think it is exposed high beyond the altar, and the nuns kept it in jealous custody in their house. The Republicans sent away the nuns in the middle of the night, at ten or eleven o'clock, just as they were, with what clothes they could get made into bundles: there were carriages at the door to send them off to some other convent, without the slightest warning or notice. The poor creatures were ordered to take up their abode in the convent of S. Pudentiana. The only thing they thought of was their relic, and that they carried with them. The good nuns received them though late at night, and did what they could to give them good cheer; they gave up one of their dormitories to them, putting themselves to immense inconvenience.

When the French came to Rome, they found S. Silvestro so useful a building for public purposes, that they continued to hold it, but permitted the nuns to occupy some rooms near the church. I was in Rome while they were still at my titular church, and went to visit the nuns attached to it. Their guests asked, 'Would you not like to see our relic of S. John?' I said, 'Certainly I should; perhaps I shall never have another opportunity.' I do not suppose it had been out of their house for hundreds of years. There is a chapel within the convent which the nuns of S. Pudentiana consider a sacred oratory, having a miraculous picture there, to which they are much attached; and in this they kept the shrine. On examination I found that there was no part of the head except the back. It is said in the extract I have read to you that the front part of the head is at Rome; but it is the back of the skull merely; the rest is filled up with some stuffing and silk over it. The nuns have but a third of the head; and the assertion that they pretend to possess the head, which travellers make, is clearly false. I can say from my own ocular inspection that it is but the third part—the back part, which is the most interesting, because there the stroke of martyrdom fell. I was certainly glad of this fortunate opportunity of verifying the relic.

Some time afterwards I was at Amiens. I was very intimate with the late bishop, and spent some days with him. One day he said to me, 'Would you wish to see our head of S. John?' 'Yes,' I replied, 'I should much desire it.' 'Well,' he said, 'we will wait till the afternoon; then I will have the gates of the cathedral closed, that we may examine it at leisure.'

We dined early, and went into the chapel of the Blessed Sacrament, where the relic was exposed, with candles. After saying prayers, it was brought, and I had it in my hands; it was nothing but the mask, the middle and back portions being totally wanting. You could almost trace the expression and character of the countenance in the bony structure. It was of the same size and colour as the portion which I had seen at S. Pudentiana; but the remarkable thing about it is that there are stiletto marks in the face. We are told by Fathers, that Herodias stabbed the head with a bodkin when she got it into her hand, and here are the marks of such an operation visible. You could almost say that you had seen him as he was alive. I have not seen the third fragment, but I can hardly doubt that it is a portion of the same head, and that it would comprise the parts, the chin and the jaw, because there is no lower jaw in the front part, which is a mere mask. The only other claimant is Genoa, and its relic I have not seen. But this is exactly the portion allotted by Mandeville to that city. I have, however, had the satisfaction of personally verifying two of the relics, each of which comprises a third part of the head, leaving for the other remainder exactly the place which our old traveller allots to it.

*** Mr. Cashel Hoey, one of our learned contributors, has kindly furnished me with a most interesting corroboration of this account. It is an extract from the *Revue Archéologique*, new series, Jan. 1861, p. 36, in a paper by M. Louis Moland, entitled 'Charlemagne à Constantinople,' &c., giving an account of a MS. in the library of the Arsenal, anterior to the thirteenth century.

The following is the account of the relic which the emperor is stated to have brought from Constantinople to Aix-la-Chapelle.

'Li empereres prist les saintuaires tot en disant ses orisons, si les mist en eskerpes (*écharpes*) totes de drap de soie et si les enporta molt saintement avoec lui trosqu Ais la Capele en l'eglise Nostre Dame qu'il avoit edifiie. Là fu establis par l'apostolie (*Le Pape*) et par les archevesques et les evesques as pelerins li grans pardons, qui por Deu i venoient. Oiés une partie des reliques que li empereres ot aportées: il i fu la moitiés de la corone dont Nostre Sires fu coronés des poignans espines. Et si i ot des claus dont Nostre Sires fu atachiés en la crois al jor que li Jui le crucifierent. Et si i ot de la vraie crois une pieche et del suaire Nostre Segnor, *o le chemise Nostre Dame*.

CHRISTIANITY IN RELATION TO CIVIL SOCIETY.

By EDWARD LUCAS.

PART I.

The complicated nature of the relations which arise in old-established societies, between the ecclesiastical and civil powers, renders it difficult for ordinary men to perceive whether and where one trenches on the rights of the other. The principles involved lie so deep, that it is, for the most part, only men of leisure and such as are accustomed to profound investigations of this particular kind, who are able to penetrate and to comprehend them.

It is natural that the ecclesiastical body, both from the mode in which its members are elected and from their training, should produce more men of the class referred to, than does the lay portion of the community, although the latter is so much more numerous in itself. A chief and sufficient reason being, that among the laity, the men of leisure have little to stimulate them to the requisite intellectual exertion; while the men of action, upon whom fall the duties of government, are too much engrossed by ambition, by the labours of administration, and by the practical questions of the day and of the hour; whereas, it is the especial business of ecclesiastics to master problems deeper than any which immediately concern society. Moreover, the Church gauges with great nicety the capacities of her servants, appointing each to the task for which his ability peculiarly fits him ; so that the waste of individual force is less, and its development more certain, in the smaller than in the larger body.

Now, as a matter of fact, the ecclesiastical and civil powers seldom agree for long together. Few statesmen start with even the intention of submitting to ecclesiastical authority or advice on questions which they deem within their own domain. The consequence is, that, like other abstruse sciences, that of government is explained, and the acts of governments are defended upon theories and by arguments whose apparent depth appeals attractively to the self-conceited, while it deceives and bewilders the simple.

The necessity, however, for plain men to form a udgment on these momentous questions, is so paramount and of such daily occurrence, that one feels instinctively there must be some easy means of arriving at sound conclusions—arguments, convincing by their simplicity, and within the comprehension of most people. I propose to bring forward in this paper some, which, having been convincing to my own mind, I fancy may be the same to the minds of others. I do so with considerable diffidence, hoping they may not be deemed insufficient by men who have studied these subjects on more philosophical and logical methods. To me, they seem to go to the root of the great question of the day, viz. the relative positions of the ecclesiastical and civil governments. They conduct to nearly the same, though not quite so advanced, a conclusion, and by a different route, as the late able article in the *Dublin Review*, on the intrinsic end of civil government. The subject is one which naturally falls under several heads, of which the two chief are, firstly, the principles which regulate the relation; and secondly, the advisability, at any given time, of enforcing those principles more or less rigidly in practice. With the latter is intimately connected the intermediate question, viz. how far it is lawful to go in holding the principles in abeyance? This part of the subject has lately been brought into great prominence by the speeches of the Count de Montalembert, at Malines, and will, it is said, be treated at length from another point of view, in a future number of the *Dublin Review*. The considerations which I shall lay before you to-day come under the first head. They are based upon the intention with which the Church was founded in the first instance, and upon the mode of its growth and perpetuation afterwards. Perhaps it were more correct to say, they are based upon the Creed. They will probably sound common-place, but at any rate they have been forgotten and practically denied by men both within and without the Church. To avoid the antagonism which is frequently aroused by the use of the word 'Church,' I shall speak of it as the 'Society of Christians,' which Our Lord founded. I shall offer some remarks, firstly, upon the Unity, then upon the Universality of the Society; afterwards, I shall endeavour to show that these could only be maintained by means of an organisation which must have begun with the earliest days of the Society's existence; the object of the whole being to establish, that a society so organised, and extending for all time throughout the world, must of necessity be independent of more limited societies, whose growth was the result of circumstances rather than of predetermination. I shall dwell at some length upon the question of Organisation, thinking it impossible to refute too often the theory of writers of the school of Mons. Guizot, that in the first ages the Church was without organisation. This plan presents the double advantage of giving a less abstract form to the discussion of this portion of the general subject, and at the same time of replying to an opinion which has great weight with our opponents. Afterwards, some of the functions of the Society will be contrasted with those of civil society, in order to prove that the latter must in reality be more or less dependent on the former: in doing this, reference will be made to the above-mentioned speeches of the Count de Montalembert.*

To begin, then, with the Unity of the Society. We all know that the Christian religion was established to provide the entire human race with the means of becoming reconciled to their offended Creator, and we all know that they were revealed to a few individuals, who, at that time, were the whole of Christian Society. The revelation of the means must evidently have been simple, since it was made by one Divine Person, at one time, to one small body of men. However manifold the means might be, the revelation of them was a complete whole. How wide soever the law, its universality required that it should provide for

* In August 1863.

all the exceptions which it was intended to allow under it. It would have been a mockery to reveal a law which admitted of exceptions, without at the same time declaring what they were. Whatever number of clauses it might contain, it was only one law. It may be called a law, or a code, or a body of laws, or Christianity, or the Gospel; but no matter by what name you choose to designate it, still it was the revelation of but one law, complete and perfect in itself; with nothing superfluous, and without omissions. When we speak of the law of England, we mean the whole law—common law, Chancery law, Acts of Parliament, and all else that goes to make up what is understood by the phrase, 'according to law.' In the same way the law of Christ is all that He revealed to men, of their duties to God and to each other: and there could hardly be omitted from the revelation, either in germ or otherwise, those of individuals, and especially those of the new Society, to civil governments.

The revelation, indeed, contained something more and higher than this, viz. certain truths regarding the natures both of God and of the human soul, which are the foundations of the law, and which, being absolute and altogether beyond the influence of opinion, can in no way be affected by the outward circumstances of governments, or of any other persons. But it seems natural to conclude that, as the reciprocal duties of governors and subjects depend immediately upon that human nature which is common to both, and ultimately upon the Divine nature, from which human nature springs, the Society, which has received a direct revelation concerning, and insight into, both these natures, should be in the position to teach, rather than seek instruction from any society which is without such direct revelation, as to the reciprocal duties referred to. If you deny the position, you must deny the revelation altogether. The law, then, based upon the actual natures of God and of the soul, being one, the belief in and the submission to it must be one. There is no accepting part and rejecting part. Whoever gives only a fractional assent to the terms proposed, no matter how large the fraction may be; whoever rejects one clause of the submitted contract, by which God is pleased to declare Himself bound to any and every man, the moment he accepts it entire, cannot demand the concession of the other terms—cannot claim under the other clauses. Till a treaty or contract be signed, so as to bind both parties to it, no treaty or contract can be said to exist. And so in the subject under examination: till a man accepts the terms God lays before him, he is outside the contract. He has not even begun to fulfil the covenants. He cannot demand payment till he has delivered the goods God is willing to accept as a sort of equivalent; which goods are an absolute and entire submission to the perfect law. And so it is with the Society; it is only in virtue of subjection that it exists at all—one subjection to one law; the law being the same to one man as to another: not that all lives are to be uniform, like the impressions from an engraving or the casts from a mould. By no means; the law has practical reference to all the minutely varied requirements of humanity, whether within or beyond the Society under discussion. It is adapted to all circumstances and to all characters. It foresees, admits, and provides for all necessary modifications and for every possible breach. Otherwise, it would be a compound and therefore not a perfect law, and could not claim an undivided submission. But, being a perfect law, this is required, and can only be given by an undivided Society. Whether, therefore, we prefer to use the term Revelation, or Law of Christ, or Will of God; *that* in obedience to which men can alone belong to the Society is one, and without unity among themselves there can be none between them and the source of this revelation, law, or will.

But while the law provides for lapses on the part of individual members of the Society, and while it furnishes means for the recovery of those privileges which members lose through disobedience to the law, no provision was, or could be, made for lapses on the part of the Society itself. If the Society fell away, there would be no possibility of its return to the truth. Christianity could no longer exist. The primary object of the establishment of the Society was, that it should declare to the world certain truths which God had revealed to it. If it swerved from the truth, it would become a society of falsehood; its connection with the truth would be destroyed, and it could not possibly reinstate itself. But truth being one, and the object of the Society being to teach the truth, the Society must be one also. Division, in regard to the truth, supposes error on one side or the other; therefore, if divisions arise, the part which retains the truth is the Society: the other part or parts are cut off from all connection with it; they cannot be the Society, or portions of the Society, in any sense of the words.

Looking, therefore, to the source whence the Society sprung, to the law by which it is bound, and to the truth which it has to teach, unity is an absolutely necessary condition of its existence.

We will now proceed to the next division of the subject, viz. the Universality of the Society.

It is universal in four senses. Firstly, as to space, extending over the whole world. Secondly, as to time, lasting by the Divine promise throughout all ages. Thirdly, as to rank, excluding none, because the promises received were to all alike. Fourthly, as to the individual man in this, that no portion of his being is left unaided and uncared for by the perfect law of which it is the depository. That it was intended to embrace the whole human race requires no proof; that to do so it must continue to the end of the world is equally obvious. That it should have jurisdiction over all the faculties of man will demand some elucidation. But, first, let us go back to the earliest days of the Society, and see how its unity and universality, as to space and time, went hand in hand from the very moment that it received the power of action. When, on the Day of Pentecost, it was increased in the proportion of 3,000 to some 120, it lost not its identity by the accession. It acknowledged the same rule as before, it participated in the same revelation, it looked forward wi th the same hope.

If the small Society held certain truths, and were regulated by principles, axioms, or government, no addition of numbers could change either the one or the other. The new members had received but an elementary instruction as to the aims and meaning of the Society they joined. They were in no condition to exercise control, or to express any opinion of weight on modes of procedure, or on questions of doctrine. They were learners, not teachers; and it was in virtue of submission to the teaching of those whom a miracle proved to hold a Divine commission, that they became members of the Society, which was increased, not altered, by their adhesion. The seedling oak is the same when it has lived its three hundred years; it has developed, but has not lost its identity; whereas, had the new men, on any principle of majorities, been able to persuade the founders of the Society to swerve from the primary object of the foundation, and to teach other things as truths than the exact revelation they had received, the Society would, *ipso facto*, have ceased to exist. To repeat what has been already said, it would have been another Society henceforth. The new members, then, were absorbed, one by one, into the mystic tree which was to cover the whole world, as the particles of light, and heat, and moisture are attracted and assimilated by the trees of the forest.

And when the universality of the Society was practically commenced by the returning home to their native countries of the 3,000, each one would take with him the obligations he had contracted on his conversion. These would concern first his relations with God, then with his family, then with the Society, afterwards with the world outside and with his government.

The obligations of the Libyan would not differ, except in detail, from those of the Mesopotamian, the Persian, the Roman or the Jew. But since life is made up of details, and since the revelation was to all men of every condition, there must be some means, common to all, of ascertaining the exact duties of each under every variety of novel or of old accustomed circumstance. Every man would find himself embarrassed with all sorts of difficulties. And if the Apostles stood in need of a special illumination after three years of constant conversation with Our Lord; men converted in a short space of time must always be referring back to their teachers for rules of conduct, to say nothing of the Sacraments. In this way the Society was bound together while it expanded.

The very remoteness of outlying members, so far from causing divisions in the Society, would be a most potent means of securing union, as will more fully appear when we come to the question of organisation. Distance from the seat of authority could not alter the inherent principle by which submission to its rules was due from all. Submission to the law which held it together was the only qualification for position in the Society. And when it grew and sent forth its offshoots and branches to distant regions, the mutual relations of the various parts were not only subordinate to those of each part with the Society at large, but they existed solely in virtue of the powers of the entire corporation which alone had the prerogative of defining those relationships.

In common parlance, one says that the lesser joins the

greater, not the greater the less. Here the 3,000 converts on Pentecost joined the little Society, which being very small in numbers, was even then greater than all the world besides, by the law and revelation which it possessed; and until it lost them nothing could alter the proportions of the world and itself. But it could not lose them, because the primary intention was that it should embrace and retain within itself all mankind. The experience of nearly 2,000 years shows, if proof were wanting, that universality as to place could only be accomplished by universality as to time. The Christian Society of the Day of Pentecost is the very same which exists to-day. The reasons for its creation and the motives for its continuance are undiminished. So far as two-thirds of the world are concerned, its final cause remains unfulfilled. It stands in the same relation to those two-thirds as it did to the entire world on the Day of Pentecost. Whatever it needed then for the conversion of all mankind, it requires now for two-thirds of them. What was new then to the Romans, is as new to-day to these. What it had at that time to offer to all men, it has to offer still. If enthusiastic devotion to it were worthy of admiration then, it is equally so now. If all mundane considerations were swallowed up in an overwhelming sense of its claims, so that martyrdoms were wisely suffered then, the same is equally true at this moment. In short, if it were intended to include all men within its pale, it must last so long as mankind continues to exist.

But if it embrace men in all countries and in all ages, it embraces men of all ranks. What it has to give is as needful to one man as to another. The salvation which Christianity offers is as far beyond the reach of the beggar as of the king. The misery of the one is no more a passport than the fine linen of the other. It is only by obedience to the law of Christianity that either can attain to salvation. However wide or however narrow the limits of the Society, no rank is excluded from the benefits or from the obligations of membership. The one law of which we have spoken above, declares the one and defines the other. And, if we regard the fourth sense in which the Society is universal, it will be apparent that the same reasons exist for its supremacy over men of every rank, the most exalted as well as the most humble. This sense includes the whole aggregation of faculties and powers of which man is composed. When human nature fell in Adam, the fall was entire; every faculty of mind and of body rebelled. Thus the ear listened to, and the understanding believed, the words of the tempter; the eye beheld the goodliness of the fruit; the memory banished the command of God; the will consented to the temptation; the feet walked to the tree; the arm was outstretched; the hand grasped, the mouth ate, the fruit. The affections, the desires, the imagination, the intellect were all concerned. Every portion of his being, therefore, became degraded. The deterioration which followed the act of disobedience was thorough. As the superior faculties of the soul had put themselves in subjection to the inferior bodily powers, the disarrangement of the whole was henceforth complete, and in this state the new Society found all mankind. It was to rescue the human race from this condition that the Society was created, and if it were to act with real efficacy on the fallen nature of man, it must have a control over all his faculties as complete and thorough as was the Fall. In order to be able to rearrange, it was necessary to have the entire command of all the parts. And as the Society was of Divine institution, the powers conferred upon it could not be otherwise than perfectly adapted to their end. The family of man, then, being derived from one original, every member of it has the same nature, and no rank can possibly escape the jurisdiction of a Society whose office is to deal with every portion of that nature. So far as to the universality of the Society.

Now as to the means by which the Society was to be maintained and propagated throughout the whole world and for all time. In treating this portion of the subject, I shall, as already mentioned, give the remarks I have to offer the form of a reply to M. Guizot's fanciful theory, that the earliest Christians were 'a pure association of men with common belief and sentiments, but without any form of discipline, or of laws, or any body of magistrates.' In these phrases M. Guizot describes an unorganised body.

In reality, however, there is no society without organisation. An aggregation of units, unless bound together by fixed laws, is not a society in any sense, as a number of loose bricks are not a house. The phrase, 'society without organisation,' is a contradiction in terms. Society disorganised, i. e. with its organisation destroyed, is anarchy, not society. The common expression of an 'unconstituted society' means simply that the society does not yet exist; the materials are there, but, till organised, they are mere materials.

Now, no other society has ever yet been founded upon a plan so ambitious (if the word be allowable) as this one. The most numerous corporations, the greatest conquerors, have never, even at the height of their prosperity, proposed to themselves schemes of such vast proportions.

For the most part, societies which have exercised an important influence on mankind, and empires which have become great, have begun with no idea of their future expansion, which has resulted from opportunity rather than from an original intention. Unceasing energy working upon a fundamental principle, clearly defined and kept steadily in view, has produced results quite beyond the contemplation of founders. And it would be impossible to point to great successes achieved either by individuals or societies, without persevering efforts, systematically directed to a certain end. But men, connected together by no stronger tie than community of sentiment, inasmuch as they have no corporate existence, lack any capacity for united perseverance. Each particular member may persevere in his own line. But without organisation such a body has no more coherence than is found among a number of men who meet together at a conversazione, where topics of common interest are discussed, and who retire at its conclusion to their own avocations.

In the present instance, however, there *was* a fundamental principle, viz. to carry the Society throughout the whole earth, to subdue all men under obedience to the revelation by which it was guided, to subject them to the law of Christ. Now the very existence of such a principle presupposes a society in the true meaning of the term, constituted with all the conditions of permanence, and having powers of attraction capable of drawing within its sphere the most discordant elements. It were absurd to imagine that a plan so stupendous was launched into the world with no more provision for its success than the fickle resolution of a few men. In the moral, no doubt, as in the material world, a body once put in motion continues to move by its own weight long after the propelling force has ceased to act. But in this case, the motion was to continue even beyond the imagination of men, and the opposing forces were not only external to but were actively at work within the body itself. In order to have a just appreciation of the difficulties which had to be overcome, we must bear in mind that the necessity for a revelation having arisen from disobedience, the propagation of the new law must be entrusted to men who were not only fully acquainted with it, but were firmly determined to adhere to it, with perfect submission. Such were chosen for these very reasons, and were endowed with supernatural powers to enable them at the same time to perform their work and to keep their resolutions. When, therefore, by their preaching, other men were induced to join their body, it is impossible to conceive that they had not rules by which the new members were to be bound, and powers of enforcing those rules. When any body of men associate to carry out an object, however limited, the first thing they do is to determine, and for the most part, in these days at least, to reduce to writing, the regulations under which they shall act, and which shall be binding hereafter upon themselves and their successors or future associates. An executive, by whatever name it goes, and however constituted, is created with the power of enforcing the laws, and of inflicting pains and penalties, so far as the terms may be applicable. The first provide for admission into, the last for dismission from, the society or association. Everyone knows that this is the course adopted. Nevertheless, we are asked by so grave a philosopher as M. Guizot to believe that in the first age 'Christianity was simply an individual belief without any form of discipline, or of laws, or any body of magistrates,' and this notion is practically shared in by vast numbers of people.

The idea of twelve men setting about a work, plainly superhuman, in which they knew they would have to encounter not only the hostility of the world and of worldly governments, but the natural proneness of men, themselves included, to disobey the law whose force they admitted: the idea of twelve men of only average common sense, with these difficulties before them, thinking, for a single instant, of undertaking to conquer the world, without a plan, with no form of discipline, without laws and without an executive, is so contrary to the experience of every-day life, that it can only be accounted for upon some theory of a mysterious supernatural assistance which no one can explain, and upon which no known sect has dared in its own case to rely.

But even had the association commenced upon the impossible supposition of an absence of laws, it could not long have existed upon such a want of basis. The Gospel narrative, however, is obviously against any such supposition. A number of circumstances will readily occur to every one, which point, from the first, to an arrangement of parts altogether incompatible with the sentimental theory.

We need not encumber the text with the examples referred to. There is sufficient in the peculiar nature of the Society itself, as shown by its object and the necessary character of its functions, to make an appeal to historical facts almost needless. The instances alluded to are nevertheless mentioned in a note, in order to demonstrate that the theory and the actual circumstances of the case perfectly coincide.*

In the first place, then, the revelation and the executive of the Society were necessarily in the same hands. It could not be otherwise. With the revelation was combined the duty of diffusing and perpetuating it. The revelation being a declaration of God's will to men, both as among themselves and as between men and God, supposed these duties. Otherwise the revelation would have concerned the Apostles only, which no one asserts. Had it been only of private interpretation, the command to carry it into all nations would have been absurd. It was, then, to be disseminated; and that in such a way, as to remain for ever in the world.

* Some of the circumstances are: The appointment of Matthias, the community of goods, the ordaining of deacons, the sending of Barnabas to Antioch, the sending of Saul and Barnabas from Antioch, the decision and letter of the Council of Jerusalem.

It was not to be subject to almost total oblivion, as the old revelations had been. Twice before had the whole human race known and almost entirely lost the knowledge of God's will. But this revelation of it was to be perpetual. And as it was only by human agencies that the perpetuation was to be maintained, the duty of arranging for such perpetuation was clearly implied in the command to go into all nations and teach. Now there were just twelve men who could teach, and they would die within seventy years. But more, the twelve could not possibly superintend the details of more than as many districts at once. They must travel, instruct the ignorant, satisfy the wise of this world, exhort the lukewarm, settle disputed questions, and bring back the strayed. All would require promptness and decision. Except with themselves, neither the knowledge nor the authority existed. But they must provide for their absence and future death. What they knew and had imparted to others, without appeal to them, could not spread further. Men taught at second-hand would say, 'This which you tell us on such a point does not agree with your other teaching. We must refer to our own Apostle.' Such reference, as above remarked, could not but be a powerful means of securing unity. But absence and death being inevitable, these conditions must have been prearranged for. Provision must have been made in God's Will from the first. It was no afterthought of men. Human shortsightedness could not have failed to anticipate what must so clearly arise; infinitely less could God's wisdom. But what provision was most natural, most simple, and therefore most certainly really made? For absence a delegated authority, for death one to succeed. Now no delegated authority can be at any time independent of the power which delegates. The fact of delegating presupposes and includes the right of withdrawing the faculties conferred. When, therefore, any one of the Apostles had established the Society in any city, and finding it advisable to move to a distance, had delegated to some chosen man powers similar to those which he himself possessed, the newly elected would be responsible immediately to the Apostle who appointed him, but in the last resort, to the recognised central authority of the entire Society. If the delegation were granted solely in virtue of individual powers, it could only be revoked by the persons who conferred it. But if the grantor acted on behalf of the Society, he could not annul the appointment without its sanction expressed or implied. Now, to suppose that each Apostle had the power to appoint and maintain representatives responsible to himself alone, is to suppose the power to create not one, but twelve societies, which has been shown to be impossible. And, moreover, in such a case this difficulty would arise on the death of the appointer: the delegate would still remain in power, being answerable to no one for his conduct. From such a plan confusion must inevitably arise. For though each Apostle would teach precisely the same doctrine, yet the teaching would fall upon ears which would hear according to the idiosyncrasies of their possessors, and would consequently become changed and corrupted with very little delay, and the delegate's authority and knowledge would be unhesitatingly called in question. Every man would judge for himself, and contradictory interpretations would at once arise.

Whereas, if an appeal lay to the college or council of the Apostles, either under a presidency or otherwise, the inconvenience of an authority lapsing by death would be avoided, and the advantage would be secured of having the concurrent judgment of a number of men instead of that of one only. The mere executive of the Society could not be in hands independent of the corporation itself; and since its main object was (regarded from our present point of view) to propagate certain unalterable teaching, we maintain that in the execution of this function its officers must be as amenable to central control as in the maintenance of discipline. 'Let all things,' says S. Paul, 'be done in order.' But there can be no order without authority to ordain. It cannot here be pleaded that this expression refers to outward observances only, because these are what objectors make so light of. It is alleged that they are the result of corruption, so many departures from the first simplicity, so many inventions of interested men. But if the maintaining of order in matters of discipline were necessarily insisted on, the argument seems unanswerable that the highest application of discipline, which in its essence is the due subordination of members, consists in the appointment of teachers; that is of those servants of the Society whose especial business consisted in carrying into effect the purpose for which it was created.

Let us now take into consideration the practical difficulties which the Society would have to meet and overcome.

An appeal to history would be too long, otherwise it would not be difficult to show that the opposition which the Society has had from the first to encounter was so multifarious in its forms, so persevering, so insidious, so powerful, and, at times, so thoroughly organised, that nothing short of an organisation incomparably more multifarious in its appliances, more persevering, more cohesive, or rather so closely knitted together, that each of its parts depends upon, while it strengthens the rest—discipline being inseparably united with doctrine, and both with the innermost thoughts and intents of the heart—could have withstood the apparently overwhelming force by which it has been threatened times without number.

But such an historical survey would take us off the line we are pursuing. This, however, may be said, that the greatest dangers to which Christianity has been exposed have arisen from within itself, and have been nourished with the food upon which the Church has fed her own children. Her form of government, her maxims, the mental training by which she regulates minds, have been the most formidable weapons of attack in the hands of rebellious subjects, who, having first learned her methods, have afterwards used them in teaching false doctrine. Every one is aware of the deadly hostility with which men, whose peculiar duty it was to maintain, have assailed the truth they were bound to guard. We are not alluding to mere laymen, the sphere of whose inimical action was therefore restricted; but rather to such men as Arius, who commanded respect by their position, bewildered the ignorant and half-instructed by their subtlety, and deluded the simple by their pretence of submission to an authority which they acknowledged while in the very act of disobeying. When we read of the extent to which the Arian heresy spread, so that centuries after its rise, and when it was all but extinguished in the country of its birth, it appeared again in force in the distant West in the ranks of the barbarian invaders, the conclusion is plain, that such vitality can only have been the result of a very powerful organisation. A similar reflection presents itself in reference to the Paulicians, who, after an interval of many centuries, having been driven from the East, reappeared in the South of France in such numbers as to threaten the very dissolution of society.* If, then, the Christian Society were to be exposed to the attacks of such formidable enemies, it must have had not only proportionate means of defence, but the capacity for extending its conquests on one side, while it warded off assailants on the other; for Christianity was never intended to stand on the defensive with the world, and in fact it never has done so. The builders of the new temple have worked with one hand and held the sword in the other. Their attitude has been always and necessarily aggres-

* Sir James Stephens, formerly Professor of History at the University of Cambridge, says, in his *Lectures on the History of France*, p. 239: 'If the Albigenses had succeeded in their designs, they must infallibly have substituted for the despotism of Rome an anarchy breaking loose from all restraints, Divine and human.'

sive. Christianity came into the world as a conqueror. Its militant character dates from Calvary, and the subjection of a continent does not even modify its nature. And while the world outside was being opposed, convinced, led captive, these internal enemies, imbued with the spirit of the world, men who failed to grasp the Christian idea, and to recognise the exact concordance of part with part in the whole scheme, have set themselves up as teachers of doctrines destructive of uniformity. Against such false teachers protection was required both by those within and by those beyond the Society. The first, lest they should be deceived and led astray by plausible arguments; the last, lest, seeing contradictions among men professing to publish the same revelation, they should doubt there being any revelation at all. Now to guard effectually against these two dangers, the Society *must* have been organised upon a system capable of meeting both unintentional errors and malicious oppositions. Of the first would be the natural tendency of the human mind to diversity of opinion; and of the second, systems which, like the Arian, contained a large amount of truth together with fatal and wilful departures from it.

Now, first, as to unintentional difficulties. They would arise from endeavours to graft Christian doctrine upon Jewish practices, or upon certain existing pagan philosophies, or from pushing real and misunderstood Christian principles to unwarranted conclusions, or from drawing false scientific deductions from phenomena inaccurately observed and clumsily grouped. In a word, from opinions treated as certainties. Now opinion, being something altogether external to truth of any kind, is absolutely excluded by revelation. It is a judgment formed upon ascertained or supposed facts, and is liable to variation and modification with the increase of information. It is not truth, nor the knowledge thereof, but merely a view of what the truth must be, judging from certain data. It is in its nature undependable. The length of time during which an opinion has been held, the weight of intellectual authority, or the evidence of the senses in its favour avail nothing in the face of more accurate research. In the calculations of human science, where intellectual speculations, or where physical results affecting whole races even, are the entire stake, opinion is all that can be arrived at: it is the ultimate term of enquiry. Even if the truth be discovered, it will never be known as such. It may be taken to be so, and acted upon provisionally in that sense, but the feeling will lurk in the mind that there may possibly be a mistake after all. If opinion be allowable, it is as much one man's right as that of another. It arose, in fact, within the Society, as it was certain to arise; and had there been no organised authority to define the limits where opinion trenched upon the domain of Divine Revelation, mankind would in a very short time have returned to precisely the same religious confusion wherein the Gospel found them. The unendurable nature of this confusion had been one chief means of preparing men's minds for the Gospel; and a revelation which left speculation free as before would have been regarded, and justly so, as a mere human invention. Certainty was wanted in place of opinion—something positive upon which the soul could rely—a rock amid the quicksands of doubt. If dogmatic teaching be not presented to the mind, it will invent a dogma for itself. Guidance it must have, and in default of a true, it will follow a false, teacher. Hence the successes of those impostors, in all ages, who have laid claim to Divine direction. But these men were sure to arise, and there must be some way of deciding upon their claims. If the Christian Society were without organisation, it could have no means of enforcing its doctrines in opposition to those who pretended to act under Divine inspiration, and concerning whom any opinion might be lawful, in the absence of an established court of appeal on such questions. The same is equally true in regard to the subjects we mentioned just now; viz. Jewish practices, pagan philosophies, and the rest. But a revelation, flung into the world, and left at the mercy of every man to interpret, would have no power to correct errors of opinion. It seems as though a very little reflection should suffice to convince one, that a most complete organisation, and one which should come home to, and be felt by, all men at all times, was requisite for this purpose.

Now as to malicious oppositions. Leaving omniscience out of the question, men, with the experience of four thousand years to guide them, must have been blind not to foresee that perverse teachers would arise in the Society. There could be no room to doubt from the first that this would happen. Can one, then, imagine that S. Paul, with his wonderful genius and his practical good sense, aware of the danger, should have consented to enter an association which proposed to overcome the difficulty, let alone the conquest of the world, without a plan, laws, or government? Even had he not received the command to go into the city for instruction, which implied authority in the person who was to teach him, he could never have supposed that the stupendous work before himself and the other Christians was to be carried on by isolated individual efforts. The idea is so absurd that one is at a loss to conceive how it ever arose. One would like to see some proof, not that the Apostles actually began, but that they were justified in beginning, a work upon which the salvation of the whole human race depended, in defiance of common sense and common prudence. When men adopt an eccentric line of action, the inference is, not that they are Divinely inspired, but rather that the motive power is of another description. No one asks for a justification of prudence. It is only for actions clearly or apparently against it that explanations are required. But it would have been presumption instead of prudence if the Apostles, foreseeing malicious opposition, had not prepared against it in the only feasible way. We are not entering here into the question, of whether or no the revelation included a code of laws for the government of the Society. We are supposing a society existing, possessing and charged to propagate a certain revelation; and we contend that the only way in which it could continue to exist, and to retain the revelation intact, in spite of the malicious endeavours of some of its members to corrupt it, was by means of a wisely-planned government; and further, that this governnent could not have been left to grow spontaneously out of necessities as they arose, but that it must have been instituted from the very beginning. Necessities would have been local, while the Society was increasing in unknown regions. To meet these necessities, if local councils were held, how would their decisions become recognised as binding upon the universal Society? Still more, how could they have tended to develop into a government which should embrace the world, and have kings for its subjects? We are asked to believe the old fable of Minerva, Jupiter being absent. We are told that this Society, instituted by God, to outlive a hundred ages, was cast into the world without laws, and yet that at some unnamed epoch it appeared all of a sudden with a constitution so perfectly adapted to its long career, that its greatest enemies are compelled to admit its matchless practical excellence. The brain from which the constitution emanated is not specified.

It really seems wonderful that so many thinkers, who are searching and accurate on all sorts of collateral subjects, who clear the ground before them with the greatest industry, advancing step by step, and branching off from time to time as they proceed into the numberless byways which lead off the main line of their march, should suddenly seem to lose their curiosity or their perseverance just at the point where reason and history combine to make palpable the absurdity of their theory and the falsity of their facts.

But even these writers admit that when civilisation in Europe was on the point of being extinguished, the

Society alone saved the world from the threatened calamity. But if the contest between barbarism and civilisation were carried on upon uneven terms; humanly speaking, that between paganism and Christianity, when the former had on its side the strength of public and private opinion, backed by the force of the most powerful government that ever existed, while the latter was weak in numbers, absolutely powerless in influence, and incapable of making its strength felt even in a small degree, was a thousand times more so. Consider what a strong hold paganism must have had upon every branch of society: on the aristocracy, whose sole retention of the priestly office elevated them above the masses, and thus gave them a twofold interest of emolument and of influence; on the semi-intellectual, who being but slightly philosophical would not readily give up the beautiful fictions of their favourite poets; on the employés about the temples, whereof forty-three besides two hundred and eighty sanctuaries existed in Rome in the time of Valentinian A.D. 364; on the clients attached to the noble houses; on all who were interested, from whatever cause, in the continuance of the games and shows held in honour of the pagan divinities, and which will be seen to have had an extraordinary possession of the public mind, when it is remembered that the Emperor Trajan gave such an entertainment, in which ten thousand gladiators fought to the death; on the army, which had been led to victory under the invocation of the national gods; in fine, on almost the entire empire, which worshipped Rome as a goddess, and firmly believed in her eternity. Why, if an organisation were requisite at the later period, when the opposing forces were something like evenly matched in point of numbers, how much more so was it in the beginning, when the proportions were altogether on the side of the world and against Christianity! Against all the influences we have mentioned, with their thousands of ramifications, it would have been folly to open a contest at all, unless by an express command from God. But for a body of men unorganised and without a plan to have done so, would have been the height of folly. Now, while, on the one hand, nobody denies the command to enter upon the combat; on the other, nobody pretends to produce evidence of a command *not* to organise. The utmost that can be alleged by any writer is, that he cannot find an account, which is satisfactory to himself, of a primitive organisation. The inability may be judged of in various ways. But reflection confirms the primâ facie view as to probabilities, and the acknowledged fact of the early existence of a perfect Society, together with the untraceableness of the steps by which its parts become harmonised into a complete whole, shows, not that the government was of gradual growth, but rather that it must date from the first days of the Society.

Such are a few of the arguments, rapidly sketched, by which the necessity for an organisation in the earliest days of Christian Society may be proved. But, if the One Society were organised at first, and if it were to spread over the world, and to continue till the consummation of ages, it would be difficult to show that the same reasons have not existed ever since its foundation, and will not in all future times remain in equal force. For the purpose of the present paper, then, it may be taken as established, that the Society was, and continues to be, fully organised.

We come to the concluding portion of our argument. We have to maintain that a Society with the characteristics described, constructed after a fashion to ensure the unchangeableness of the body of doctrines it had to impart and by which it was bound together, must not only be independent of all other societies and bodies of men, but must claim a legitimate control over their action in many particulars.

In the first place, then, it is to be remarked that this Society grows upon laws of its own, and that its operations are regulated on principles inherent in itself. The particular form of its growth, and the direction in which it spreads, may be modified by the fostering care of external powers, or by the storms of persecution; just as a tree is sheltered, yet bounded by the wall near which it is planted, or is bent from the direction of prevailing winds. But this eternal tree outlives alike the decay of shelter and the perseverance of storms. It borrows warmth, not vitality, from outward protection; and as for the effect of the hurricane, the harder it blows the more firmly does it root itself.

Yet the mass of even Christian politicians start upon the idea of keeping or bringing this independent Society under the control of the State; not of any particular State, but of 'the State' in general. The abstract idea of 'Christian Society' is to be made subject to the abstract idea of 'the State.' That Society which we have described, and which, as a matter of history, has completely changed the whole face of society at large, both within and beyond its pale; which for hundreds of years grew in spite of the State; whose spread was in no way limited by the frontier lines of empires; which having first conquered the conqueress of the world, afterwards subdued her savage despoilers, making the obligation of gentleness of manners so universally recognised, that men of enlightenment wonder it is not felt even in pagan countries; that Society, which, by teaching governments and peoples their duties to each other, has given stability to the former by teaching them to look to the love rather than to the fear of their subjects; and in so doing has altered the whole code of political maxims, thereby showing itself superior in wisdom to the State by how much the teacher is better than the taught; that Society, whose principles form the basis of all modern law, is declared to be subservient to the State, and to possess only so much freedom of action over its own subjects as the State may choose to permit.

Of two things, one must be affirmed by these politicians: either that Christian Society is subject to the State in the widest sense of the term, or that it is subject to the Christian State. If the first be said, the result must be that the very existence of Christianity would depend upon the will of its enemies. There is scarcely a pagan or infidel country where the State has not persecuted and attempted to annihilate it. It was so throughout the ancient world: it is so now in the East.

The martyrdom of fifty thousand Christians in Cochin China is a somewhat strong expression of State opposition. But the position is untenable. No one but an avowed enemy of the Cross would maintain such ground in plain terms. There is, indeed, a sort of middle line, which it is possible to take, viz. to ask of the infidel State to place Christian Society on an equality with other societies, in accordance with a principle which was invented by the enemies of Christianity and of God. I confess, this seems to me to be abandoning the prerogative which of right belongs to the one universal organised Society, and making its freedom dependent upon the forbearance and consistency of its most malignant opponents. It is only another way of asserting the subjection of the Christian Society to the State. You may conceal the principle under eloquent phrases, and with a flow of enchanting oratory, but there it is, and with a little trouble will be easily detected. Whether or no the late speeches of the Count de Montalembert at Malines contemplated this principle, cannot be decided here. But several phrases which he uses, such as 'renunciation of privilege,' 'reciprocal independence of the two powers,' 'free co-operator,' seem to imply such a principle. Used in the way in which the Count employs it in reference to Christian Society, the word privilege grates upon the ear. Consider the meaning of the word. Privilege is an exceptional advantage granted. But who is the grantor in this case? The State? Then Christian Society takes a boon from a superior power! But it is Christian Society which has exceptional advantages to offer, as will be seen developed at some length in the following lecture. 'Reciprocal independence!' There must be *some* appeal *de jure* in the last resort whenever any two persons enter into collision. Then where is the independence in the present instance, wherein one or the other must be, and where both claim to be, supreme? On one side or the other independence ceases the moment the two powers come into hostile contact. It can hardly be intended that in such cases the infidel State is to have freedom of action over Christian Society. Both cannot be free: one must obey. Shall it be Christian Society? No Christian, certainly no Catholic, dare say so. We are speaking of obedience on questions concerning the welfare of Christian Society. Shall the State be called on to yield? If so, Christian Society *has* a privilege. It has indeed a privilege, granted by God when He revealed the one perfect law. That is a privilege which there is no right or power to renounce in the face of the infidel State. The Universal Society may for a season withhold its demand for freedom of action in the full exercise of its right, but it cannot 'protest clearly, boldly, publicly,' against a return to what has been conferred upon it, not for the benefit of France, or of Germany, or of Europe, but for that of the entire world. The right is inalienable, and has attached to it an obligation which Christian Society can no more escape from, than the individual Christian can evade the responsibility of his Christianity by an act of the will. We know that the obligation only arises with the advent of power. But being in a condition of weakness, if such be really the state of affairs, is Christian Society to protest that when power returns, it will forego a privilege which is a part of its very constitution? For such it is: as will more clearly apparent when we come, in the next lecture, to compare the modes in which power is conferred upon the two governments. But confining ourselves to the points we have established hitherto, it seems evident that the Unity, the Universality, and the perfect Organisation of the Society, suppose faculties and rights beyond any which can possibly belong to smaller bodies. Now, the State has the right to extend or curtail the action of smaller Societies within itself: it may and it must widen or limit the freedom of its individual members. It interferes of necessity with them in various ways. And in a similar manner the Universal Society not only may, but must, exercise a prerogative, which is a right or a privilege according as it is regarded in relation to other smaller constituent Societies, or to God, Who conferred it. We know, unfortunately, that practically the history of the relations of State Churches with even the Christian State is one of the concession of rights on the part of the Churches. But it is hard to convince oneself that this is a reason or a justification for the assertion of principles in regard to infidel States which are contrary to the very nature of the State to which they are applied.

There is no time to pursue the question further in this direction. So far, then, for the present as to the infidel or pagan State, and to that purgatory or 'middle State' to which we are led by good men propounding policies based upon principles which are neither pagan nor, if I dare say so, quite Christian. But if it be said that Christian Society is under the jurisdiction of the Christian State, the declaration carries its condemnation on its very face. It is Society out of which the State is formed, not it out of the State. Society is the greater, the State is the less. Society embraces all States. It is the generic term of which States are the species; as life includes vegetable, animal, spiritual life. Society existed before the State was thought of; and *à fortiori* Christian Society before the Christian State, which exists solely in virtue of the submission of each of its members to the law of the Society. There was no Christian State till the sovereign submitted, nor any Christian Government till the ministers submitted to the law of Christian Society. At what period and by what means did submission become changed into command? There are but two ways in which men, whether kings or subjects, can become members of the Society of Christians. One, by an humble request to be enrolled among the members; the other, by baptism in infancy. In the first case, if submission be promised on condition of reception, how does a king, more than another man, acquire the right to break his promise? In the second, there can be no pretence for rejecting the authority of a Society to which he claims to belong, and which, by the very nature of the supposition, existed before him. He may renounce allegiance; but that sort of independence is not very enviable. We are not asserting here the right of any particular Church to his obedience. We are speaking of the Universal Society, and we say, that out of it, at some time, arose the Christian State, every member of which was, and is, bound by the laws of the Society.

Look at the two powers from another point of view. The first law of nature is that of self-preservation. Now, the Christian law has to do, primarily, with conscience: it is only through conscience that it acts on the outward forms of society; and the moment in which the last conscience should throw off the yoke of that law would be the same in which the law would cease to exist in the world. The State, on the other hand, has, as such, nothing *primarily* to do with conscience. The business of the State is to maintain order and security. All that the State knows of conscience it has derived from Christian teaching. Before Christianity, the idea of regulating State affairs upon considerations of conscience was nearly unthought of. Conscience may be said, in a certain sense, to have been the creation of Christianity, at least it was this which awakened it out of its long lethargy; and to the present day it is scarcely regarded beyond the limits of Christian Society. But it embraces the whole body of Christians. The laws which regulate it, and which depend for their subsistence upon the submission of conscience, must of necessity overleap State barriers. It is not bounded by rivers or chains of mountains, far less by the ever-shifting landmarks of States. When, therefore, the Christian State, from a notion of what is requisite for its own self-preservation, enacts decrees of any kind, the Christian law steps in and asks, 'Will these decrees destroy conscience, upon which I live?' And if it be urged that the State is the best judge, in its own case, of what self-preservation demands, at least an equal liberty, in this respect, must be conceded to Christianity. If Christian Society know not what its own interest requires, how can the most Christian State conceivable know? seeing that all its knowledge of Christianity is derived from the organised Society of which we are speaking. And if the most perfect individual Christian is he who is most submissive to the Christian law, does not the same hold good of States? Then, again, the safety of the Christian State will be seen to depend, in a great measure, upon its own retaining its just position between organised Christianity on the one side, and individual Christians on the other—from this: that so long as the State regulates itself after this manner, it can appeal in its own behalf to the individual conscience; whereas, insubordination, on its part, shuts the mouth to such appeal. But statesmen, judging by their daily experience of human nature, attribute to Christian Society and to its executive ministers a selfishness which they see to be all but universal. Occupied with the difficulties of office, influenced by the apparent exigencies of a crisis, and pressed upon by the clamours of contending parties, statesmen perhaps do not perceive where they overstep the line of submission in listening to a policy urged upon them by powerful classes of men—Christian, like themselves. They overlook the sacred character of the Society with which they are dealing. They attribute to it the faults of individuals; nay more, they see personal selfishness, where, in reality, there is only devotion to Christianity. While quick to detect selfishness in the rulers of Christian Society, they do not perceive it in themselves. They argue, because every individual may and does err, that therefore the corporate Society does the same. They forget that all power upon earth has been given to the Divine Head of the Society, which is bound together by a holy law; whereas, the State can make no such pretension. It does not seem to occur to them as unreasonable to ask a society regulated by a Divine, to submit to one which acts only under an inferior, law.

They seem unconscious that for the Society to do so would be to declare with one breath that the law is binding upon all men, and with the next that a certain class is exempted from obedience to it; that it would be, at once, to affirm and to deny that the law defines the relations of all men to each other. Yet, in all the contests between the two powers, the whole question at issue turns upon that very point. The one asserts and the other denies a Divine commission to declare these relations. But, in so doing, the State is most inconsistent. It admits the right up to a certain line, and there it stops. It allows that every member of the State, including the statesman himself, must bow (in his private capacity) to the authority of Christian Society. It asks, nay, it demands, the assistance of the Society's executive to enforce those rules for the maintenance of order in the mutual relations of men among themselves, and of submission to the civil administration which the Society has laid down. It requires the Society to act as a sort of police in its behalf. The State says to it, 'You have the right to control consciences. It is your duty so to regulate them, as that men shall aid and not thwart me in my efforts for the benefit of all.' But when these beneficent intentions, having become converted into oppression, or the State, from notions of its own self-interest, having set itself to interfere with conscience, the Society demurs, and claims to exercise on behalf of its subjects those controlling rights over conscience which the State had insisted on in its own favour, immediately they are declared null. The State then proceeds to define conscience; and the same men who as private persons acknowledge the authority of the Society, as statesmen refuse to obey it. Whereas, it is clear that any executive, whose powers of enforcing respect are played with in such a manner, must quickly become an object of contempt, and therefore incapable of performing the very work which the State requires at its hands.

It may or may not be true that the One Society can err in matters of policy. It is certain that it does not lay claim to infallibility in these matters, in the same way as on questions of doctrine; but that cannot release statesmen or governments from the obligation of obedience, which springs from the very nature of the Society, and which arises prior to any action, good or bad, on its part. This debt, being already at this moment incurred, for every Christian who shall hereafter be born, cannot be thrown off. The tyranny of a parent may drive a child into lawful disobedience. But here we have a Society founded upon the truth, whose existence depends upon the spread of a knowledge of the truth; its preservation of the truth guaranteed by Divine promises; its organisation expressly fitted to defend the truth against all attacks, both from without and from within. Such a Society cannot allow the State to exercise an authority independent in the last resort of its own. Because, whether in relation to subsects or to other States, it must be bound to act upon the maxims of truth, of which it knows nothing but what it learns from the Society with which alone the truth is deposited.

But, even looking merely at the relative powers of judgment which one may reasonably expect the leaders of the two orders to possess, one would, on natural grounds alone, give the palm to the leaders of Christian Society.

The statesman's vision is more or less bounded by the outlines of his own State. What he sees beyond, he looks at *ab extra.* He must bring all foreign questions to the tests of the local interests of his own community. His traditions date back but a few centuries. For him the circumstances of different epochs are so unlike, that he has in each to work out a new experience for himself. His freedom of action is checked by other independent powers. He judges upon partial and interested representations.

On the other side, the Christian leaders are men of a high order of intellect. As statesmen and philosophers they are almost, if not quite, unsurpassed in this respect. For them the world is a home; no place is foreign to them. They are, therefore, necessarily men of large views, and accustomed to taking a survey over the broadest possible field of affairs. They have the most ancient traditions to fall back upon. With them the experience of one is renewed in every succeeding age, for it is their business to understand and to deal with human nature, which is always the same. They administer the affairs of a Society with ramifications, and consequently with conflicting interests, all over the world. The vast variety of circumstances which must for ever modify decisions, is constantly before their minds. They can never forget that they are the successors of the men who led the infant weakness of the Society to war with all the powers of the world, and who won the fight.

The further the contrast is carried out, and the more minutely the respective characteristics of the two parties are examined, the more will the advantage appear to be on the side of the leaders of Christian Society.

Then, again, still looking at the matter from a purely human point of view, there seems no reason why corruption, and the abuse of power, should more readily arise among them than among laymen in authority; while viewing the probabilities in reference to the objects for which the Society has been founded, and to those safeguards against lapses which are naturally to be expected in a Divinely appointed constitution, one would say the danger of excess would be far greater among lay rulers than among ecclesiastical.

These are a few of the ideas which strike one on a vast subject, which requires a much more elaborate treatment than can be given to it in one or two essays. It is a subject demanding examination from many points of view, in order to close the way to classes of objections which only seem grave because they are not met in full front by arguments which are not intended to, and therefore do not, apply to them. It appeared to me that the strongest and plainest arguments were to be found in considering the distinctive marks of Christian Society. I have, therefore, endeavoured to trace its growth from its foundation, not historically, but as it must necessarily have happened; and it will be found that the conclusions which I have aimed at establishing in this, are of the greatest importance in further developing the subject, as I propose to do, in the following Part. The same remark applies to the more scattered observations at the latter portion of the above pages.

PART II.

In the former paper I endeavoured to show, from the nature of Christian Society, from the object of its foundation, and from the mode of its growth and perpetuation, that it must needs be independent of civil governments. After pointing to the Unity of the Society, and to its Universality as to time and place, I proceeded, at some length, to establish that these characteristics could only be maintained by means of a very powerful organisation, whereby the whole is united in such a way as necessarily to place it beyond the control of the State: because the latter, being circumscribed and constantly subject to changes of limit, can have neither power nor jurisdiction over a body which is nowhere conterminous with its own bounds—in other words, because the less cannot include the greater. I remarked that the number of members of the respective corporations in no way affects their comparative greatness. That the one hundred and twenty Christians on the Day of Pentecost were a society greater than the whole world besides, because of the Divine law and revelation which it possessed, and because of the Headship of Christ, which neither is, nor can be, claimed by the State. Starting, then, from the basis of the one Universal Organised Society, I called attention to the tendency of even Christian politicians to aim at making this Society dependent upon the State, not on any State in the concrete, but upon the abstract idea of the State. It was pointed out that to make Christian Society dependent upon the State in the widest sense of the term, would be to place it at the will of its enemies: while to put it under control of the Christian State would be to place the teacher under jurisdiction of the taught. But a middle line was alluded to, namely that which seems from certain expressions to have been intended in the late speeches of the Count de Montalembert at Malines, wherein, without expressly saying so, the infidel State of modern times is by implication asked to grant an equality between the one Divine Universal Society and other societies which have no Divine foundation, as if the State were in a position to give, or the Society were at liberty to accept, equality. Having made this digression, I returned to the relations of the Society with the Christian State, remarking that the State having become Christian in virtue of the submission of each of its members to the one law of Christian Society, could hardly turn round and seek to exercise constraint upon that corporation. That by allowing such constraint the Society would abandon the function for which it was created, and by so doing would, *ipso facto*, cease to exist. It was said, that the Christian law acts on society only through conscience, and that the moment wherein the last conscience should withdraw its allegiance would be the same in which the law would be banished from the world. It was further remarked that conscience being world-wide, the one organised Society could only act effectually upon it provided the Society itself were independent: that the security of the State depends in a great measure on the action of the Society upon consciences: that the State weakens its own position by weakening the hold of the Society upon consciences: that as a matter of fact the State is inconsistent in taking that line, because it is continually appealing to the organised Society to influence consciences in its behalf, and that it not unfrequently reproaches the Society for neglect in this respect. It was said, that any errors or supposed errors of policy on the part of the Society, could not release statesmen or governments from the obligation of obedience. Because, as for statesmen, their obligation, as members of the Society, begins prior to any action, good or bad, on the Society's part; that it is in fact incurred at this very moment for all who shall hereafter enter the Society; and since governments are made up of individuals, and since they know what is the true relationship between themselves and their subjects from the Society alone, they cannot escape the obligation in any way. In conclusion the leaders of the two powers were contrasted together, in order to show that, as a matter of probability, selfishness and incapacity, which are the pleas usually urged against Christian leaders, are less likely to be found among them than among the leaders of civil society.

It will be observed that the conclusion arrived at in speaking of conscience, is more advanced than was at first proposed. This was inevitable. The independence of the Society cannot well be established conclusively without going a step further, and asserting the dependence of civil society. To establish this will be partly the object of the present paper. I propose to bring forward some arguments on the power of Christian Society, as derived from its nature, according to the explanation previously given: thence I shall, in conclusion, proceed to the practical question, how far it is wise, or even allowable, because of the hardness of the times, for the Society to descend to curry favour with civil governments by the abdication of a prerogative which has been conferred upon it, in view of such contingencies. The term Christian Society, or Organised Christianity, or Christian Government, will be adhered to throughout as a concession to modern democratic notions. Because every man who is a Christian can feel no jealousy or fear of admitting arguments which are at least as much in his own behalf as any that can be used on the other side. He is indeed more unalterably a member of Christian Society than he is of the State: for while by removing to another country he ceases to be a member of his own, and becomes an alien in his adopted State, his Christian citizenship remains always and in all places the same. I am defending the rights of all Christians alike, those of one neither more nor less than those of another, be he who he may. To claim as rights on either side what are not so in reality, would be as great a folly as to deny to either side what is due to it. That which every wise man must wish to see, is a just position, a perfect equilibrium, maintained by every party; by individuals, by civil governments, by the government of Christian Society. Where the latter is to be found, is a further question; and if, to any person, the answer arising from the nature of the Society, as before explained, should lead to a conclusion which goes against the grain, the validity of the arguments we are to consider to-day cannot, with any show of reason, be therefore impugned.

To begin, then, at the very beginning of the subject. No one of those to whom these remarks are addressed will deny, that all power comes from God, both the power of the civil government and that of organised Christianity. That the two powers come in totally different ways seems to me equally manifest. As to the first, it appears clear, both from the practical origin of civil governments, from the various forms they assume throughout the world, and from the changes out of one form into another, which have been of such frequent occurrence as to prove that it is in the very intrinsic nature of civil governments to be subject to transformations; it seems clear, I say, from these three considerations, that the power which they hold, although coming from God, does so in an indirect way. For, first, in the transition of society from the patriarchal to the civil system, it was necessary that men who were really independent of each other should, from the motive of some mutual advantage, have consented to place themselves under the jurisdiction of an authority whose title did not exist till after the consent was given; and the independent parties must have been competent to choose one form as well as another. In the next place, the fact of a great variety of forms having at all times existed shows, that all are allowable unless some direct revelation can be alleged, condemning or sanctioning any particular form. That such revelations have been made, as to particular governments, is admitted. But they have been made to one nation only, and never, as if the form prescribed were binding upon any other people. With this exception, if the general position be objected to, the Divine right of civil governments must be asserted, for it would be a contradiction to deny the Divine right of a power derived directly from God. The theory has, however, been maintained in ancient times on the plea of pretended revelations, and in modern times by certain tyrannical princes and their partisans.

But, the compact having been entered into, authority once firmly established under it, and society settled upon the basis of such authority, the power is truly declared to be from God, because by it alone justice, of which God is the head, can be maintained in the civil relations of the subject members. Under this authority, rights arising out of the compact are established, property is acquired, and natural liberties ceded in return for equivalents which the authority guarantees. To overthrow such authority, therefore, is to infringe rights, to invade property, and to deprive ceded liberties of the retribution which is their due—in other words, to banish justice. It is only when the authority, itself unmindful of its proper function, and having itself discarded justice, that justice itself, acting through the once subject members, displaces the old and substitutes a new authority, to which, henceforth, they must submit, the new authority or power holding its place in virtue of that justice, to which its subjects appealed in effecting the change. And God Himself, being the Author of justice, the power is manifestly from Him, though conferred in the indirect manner described. The civil Government has, therefore, a Divine right, and the error which has been made has not been in the use of the term, but in attributing the Divine right to individuals, instead of to the office. Of practical errors on the other side, there is no need to speak here.

I am quite aware that celebrated men have maintained the theory of the civil power being derived directly from God. But one fails to see how it is directly conferred, in the absence of special revelations, or of a revelation once for all, declaring, as in the case of the sacraments, when and at what moment the power descends, and by the action of what legitimate authority it becomes binding upon subjects. Moreover, though the theorists are celebrated, they are not numerous, nor by any means of such sound reputation as those who hold the indirect opinion. The mere fact of changes being lawful, not to say quite inevitable, seems to me to preclude the possibility of the 'direct' theory, without supposing direct revelations on every occasion of change. But changes are, for the most part, the results of injustice, which God indeed permits, but cannot prescribe. The injustice, then, having been successfully carried out, and the new authority established, the old process with regard to rights, property, and liberties, is repeated, and Justice—that is to say, God—requires submission to be yielded to the new power. But the power arises in the most indirect way.

Again, civil governments are very numerous, and, by the nature of man in his present condition, conflicts between different governments are of frequent and unavoidable occurrence. But, if the right of one be Divine, so is that of all; and in these conflicts we should necessarily have one Divine right directly conferred, fighting with another Divine right directly conferred, which is absurd. Each has its Divine right, founded on the natural justice we have described, and having for its object the good of its own particular portion of society, the whole being presided over by the Divine Justice. But human nature requires that men should live in society, and is therefore of necessity provided by the Divine Justice with the means of making society possible, which can only be done by the establishment of civil governments. But the particular forms, both of society and of governments, are within the choice of men themselves and cannot be said to be in any way Divine.

Organised Christianity, on the other hand, stands in an altogether different relation to God. It was founded by God Himself, and, as we saw in the former paper, is bound together and exists solely in virtue of a law directly revealed by Him. The law and the Society are coextensive. If the former were taken away, the latter would go with it; if the latter were dissolved, there would be no subject for the operation of the former. The Society consists of three parts, viz. Christ, who is the Head; the human members, who are the body; and the law, which is the soul of the Society. The power which it holds, therefore, comes in the most direct manner conceivable. It dwells, by the Divine nature, in the head, and is communicated to the body through the law. If the law were without power, the body would dissolve into its elements. If the body were without power to maintain the law, the latter would cease to exist. Power, therefore, is an essential attribute of the Society; and since the Society is no society without Christ, the power it possesses is truly Divine.

But civil society exists independently of Christ; because it was before Christ came, and it continues where He is unknown, and even where, being known, He is rejected. This may be considered sufficient on the remark that, although the two powers come from God, they come in two totally different ways.

In the next place, the observation is an important one, that it is almost impossible to state too absolutely the power which any government possesses, *in principle*, under certain circumstances. That this is the case is stated by a modern writer of authority in treating of the powers of the most democratic constitution extant. He declares them to be actually unlimited. The expression is a strong one; nevertheless, if we examine the powers of the civil government in detail, we shall see that it is scarcely, if at all, too much so. Thus, the questions wherein it is of the greatest moment that the limits of these powers should be strictly observed, are questions of life and death; and especially of the life and death of the executive members of organised Christianity. Personal liberty, property, the right of declaring war, and all other subjects, are less momentous than questions of life and death. Now, in the absence of Christian, it is clear that the civil, government has the most absolute power of life and death over its subjects. Because, although it can act only in conformity with its own laws, yet the legislative power rests with itself. It alone can define crimes; and if it be said that the civil government is restrained by the natural law to which it owes its origin, the reply is conclusive, that, in the absence of an independent court of conscience, the State is the only possible interpreter of that law. But if, Christian Society being constituted, an exception be claimed on behalf of its executive members, I answer that there are certain extreme cases where the Society's executive is powerless to control its own members, and that in such extremities the civil government has a lawful power to act even against the life. The civil government has a lawful control over the lives of all its subjects, under some possible circumstances or other. It does not weaken the argument to admit that, in the extreme cases supposed, both governments must be in agreement. Because, the right of action is a natural one, and is not derived in any way from organised Christianity, but from the necessity for social existence which supposes the right of taking the steps needful for its own preservation.

It is of importance to recognise this principle in regard to civil governments; because the argument will be found to tell with equal or greater force on the other side, by-and-by. I am anxious that the widest extension of which they are capable should be admitted on behalf of the rights of the civil government; and I do not see what other right can be demanded larger than the one now in question.

Let us now regard the relations of the two powers from another point of view. Government, practically speaking, is an art; the art of regulating society, of producing an harmonious action among its members for the general peace and well-being of each and all, individually and collectively. In another relation government may be called a science; but *practically speaking*, it is strictly an art. Now, all art is the result of experience. While it bears certain relations to both nature and revelation, art is subordinate to both. It acknowledges in each fixed laws, which it must apply, but which it cannot alter. The province of science is, to study nature. If I may so speak, it seizes hold of nature, turns it on every side, examines it minutely, tests one phase of it by another, experiments upon it, and so endeavours to master the laws by which it works, and to understand the connection between them and the phenomena which result from their operation. This being done, art proceeds to frame laws for enabling men to make use of those natural laws of which science has discovered the existence and mutual bearing. To become an artist, i. e. one thoroughly versed in his art, a man requires to acquaint himself with the theories, the experience, and the rules, of those who have gone before him. He treasures up the sayings and views of former artists: he heaps together facts, groups them, generalises upon them, and aims at finding out wherein, why and how far his predecessors have failed: the whole range of human knowledge is not too wide for him, because from any side a ray of light may penetrate the twilight in which he works. To perfect himself in the art of government, the statesman confines himself to no country, to no age, to no language. He finds practical illustrations in his own country, and in his own epoch, of the maxims of ancient times and other nations. He calls to his aid the poet, the philosopher, and the historian. He builds up from their records a theory more or less applicable to the circumstances in which he is placed. But when all is said and done, he has, and can have, no code to which he can refer, as if it were perfect. At the best, his work is but a compromise between the desirable and the practicable. His experience, so far from teaching him to look for perfection in any system, shows him the impossibility of finding it at all. Other arts, dealing with matter only, leave durable monuments to be seen and handled, and as examples open to all the world, to be emulated and improved upon for thousands of years.

But the art of government has to deal with evanescent combinations of circumstances, which are never precisely repeated in history, and with minds operating upon and operated upon by facts and changes, whose proximity gives them false proportions in the eyes of men naturally ignorant of matters which do not concern their daily life. Nor is it necessary for the statesman only to acquaint himself with the history of former times, and with the causes of present manners. He must, as Cicero says, never cease from studying and cultivating *himself*—for the mind of the governor is reflected upon the governed: and the success or failure of his government will depend upon whether he make a true or a mistaken estimate of the work before him, and his judgment will depend upon his natural character, his education, and his habits. He must, then, learn that never-perfectly-discovered problem, to know himself. So that, if not even material arts can be brought to a state in which they are incapable of further improvement, much less can that of civil government, with all its complications, public as well as personal. If we consider the various forms it assumes, we shall acknowledge, as Cicero continues, that each has a precipitous and slippery passage down to some proximate abuse; and that every form is but an imperfect system of checks upon both governors and governed. But the government of the Christian Organisation is no art, it is a science, and one not based upon experience or investigation. All the investigations of ancient times ended in the most disheartening conclusions; and no progress has been made in modern times apart from revelation to render experience more fruitful, or investigation more successful, in results. I endeavoured in the former paper to establish, that Christian science embraces, not only the knowledge of God's will to men, both as among themselves and as between Him and them, but in addition certain rules, either in germ or otherwise, for the government of the Society, which would enable it to last through all time, to extend throughout the world, and to overcome every kind of hostility. There was no room for investigation: the Society was placed in the world composed of men—ignorant according to worldly knowledge—but yet bound to carry out a programme which required the very perfection of wisdom. With such a Government, investigation could add nothing to the adaptability of its laws to their intended object. It could only prove how perfect were the rules revealed, and how certainly they would, if simply followed, work to a successful end. Experience could only be a light shining out of the past over the present and the future, and lending a natural clearness to the supernatural certainty of faith. Experiment could hold no place in a system provided from the beginning against every possible contingency. From this point of view, then, it is plain how far superior one government is to another; the government of the Christian Organisation to that of civil society. The superiority can only be denied by first replying to the arguments by which the primary organisation of Christianity was established in the former per.

We will now examine some of the pleas put forward

on behalf of the civil power, in proof of its superiority to the spiritual, in matters of State; and we shall find that, so far from confirming the position they are intended to maintain, they lead directly to the opposite conclusion.

The first is a semi-philosophical allegation, to the effect that it is the State which protects all citizens in their rights to life, liberty, and property, which the citizens therefore hold, subject to the supreme protector's claim to take them when the public welfare demands their cession. The plea is specious, and contains more truth than its propounders probably imagine.

It is, no doubt, true that the supreme protector (such is the phrase in use among asserters of the civil prerogative) has the power of life and death for the public good. It is declared above that the State has these rights, even over the Christian Society's executive, and one reason has been given, which seems conclusive on the point. We cannot get away from the fact, that the power of the civil Government is Divinely conferred. Of the pretence, that its power comes from the people, it need only be remarked, that the arguments used above, seem to undermine the ground upon which the advocates of this notion take their stand. It may be added that, to give force to any argument on the subject of rights, an appeal must be made to justice. Even perverse men, in seeking rights by crooked methods, appeal to the justice of their cause. As Brutus says of the murder of Cæsar, 'What villain touched his body, that did stab, and not for justice?' Now, the court of appeal is, in all cases, of higher authority than any appellant. Since, therefore, the civil jurisdiction appeals to, and, as said above, is based upon justice, it can only be said to be derived from the people, *who are appellants*, in a secondary sense. To say so in an absolute sense would be an obvious fallacy. But God and justice being one, the civil power comes from God, though indirectly. Let there be no misapprehension. While anxious to give the civil power all the prerogative it can claim, and to magnify its office in presence of the Christian Organisation to the utmost possible extent, consistent with truth, I have declared that the Divine right of kings has been unduly insisted on. But now comes the question, Which of the two powers is in reality the supreme protector? It will be remembered, that in allowing extreme penalties to rest in the hands of the State, the admission of the undeniable fact was not based upon the character of supreme protector which the State claims. That could not be done with any regard either to the facts of history or to reason.

The history of the world furnishes numbers of instances wherein the State itself has required a protector; wherein it was utterly incapable of defending itself against attacks from without, and against dissolution from within, when it has been unjustly absorbed by more powerful States, and when it has fallen to pieces from inherent weakness. But nothing of the kind has taken, or can take, place, with organised Christianity. True it is, that countries once Christian, have become again infidel; that branches have been lopped off the mystical tree; but the life and organisation of Christianity have not been impaired or affected thereby; for while these very events were occurring, the growth of Christianity was more rapid in other directions; its organisation was developed, and it was enabled to exercise, with greater plenitude, that jurisdiction which it always possessed, but which, in its infant state, remained in abeyance; just as the Divine power of its Founder, plenary though it were in the crib of Bethlehem, was not exhibited to the world till He came to manhood. But scarcely was Christianity recognised as a power by the State, when it was called upon to take the State under its protection. It was within one hundred years of the conversion of Constantine, and within fifty of the death of Julian, that the invasion of Alaric took place. The civil power, having at its command all that it could collect and concentrate of the material force of the State, was powerless to repel the invader. The very capital was sacked and burned to the ground. Then was seen how organised Christianity wielded an influence more potent than the State in defence of the State, over which it threw its shield. It was at this time that S. Augustine, an eye-witness of, and a sufferer by, the barbarian invasions of Africa, which ended in leaving the country an easy prey to the Saracen hordes, was writing, taunting the heathen with the powerlessness of their gods, and appealing to well-known facts of recent occurrence, in proof of the power of Christianity to protect even its enemies. 'Are not,' he exclaims, 'these adversaries of the name of Christ, the very same men whom the barbarians spared for Christ's sake?' The sepulchres of the martyrs, the basilicas of the Apostles, which, in the devastation of Rome, received even their enemies who fled to them, prove what I say. So far raged the bloody foe; there his murderous fury was stayed. Many falsely assumed the name of Christian in order to avoid the present penalty. How many would have escaped but that they feigned themselves to be the servants of Christ? 'Look now,' he continues, 'at the history of the wars before and since the foundation of Rome. Read, and show of a city taken by strangers, who spared those whom they found in the temples of the gods.'

He then gives a number of instances to attest the weakness of the old religions—I do not say to protect the *State* in its utmost need, but even to defend *themselves*. On the one side, he says, were murder, devastation, spoliation, affliction; on the other, the very barbarians themselves, choosing out the largest basilicas, as places of safety for the conquered—whence none might be taken and where none might be molested—in short, the right of sanctuary (whatever modern calumny may say) actually enforced, even against the enemies, not only of Christianity, but of the State, which lay at their mercy. One need scarcely go further to prove which of the two powers is supreme protector in the last resort. Nevertheless, I will quote two writers, both more or less hostile to the Church, in support of my argument, looked at historically. The first shall be M. Guizot, and the second, Mr. Hallam.

Speaking of the times in which S. Augustine lived, and a little later, M. Guizot remarks that 'Had there been no Christian Church, the whole world would have been abandoned to material force. The Church alone exercised a moral power: she did more, she kept up and diffused the conviction of a rule—a law, superior to all human laws. She professed that belief, so essential to the well-being of mankind, that there exists above all human laws, another law, at different times, and from a difference of morals, sometimes called reason, sometimes the Divine law, but which everywhere and always is the same law under different names.' Such is M. Guizot's appreciation of the protecting power of organised Christianity, for he admits a complete organisation long before this period. Christianity alone saved the world from the domination of brute force; and in so saving the world, she saved the civil government, which could never continue to exist upon a system of mere brute force. Following in the same line, Hallam corroborates the declarations of Guizot. After many pages of hostile remarks, he at length admits, that 'the influence of the bishops upon the barbarians wore down the asperities of conquest, in the fall of Rome, and saved the provincials half the shock of that tremendous revolution.' He continues, 'As captive Greece is said to have subdued her Roman conqueror, so Rome, in her own turn of servitude, cast the fetters of a moral captivity upon the fierce invaders of the north.' In illustration and corroboration of this observation, it will be enough to name S. James of Nisiba, S. Loup of Troyes, S. Aignan of Orleans, the same S. Loup and S. Germain l'Auxerrois in this country, and Pope S. Leo in connection with Genseric and Attila. But if the external enemies of the empire were held in check by the rulers of Christian Society, it is no less true that the internal ones were equally so. When S. Ambrose, by refusing the Holy Communion to the Emperor Theodosius, compelled him to make what public amends were practicable for a barbarous massacre, he took the best way possible to save the Government from the effects of its own crime. He, and Christian Society in his person, held the shield of justice between the State and that violence which its own act countenanced and invited. There was no question of humbling a monarch, probably not even of serving the State. As a Christian teacher and ruler, he had a simple duty to perform, between Christ, Whose officer he was, and the Emperor, whose subject he was, and in performing it, he consciously or unconsciously did the State a material service. He read a lesson not to the Emperor alone, but to society at large, in that higher law to which M. Guizot refers, and which, while guarding subjects against the oppression of princes, saves the State from the consequences of that despair which subjects feel who lie at the untempered mercy of rulers. It may be said that this was but an instance of individual independence in a subject, acting upon the mind of a prince truly noble in character. But such is not the case. S. Ambrose acted not as a subject of the State, but as a ruler of Christian Society, not as the nominee of the civil power, but as an executive member of the great Christian Organisation. As an imperial delegate, he must yield or run the risk of degradation: as delegated by the central authority of Christendom, to yield would be to incur degradation. To allow men in high positions to exhibit contempt for the religion of which the bishops were the heads, would have been fatal to society. I believe it would be impossible to point to an instance of a single nation which has become great, whose greatness was not founded upon a strict obedience to some religion. But at the period of which we are speaking, the old religions had fallen into contempt; there was little or no practical reference in life to supernatural government—men lived without God in the world. Christianity had, however, stepped in, and with marvellous activity had seized hold of society man by man, giving to each new and more exalted notions of duty, purifying the unselfishness which had made men ready to sacrifice themselves for the State, by presenting to them a higher object for which to make a more complete sacrifice, and in so doing had created, or rather had become, a power in the State which could alone save it from utter anarchy. At such a moment especially, to allow a relaxation of the laws of the Society must have had a most pernicious tendency. And the history of S. Ambrose and Theodosius is only one out of a thousand instances, daily occurring, wherein the Society enforced its rules with a perseverance and a minuteness of detail absolutely necessary, but at the same time perfectly efficacious for the permanent maintenance in the Society of the influence which it exercised with such wonderful results at that desperate epoch. We come back once more to the point from which we started, viz. that the Society was founded to teach the true relations of men to each other and to God, and we may well say that a corporation which is able to cause these two relationships to be observed between governors and governed, under such circumstances, is a protector far more deserving of the title of supreme protector, than the State can possibly be; and we may confidently appeal to history in proof of our contention.

But while referring to history, one feels that the reference is almost superfluous. The homage which every statesman pays to religion by appealing to the people's sense of religion on every suitable occasion, is an admission more conclusive than any argument drawn from history, that civil rulers themselves acknowledge its superior power. Indeed, unless religion be a sham, there can be no power equally potent to prevent excesses, either on the side of the people or of their rulers. And it is in the avoidance of excesses that the security of States consists. This portion of the subject has already been dwelt upon in reference to conscience, and I therefore pass on now, merely remarking that if the power of *any* religion be as great as I say it is, that of the Christian religion, with its Divine origin and its perfect organisation, must be indefinitely greater.

If, therefore, it be true that the supreme protector, and no other, has, as such, the power of life and death over subjects for the public good, it would follow that jurisdiction would lie not with the State at all, but with the State's protector—a conclusion altogether at variance with the theory, on which we shal have something to say presently, of the mutual independence of the two powers. It will be borne in mind that in stating this plea on behalf of the civil government, I have exactly copied the words of an existing constitution entirely opposed to the idea of a church. On the other hand, while admitting the truth of the plea, and while allowing in accordance therewith the power of life and death to rest in organised Christianity, it is necessary to call attention to a most important distinction which exists between jurisdiction and the exercise of it. It is desirable, on this point, just to quote the memorable saying of Balmez, where, in repelling an old and well-known calumny, he says that although 'armed with a tribunal of intolerance, the popes have not shed a drop of blood.' They had the power and the opportunity, which does not always accompany jurisdiction, but they did not employ it; or rather they used it to save, not to destroy life—to reprieve, not to condemn.

In the same way, though the powers of the President of the Federal States of America, like those of the Roman Dictator of old, are declared to be at certain times unlimited, and very dangerous, and though he could not be impeached for illegality in practising excess, yet is he restrained by prudence from the harsh use of faculties he unquestionably possesses. Having mentioned this distinction, I hope I have sufficiently guarded myself against misconstruction, and I sum up on this branch of the subject thus: If the highest functions of government belong to the highest powers, the Christian Organisation must have jurisdiction over the State, so far as the character of supreme protector gives it jurisdiction; for the title cannot be fairly claimed by the State in any but a secondary sense, which must be apparent to any-one.

We will examine but one other, and that the most popular, allegation in regard to the two powers. It is urged with an appearance of high principle which would be captivating were it not absurd, and ludicrous were not so many people deceived by it, that the government of Christian Society, having to do with spiritual affairs only, must not mix itself up with secular questions, which come only within the cognisance of the civil government. Now, as far as the two governments are concerned, it is difficult to see in what way one is more immaterial than the other. Government is not in any correct sense of the term a thing to be looked at and handled. Essentially it is an operation of the mind. It is mind that governs. Macbeth talks perfect philosophy when he speaks of 'the mind I sway by.' Where superior mental capacity is wanting for long together, government ceases. Exalted intellects survey the condition of inferior understandings, and of material objects, and upon the view taken proceed to regulate the relations of each. It is the same with both orders. The ruling mind issues its commands in words almost as immaterial as itself, and forthwith inferior minds proceed to execution. In whatever way the ruling mind is enlightened, there is nothing material in either case. Those ruling minds which regulate secular and material affairs, do so by a purely intellectual operation. Except in barbarous states of society, the ruler is not the executive. He does not personally enforce obedience to his own laws. He works with the hands of others; and the whole difference between him and the spiritual ruler is in the mode of employing the same tools. The former acts through the general and the magistrate, the latter uses the same officers through the civil ruler when coercion becomes necessary. But coercion, either for spiritual or secular ends, is rendered for the most part needless by moral convictions. The knowledge that force will be used saves its employment in the general business of life. Its use is exceptional even with the civil ruler. The spiritual ruler, no doubt, brings convictions of a higher order, and such as are out of the reach of the civil governor, to bear upon subjects. But that by no means excludes him from the aid of those which are within the domain of the civil ruler. The employment of supernatural does not exclude that of natural fear by the spiritual, any more than that of material excludes that of moral force by the civil, ruler. There is, therefore, nothing in the material nature of the one and in the immaterial nature of the other which can be adduced as a reason for dividing the sphere of their operations. Furthermore, man being a compound existence, there is nothing so spiritual as not to have for him its physical, nor anything so material as not to have its spiritual, connection. To endeavour, therefore, to cut off the spiritual government from a voice in the secular, is not only contrary to that natural order of things whereby the inferior is subordinated to the superior, but it is even to abridge the superior of its connection with the inferior, by one half the object of its creation, viz. that of teaching and enforcing the duties of men among themselves. If the duty of man to God could be separated and marked off by a broad line from his duty to his fellow-men, there might be something in the pretension. But so long as it is admitted that Christianity has to regulate duty to neighbours, it is absurd to deny to the Organised Society a voice in, and even an appellate jurisdiction against, the secular Government whose whole and sole function is to regulate human relationships, except when called upon by the Christian Government to exercise a higher office. When under the old Pagan governments decrees were passed in honour of the gods, the object was purely civil: to honour them for their own sake was not contemplated. The worship had in view the protection they were expected to afford to the State in return for the homage offered. The welfare of the State was the ultimate aim. There was no religious jurisdiction, independent of the State, to which appeal could be made as against the State. The very laws which established the particular religion were the creation of the State. The gods themselves were many of them only immortalised men, who were reputed to have deserved well of the State. But when Christianity arose, a power was called into being independent of, and therefore above, the State: it received a law from God, which it communicated to the State, and to which the State and every member of it is amenable. This is not denied within what men of high principle are pleased to call the domain of the spiritual power.

But it is contended that the civil has a jurisdiction independent of the spiritual power; and this is to a certain limited extent true. It is not deniable that even the inferior officers, in an army, in a municipality, or even in smaller self-governing bodies, have certain rights and exercise certain functions without reference in a general way, and in ordinary times, even to their immediate superiors, much more so without reference to the commander-in-chief or to the head magistrate or functionary. If this be allowed in the case of such inferior ranks, the first officers of the State, having a wider range of duties and more important and multifarious interests to secure, will naturally have a so much wider liberty of action. If, however, the inferior officer overstep the limits of his authority, and an appeal against him be carried to a much higher tribunal, it will be vain for him to allege the superior exaltation of the court and to say: 'Your business is to legislate, to declare war or to maintain foreign relations, and generally to attend to the highest duties of State, and not to interfere with me. I appeal to men of my own rank: let them decide: you have no right to meddle with such small affairs.' In the same way there is no question of the Christian interfering with the civil government, till the former has passed, or is about to pass, a line within which its action is free. It is only when interests are affected altogether within the cognisance and control of organised Christianity, that the latter protests; and for the State to demur to its decision, on the plea of the purely spiritual nature of its functions, is to set itself up as judge of those many spiritual questions which in the same breath it acknowledges to belong to the other power. Two strangers are independent of each other, but if one sees the other commit violence upon a third, the mutual relations are changed; the independence ceases, and the peaceful man becomes an officer of justice as against the wrong-doer. In such a case, who would listen to the violent man's protest against the interference of the stranger? Now, this would be the relative position of the two powers, were the State really a stranger to the Christian government. But this is not the case. If changes are made in the civil law concerning marriage or education, for example, such changes are declared to be in accordance with Christianity. Even questions regarding the holding or confiscation of certain property, are discussed on a professed respect for the interests of Christianity. The State, therefore, is always to a certain extent under Christian tutelage. And if it proceed to act in violation of that revealed law which is deposited with organised Christianity, the latter has a right of interference tenfold greater than the peaceful has over the violent citizen. But, observe, its only mode of interference is by exercising an intellectual and moral influence over its own subjects. If the State refuse to place its material at the command of the spiritual power, the latter has no means of compulsion; it can only persuade. Passive obstruction may be offered, and even in extreme cases the supreme protector may call upon subjects for support as against the rebellious State. It will be for the supreme protector to decide at what point the case has assumed gravity enough to call for the exercise of such opposition. But it would be absurd to ask the spiritual power, the supreme protector, to decide whether the Christian religion would suffer most by blind submission to the State on questions directly affecting that religion, or by the probable troubles arising from opposition to the State. To propose such submission would be equivalent to asking the Christian government, the supreme protector, to abdicate its functions. And as the only possible weapon in the hands of Christianity would be a spiritual one, it is difficult to see upon what principle its use could be objected to, consistently with the assertion that the domain of the spiritual power must be strictly spiritual. Remember, we are not talking of this church or of that—but of that organised Christianity the necessity for whose existence we proved in the former paper; and we say that if to the spiritual weapons of the Society, the State oppose its material ones, it may be able in a great measure to destroy the Christian Organisation in that particular State, but in so doing the State ceases to be Christian. It throws off its obedience to that government which holds the Divine revelation. And any Christian subject of the State has a right to exclaim: 'Much as I prize my allegiance to the State, I value my character of Christian more, and I call upon the government of Christian Society to defend me, my friends, and my posterity to the best of its ability against the encroachments of the State, and I say that if it fail herein, I stand unprotected and at the mercy of an infidel power. I do not ask the State to judge for me on these spiritual questions, because if *it* were able to judge I should be no less so, having as much light as the State. I demand, then, of the Christian government to judge for me; to let there be no doubt as to the line of conduct my duty demands. I speak in my own interest, apart from any I may feel for the Society. If I have a right to call on the State to protect me against outward violence, I have an equal or a greater right to protection on the other side against the violation of my conscience, and I require it at the hands of the Society with all the energy of my soul. I do not lie at the foot of an ambitious clique of spiritual usurpers. I do not surrender my intellect to a set of designing men. On the contrary, I use it with all the keenness I may possess, and I conclude that if God meant the revelation to have been in the hands of the State, He would have said so in plain terms. I weigh the accusations of ambition and such like, and I perceive that the very men who bring them are themselves inflated with ambition, and full of designs for their own aggrandisement. I perceive also a curious phenomenon, viz. that these external supporters of the civil as against the spiritual power are no real friends of the former, but only as against the latter, being ever as ready to overthrow the one as the other—men who hate all authority, and who only seem to take the side of the State because it, too, is impatient of control. I see moreover that one State never appears to question its right to interfere with the purely internal affairs of another, whenever a party can be found in the other State, either truly or falsely to declare itself oppressed. The only doubt is as to the policy of intervention. That once settled, the indefeasible right to come to the aid of the oppressed is acted upon without the slightest misgiving, and no party in the transaction protests against the principle. The ordinary grounds of demur are themselves an admission of the right. It is answered that the oppression is imaginary, or else that severity is rendered necessary by the turbulence of the complainants. But the natural right based upon the fraternal bond which unites the whole human race into one family is not denied: governments perfectly unconnected with the subjects, and having no authority over them whatever, demand redress of other governments as independent as themselves, and failing to obtain satisfaction proceed to enforce their demands by arms. Nevertheless, so soon as the spiritual power, the government of organised Christianity, protests on behalf of me, its own subject, against the tyranny of the State, immediately the cry is raised of usurpation, arrogance, *imperium in imperio*, allegiance to a foreign power, national rights, independent power, and the rest. As if it were not quite as natural, and a thousand times more imperative on the Christian government, to defend its own subjects, and to enlighten and safeguard their consciences, than it can possibly be in any State to act on behalf of strangers. In one case there is a natural right, but certainly no necessary obligation to interfere; in the other, intervention is a condition of the existence of the Christian Organisation, and that not only in obedience to the natural law of self-preservation, but in the sense of duty too.' Such is the language in which any Christian has a right to plead on his own behalf.

From what has been said, it would appear that the

Society, so far from holding the position of being dependent upon the State, occupies precisely the opposite relation of having the State dependent, in a great measure, on itself. If time allowed, it would not be hard to prove that this is, in reality, the case even in countries whose governments have thrown off all connection with the one Universal Organisation.

There are many other points which deserve examination, and which, indeed, ought to be debated, as to the principles upon which the relations of the two powers repose. But time presses, and I hope those already laid down are sufficiently marked out (notwithstanding the obvious incompleteness of their treatment), to render clear the truth of the remarks I now proceed to make on the Malines speeches, according to the plan announced at the beginning of this lecture.

We have now the two Governments, civil and Christian, fairly before us, and before each other, face to face. Both administered by fallible men, but, the former, many in number and various in form; the latter, one: the former, bounded by seas and rivers; the latter, universal: the former, liable to change and destruction; the latter, indestructible and incapable of change, as is the case with everything Divine: the former, subject to human laws; the latter, to the one Divine law: the former, having for its end the preservation of human justice; the latter, having for its end to repair the infraction by mankind of the Divine justice: the former, frequently in the hands of men rebellious to the law of Christianity; the latter, organised expressly to enable it to grapple successfully, not only with rebellious civil powers, but even with the defection of its own officers: the former, an imperfect result of imperfect experiments, and worked out upon an imperfect knowledge of facts; the latter, founded by God upon the most perfect knowledge of all the facts, and constituted for the purpose of acting in reference to them; one of the foreseen facts being, the imperfections, the weaknesses, the ignorance of administrators: the former, holding a power derived from God through its subjects; the latter, invested with power immediately from God: the former, incapable of maintaining itself without the aid of the latter; while the latter, having fought its way against all the power of the former, for hundreds of years, became, from the moment of its ascendency, even by the admission of enemies, the supreme protector of the former, and yet there is a question of the so-called mutual independence of the two Governments, and even of making the Christian subordinate to the civil power; of giving up the ground conquered by thousands of martyrdoms, and held against the enemies of the State itself for so many centuries, because an hostility arises, which is as a mole-hill to a mountain, when compared with the threatened subversion of society, at a time when the spiritual power had but just emerged from what one may call its infancy.

It will be observed that the contrast, so far as it is here presented, only extends to those marks of the two Societies which have been treated in the foregoing pages. To complete it, the holiness of Christian Society, and the want of this characteristic in Civil Society, require elaboration. I intend to make this the subject of a future paper or papers.

In the former paper, I called attention to certain phrases, which seemed to imply a whole set of ideas altogether at variance with the intrinsic natures of the two powers, as explained or hinted at in both lectures. I will now bring before your notice other expressions of the same kind; and after referring to explanations which have been given of the use of these phrases, I will point out wherein the fallacies they contain appear to me to consist. This can only be done, too shortly, in the few minutes which remain. I will, therefore, without more loss of time, plunge *in medias res.*

The Count de Montalembert begins by enunciating a motto, which it is impossible to translate into English in accordance with the principles we have been considering. His title and motto is, 'L'Église libre dans l'État libre.' That must either mean *a* free Church in *a* free State, or *the* Church free in *the* State free. The first form would be to ignore the Universality of the Church. Speaking of the Christian Organisation, you cannot use the particle '*a*.' It is the only entity of the kind: other organisations are partial; this stands alone, and must have the definite article. The expression, 'A Church,' would imply either that portion of the Universal Organisation which exists in any given place or country, and whose local rights we are not discussing, or a sort of courtesy-title, allowed to some aggregation of men who profess to belong to the One Society, but who do not in reality belong to it. We may, then, dismiss this translation. The other is as objectionable for an opposite reason. The Church in the State. Here, 'the State' must be either an individual State, or the State in the abstract. In either case the formula would put the greater in the less, the universal in the particular, the Divine in the human. In the first translation, the Church is reduced to the dimensions of a State; in the second, the State is expanded beyond the dimensions (if it have such) of the Church. When, therefore, the Count announces that the phrase has become and will remain for ever historical, one may be permitted to hope that it will, with all convenient speed, be consigned to that portion of history which is past. In selecting a device for the banner under which we are to fight, it is of the first importance to choose one whose meaning shall be in no way equivocal; one which can be defended on all grounds and against all attacks, and this seems to me to be more than can be said of the one in question. I venture to suggest that it has not yet taken sufficient hold of the public mind of Europe for it to be considered as the watchword to which all defenders of Christianity are bound to rally. Let us trust that this misfortune may not become an accomplished fact.

But it may be thought that I am hair-splitting, in dwelling upon a phrase which most people think they understand. Unfortunately, such is not the case, for the Count expressly says, that the formula is the 'symbol of our convictions and of our hopes,' by which I understand, 'an abstract, or compendium; the creed and summary of his politico-religious faith,' and nothing in the character of the author warrants us in doubting that the words have been well weighed, and carefully rehearsed, before they were given to the world. It seems a certain portion of the audience before whom the speeches under consideration were delivered, applauded the sentiment, which was immediately followed by the declaration, that by the motto he intends, 'the liberty of the Church founded upon public liberties.'

Now, I showed before, that so far as the beginning of modern society was concerned, organised Christianity was its defender and preserver. The subject might have been pursued there, but that I had it in mind to quote the words of our President, where, in the third lecture on Concordats, delivered at Moorfields in 1855, His Eminence says: 'So far were our ancestors from any jealousy of the liberty of the Church, that they considered the very first step towards obtaining civil liberty, was to grant to the Church the utmost possible extent of that gift; and there is scarcely a charter to which we look back, as a noble monument of our ancestors' love of freedom, which does not base the whole of its system of enfranchisement of the thrall and liberty of the subject upon a firm basis of liberty for the Church, and the full exercise of all her rights, untrammelled and unfettered;' and this assertion is proved by convincing quotations.

Are we, then, willing to reverse the old-established order of things, and in place of public liberties, founded upon those of organised Christianity, to allow political liberties to be regarded as the basis of those of religion? Are we to enter upon a course precisely the opposite of that which history proves to have succeeded during so many centuries? Are we to experimentalise upon an idea diametrically opposed to that of a Universal Society capable of withstanding all the shocks of time, all the hostilities of States, all the aberrations of even its own rulers—a course, besides as fatal to political as to religious liberties? The proposition is one which, if seriously intended, goes to establish the permanent upon the changeable—the house upon the sand. But it may be we are misapprehending the author's meaning. Perhaps it is so; but we are told almost immediately of the 'reciprocal independence' of the two powers. Now, reciprocity means a giving up on both sides, and implies, therefore, a certain dependence on both sides. Consequently, to talk of reciprocity between the two powers, is to suppose the temporal able to give something to the spiritual, equal in value to what the latter gives, and which the latter is supposed to give in return. Now, this is a great mistake. The Christian Organisation, as we tried to show, is not only independent of the State, but actually has the State, in a great measure, dependent upon itself. The State has nothing whatever to give or to withhold which is of any value to the spiritual power; and the latter has nothing to hope or to fear from the State. The State is either Christian or infidel. If Christian, it must, both in the persons of its members and in itself, submit to the Society out of duty. The gifts the statesman bestows, in bestowing them upon Christian Society, he bestows upon himself, as a member of the Society, and what the State has to offer it has already received the power of giving from the Society. It gives protection by means of laws based upon the Divine law of the Society; or, at the least, upon the natural law interpreted by the Christian revelation. It has to invoke the influence of the Christian code upon conscience, in order to convince subjects of the justice of its own code; for without such a belief, submission would not be yielded, nor could it be enforced. So that the Christian State can only return what it has already received from the Society.

If the State be infidel, as indeed nearly every State is, either it gives nothing, or it gives persecution, or it gives just so much protection that it hopes to receive more of some sort in return. It gives what the power of the Society can make it part with, if one can use the expression; for in reality it parts with nothing. In the first case, nothing can come of nothing. In the last, the bolder the stand made, and the greater the vigour and force exhibited by the Society, the more will be conceded. But of the second case it will be said, if the infidel State misapprehend the attitude of the Society, it will probably proceed to persecution. Well! certainly the Society will never tear down the imperial edict—it will act with all possible prudence and circumspection—but it is more than doubtful whether the Society has ever lost anything worth saving, by any persecution. For *individuals* who are capable of being persecuted into abandoning their faith, are a bad leaven which will sooner or later infect surrounding members; and *societies* which are so capable are already infected past cure. Martyrdom, as the Count quotes, was an invention of Heaven to conquer the lords of the earth. Nevertheless, that is no reason why martyrdom should be invoked and persecution courted. But in order to avoid either the one or the other, it is not allowable to propound erroneous principles; and it is to an inexactness of expression, which, with the majority of minds, and especially with the young (to whom the Count particularly addressed himself), would lead to false conclusions, that I am at present objecting. It is too grave a danger to encounter, according to my apprehension, that of educating whole generations of men in the habit of using vague and ambiguous language on these all-important topics; and of defending before enemies their candour, and the straightforwardness and honesty of their intentions, in the profession of principles which will not bear scrutiny by either party. I can conceive no better mode of preparing society, ages hence perhaps, for arriving at a condition as incapable of withstanding a persecution carried on by men of enlightenment, as were the people of this country in the sixteenth century. I do not now find fault with any principle M. de Montalembert holds. It is no business of mine to judge him. He is besides too tried a champion of the cause for which we are all fighting, to be open to anything even distantly approaching to hostile criticism. But when expressions are employed which are at least liable to misconstruction, and their continual repetition counselled, one is at liberty to call attention to the danger into which he is leading his followers.

What could anyone possibly understand by the

assertion that 'the Church can no longer be free except in the midst of general freedom,' than this, that its freedom depends upon some cause outside itself? Whereas the Christian Corporation was from the moment of its constitution self-existing; that is to say, having Christ for its Head, and being assured of a continual accession of members to its ranks, it became imperishable. So that it could never be anything but free. It will be said this is true in a certain sense, but not in that in which M. de Montalembert writes. I shall reply to that objection presently, merely remarking in the meantime that the so-called reciprocal independence is a favourite idea in France, dating back at least as far as Bossuet's posthumous work, 'The Defence of the Declaration of the Gallican Clergy on the Ecclesiastical Power;' that it is found in various French writers since his time, and at the present day; and that it is also the Protestant notion of the relationship of the powers in question.

So far, then, there is no hair-splitting. We have had 1stly, the formula; 2ndly, the formula described as the symbol of our convictions; 3rdly, the liberty of the Church founded upon public liberties; and 4thly, the reciprocal independence of the two powers. All seems consistent, every point agrees with its predecessor, and will be found to agree with what follows, viz. the necessity which is said to exist for the 'suppression of privilege' for the Christian Organisation. In the former paper I pointed out that the freedom of the Christian Corporation is a right, and not a privilege; that to call the full practical recognition of its rights a privilege, is to suppose the State possessed of a power and position superior to that of the Christian Corporation, which we have seen to be untrue and absurd. It was pointed out, that to call this body privileged is a correct expression in relation to God, Who has, indeed, conferred upon it privileges far superior to those of any other corporation; but for that very reason, the term is incorrect when applied to it by the State, or by men speaking of it as politicians, and also because none but a superior can confer privileges, and the State is certainly not that superior. Now to speak, as M. Montalembert does, of the 'suppression of privilege,' involves the idea of privilege, in his sense of the word, actually existing somewhere. This can only be in a country wholly or almost entirely Christian, where to suppress it would be deliberately to place Christianity on a worse footing than it at present occupies; and this is what I understand to be desired in view of certain contingent advantages to be gained elsewhere, though what precise advantages would be gained by banishing so-called privilege from such countries, one does not quite see. But very possibly this is not the Count's intention, for I do not know that any single passage can be quoted to the effect supposed. At the same time, it cannot be well denied that to ordinary readers, the impression I have suggested would certainly be conveyed. If such be not the speaker's wish, it would be well to have an explicit denial on an early occasion. Because it is certain that unless this be really his meaning, a misapprehension on the point is very widely prevalent. The question is one of too much importance to be left in doubt; it ought to be cleared up with as little delay as may be convenient. It is the more necessary this should be done, because the same ambiguity of expression presents itself when M. de Montalembert comes to treat of liberty of conscience. Thus, on the one hand, it is applauded in the most general terms, and the triumphs of religion in America and England are favourably contrasted with what are denominated its ephemeral and equivocal empire in Spain, where Protestantism has hardly ever set its foot; and on the other the Count de Maistre is quoted approvingly, as saying that it is almost too trivial a truth to repeat, that to allow Protestantism to enter a Catholic country is a misfortune. We seem to see just where the author's religious instinct prevents him from logically carrying out the principles involved in his own formula, and in the other phrases I have quoted. But the language is not exact, and we know not whither he would lead us.

At this point he seems to have fallen into a singular misconception, such as one would hardly have expected to meet with in a French author. He says, that liberty of conscience was created and put into the world on the day when the first pope replied to the first of the persecutors, 'Non possumus: we cannot but say what we have seen and heard, we cannot but obey God rather than men.' To my apprehension, that was the very day when conscience, which had been only too free before, was declared bound. Freedom of conscience was at an end. It was no principle of liberty that was invoked. What S. Peter alleged was, a revelation from God, and a strict command to publish it. He announced, not conscience at liberty, but conscience bound to speak. As against Pagans he could demand liberty for Christians; but not as a principle for Pagans and Christians alike. He was commanded to speak; and as God requires nothing impossible, the command implied the right to liberty. On the other side, there was no command to speak: and therefore, a liberty of the same kind and derivation could not possibly be implied. Depend upon it, nothing was ever further from the mind of S. Peter when he said, 'We must obey God rather than men,' than to assert a liberty which should allow a Christian State to permit the entrance of heresy within its borders, because of possible advantages in other countries, arising from the fact that Christian leaders are able to point to such liberal conduct in Christian States.

Such are the principles against which I protest, and which appear to be announced in the speeches delivered at Malines. I do not say that the Count de Montalembert holds such principles, nor even that he has expressed them unintentionally. All I say is, that to me they seem to be involved in the words employed.

Two explanations are offered of the line taken by the speaker; but it is not easy to adopt either. The first is to the effect, that the author may not have sufficiently correct ideas on subjects to which he has not specially applied himself; the second runs in this way. Do you not see that you and he are talking of different things altogether? You are talking of scientific principles—he only of certain practical questions touching the conditions of modern society, and how the difficulties, dangers, and facts of the age are to be met and combated. When he speaks against the Inquisition, persecution, and privilege, he is throwing dust in the eyes of our adversaries. On these points he does not mean what he seems to say. He is advocating your cause. He is a special pleader in your behalf, and it is not wise to expose the fallacies his phrases seem to contain.

Such explanations place one in a dilemma. Of the first I will only say, it is a personal explanation, which may be allowable in the mouths of those who have proposed it. As to the other, to imagine that it is part of his plan to give expression to sentiments which he does not entertain, and that in such language as scarcely admits of a double interpretation, would be to suppose a want of candour quite unworthy of the man. And, besides, his own declaration is so pointed, that one cannot accept the explanation suggested. He says distinctly, 'I am, then, for liberty of conscience, in the interest of Catholicism, without *arrière pensée*, as without hesitation. I accept freely all those consequences which public morality does not reprove, and which equity demands.'

We are, then, driven to the conclusion that it is the Count's wish, merely to propound a policy applicable to the times, reconciling the principles of the Christian Organisation with those of modern society. But the idea of endeavouring to reconcile Christian principles with the theories of the world and of the enemies of Christ, is so repugnant to one's every notion of the functions of religion, that one is at a loss to understand the advantage of making the attempt. And when we are told that in order to exercise a salutary and fruitful action upon it, we must know how to accept the vital conditions of modern society, and when we are further told how necessary it is clearly, boldly, publicly to protest at every turn, against a return to what irritates and disquiets modern society, I cannot but repudiate the sentiments so far as I comprehend them. It is undoubtedly true, that, in order to exercise a salutary influence on the society of any epoch, its tendencies must be studied and thoroughly understood. What it may be to accept the vital conditions of modern society, I do not quite know. And as to the society of the present day, if it be in so highly excitable a state as to be easily irritated and disquieted, why I do not see that we are called upon to watch it, or to hang upon its lips, or to stand and crouch under its testy humour. If, with all its enlightenment and science, it do not understand what are the vital conditions of the Christian Organisation, or if it refuse to make itself acquainted with the requirements of Christianity, it must be made to learn. The truth is, modern society knows a great deal more than is supposed. Look at its composition. It is divided into three great classes. Those who belong to the Christian Organisation; those who, not belonging to it, are men of good will, and from among whom the Organisation gains its recruits in all parts of the world; and those who are its avowed enemies. Of these the first and the last understand it well enough. It can hardly be pretended that the first class will be scandalised by a denial of modern notions respecting freedom of conscience, coercion on behalf of religion and peculiar privilege as it is called. If they would be startled at the utterance of right Christian principles, the reason is, they have been so surrounded by enemies, that they have not heard the truth on these questions fairly discussed. The remedy so far as they are concerned is, not to join in the cry which is for ever raised at the sound of names which *seem* to convey ideas, but which only *do* excite blind passions and prejudices; but rather to grapple with these false and rash judgments, to demonstrate their fallacy, to expose the hollowness of their foundations; to repeat constantly, at all seasons, in all societies—on every possible occasion to reiterate, that the history and principles upon which they are built have been falsified for centuries upon a plan, deliberately and of set purpose; that many of the prominent notions of the day, which have been elevated into principles, are mere questions of expediency; that it is absurd to yield up independence of thought to bow before a tyrannical public opinion, which may change at any time, and which for that, among other reasons, has no claim to respect; that the true line to be taken by Christians, is to turn the weapons of our enemies against themselves, by exposing the untruthfulness of their gravest authorities, and the ignorance, the inconsistency, and the hypocrisy of their leaders: in a word, that our attitude must not be one of defence and apology, but of attack and exposure, of taunt and of ridicule. By this means at least two good effects will be produced: one, that a more manly tone will come to pervade the weaker portions of the Society. Such members will acquire the 'arts of self-reliance, and of self-control.' It will no longer be true, as the Count says, it is at present that 'incessantly and everywhere they are excelled, surpassed, conquered, and duped, by their competitors, their antagonists, or their oppressors, sometimes by unbelievers, and sometimes by Protestants, here by democrats, and there by despots.'

They will no longer experience embarrassment and timidity in face of modern society; they will neither love it, nor fear it, nor fall into its ways. And why should they? What have they to gain by so doing? M. de Montalembert himself supplies us with an answer when he says, 'The less solidarity exists between the Church and any power whatsoever, the less she invokes the support of any external power, the stronger and more popular she will appear.' That is perfectly true, and, therefore, boldly to face the power of modern society, and to refuse any solidarity whatever with it, is the way to give courage to our own brethren, and at the same time to prove to the second of the two classes that her and our independence is thorough: independence of despots on the throne; of despotic democrats; and of that social despotism, by which every one of us suffers, but which must be braved and overcome. The respect of these people will be gained, and, as a certain consequence, their prejudices will be removed. The very shocks they experience in the constant encounter will lead to research and conviction, gradual, but sure. We speak of an every-day experience, not as in estimation of what may be, but of what we know is set down in the history of the last twenty years in this country: here, where the fight has been all up-hill, against an overwhelming majority; against unreasoning hostility and genuine fear; against political tradition and social ostracism. It may be safely said that the bold policy has been the successful one in England. It is, therefore, with regret one sees proposed anything in the shape of a compromise with modern society on the Continent; where the three classes are in quite different proportions; where the second class is in a small minority, existing chiefly in certain large cities and districts, and where the fight has to be carried on between the Christian Organisation and a minority of avowed enemies of all religion. These are men with whom it is impossible to keep any terms. To conciliate them is impracticable, and they do not require convincing, for a large proportion of them, the leaders especially, know well the truth against which they are sworn, or in league. This is that destructive democracy of which the Count speaks, and whose other name is 'the Revolution.' It is a class whom we have to consider no further than as a powerful unscrupulous foe; but whose strength consists, first, in the secrecy of their movements; and, secondly, in the ignorance and timidity of their opponents. To combat these with success, there is no need to adopt their principles and demand their application to ourselves. We know that when in power they will never grant our demands; they will falsify their principles without hesitation against us; they not only *will*, but they *do*. The Count declares it. It is to *us*, he says, that are refused freedom of education, freedom of association, liberty of the press. And, therefore, it were a waste of time, and a great mistake to *appear*, even, to ask for any one of these things, as for an inherent right belonging to all and every citizen, in virtue of his citizenship or of his manhood. For no conceivable reason, except inability to hold out against us, will this party ever allow free scope to organised Christianity in these respects. All we can do, therefore, and all we have a *right* to do, is to overwhelm them with argumenta ad hominem; for, dishonest as they are, each one tries to conceal his character. It is not easy for them to look one another in the face while proposing or upholding a direct palpable breach of principles, which are incessantly invoked. No! Falsehood ever puts on a goodly outside. And *our* strength consists, not in suing for equality of privilege, but in tearing the mask from the face of hypocrisy. Moreover, there is, in demanding equality, where we have a right to superiority, upon a hundred titles, a most discouraging confession of weakness. The condition of things is this: we are in danger of being dispossessed, and of relapsing into the régime of sixteen hundred years ago—when our forefathers in the faith were asking for equality before the State, which, till then, had found no superior. Our Divine Society, having conquered the old, and having raised up, out of conflicting elements, a new human Society, leavened by the Divine power, and as nearly perfect as any Society that is ever likely to exist, may naturally conceive that, apart from its Divine nature, it has claims to superiority over all new comers and experimentalists; claims founded upon social benefits bestowed on mankind. At any rate it was in undisputed possession, when, some century ago, or less, certain perverse men arose, who proposed to more than undo the work of over seventeen hundred years. They determined not only to overthrow the Society, but, with it, all religion whatever, to banish God out of His own world, and to create such a Society as has never existed since the Deluge, if even it did before. These are the men who propounded the principles of Eighty-nine. They have attracted to themselves a body of adherents all over the world, from Santiago, in Chili, to Moscow; they have seized upon Governments, which they possess, and which they use to enable them to seize others. And it is for fear of these new men, these usurped Governments, that we are counselled to renounce privilege once and for ever; being told that to claim for our Society a privileged liberty is to create for it the most redoubtable of dangers. We are invaded, besieged; our patrimony spoiled, and we are called upon to make terms and truce with our foes, the enemies of Society and of God!

It appears to me, that if the Count de Montalembert has been inaccurate in the use of certain expressions, he is even more mistaken in the policy he advocates. I say this, while fully admitting, what one must be blind not to see, viz., how full the speeches are of excellent, accurate, and profound observations; how many original remarks they contain; and how much may be learned from a diligent perusal of them. And I speak with the more confidence, as knowing that, if my criticism has been in any respect erroneous, in the opinion of more competent judges, they are here to correct me.

There is no time now to enter into a discussion of the real principles which should regulate liberty of the press and of association, power of holding property, freedom of education and worship, and of using the secular arm in support of the spiritual power. They are all questions which should be gone into in detail in connection with these speeches; and they are all intimately connected with the practical working of the principles upon which the relations of the One Universal Organised Society with the civil power have been shown to be founded. Great advantages are to be gained by the dissemination of definite notions on all of them. We have been accustomed to hear praise or blame lavished in so absolute a fashion in reference to them, that it is impossible many among us should not have been carried away by one or the other.

But out of a mass of matter, only a selection can be made in a paper like the present. I shall therefore conclude by calling attention to an idea which seems to run through the whole of the speeches. The Count appears to take it for granted that a uniform policy can be wisely applied in every European country. Is not this a fallacy?

In Spain, where, in spite of certain despotic acts committed at distant periods, and notwithstanding the persecution which religion has suffered there, heresy has never been able to gain a footing among the great body of the people: in Austria, where Protestantism, having once become established, is treated with justice, and has no present or hope of acquiring future power of persecution: in Prussia, where, though Protestantism is in the ascendant, the press is as free for the Church as for the sects: in Sweden, where there prevails a rigour in order to the exclusion of the faith more tremendous than the Inquisition: in England and America, where, politically speaking, with some exceptions, perfect liberty of the press, of association, and of worship exist, it appears impossible to adopt a policy which should be suitable to each one of these diverse conditions, and should at the same time be applicable to France and to the Italy of to-day, where the press is free except on the side of the Church, where all sorts of associations are allowed, but where charity is put under the ban, where in short the revolution is on the throne and where religion is systematically persecuted. The conditions of each country, the temper, the power, and the proportionate numbers of the different parties, the wishes of the people in regard to liberty of speech and action, their political constitutions, and their more restricted local circumstances, are so various, that no policy could be invented to embrace the whole. Everywhere, as before remarked, there are two parties outside the Church—one to be opposed, the other to be conciliated. Is it to be imagined that the former can be made more bitter and hostile by any line that can be adopted, or by any argument that can be brought forward in support of Christian principles? Can one trace the present oppression in Naples to the conduct of Ferdinand I. or Ferdinand II.? the suppression of the religious houses in Piedmont to the repressive system of Charles Albert? or that of the Society of S. Vincent of Paul in France to any repressive acts past or anticipated in that country? I think not.

The only real danger to be guarded against is this: that the hostile should gather strength from the neutral party, in times when the public mind is excited, and thus be enabled to carry measures into effect for which their own unaided strength would be unequal. But in one country more liberty, in another less, may be taken with the prejudices of those outside the Christian Organisation. It is a question for each country on each occasion.

In this country friendly outsiders are coming over in considerable numbers: in France itself, especially in Paris, a more rapid increase of strength is visible: in Spain the Government, formerly so hostile, has put itself in agreement with the great body of the population, who were never unsound: if in Germany less movement in the right direction be observable, the cause is to be sought in the religious indolence of the people, not in disabilities from fear of Christian principles. In these, as in all countries, political maxims, public law, and civil liberties may and must be used in order to gain recognition of the rights of organised Christianity, or to extort them when needful. But nowhere and at no time should members of the Society let the idea enter their minds that the rights in question depend in any way upon the constitution, or the forbearance, or the patronage of States. To guard effectively against such a notion becoming current, it should never be forgotten that in throwing dust into the eyes of our enemies, the danger is incurred of blinding our friends.

INDEX.

CPSIA information can be obtained
at www.ICGtesting.com
Printed in the USA
LVHW101937050422
715402LV00003B/76

9 783752 588255